Toot-Toot-TOOTSIE, GOOD-BYE

Toot-Toot-TOOTSIE, GOOD-BYE

RON POWERS

DELACORTE PRESS/NEW YORK

Published by
Delacorte Press
1 Dag Hammarskjold Plaza
New York, N.Y. 10017

Manufactured in the United States of America

Designed by Terry Antonicelli

First printing

Library of Congress Cataloging in Publication Data

Powers, Ron.
    Toot-toot-tootsie, good-bye.

    I. Title.
PS3566.093T6   813'.54   80-19770
ISBN 0-440-08190-4

Acknowledgment

For L. C. Fanning's play-by-play re-creation in Chapter XX, the author is indebted to the eloquence of the late Russ Hodges, who broadcast Giant baseball over radio stations WMCA in New York and KSFO in San Francisco for twenty-two years until his death on April 19, 1971.

The author also wishes to thank Monte Irvin, of the office of the Commissioner of Baseball, for supplying from his personal collection a recording of Hodges' great moment. It should be remembered in history that Irvin hit a home run the day before.

—R. P.
New York
April 4, 1980

Dedication

To the memory of my brother, Jim (1945–1977)

"That is no country for old men . . ."
—WILLIAM BUTLER YEATS

"You can't beat fun at the old ballpark!"
—HARRY CARAY,
Baseball Announcer

Toot-Toot-TOOTSIE, GOOD-BYE

OCTOBER 3, 1951

I T TOOK OFF AGAIN!
*That much he never doubted;
that much he knew. He had seen it, alone perhaps among all the
men who had ever existed in time. The ball leapt off Thomson's
bat and rocketed out to left field, a sinking line drive. In the instant of perception that was allowed him, he saw that it was going to
hit the high wall for a double, or maybe only a single, because Pafko
played the wall good. . . .*

But it took off again!
*The ball actually rose in flight (a fact never mentioned in any of
the next day's newspapers nor ever, in history). He had seen it. And
. . . it's in there . . . it slipped, darted like a dove, in under that
jutting left-field facade, and vanished into the lower stands.*

And Pafko . . .

*And people turning to stare at one another, stunned . . . writers
ripping up their leads . . .* and Jesus Christ it's over!

There is an instant of silence.

And: "Toot-toot-tootsie, good-bye!

"Toot-toot-tootsie, good-bye!

"Toot-toot-tootsie, good-bye!
"Toot-toot-tootsie, good-bye!"

(How he stood there, then, in the damp autumn booth, at the peak moment in American time, earphones askew, yelling himself silly, the words following the ball out on its sacred trajectory, the words expanding to fill that cloudy Indian-summer day, to fill a city and a nation—coast-to-coast hookup—the words to follow him down the decades and bind him forever to history; to make him as famous as the drive made Thomson himself; a litany forever in demand at Knights of Columbus halls and Rotary luncheon halls; "Give us that old 'Toot-toot-tootsie,' L.C.!", and him always obliging. . . .)

But, yes, that ball took off again. *That was his secret, a revelation rendered only to him (not even Thomson himself was ever aware of it) . . . he had been chosen as sole witness to the final ordered instant in the game that was (his blood knew, his sleeping brain knew in a realm far beneath and apart from his ability to connect the knowing with words) a simulacrum of America.*

He did not mention the fact on the air that afternoon in all his whooping celebrations; he did not tell the nation he had seen the ball rise. On the same day, the United States revealed that Stalin's Russia had exploded an atomic device. . . .

It was the last stroke in the last pure season, a comet, rising and rising again, to bisect the American century. The world was never the same again. The leagues that had stood inviolate as empires began to wander and drift; the teams that had been city-states became nomadic tribes. All was in upheaval. Television came in. Eisenhower was elected twice but it didn't seem to help any; people hated and mistrusted one another now. There were gaping raw holes on the surfaces of cities where the old teams had been, the old stadiums; and then the cities flowed over the raw holes, and all that was left of the crime of their uprooting was a free-standing crime that hung like a dark cloud on the deserted streets, and dissolved into a billion crimes.

After a time he ceased paying attention to what was happening in the alien nation outside, and turned his attention inward, to the unchanging imperatives, the guaranteed renewals, of the game itself.

And all he knew was that Willie Mays would have been up next.

CHAPTER 1

"Now you don't figure it's gonna happen outside of a place like Tommy Eagle's, right? I mean even at two, two-thirty in the morning."

"No way."

"Right there at Fifty-second and Park. And all right, I'll admit I'm not feeling a whole lot of pain—"

"You was *knee*-walkin'."

"No, but I—"

"You was burnin' with a low blue flame, hot dam'." Turtle thumped the steering wheel.

"No, but I've had a highball or two in me. And criminy—it happens so quick you don't even have time to—"

"They was up*on* you."

"Two of the sons-of-biscuit-eaters, and they're—" Fanning exhaled White Owl smoke. He leaned over to Turtle Teweles's ear and lowered his voice, although the chances of being overheard were dim, seated as he was in Turtle's Lincoln Continental as it barreled along the FDR with the windows up and the air on. "—they're *black as the ace of spades*!"

"They was *black* sumbitches."

"And one of 'em has a god damn snub-nose thirty-eight, and before I know what hit me why I'm backed up against the wall there in the service driveway."

"Now you're twixt a rock and a hard place."

"And it's two, two-thirty in the morning. Now who's gonna get me outa this?"

"*Now* you're 'bout down to the short strokes." Turtle, his Marlboro glowing like a bullet in the center of his lips, gunned the Lincoln across two lanes of traffic just in time to catch the exit for the Triborough Bridge.

"And, you know, one of 'em says, 'Le's have yo' wallet, you so-and-so'—you know the language they use." Fanning threw an arm across the back of the seat. The cream vinyl felt warm from the April morning sunlight. Today was going to be the right kind of day to get the thing, the rhythm, started. "So I think, this is it, this is church. You ever had a gun in your ribs?" he turned again to Turtle.

Turtle sucked his Marlboro and appeared to search his memory from behind his Polaroid Cool-Rays. They both had on their Polaroid Cool-Rays.

"I can't rightly say as I have."

"Lemme tell you something, pal," said Fanning. He covered his mouth with the back of his hand to cough, a deep broadcaster's cough. "Anyway, I'm thinking this is it for me, this ends the inning, no runs, no hits, no errors, nobody left. I mean these cats look like they're gonna cut my eyeballs out and eat 'em for *grapes*."

"These cats come to do bidniss," said Turtle.

"So I put my hands up and I say, 'Criminy, fellas, I'll give you anything you want, just for God's sake don't shoot me.' And you know what happens?"

They were approaching the Triborough toll plaza. Both men reached up to remove their Polaroid Cool-Rays and tuck them into their outside jacket pockets. Turtle started to feel in the pockets of his green pants for quarters. Fanning handed him a folded dollar bill. Turtle swerved into the attendant lane.

"Cat opened up and blasted you to glory."

"No . . ." A lime-colored Volkswagen Rabbit was pulling alongside them in the lane to their right. Fanning turned and looked at the car intently. There was a family inside; Dad in his striped alligator shirt, Mom with her hair tied up in a scarf, three boys in the backseat wearing plastic Nat batting helmets. Obviously heading for the ball game.

Fanning continued to stare at the people inside the car until one of the small blond boys in the back noticed him. The child frowned. Then his eyebrows shot up and he began waving and pointing toward Fanning. The other members of the family now were looking over; the father and mother smiled and fluttered their hands.

Fanning beamed back at them. Rule one. You never let down your public. Turtle was easing the Continental past the attendant booth now. "Hey, ole buddy," he boomed at the man in the window. The man's sour mouth widened into a grin.

"Turtle Teweles! L. C. Fanning!" He leaned down so that he was eye-level with Fanning. "Hey, 'Toot-toot-tootsie, *good-bye*,' right, L.C.? Go get 'em Nats!"

"Atta boy," said Turtle. "Keep change." He floored the accelerator.

Both men reached into their jacket pockets and replaced the Polaroid Cool-Rays over their eyes. The Lincoln Continental surged along the great concrete causeway in the spangled April morning, against the last crawling dregs of incoming commuters.

"So anyway, you know what happens next? The kid hears my voice and he says"—Fanning rested a ham hand on Turtle Teweles's knee—"he says, 'Hey, mo' . . . *thass L. C. Fanning!*' He says, '*Mah main maaan.*' He says"—Fanning had to fish out his handkerchief and wipe his eyes with it, he was laughing so hard now he was crying—"he says, 'Hey, mo', how 'bout gettin' me a coupla tickets to the *Giant* game next week?' Oh, cripes . . ."

"That cat *recognized your voice!*" Turtle Teweles leaned on the Lincoln's horn. Both men opened their mouths wide and let the laughter cascade.

Yellow patches of early-blooming forsythia flashed against dirty stone embankments as the Lincoln bounced and rocked along the Grand Central Parkway. "The *Giant* game." Fanning laughed weakly. "The son-of-a-biscuit-eater was gonna ventilate me. . . ."

His story had been a great hit with Turtle. It had been a great hit each time he had told it over the last seven years, on the way to Flushing Stadium for Opening Day.

The parking lot that formed a crescent around the rear of Flushing Stadium was already one-third full when Turtle guided the Lincoln onto the asphalt, gently honking the first ambling fans out of the way. It was 11 A.M., two and a half hours before game time. Already people were forming lines at the general-admission windows. Vendors had set up their stands. The austere plaza around the stadium—a businesslike grid of molded concrete and Cyclone fencing—was rendered festive by a procession of balloons and Nats pennants in the "official" colors, a navy field with orange lettering trimmed in white.

"Lookit all the chickabiddies," said Turtle. "I didn't know the school system had an open date today."

"Didn't you ever sneak out for a ball game when you were a kid, crawl under the fence?" Fanning felt expansive; Opening Day always did it to him. It was part of the rhythm.

"Oh my yes. But dam'. In Arkansas we never had to ride on any dam' *A* train twenty miles outa town. Hey, you show me the kid that's gonna crawl under this ballpark. Kid'd have to have a god damn demolition squad with him. Kid'd have to have a god damn jackhammer for a nose."

"Kid's gonna have to pay his way, isn't he?"

"Not to take anything away from that kid."

It was true. Flushing Stadium sat on a scar of asphalt with all the elegance of a giant washer glued to a sheet of sandpaper. It was one of the new stadiums built for the major-league expansion boom of the 1960s. It was expensive, efficient, architecturally impeccable. It formed a perfect circle around the playing field, with its symmetrical cone of an outfield: exactly 375 feet down the lines, 410 in straight-away center. There was not a bad seat in the park. No fan sat behind a post. There was a three-star French restaurant for the season box-seat holders, with windows that afforded a view to the field.

There was, above all, the scoreboard: 180 tons of computerized technology. (Danny Breen, the Nats' public relations man, called it an "Information Center.") It had the nickname of every player in the

National League stored in its memory circuits. It had a giant closed-circuit television replay screen. Its massive black slate could flash Technicolor messages of welcome to the network telecasting crews, to groups of Nat ticketholders; it could provide baseball trivia quizzes between innings, the questions posed by an animated version of the Nat mascot—a cute Revolutionary War drummer boy with a bandage on his head. The scoreboard could sound the cavalry "Charge" in stereophonic sound during Nats rallies and could deafen the stadium with an amplified recording of L. C. Fanning's voice yelling, "Toot-toot-tootsie, *good-bye*," after a Nat home run—to the animated accompaniment of a straw-hatted figure with a cane. It could produce an undulating full-color representation of the American flag. It could render animated parodies of any one of fifty-six computerized "game situations." It also gave the score.

"Someday you and me's gonna come to work and find out that electric mother's got our jobs," Turtle had said once. "What's the penalty in this state for murdering a scoreboard?"

In short, Flushing Stadium was an oppressive place in which to watch a baseball game.

Fanning would never say so on the air. "Beautiful Flushing Stadium" he called it on the air; he wasn't out to hurt the Nats' attendance totals. But criminy. He'd come up in the days of the great old upright neighborhood ballparks—Ebbets Field, the Polo Grounds, old Sportsman's Park, Crosley Field—the old square-bottom parks that were crafted in the first twenty-five years of the century, fitted like tiles into the existing mosaic of the city (hence, the lopsided sag of certain elderly outfields) and settling, over the decades, into the stew of summer urban life, absorbing the aromas of sulphur and soot and barroom beer and gasoline from the neighborhoods around them, and in turn investing the neighborhoods with the particular aroma of the ballpark, an aroma elusive to description, but an aroma drawing upon rich dark majestic vapors, dank and hot and sweetly molting; an aroma compounded of stale popcorn and beerfoam and the sweat of men and the holiday perfume of women. The best of these ballparks came to form the spiritual centers of their cities, with their lines of pennants above the treetops by day and, by night, their hum of human energy, of common human hope, the hum broken now and again by the great orgiastic roar, the giant intake of breath, followed by the notes of organ music as if from afar; and all of it encapsulated in the milky electric upshining of the stadium lights that glowed over the city like a corona. Some of those ballparks still stood, by the grace of God; most of them were gone, departed friends, high-rise apartments where Gibson had faced down McCovey on fastballs with the bases loaded.

There was a thumping on the window on Fanning's side, and he gave a start. Somebody's grinning face pressed its nose against the windowpane, a hand waved, and the face was gone. He flashed a smile, a moment too late. Turtle had seen to it that the Lincoln had a fresh wash and wax job, and Fanning knew that the black finish gleamed under the cloudless sky, drawing attention, as Turtle eased his way down the asphalt toward the Cyclone gate marked Press.

"Natives are restless," he remarked with satisfaction. They both removed their Polaroid Cool-Rays. "Here I am, quail," sang Turtle into the dashboard. "This here's yer sweet-talkin' daddy the radio baseball man."

A uniformed attendant in white gloves sprang to open Turtle's door, then sprinted around to Fanning's side.

"Welcome to Flushing Stadium, Mr. Fanning!" The man, touching his visored cap, was a florid Irishman, formal in the old way. "I seen where you picked the Nats on top, sir!"

"You got it, pal." Fanning stood by the car door hitching his trousers up over his middle; his eyes were fixed on the curve of the stadium's rim across the shimmering asphalt.

Standing, he carried his hamshaped belly high. It sat comfortably atop a pair of pipestem legs that gave Fanning a few inches' edge on most men. In his younger days Fanning might have passed for a distance runner. He still liked to accentuate his vertical lines by having his pants fitted snugly at the seat, waist, and crotch (though they chafed like hell on hot days in the booth) with creases as sharp as the edges of a woman's fingernails.

His face, still reddish brown from Florida, was a miniature version of the ham belly—widening as it descended from crown to jowl. The face of a man with a cannon for a voice. His hair was smartly combed, even the thinning strands on the top; over the ears he had let it flare fashionably—vestiges of yellow softening into white. Razor cut. Fanning was a man who thought about his appearance.

"When we got Humphries," said the attendant, lifting a white finger, "I says to my wife, 'That puts the *p* in pennant.' The *p in pennant*, Mr. Fanning."

"He'll get us some runs, won't he," murmured Fanning, but his mind was not on the conversation.

"He'd better. We're payin' him five hunnerd grand a year." Fanning scarcely noticed that the attendant's voice had turned cold. "Five hundred thousand dollars," he repeated, his eyes, for some reason, fixed on his white gloves. "Mother of God, I remember the year Musial signed for a hundred grand. I thought the millennium had come. Now that was a swell fellow, Mr. Musial."

"He'll get us some ribbies," said Fanning. He was gazing at the stadium, and tucking his shirt into the waistband of his pants, and the attendant's voice came from a great distance; it was all happening again inside him.

The rhythm of it was starting, like the stirring of strings at the beginning of a symphony; the great quotidian rhythms of the baseball cycle were moving inside him, and he couldn't help it, he jus. had to stand there a minute and feel it. Forty-two years in the business, *Mister* Play-by-Play, the coast-to-coast hookups, the World Series assignments (sharing the mike with Barber, with Allen, with Pelham himself, the man who invented it), the pennant call for the Giants in '51, riding Thomson's shot into history on the airwaves, the best table at the Copa, golf with Jimmy Durante, the day he got Ike in the booth to call an inning, "playing himself" in that Martin and Lewis movie, oh God, even the long nightgame years with the second-division teams, these Nats in their outlandish uniforms who didn't have a prayer, this perversion of baseball on blue chemical grass, he loved it. Between the white lines the game was still the same; the other sides of the lines, he didn't care to think about too much. The shirting under his armpits and on the small of his back was getting damp. He was leaning against the Lincoln with his weight on his hand. Turtle—short, burly, and bald, the textbook catcher—was scowling at him.

"Come on. Don't leave your game in the bullpen," the old catcher said softly. He sensed what was going through his partner's mind.

It all had to be just right. There were patterns to be observed. Rhythms to be kept. Certain amenities to be respected. Opening Day for Fanning had always been a ceremony of small gestures, an etiquette of colors to be worn, verities spoken, authority affirmed, jokes told, aromas savored; a thousand elusive balances to be plumbed and adjusted, currents tested—it was as though the baseball season were a tangible instrument, a craft, rounded and oddly delicate, which must be launched on a clear pool, with touches of the fingertips, while the nation held its breath. A continuity was at stake; of that Fanning felt sure, although he could not define it: a continuity of the country and the sport and the airwaves intertwined, for he had come, after all the decades and the color guards and the generals home from Europe demonstrating their curve-ball grip, and from the knowledge of his own descriptive voice at large on the rapt continent at night—he had come, after all the decades of all of this, to regard the three entities as mutually supporting, equal in value: the country, the sport, and the airwaves.

It all had to be just right. The rhythms of the season had to be launched with exquisite care. The thread with the past, the precious continuities, must not be destroyed. Especially this season. This season above all, this final, closing Opening Day.

He had known that it was going to be his last one only since February—just a day before the annual Baseball Writers Dinner in New York. He had come in to the doctor with kidney stones. The doctor was just a young blond boy. Easy and methodical. (Good temperament for a relief pitcher.) He had run tests on Fanning—X rays and other things, Fanning didn't follow all of it. Then on Fanning's follow-up visit the kid had sat back in the padded easy chair behind his desk and pulled a gold Eversharp out of his shirt pocket and sat there turning it over and over in his fingers.

Fanning would never forget the way the young doctor slipped his hand in there and pulled out that gold pencil. Like a pitcher wiping his hand on his jersey; just a ritual move to shake off the tension.

Because that was when the doctor told Fanning about the lung.

The kidney stones, the kid said (as though he were talking about some pitcher's sore wishbone), were a typical endocrinal reaction to the other problem; it makes a man run high calcium, which translates into kidney stones.

But the big problem was in the lung.

For a man of sixty-three, a heavy smoker, it was simply not that unusual, that was all. Fanning felt hardheaded about that fact. They could cut on him when the time came. He wasn't going to whine. In the meantime it was his private knowledge and no one else had to know anything about it. Not even Turtle. Especially Turtle.

He announced his retirement at the Baseball Writers Dinner. Effective at the end of the season (barring postseason play).

He did not announce the reason.

It had made a moment. Cries of "No, no," in the smoke-filled banquet hall. The orchestra had struck up an impromptu version of "Toot, Toot, Tootsie! Good-bye." A standing ovation. And of course the papers played it up the next day.

Perhaps he should have stepped down right there and then. (It would have made a bigger moment.) God knew, it wasn't as though L. C. Fanning needed the work. Forty-two years on the air—beginning as a Boy Announcer—were about enough for anybody, he figured. (He would like to have made it to fifty, but a man ought to know when he's reached his time.)

Besides, he had his contacts in Florida. Business opportunities. A friend of his owned a small daylight-hours AM outlet in the Tampa-St. Petersburg area, where the Nats trained in the spring. He could look forward to an hour or so a day on the air, maybe one of those little coffeepot interview shows from a local restaurant. Nothing to strain the vocal cords. Visiting celebrities. He had his following down there. Lifetime ball fans, God bless 'em. He'd have lots of time left over for golf. Lots of nothing but time.

But St. Petersburg would have to wait until the end of the regulation season. (Fat chance for postseason playoffs.) Fanning would give it one last whirl.

He wanted to go out with his Day.

Most people have their vanities. Fanning guessed that his was that he wanted to go out with a Day: The marching band. The ballplayers lined up along the baselines. Some of the old Giants on hand, people like Thomson. And Turtle, of course. Member of that '51 team, now Fanning's partner—the best friend that Fanning ever had. It wouldn't be Fanning's Day without Turtle there.

And the microphone at home plate, plugged into the P.A. system.

The dignitaries. Commissioner of baseball, couple of entertainers. (Could they get Sinatra? Frank had "done" an inning once in Fanning's booth.)

He wouldn't even mind a little bunting.

The telegrams—from the mayor, from the governor of Michigan (his boyhood home state), perhaps from the President. The President was a ball fan. "Avid," was the way Fanning had once heard him describe it. The chief executive taking time out from his busy routine . . . it wasn't beyond the bounds of reason.

And the gifts. The golf clubs, the ticket to Honolulu, the appliances. The savings bond. He didn't care about the gifts. He'd give the gifts all back. God help him, he just wanted a chance to stand there at home plate and throw his arms up and wave good-bye to it all, after forty-two years in the business. One final flourish for the fans, God bless 'em. Greatest people in the world. One last rendition of his trademark home run bellow, that had become so famous down through the years.

"TOOT-TOOT-TOOTSIE, *GOOD-BYE!*"

He could hear it echo through Flushing Stadium's silver spires and girders every time he thought about it. What a moment. A farewell moment in baseball history to equal Gehrig's . . . it gave him gooseflesh.

A Day certainly wasn't too much to expect. He was the dean of this business now that Pelham was retired, no doubt about that. Brickhouse in Chicago had a claim, but Brickhouse had come up in television. The hell with that noise—no reflection on Brickhouse. (Come to that, they had given Brickhouse his Day. And if a television man deserves a Day, there's no way they can't hold a Day for a radioman. Radio was where all the art was.)

So much for the Day. He wanted it, he'd go through Hades to get it. And broadcasting one more year of major-league baseball was not exactly L. C. Fanning's idea of Hades.

What made the whole shooting match a trick call, though, was the matter of the laryngeal nerve.

The lung thing was beginning to affect this nerve. The young doctor had said so. (Twirling that blasted Eversharp.) There was going to be some paralysis, the doc had said. (If that arm stays sore, you may have to miss a turn or two.) There was going to be some fading in and fading out of the voice before it got to be totally bad.

Now there was a joke. Fanning's voice box burning out. Like a piece of old radio equipment. Well, why not? Wasn't that what he was?

Meanwhile, here he stood in front of Flushing Stadium on his final Opening Day. With its rituals to be honored. What would the baseball world be without rituals?

He'd had to tell the stickup story again to Turtle. The attendant had to be there waiting for them (the white gloves were important). And the hat. Criminy, he had to have the hat along to jam on his head for Opening Day.

It was the first thing he had bought in New York City when he got the Giants assignment in 1948: a $7.50 Ambassador with a two-and-three-quarter-inch brim, satin lining. He'd bought it at Worth and Worth on Madison Avenue. It was a hat meant to be worn by a sportscaster, with just the right creases, the right dents in the crown; a daredevil, Johnny-on-the-scene hat that had made him feel immediately a part of the sporting world. He'd put it on as soon as he was out of the store.

Over the years he'd preserved the hat as though it were a part of his physical self. Changed the lining he didn't know how many times. Worn it stubbornly after brims got shorter, then after men stopped wearing hats at all. He loved the damn thing; it said something about his line of work. He still got it out of mothballs for special occasions. The fans depended on it.

Now he grasped its soft crown tenderly and arranged it over his skull just so. Just the right tilt. He was ready.

He looked at his wristwatch. Good God. Where had the time gone?

He motioned to Turtle and they started across the asphalt.

"Hey boys! Ain't you forgettin' something?"

The attendant's voice stopped them. Fanning and Teweles gave each other a quick inventory. It was essential that nothing be out of place, that no ingredient be missing from the construction of their Opening Day ritual.

Fanning patted his shirt pocket. He had his White Owls. Turtle had his false teeth in his mouth. They both had on their Polaroid Cool-

Rays. In addition to his hat, Fanning wore his trademark red polyester blazer with the white nylon open-collar shirt underneath, the one finished off with clusters of red checks. The fans had come to expect something red in all of Fanning's ballpark ensembles. Turtle had on his own "Total Look" concept, which involved a plain green jacket over a body shirt unbuttoned wide over his hairy barrel chest to show off a concatenation of turquoise neck jewelry. Turtle's color concept on this day was built around green. They both had on their Nunn-Bush tasseled white loafers set off by black ribbed silk support hose.

Fanning was carrying an attaché case in which there resided a National League Green Book, the New York Nats annual Information Guide, his own personal bound baseball scorebook, a three-minute egg timer, a tin ashtray coated with flecks of green paint, a Bic lighter, a stopwatch, a pair of binoculars, a sheaf of the afternoon's commercial announcements encased in clear plastic binders, ten felt-tip pens each in a different color, and half a package of Velamints.

They were two killer broadcasters. No mistake.

They both turned and looked back. The attendant put his fists together, raised them above his head, and made a wild circle.

The net.

"Damn me," muttered Turtle and started back for the Lincoln on a dead lope, rummaging in his pants pocket for the keys.

Fanning pounded his forehead with the heel of his hand.

"Pal," he wailed, "you just made the fielding gem of the afternoon. Here, I wanna give you a little token of my appreciation." He reached in his own pocket for his money clip.

How could he have forgotten the net? Without the net, his Opening Day ritual would have fallen apart at the center. The net was as much a part of L. C. Fanning's identity as the red sport coat, the high baritone pitch of his announcing voice, his trademark "Toot-toot-tootsie, *good-bye!*" The net was a brilliant theatrical stroke, a prop that set him apart from every other announcer in the major leagues.

An aluminum butterfly net with an elongated handle, it rested on the shelf of Fanning's broadcasting booth, in plain view of the crowd, its deep webbing visible against the yellow WERA broadcast banner. It went where Fanning went, from city to city across the National League.

When a batter hit a high foul that arced back toward the pressbox, L. C. Fanning would seize the net and make a great show of attempting to snare the ball in flight. Sometimes his efforts would cause him to lean far out of the booth, in apparent defiance of a free fall to the loge seats. In that instant the attention of every fan in the stadium would shift from the game to Fanning with his net. Crowds at Flushing Stadium and in the ball parks around the league had long since learned to accompany the moment with a drawn-out cry of "OooooooooOOOooOOH!" When Fanning actually succeeded in bagging the ball—maybe twice in a season—the crowd would top off its cry with a shriek of *"Olé!"*

When that happened, Fanning would raise both arms over his head and welcome the crowd's tribute like a Roman gladiator, turning this way and that, shaking the net, a small red dot high in the bosom of the stadium, drawing the energy of the throng into himself with such force that often the game itself would come to a halt. The television cameras from both the New York and the visiting team's station would swivel around to train on the Nats' radioman, until he fished the ball from the webbing and tossed it down into a forest of hands. The routine had become so famous that New York fans began showing up at the stadium with their own nets. Then, a couple of seasons ago, Danny Breen, who didn't miss a trick, invented a promotion called Nat Net Night. On Nat Net Nights, small plastic replicas of Fanning's net were handed out to every child under the age of thirteen accompanied by a parent. Fanning had not been so sure he liked Nat Net Night. There was something in it of the blue chemical grass on the outfield floor. But he went along with it. He was, after all, a company man.

So how could he forget the net here on Opening Day? The question troubled him.

"Here, pal. . . ." Fanning held forth a five-dollar bill.

The attendant turned his eyes away. His expression darkened. "I don't want your money, Mr. Fanning," he said in a low voice. "Not everything in this here park is done for a dollar."

A car door slammed, and Turtle was back with the net in his hands. He draped it over Fanning's head.

"This way you'll always know where it's at," he drawled.

"How about this guy," Fanning appealed to the attendant. But the man was still looking away. Fanning put the five-dollar bill back into his pocket. Fanning knew that he had violated something unspoken but essential between the two of them, some leftover bond from the old days when the man had worked the lot at the Polo Grounds. He hadn't meant to, but he'd done it anyway. That, and forgetting his net in the first place, threatened to upset his balance, to get this season of all seasons off on a wrong foot.

He wouldn't let it happen. Nothing was going to destroy his Opening Day mood.

He took the net off his head; it had suddenly felt too real. "Come on, Turtle. I'm gonna show you how to talk into a microphone."

CHAPTER

2

EVERY TIME FRANKIE WILDE had to walk past Jeffrey Spector's office doorway, he got the cold flashes. He'd had to make that walk often over these past three months. Jeffrey's new office was situated between his own and the WERA executive office latrine. Frankie Wilde had to use the WERA executive office latrine a lot lately—mostly as a result of the water he gulped to wash down the varieties of pills he took to smother down the anxiety symptoms engendered by the presence of Jeffrey Spector next door. It was what they called a vicious circle in technical language.

"Hiya, Chief," he called to the slight figure seated inside, beyond the secretary's alcove, and stepped lively on down the corridor as though he were in a hurry to get someplace. (Where? Past his office was a dead end. In more ways than one.) Someday, he knew, he was going to walk into Jeffrey Spector's narrow line of sight and Spector was just going to slide back that plate in his skull and flip on that laser beam that Wilde knew he had screwed in there, and that was going to be the end of Frankie Wilde. There wasn't even going to be a stain on the goddamned rug.

"Frankie, can I see you for a second?" Frankie Wilde stopped dead in his tracks and his shoulder blades did this weird thing they'd been doing lately; they drew up together like somebody's ass, and convulsed. Wilde knew that Jeffrey's bluejeaned secretary had seen it, and he knew it was not a sight you'd ask to see. Frankie Wilde had these big beefy shoulders; he had, after all, fought in the Korean conflict (which fact he liked to remind these new kids of in a number of ways, such as by calling the WERA executive men's room the "latrine"). Frankie Wilde wasn't even his real name; he'd chosen it in his deejay days back in the fifties because he thought it fitted his rugged image. The point was, Frankie Wilde was nobody's pussy. *But god damn!* This kid Spector was enough to send anybody screaming out into the streets.

"What's on your agenda for this afternoon, Frankie?"

"Well, I . . ." *Tell the truth. He can read your mind anyway.* "I actually thought I'd do a little tour of duty out Flushing Stadium way. Spend two–three innings with L.C. and Turtle. Make sure things are running smoothly. Season lid-lifter out there, you know." He jingled the change in his pockets, and then stopped. Jeffrey Spector, he had noticed, never jingled the change in his pockets. Wilde wasn't even sure that Jeffrey Spector had pockets.

Jeffrey Spector nodded thoughtfully, and the thing that spooked Wilde the most about him drew into focus again. *He looked like a child, sitting in that chair!* A terrible, scary child. The thin, almost emaciated body, the long white neck with its bobbing Adam's apple emerging from the improbable western-style plaid shirt, the mop of dull brown hair, the staring, slightly walled eyes behind the dark-rimmed glasses—he looked like the Boy Genius on *Mr. Wizard.* ("Gosh, Mr. Wizard—take *that,* and *that,* and *that!*" "*Aaagh . . .* Jeffrey, I told you . . . not to tamper . . . with those circuits . . .")

Twenty-three years old, and executive vice-president/general manager of Radio Station WERA, the flagship station of MetroCom Broadcast Communications, Inc. It was obscene. It was a violation of nature. It was, in its way, an eerie affirmation of the message that Jeffrey Spector had hanging on the wall behind his desk—a message written in clusters of type on computer printout paper:

REALITY IS ONLY WHAT
YOU PERCEIVE IT TO BE

"You like baseball."

Spoken flatly, the remark was nonetheless a question, Wilde knew. No. It was cross-examination.

He shrugged his big shoulders, which was a mistake; they bunched and did their ass thing again. "Well . . . you know . . . they . . . a few innings now and then. Got to look out after our guys. . . ."

What was he being so defensive about? Of course he liked baseball. He loved baseball! What the hell was the matter with liking baseball? What was wrong with going out to the ballpark and looking at broads for a few hours? Besides, as the station's program director, it was his duty to keep a tight rein on all phases of the broadcast operation.

Jeffrey Spector was turning a ball-point pen over and over on his desk top, sliding a thin thumb and forefinger down along its shaft, letting the pen drop, picking up the bottom end and starting the process all over again. In the silence of the vice-president's office, the pen went *"Thack . . . thack . . . thack."*

Wilde realized he was staring at the pen as though it were a gavel.

"Your energy blows me away, Frankie. I can relate to it." Jeffrey's own eyes were on the pen; Wilde could never be sure whether the kid was putting him on or not. In his flat, slightly bored voice, Spector continued: "While you're out there, I have a little number I'd like you to lay on the guy who owns the Nats. Sonderling?"

"Sonderling."

(*Goddamn right Sonderling, you little punk,* thought Wilde; *M. Jerrold Sonderling, the biggest real estate developer in this freaking town since the Pilgrims. . . .*)

"Right; well, tell Mr. Sonderling that we're interested in unloading the Nats games, as early as July if we can work out an arrangement that is mutually agreeable. . . ."

Frankie Wilde sucked in air. He had to bite his tongue to keep from yelling that that was the craziest, most insolent, most harebrained freaking notion he'd ever heard of. WERA had only broadcast Nat baseball since the Nats were created in 1960—since Jeffrey

Spector was three years old. The Nat broadcasts were the cornerstone of WERA's identity in New York. Jeffrey Spector had held his exalted new position for the sum total of three months, and if this little android expected to get away with this kind of wholesale . . .

Keeping his voice pleasant, like an uncle trying to talk a favorite nephew into placing the blowtorch carefully back on the workshop bench, Wilde said:

"Jeffrey. Have you checked this out with the group management people at MetroCom? You know that the last thing Silvers did here was renew the contract with the Nats."

Silvers was Spector's predecessor.

"That is one reason Mr. Silvers isn't here anymore, Frankie."

"The point is, *we're locked in*! We're paying Jerry Sonderling half a million a year to carry Nats baseball. There's not another fifty-thousand-watt station in this city that's going to give him that kind of deal."

"You don't have to convince me of that," said Jeffrey Spector dryly. "Have you looked at last year's Arbitrons for the Nat broadcasts?"

Frankie Wilde made circles with his hands. "Okay. They didn't get the greatest numbers in the world."

"They didn't get the greatest numbers in the neighborhood. Six points per quarter hour. And the points they did get were mainly people over fifty. Look, WERA just about broke even on the Nats baseball thing."

"God dammit—" Wilde realized he was on dangerous ground; he was talking to a kid who could terminate his career at any moment and not look back. At age forty-eight, with alimony, Frankie Wilde needed a career. But what this kid was proposing amounted to an act of lunacy. "God dammit, Jeffrey, the Nats games were never *supposed* to make big money. They're a *goodwill* gesture; they're something people *identify* with WERA; they're a *building block* . . ." He let his voice trail off.

"Goodwill." Jeffrey Spector turned the words over in a toneless voice, as though they comprised an interesting phrase he had found in a pocket foreign language guide.

Frankie Wilde shifted his ground.

"Why do you want to risk pulling down heat from the brass at

MetroCom with a stunt like this? Hey. Across the board we're holding our own.''

Jeffrey Spector searched Frankie Wilde's face with an appraising
look that made Wilde's heart pump. With his thin right hand he fur-
rowed in a drawer beneath his desk. The hand came up with a thick
sheaf of papers: the winter Arbitron sweeps. Spector let the sheaf fall
with a heavy thud on his desk.

"We're not here to hold our own, Frankie. We're here to grab
from others. That's why you have an outrageous kid like me for a
boss now. That's what the people at MetroCom are interested in.
Movement. And the fact is, Frankie, we are *not* holding our own.
K3Q is taking numbers away from everybody in town. Us included.
That ain't holding steady.''

K3Q. How Frankie Wilde had come to hate those affected call-let-
ters. Thirteen months ago K3Q was an unknown FM station broadcasting wallpaper music from a second-floor studio up above an ice
cream parlor. It couldn't get an Arbitron rating with sonar equipment.
Then one sunny day the program director got a bright idea and told
his stock boy to pick up four hundred dollars worth of albums during
his lunch hour.

The albums could be by any artist or group, the program director
specified, as long as they featured a certain musical rhythm that was
becoming popular with Hispanics, blacks, gays, and other subcultural
groups.

The rhythm sounded as follows: "*Got*-cha, *got*-cha, *got*-cha, *got*-
cha.''

The program director's hunch proved to be a good one. Within six
months K3Q was the number-one-rated station. Not FM station: radio
station. Not in New York: in the country.

Four months after that MetroCom Broadcasting made some trade
headlines of its own. It promoted a twenty-three-year-old programming whiz named Jeffrey Spector to the position of vice-
president/general manager of its flagship station, WERA, the
fifty-thousand-watt sports-and-easy-listening behemoth of mid-
Manhattan. Spector was the youngest station executive, by twenty
years, in the history of MetroCom.

Spector's promotion seemed like a good thing for Frankie Wilde at
first. It created a vacancy at program director. At the time Frankie

had wanted program director. With twenty-four years in the business under his belt he knew his on-air glory was behind him, and he wanted to step into a more institutionalized kind of gig. He knew scheduling. He knew the WERA listener market. He thought he would be happy puttering with the flow of WERA's daily sound, and filling in as a relief man on the air from time to time.

In reality, Wilde's new opportunity had not proved to be quite so pleasant. His title carried with it a $50,000 salary, but still it was a nominal title, words on a desk plate. The real program director was Jeffrey Spector. Spector was also the de facto music director, news director, director of community affairs, editorial director, sports director, and director of public relations—although other people answered to those titles and drew paychecks. Frankie Wilde was, in fact, one of several personal caddies for Jeffrey Spector.

Wilde should have sensed what he was in for on the first day that Jeffrey Spector took command. But now it was too late.

Now the lad was lecturing Frankie Wilde on the nuances of programming strategy. Calmly, with no outward sign of condescension: a technician reciting dry facts.

"There is no alternative for us, Frankie. K3Q has us all playing defense. We're all adjusting. The station that adjusts the best will be the station that can counterattack the soonest. Look at WABC. Seventy percent pop. I mean, what can I do? I don't like to play defense, but the figures are in front of us."

"The Nat games are holding their own," Frankie said "They averaged a six share last season, what the hell's wrong with that?"

Spector held up a bony finger.

"Number one. That was last season, when K3Q was still taking off. If you look at the September figures—when the Nats were busy finishing last, by the way—you'll find a thirty percent drop over the April figures. All right?"

"But that's still—"

A second bony finger joined the first.

"*Number two*. We're dealing with incompatible audiences, man. The kids who tune us in to hear Contemporary just *flame out* when the *ball* game comes on. They're not into *ball*, see. And the people who follow the ball games don't relate to Contemporary."

"The sales department likes baseball games, Jeffrey. They're easy to sell."

"Yeah. Right." Spector made a show of checking his digital wristwatch. "To specialty advertisers who don't buy time the rest of the day. Ice hockey was a very big item on WMAQ in Chicago. It also buried the station. Look," Spector said, "there's no way to say it nice, Frankie. Sports audiences are Poly Grip audiences. They're thirty-fives to forty-nines. I'm not here to deal with thirty-fives to forty-nines. Am I communicating with you?"

Frankie Wilde nodded. It occurred to him that he was forty-eight. He ran a hand through his curly hair. He cleared his throat and made himself say the next, dangerous thing.

"Jeffrey, excuse me, but I asked you a question a minute ago, and you didn't give me an answer. *Did you clear this with the brass at MetroCom?*"

For the first time since Wilde had known him, Jeffrey Spector smiled. It was not a nice smile.

"If I didn't," he said, "and if my strategy falls through, then you'll be sitting in this chair by the end of the summer, won't you?"

And if it doesn't fall through, I'll probably be broadcasting for All-City Taxi, Wilde thought.

"You'll speak to Mr. Sonderling, then?"

"Sure I will, Jeffrey. If that's what you want."

Frankie Wilde opened a desk drawer. What he took out was not a stack of Arbitron ratings, but a warm chicken salad sandwich on whole wheat bread, wrapped in waxed paper. He unfolded the paper moodily, like a man opening a letter that he knew was bad news.

Things had certainly changed around WERA in the last six months. You wouldn't know the place. Before, the station had had a reputation in broadcasting circles as a great place to work, to carve out a career.

In the hierarchy of New York radio stations, WERA was known as a safe long-term investment—not a glamour stock like WABC, but a solid, respectably profitable institution. Its audiences were people who had *grown up* on WERA. WERA was a "family" station, one of the last few remaining: all dark mahogany paneling and institutional carpets. It was famous for nurturing personalities and making them into stars, personalities like L. C. Fanning and Parks Madison, the "zany" morning man of seventeen years, and the legendary Whispering DeWitt (no one knew his real first name), whose ethereal voice had kept New York's "night people" spellbound for as long as anyone could remember. It was said that Whispering DeWitt was a disinherited socialite who appeared at the studio each midnight clad in a velvet cape with a red lining. Actually, Whispering DeWitt was a short and grossly overweight former piano tuner named Hy Potash. That was one of the best-kept secrets in radio history. Oh, God, WERA had been a wonderful place to be. An ideal place for a guy like Frankie Wilde. But now it had all changed.

The sign posted by Jeffrey Spector in the main studio said it all:

Shut Up And Play The Hits

The irony was that Frankie Wilde found part of the change exciting. It was the natural energy of radio awakening from a long sleep, reclaiming some of the freshness and diversity that television had bled from it in the 1950s. Frankie Wilde was the last person to object to that. He was a radio purist; he had waited years for this to happen. American radio was on the move again, billings were up, program formats were expanding, even the mystery shows were coming back—that was the good part.

The bad part was the excess. The people coming through these doors now—Jesus, Wilde had had a hard enough time dealing with Jeffrey Spector's predecessor as general manager. Silvers was a hotshot out of Los Angeles who had done big things with a sleepy fringe station in the San Fernando Valley called KULT. Silvers had switched KULT's mellow-rock format to all-country music. He had promoted the change with bumper stickers, T-shirts, and television commercials. He had flooded the station's airwaves with a succession of cash giveaways. Thousands of dollars were doled out each week in "jackpot" phone calls that depended on the recipient's answering with the phrase, "KULT's gonna fill my pockets!"

Rival station managers shrieked that Silvers had bought their listening audience. Which he had. When he left KULT for New York, the station was number two in the market.

Silvers blew into WERA with plans to strike gold again with the same formula. That was a year and a half ago. But he reached too far. Silvers hired as his program director the young Jeffrey Spector, whom he proudly described as "my protégé."

Within eleven months Silvers's "protégé" had quite simply eaten Silvers alive. No one could even find out where Silvers had landed after the coup. Now, with Jeffrey Spector in total command of the station, WERA was starting to learn what the word *change* meant.

Spector's first morning as vice-president and general manager lived in infamy as the Day of the Seven Little Soldiers.

On that morning Spector summoned into his office, one by one, seven of the key people at WERA: three on-air personalities and four department heads. Each of them had been hired by Silvers. On his desk Spector had arranged seven hand-painted wooden toy soldiers, all in a row.

The first man into Spector's office was the happy-go-lucky morning man. When the man emerged, he was not laughing. One of the soldiers on Spector's desk had been toppled over.

So it went until all seven soldiers were lying face down. Not a word was spoken during the entire proceedings.

In the three months following the Day of the Seven Little Soldiers, Jeffrey Spector set about to complete his lobotomization of WERA.

The pop sound had taken over more and more segments of the broadcast day. It saturated the morning drive-time hours, where call-in shows and middle-of-the-road tunes had once reigned. It had moved into the late afternoons, replacing a popular women's gossip and phone-in show. Now it was licking at the timeslots reserved for Nats baseball broadcasts.

Frankie Wilde took the limp chicken salad sandwich in his hand and squeezed it until the filling ran out over his fist. He pretended that the sandwich was Jeffrey Spector. The filling felt good on his hand.

He got up from his desk, wiped the chicken salad from his hands, rolled down his sleeves, and reached for his natty brown blazer. It was getting so he felt sheepish wearing a blazer around here.

Frankie Wilde did not like what he was going to do at Flushing Stadium that afternoon. Among other things, he would be sticking a knife in the ribs of L. C. Fanning and Turtle Teweles. He and Fanning went back a few years together in this business; they were part of the WERA ''family'' well before Turtle joined the broadcast team. And if Sonderling agreed to Spector's outrageous request, there was no guarantee that the next station would pick up Fanning's contract.

Hey. He didn't have a choice.

''Get into that game, Frankie,'' came Jeffrey Spector's voice as Frankie passed his office doorway. ''Go Nats, or whatever.''

''I will,'' he called back. But already he felt like he was out of the game.

CHAPTER

NOW IT BEGINS.
        Nearing the press gate
turnstile, Fanning felt the rhythms take hold of him. It was a thin and
delicate moment, this first walk to the stadium. It depended upon
morninglight reflecting on steel and chrome; it depended upon an
external sense of himself and Turtle Teweles, their correctness of
shined shoes and wristwatches, their erudition of Florida tans and
clean fingernails.

Passing the northeast curve of the stadium, where the bleachers
abruptly fell away in a vertical sweep of exposed girders, Fanning
caught a glimpse of the playing field. It was a slice of brown infield
earth, smooth as mahogany, the crescent of dirt behind second base
that gave way to the outfield sward as abruptly and cleanly as Indiana
gives way to Ohio. Heaped above the pristine playing field were the
far grandstands—a perpendicular suspension of seats, tiers overlap-
ping tiers, like a frozen avalanche, deep and shadowed. He saw the
horizontal lines of color that delineated the vertical sweep: the cream-
colored section at playing field level that contained the box seats, the
red seats of the loge section stacked above it; above that, the blue of

the mezzanine; then, rising to the distant rim of the stadium, almost melancholy in their arid isolation, the green rows of the upper level.

Fanning let his eye drop quickly again to the slice of playing field. It was utterly familiar and yet impossibly removed, a battlefield from an ancient and constantly changing dream.

"Come along," said Turtle, who had trudged several paces ahead. "If I don't start suckin' beer in a few more minutes I ain't gonna be in no condition to face the 1980 edition of the New York Nats."

"You know, old pal, you might have made the Hall of Fame," muttered Fanning, "if they had installed a courtesy tap in it." An old joke between them. He started walking again, but his eyes remained fastened on the slice of infield until the right-field bleachers blocked it from view. He couldn't say what was on his mind to Turtle. What was on his mind was the feeling that as long as that particular crescent of the second-base area stayed exactly the way it was, a man might not succumb to the erosion of time.

At the press gate now, they were waved through the turnstile by an attendant before they could produce their press cards. Handshakes all around. "Don't let Brickhouse through unless he knows the password, Tommy." The Chicago Cubs were the Opening Day hostiles. "Ha-ha, right, Mr. Fanning." A salute. "You and Turtle bring us a pennant now." All correct; all part of the rhythms.

Inside the stadium now; its innards like an exposed skeleton; a great dusky intelligence of girders, crisscrossing pedestrian ramps, coils of pipe; the dusk broken here and there by the sudden portals affording a glimpse of blue sky, pennants, the outfield sward; or by the isolated glow of a refreshment stand, with its sign demanding Please Form a Line. The stadium's intestines formed a transit system that mimicked the great highways of America. Whereas the old ballparks offered narrow walkways, two-lane blacktops to the hillside meadows that were the grandstand seats, these modern structures seemed engineered for fast and constant travel: wide, efficient slabs of concrete that dipped and soared among the various levels, the section numerals posted like exit signs. There was a constant volume of pedestrian traffic on these throughways, Fanning had noticed, even during the heart of a ballgame: people wandering, strolling, hurrying, clustering about the refreshment stands like tired drivers at a roadside oasis, departing again, in circling motions, yet detached from the event that drew them there. Moths around a flame. Where did they think they were going? Many of them carried transistor radios. Did they listen to the game as they strolled? The sight of all the radios pleased Fanning. The radios made him think of his own voice, floating up as it must have from the warm dark dashboards of countless thousands of automobiles over all the years. He imagined his voice in the moving hum of summer evenings on the road, his voice the voice of summer itself, filling the minds of tired salesmen, boys in jalopies, a young couple out on a date, taxicab drivers, stevedores heading home, the men in the neighborhood out for a beer, all the pilgrims of the American road—himself a guest in their intimacy, filling their minds with the imagery of infields blazing under arc lights, of quick strapping men with legendary names who strained against fast balls and dove for sinking line drives on behalf of all the people on the road.

With Fanning's voice to unify it all: connecting the grids and patterns that are the ball game to a waiting, restless world, a world dying for grids and patterns. It was one of the recurring images that kept his life's work from ever seeming stale—that kept it, in fact, tinged with majesty.

"Now that's a great invention, isn't it, the portable radio?" he remarked to Turtle, expecting nothing more than Teweles's contented grunt of affirmation. But instead, a cloud passed over the old catcher's face, and he remarked with unaccustomed vehemence:

"It's *tit*."

Fanning had to stop and look at his partner to make sure he heard right. "It's *what*, pal?" he asked.

"It's *tit*." Turtle was serious. His fierce eyes swept the people around him.

"Portable radios is *tit*. These sorry people cain't leave their house without stickin' a radio in they ear. Ever time I see some asshole with a portable radio I say to myself, there's one sorry bastard that's suckin' tit."

"Turtle. Criminy. If it wasn't for portable radios you and I'd be talking to ourselves."

Teweles eyed Fanning for a moment and then turned his head to spit, a gesture that he had effectively used to wither umpires in his playing days.

"L.C., Jesus Only God you don't think they's listenen to *us*, do you? You ever pay attention to the slop that comes outa them things? It ain't nothin' but Porter Rican rock an' roll. It ain't nothin' but *tit*."

"Tit. That's fine, Turtle. That's fine talk."

Turtle was unchastised.

"Portable radios is *tit*. Candy bars is *tit*. Dogs on leashes is *tit*. Motorcycles. Ever'body in this candy-assed country's gotta have their tit along before they can have any fun. Americans are desperate for tit. Lookit all these fat titsuckers. Hell, L.C., I've studied it. You ever wanta hear about it, I got me a whole philosophy of tit."

Fanning was just starting to believe that maybe his longtime running mate was talking serious for once in his life.

When the old catcher pulled up his shoulders and uttered the baseball announcer's most cherished qualifier.

"Not," said Turtle, "to take anything away from tit."

The two partners stretched their mouths and brayed into one another's faces.

"You old son-of-a-biscuit-eater. Come on, I want you to explain to the WERA listening audience about tit."

"I will, too, by God, you just gimme the sign."

The fans were becoming aware of them now. In their bright announcers' clothing, Fanning and Teweles were distinct from the dull festivity of the workingman fan: the notch-sleeved white shirt with the undershirt visible, the dutiful suit-coat folded and draped over one arm, or the functional nylon Windbreaker, the kids in their sloganed T-shirts, and every twelfth fan with a fielder's mitt. (The crowds at Yankee Stadium were different, Fanning had noticed from his infrequent visits there—raucous fiestas of dark slick strutters in platform shoes and wide-brim fedoras; sweet wine and marijuana took precedence over red-hots and popcorn. Fanning tried not to be judgmental. It was not as though he was prejudiced; some of the finest young ballplayers he knew were latino and black. But . . . he was at home, that was all, with the white ethnic working-class clientele at Flushing. They were the Fans Eternal. Like the game itself, they had not changed, in essence, from the old days, from the days before Bobby Thomson hit that home run.)

"Heyyyy, L. C. Fanning! Turtle Teweles!"

"Wouldn't be a ball game without you, L.C.!"

"Hey, Turtle, sign my card, baby!"

"Lessee the net, L.C. Gonna get a foul ball today?"

"Give us the old 'Toot, toot,' L.C.!"

It added to the rightness of things. He heard Turtle's guttural drawl of response beside him, and he felt good. Striding toward the elevator to the press level, Polaroid Cool-Rays in place, correct and official, both of them, but never too absorbed to return the waves of fans, the salutes from daddies in their go-to-hell Bermudas showing blue-veined calves, their families clustered under Nat pennants like lost regiments. He loved to walk among the fans. Face it: He didn't mind being recognized.

But Fanning liked it almost as much when the fans recognized his partner, Turtle Teweles. Few people, of course, remembered that it was L. C. Fanning who gave Elvin Ray Teweles the nickname "Turtle" during the Turt's playing days. It happened during a Giants game at Crosley Field in 1948 when Teweles, who was then catching for the Reds, was knocked spinning at home plate by an onrushing Don Mueller. On his back, with the ribs of his chest protector turned toward the sky and his stubby arms and legs flailing, Teweles resembled a large turtle that had been tipped upside down, and Fanning said so. The nickname stuck. It contained, after all, a larger aptness. Teweles, the unlettered (and then virtually mute) Arkansas farmboy, shuffled and dragged his way through most phases of his life with the ungainliness of a turtle on land. Ill-mannered, ill-spoken and un-kempt, he was one of that legion of unbelonging men born with the aptitude to play this unlikely game, this game so disconnected from evolutionary skills yet so deep in the blood of American men. He was an organism designed by nature to be a catcher or nothing at all. ("The tools of ignorance match the ignorance of Teweles," one scribe had angrily penned after a disastrous attempt to interview the then-rookie in 1946.)

But when Elvin Ray did in fact don his "tools of ignorance," his mask and chest protector and shinguards, and make his way onto the major-league diamonds of America, a remarkable transformation oc-curred. Like a turtle slipping into a stream, he acquired a brute sort of grace, a rough padding elegance behind the plate. His skills were primal. He never batted for a high average. But his hits had an un-canny timeliness about them (a notion promoted by the young announcer L. C. Fanning). Teweles was a hero to Fanning, and it was Fanning's encomiums that inspired the Giants to trade for the Turtle in 1950—assuring Teweles a place on the Miracle Giants of 1951. Thomson's team. It was Fanning, too, who persuaded the laconic athlete to come up into the broadcast booth and develop himself into a color announcer at career's end. The old catcher, spared the lingering half-life that awaits most men who express themselves with their bodies, came to regard Fanning as something of a messiah. The two men idolized each other, and became, in no time, quite the vogue on the New York sports airwaves.

They were at the press elevator now, and Turtle was in a hurry to get on up to the pressbox and start slapping backs and chugging free pressbox beer. Not Fanning: "You go on; and fer cripes sake save a little for me." Fanning's heart was starting to pound. He headed for an unmarked door on the ground level, where a single Andy Frain usher sat on a folding chair tilted against the concrete wall. Fingers to the brim of the hat: *Good to see you, Mr. Fanning.* He opened the gray door and L. C. Fanning entered Eden.

Down a gray corridor lit by naked light bulbs, through another door and into the runway that leads to the Nats' dugout. He was walking on wooden slats now, which yielded to the spikes of baseball shoes. He felt his body expand, his stride loosen. He listened to the sounds of his own feet pounding the boards that major-leaguers trod. Willie Mays had walked through here on his way to work. Musial in his last days. Seaver, Bench, Rose. Drysdale, Big Double-D, now an announcer himself. The National League walked these boards. And L. C. Fanning. Fanning knew them, knew them all. They knew Fanning. He had walked among them. One thing was sure: the thing inside him, the wearing out of parts, as he thought of it—like the fading of a good radio tube—it couldn't rob him of this life, this universe, nor of his relationship to it. His contributions. It was why he felt no sorrow. There was light up ahead, the white refraction of sunlight. The dugout. Men's voices. An inventory of yellow Adirondack bats. Blue plastic batting helmets stacked military style. Rolls of adhesive tape. A clipboard. A black telephone receiver mounted on the wall, for calling the bullpen.

Fanning strode toward the entranceway leading into the dugout—

and nearly buried his nose in a swatch of gray woolen underjersey. He heard a deep fluid voice say *"Dam'."* He felt a rock-hard torso, reacting by a lithe instinct, pull back to soften the collision. Looking up, Fanning realized he had inadvertently brought his net down over the head of a ballplayer. He stared into the unamused eyes of a hard handsome black face. He recognized Lionell David "Bogart" Humphries.

"Man, ain't you heard niggers are out of season?"

It was muttered without mirth. The ballplayer lifted the net back over his head—brushed it away, really, as though it were a cobweb— and pushed on past Fanning, heading for the clubhouse.

It was the second time in fifteen minutes now that Bogart Humphries had figured as a jarring note in Fanning's Opening Day rhythms; the second time, for that matter, that Fanning's net had befouled him. Again, Fanning sensed a gathering discordance. Again he suppressed it. He hadn't yet formally met Humphries. The slugging outfielder, an American League superstar for years, had come over to the Nats in an unexpected trade after spring training. He had a reputation as a talented but sarcastic troublemaker. It was not an auspicious meeting for the two of them.

At least nobody had seen the incident, thank God. Fanning gripped his net by the neck, in the same hand that held his briefcase, and strode through the entranceway into the Nat dugout. "Hey, Voice." A player clapped him on the shoulder. A rookie. Pendleton. A strong-faced kid with wild yellow hanks of hair. The kid had a wax cup of Coca-Cola in one hand. He smelled of liniment. For an absurd instant Fanning felt grateful to the kid to the point of tears. He wanted to smother his face in the tundra of strength and assurance that was the kid's chest. Immediately he was redfaced at the private thought. "Hey, pal." His voice was suddenly deeper than it had been all day. He loved these kids, their wonderful agility, their clean-cut ways—that's what he told himself. And he glowed (cripes, after forty-two years) at that term, "Voice." *They* recognized *him.* A nickname, acknowledged by professional ballplayers—well, it was about all that anyone had a decent right to expect out of life. The rhythms of the day reasserted themselves.

He was in the midst of ballplayers now, a scattering of Nats who were not involved in batting practice. (On the far side of the field, beyond the batting cage, the Cubs were throwing on the sidelines, big easy men in blue uniforms, visible from the dugout perspective only to the waist, as though the Flushing infield encompassed the curvature of the earth.) Fanning had never accustomed himself to the immediacy of major-league baseball players in uniform. He felt their presence almost as a mild physical shock. They seemed to him as casual and terrible as dismounted cavalry, the perfect whiteness of their home jerseys like calcimine banners, set off with numeral trim and striping as precise and delineated as the grids and patterns of the stadium itself.

There was a ululation of voices around him. Men who were dressed with the same hopeful show of flamboyance as Fanning, but whose encumbrance with the straps and wires of portable tape recorders gave a workaday cast to their insouciance, were moving among the players, seeking interviews. A couple of these men wore short-brimmed canvas hats, in pastel colors—a pitiable giveaway. These fellows, noticing Fanning, called to him and strode over to shake his hand. Fanning returned their greetings, politely but with a certain distance; they were press from smaller cities around New York, tourists here for Opening Day; their temporary credentials swung from their coat buttons like price tags. As a mandarin, Fanning had to apportion his cordiality in subtle degrees according to rank; it was part of the unspoken etiquette of the baseball press corps.

He had taken a satisfied survey of the playing field—which he would shortly tour, slapping players' rumps; it would be a peak moment in his pregame rhythms—and had slid onto the bench next to a reserve Nat infielder, a kid named Chavez. He had folded his arms in the accepted way to begin a low-key ballfield conversation (both parties staring straight ahead, deadpan; making eye contact violated the ballplayer's notion of cool) when he heard a voice call:

"L.C."

A young man's voice. Possibly a cub writer who needed a few quick notes for a sidebar piece, or maybe a young announcer wanting some tips on how to crack the New York market. It was a bending of protocol, but L. C. Fanning was no snob. He was a young guy starting out in this business at one time himself.

Fanning looked to his left, toward the entranceway. But it was no young man who stood there. It was Mel Pelham.

Fanning shuddered. Fooled by the voice. He suspected that he might run into Pelham before the day was over. Pelham was another Opening Day fixture. Theoretically, Fanning should defer to Pelham; he was one of the Founding Fathers of the trade, a genuine baseball announcing pioneer.

But Fanning knew what Pelham would be wanting to talk about. It was his duty, in a way, to listen. He just wished it hadn't come so soon, right amidst the most crucial rhythms of Opening Day.

"Why, hello there, Old Sergeant!"

"Hello, L.C."

Mel Pelham lifted up a limp speckled hand. Fanning gripped it and made his own voice sound hearty.

"Why, you old owlhoot. Ain't seen you in a coon's age. What are you now, playing golf every day of the cockeyed year?"

The young shortstop slid unobtrusively away.

"I always come up for Opening Day, L.C." Pelham looked as though he had been stuffed into his black suit by a mortician. The folds of his neck funneled into his starched white collar. His necktie was held in place by a gold stickpin, in the old style. An American flag was pinned to his lapel.

"Aha. Uh-huh. Why sure."

The flesh on Pelham's face had turned waxy in his dotage; it seemed to be gathering itself into heavy droplets, like tallow from a candle. Like the folds of uniforms from the extinct teams that Pelham used to cover, play-by-play.

But his hair was still black as an anvil, and Pelham had it slicked straight back over his head. And the voice—God, the voice! Seventy-something, and Pelham still had the pipes of a twenty-year-old. It made Fanning's skin crawl; Fanning could not meet Mel Pelham without a horrifying sensation of meeting himself face to face—his self, past and future.

"Well, what the hell, Sergeant"—Fanning was booming now, jovial in his own famous voice—"why don't we see you up here more often? Hey, folks"—turning to include the dugout at large—"we've got a celebrity in our midst. Mel Pelham, one of the great announcers of all time!"

The players and the lower-echelon press all seemed to be busy with interviews.

"You know I don't get up a great deal anymore, L.C. You know I lost Catherine last April. God rest her soul."

"God rest her soul." Fanning was thinking of his own Eleanor, gone these seven years. He forced his thoughts back to Pelham, to the young Pelham, the dashing announcer he had admired in his own youth: a name as big as Ted Husing's, a household name, broad fedora cocked low over an eye, thrusting sausage-shaped microphones at Baseball Immortals for the benefit of Sunday-supplement photographers. Fanning remembered that he'd patterned his own style on the airy singsong of Mel Pelham.

"God rest her soul," he repeated quietly. He wished that the little old man had not hunted him down.

"Ought to be a great day for a ballgame," he said desperately.

"The Baseball Announcers Hall of Fame vote was in February," said Pelham.

Criminy. Here it came.

"I ought to have made it this time, don't you think, L.C.?"

"If anybody deserved it you did, Old Sergeant."

"Allen's in. Barber's in. Elson's in. Christ, L.C., I was there at the beginning! I invented play-by-play. I invented the *'Heeeee's out'*!"

"That's right, Sarge." Fanning was looking away.

"Forty years. Forty years straight announcing big-league baseball. Fourteen World Series on the networks. Another twelve for the Armed Forces Radio, L.C. . . . football games anywhere you want to mention. All the big ones. The Rose Bowl, Orange Bowl, Gator, Sugar, Army-Navy."

"That's right, Sergeant. All of us owe a great debt to—"

"Fights, L.C. I did the big fights. Carmen Basilio was a personal friend of mine. I met Eisenhower. I met Churchill. I interviewed Connie Mack. . . ."

Fanning was starting to perspire. He was not going to go out this way, pitiful, clinging to the past. The past was important, but L. C. Fanning was a man who lived in the present. He was going to make a clean break and walk away from it.

He fumbled in his pocket for a White Owl.

"You sure knew the great ones, Sarge."

"Oh, God, the *accolades*." The young voice was a whine. "I had the accolades, L.C. I invented the god-damn craft."

"We all owe you a great—"

"They voted Allen in, Barber in. Elson made it a couple of years ago. I just want to be voted in while I'm living, L.C., that's all. I belong in the Baseball Announcers Hall of Fame." Pelham lived alone in some spring training Florida town, Fanning knew. He hung out at the wire fence with the other old men during the March exhibition games and chased foul balls across a busy four-lane boulevard.

"You ought to be automatic," Fanning told him. He blew a plume of blue smoke. "You were an all-time great. Say, when are they going to get this show on the road?"

After Frankie Wilde left, Jeffrey Spector sat behind his desk and stared for a long time at a novelty device on the desk's surface. A slender silver rod was balanced on a cylindrical base. The rod was weighted on one end; on the other end were attached two small silver airplanes. When there were subtle vibrations in the room, the rod swung from side to side, making the airplanes appear to fly. The device had given Jeffrey Spector many happy hours of absorption.

Jeffrey tapped on his desk and watched the planes bob and circle. His lips were moist and parted, like a child's. His bluejeaned secretary started to come through the doorway, saw Jeffrey Spector's rapt face, and retreated. She knew better.

After a long time Jeffrey Spector nodded to himself. His eyes still on the small circling planes, he reached into his desk drawer and withdrew the Sunday magazine that he had been saving from a Long Island newspaper. A beautiful woman's face was on the cover of the magazine. Jeffrey Spector turned his gaze on the woman's face and studied her as intently as he had the silver airplanes. Then he touched a button that summoned his secretary.

"Find out who her agent is," he instructed, holding out the magazine. "And have him call me. Today, if possible."

On the playing field now; up the three steps from the Nats' dugout, leaving Pelham behind to stew in his memories. Out into the sunlight. The air around him was full of satisfying little cracks: bat meeting ball, thrown ball slapping into glove. Infielders leaned low and whistled through their teeth. Some player called, without looking his way, *"Hey you, Voice."*

Fanning felt his body loosen. He rolled his shoulders a couple of times as he strolled, as if to relax a neck muscle, the way Jesus Alou used to do at the plate. He felt his strides growing longer, in the manner of the players, and when he paused to trade a handshake with some of the writers around the batting cage, he knew that his white shoes were planted wide apart, toes out. He couldn't have changed it if he'd wanted. Everybody else's white shoes were planted wide apart, too. It was simply a part of the way you felt, down there on the field with the players, on Opening Day.

"It is simply a *mind-blowing* concept."

"Shall we set up a lunch and talk it over, Mr., uh"—Jeffrey Spector glanced quickly down at the note pad in front of him—"Bland? Bandle?"

"Bil*and*ic. Well, I mean, this is all right out of the . . . I mean, I can't guarantee Robyn's availability this summer, we have some prior commitments down on paper . . ."

"I appreciate how busy she must be. Well, thank you anyway, Mr. . . ."

"No, I mean, hey, I'd like to keep the option open; I mean it's just such an absolutely *nutbar* concept, I mean it says *different,* it says *playing against type.* . . ."

"It would look good in her portfolio."

"It would look *très* good in her *portfolio.* . . ."

"Well, then, perhaps we have a—"

"Would there be TV?" The voice on the other end of the line was suddenly matter-of-fact.

"I couldn't guarantee her TV. Not right at first. As you may know, we have a working arrangement with Channel Six. . . ."

"I know that if I could sweeten this concept with the possibility of the TV element, and took *that* package to Robyn . . ."

"On a scale of one to ten, Mr. Bandle, I'd say the chances were better than fair. . . ."

"Bilandic. Bobby Bilandic. Well, hey, I mean, this is all *très* preliminary, of course. . . ."

"It's very preliminary. From our end too. I want you to be aware of that."

"Outfront. Well, I mean, hey, it has elements of the kind of vehicle that we like to see Robyn involved in . . ."

"Not long-term, of course."

"*Not* long-term. But I think if she could hear somebody talk a little TV . . ."

"Why don't you get to her with this, then, and we'll get back to you. Or you get back to us."

"I'll get back to you. Just a *bitch* of a concept, man. You guys down there must be just an absolute bunch of *raving ninnies.*"

"Thank you, Mr. Bilandic. That's very nice of you to say."

Up in the elevator now, heading for the press level. A garland of sweat in beads over his eyebrows from his tour of the playing field. Clutching the aluminum net and the attaché case, ready now to get to work, get back in front of that Electro-Voice 635 directional microphone and do the thing that had made his one of the most famous names in American sports.

Baseball on the radio.

Let the others, the pretty boys, have the TV side. There was no art to it. (He knew—he'd tried it once.) The TV camera had ruined sports announcing, as far as L. C. Fanning was concerned. It took away the art. The description. Criminy, you had to watch the blasted little screen instead of the real game in front of you, to be sure you were talking about what the people saw. What you did on the TV side was you "supplemented" the picture. Well, the blazes with "supplement." Fanning was a broadcaster. A professional. He did his best work on the radio. And the public appreciated that. His public. His audience. He felt a sudden loyalty to them that raised a lump in his throat. (A lump in his throat. Now there was a figure of speech.) The elevator doors slid open and the crowd's raucous din hit him on a wave of damp wind, whipping about the curving concrete causeways. The press level was just above the loge, part of a rind of compartments that ran around the interior rim of the stands. There was still an hour to go until game time. In a few minutes he would join Turtle in the press lounge for a beer. But right now, still moist from the playing field, still trembling with the rightness of the rhythms, he wanted a few minutes to himself.

He walked over to an unoccupied compartment—some corporation's seats, he supposed—and sat alone in a folding chair. On the field below him, batting practice for both teams was over. The Cubs were taking their infield, and a marching band was drilling in the outfield. The stands were more than half filled. He judged the crowd would be around forty thousand—not a sellout, but not bad for a last-place team on Opening Day.

From where he sat, Fanning could see the transistor radios that so many of the fans were carrying. The sense of loyalty, of *duty* to these people, returned. *They were going to hear him describe what they themselves were seeing!* He never got over that.

He took out a handkerchief and mopped his brow. People asked him from time to time: Don't you get tired broadcasting baseball games year in and year out? He always had to laugh. He couldn't find a way to answer them so that they would understand. He was not an egghead. No deep thinker. What he felt about his broadcasts would have to go unsaid, or else show up somehow in the broadcasts themselves.

He sure as hell didn't need the money. For years, in the old days, he had done professional football games in the off-season, the New York Giants games. But he quit that. After a while he didn't need it, and it was nothing like the lift he got from doing baseball.

No, money was not the question. He'd put some money away. He'd gotten rid of the place in Connecticut when Eleanor passed along. He had loved that house. It had a den where you could entertain, fix a guest a highball, and show him the souvenirs: the framed newspaper articles and magazine covers about him that Eleanor had saved and put together over the years, the telegrams from famous politicians, the citations, all the photographs of him interviewing the great ballplayers, shaking hands with Ike, posing with Bobby Thomson. . . .

Mel Pelham's face came into his mind's eye.

. . . But blast it, the point was, he could *walk away* from all that. With Eleanor gone and the son, Matthew, off in Michigan doing the thing that humiliated Fanning whenever he thought of it—with these last anchoring links to family obligation cut away, Fanning had been free to rise on the ballast of his radio persona into a stratosphere of the soul, a kind of ascetic purity. Now his home was on the airwaves. The New York Nats were "his" team and the subject of his artistry, and he felt himself as involved in their games as he had ever been as the Boy Broadcaster of the Giants. But in the last seven years he had felt a widening detachment from the consequences of their victories and defeats. Now they were colors on his palette—he had dedicated the remainder of his career to purifying his airwave Voice, toward making each broadcast a subtle variation on a beautiful theme, the elusive, irresistible twinings of baseball and radio and American yearnings. A woman he had once known, a powdered stately widow who had "cultivated" an interest in Nats baseball through listening to his play-by-play, had taken an interest in Fanning and tried to expand his interests into the wider world of art. Over tea—foreign substance!—in her Park Avenue apartment, she had told him of a French painter named Monet, a man who, as he had aged, had returned again and again to the simple subject of a curving Japanese bridge over a lily pond. This artist had painted the same scene many times, jabbing at the canvas with thousands of tiny excruciating strokes, trying with each composition to alter the play of light, the relationship of colors, the sense of space among the objects in the scene. The story had bored Fanning at the time, and he had devoted most of his attention to the thin vertical slit between the buttons of the widow's blouse— how it yawned open then closed as she swayed in the brimming effervescence of her little seminar. The ballplayers' influence; he couldn't help it. He had left the place spewing insistences of Dinner Sometime. He had never called her again.

But the image of this Monet germinated in him, and as the seasons went on, he began to see the primal baseball diamond as his lily pond, each Nat contest as the variation. There were so many things he wanted to say. The truth was that he could not wait for each broadcast to begin. He had an artist's manic urge to seize materials and synthesize, to create out of disparate materials something that was not there before, and could never be again. Turtle Teweles was his unwitting leavening agent; the color man a thinner for his colors. In Cincinnati he would stroke in a pigment gleaned from a black Shriners convention at the Rhinelander Hotel (epaulets and scimitars flashing before indifferent desk clerks). In Los Angeles, a shade of the astonishment he'd felt upon glimpsing, from the window of his passing car, the star of a 1950s TV detective series cutting his own grass with a hand mower on Sunset Boulevard. In St. Louis, a lurid splotch of workingclass softball under the lights at Carondelet Park and how the moths buzzed against fastfood marquees along Lindbergh Boulevard. In Chicago the scarlet line of a fistfight between a business-suited youth and a black parking-lot attendant on Rush Street.

There was always something more to add to the game descriptions, some details from the American maw to synthesize. And as his anchoring links loosened, he became a citizen of the airwaves. He floated on an endless Gulf Stream among the cities, and once, in Pittsburgh, his engineer looked up from his headset between innings and said, "Your station says to cut out the descriptive crap and call the game," and Fanning ignored the order, and no one ever mentioned it again.

A night game in Houston:

"We roll along into the bottom of the fifth inning . . . the Nats holding onto a one-run lead. . . . The Astros will send up Scott, Washington, and Mendez, and if anybody gets on, Baum and Vinnie Smith. Well, Turtle, old pal, we're here in Texas for three games. . . . I see where a fellow over in San Antonio . . . astronomer . . . here's Beasley's first pitch to Scott . . . down low for a ball . . . an astronomer at Trinity University has come out and said that the earth is the only planet in the universe with intelligent life. How about that, Turtle?"

"Well, they . . . I thought they already had that figured out, L.C."

"Here's a strike, a fastball, over the inside corner of the plate. . . . Bill Beasley with that nice fluid overhand motion . . . sometimes that fastball of his will sneak up on a hitter. Outfield straightaway. One and one. . . . No, Turtle, the scientific community as I understand it . . . has been divided lo these many years on whether we have intelligent neighbors in our cosmos or not. . . . Nats talk it up around the horn."

"I'll be a sonofagun."

"Beasley rocks . . . aaaaand . . . Scott chops a sharp one-hopper down to first . . . Dobson scoops . . . steps on the bag . . . and there's one away. That'll bring up Tater Washington . . .

power-hitting veteran outfielder for these Astros. . . . Big T has already bruised Mr. Beasley's feelings with a screaming one-out double back in the third, scoring Leonard. . . . So anyhow, this old planet Terra Firma may be the only candy shop that's open for business in all the dark reaches of space, ladies and gents . . . and when you think about that . . . why it makes the current Nat four-game losing skein seem like pretty small potatoes after all.''

"And, L.C., I guess it don't do one darn bit o' harm to the stature of the World Series.''

Now, in this last season, he would bring his art to its fullest measure. He would render his broadcasts at once material and abstract. Spine-tingling play-by-play action for the meat-and-potatoes baseball fan (never abandon your basic audience) and yet, at the same time, a linkage: an attempt to blend the ball games with his notions of the larger pageants and pulses at work in America. With a steady daubing of well-aimed asides, fantasies, associations, improvisations, yarns, rumors, comments, and fables, L. C. Fanning intended to turn the airwaves—his airwaves—into a canvas of the national life. A work that all Americans could be proud of.

Fanning pushed himself up off the folding chair, dusted the seat of his pants, and grabbed his aluminum net and attaché case. It was time for the last ritual before the game started; probably the ritual he liked best of all. It ranked right up there, he figured, with strutting around on the playing field.

This was the ritual of the press lounge.

When the guard opened the door for him, Fanning just stood there for a moment, taking it all in.

Fanning looked in at them, the big softbellied men with their cheeks filled with food, blessing each other with one-liners and horselaughs. He felt something like love. He understood it. He understood that this press lounge, with its paltry free food and drinks, said more to these men about their privileged occupations than even the cross-country jet trips, the paid hotel rooms, the expense-account dinners all summer long: because this press lounge was an inner sanctum of the stadium itself, part of an impossible childhood myth, now attained.

He heard his name bawled, set down his net and case, and plunged joyfully in.

"*Real* fine, *real* fine."

L. C. Fanning moved into the press lounge like a paddle-wheel steamer. He seemed to propel himself by his upper body alone. With each movement forward, one of his churning big hands came down on the shoulder of a compatriot. There were Jack Brickhouse and Lou Boudreau from the Chicago announcing team; big jolly men, mandarins like himself, all aftershave and pinky rings.

"*Real* fine, *real* fine. Hey, sign Brickhouse's name to my tab, there, Teddy, and remember, Jack, *I'm a big tipper!*" Brickhouse roared. Oh, God, it was fine.

He chugged along quickly, navigating this way and that around the shallows of grinning men clinking ice. Faces turned to him, faces of old friends. There was Frankie Wilde from the station: nice guy. Frankie nodded, then turned quickly away. Fanning made a mental note to get down to the station more often, see the gang. There had been a lot of turnovers, some new management. Some kid running the store now, young phenom. He didn't keep in close touch with the station like he used to. On the road in summer; Florida now, a lot of the winter. But oh, there used to be a swell gang at the station. You can't beat radio people.

There was a steam table in one corner. A black waiter wearing a tall chef's hat was forking up free frankfurters and sauerkraut to a line of Working Press holding paper plates. "Hey, Dick—they tell me you haven't eaten since the World Series!" Real fine.

He walked among the men, slapping shoulders, shaking hands. He came upon a conversation between a writer from New York and a writer from Chicago. The New York man had his finger in the Chicago man's chest, and he was saying:

"Burger Beer, Burger Beer. Burger Beer sponsored the goddamn broadcasts. The Burger Beer Baseball Network. Oh, Christ, I can remember his voice just as plain as day. I'll think of his name in a minute."

Fanning walked away from that one.

He spied Turtle. He saw at a glance that Turtle was already giving grief to the girl from the *Times*. The girl from the *Times* was standing on the fringe of a group of writers and on-air men; she was obviously trying to join the conversation, and Turtle—well into his fourth or seventh beer, Fanning saw—was giving her grief.

Turtle was pretending to have a sneezing fit. "Cutcha*sack*off!" exclaimed Turtle, holding a finger under his nose. "Horse*shit!*" "Oh, ah, squeezey*anuts*off!" "*Ah*shit!" The men around him were making a show of trying to hold back their mirth. The girl from the *Times* was clearly embarrassed, but holding her ground. She was a thin girl who was wearing some sort of mock army fatigue shirt with little buttoned flaps to hold up her rolled sleeves. Fanning hated to see Turtle behave like that, but the truth was, he didn't think the girl from the *Times* had any place in the pressbox either. It wasn't that he hated women; but girl sportswriters weren't natural. They upset something; violated some pattern. Broke the rhythm. Well, hell. They shocked him, to be truthful.

He made a mental note to talk to Turtle about his language toward the girl. No point in cruelty. Cruelty shocked Fanning, too.

He reached the curved bar and ordered himself a draft. A small pink-skinned man with gold wavy hair was leaning against the bar, talking to one of the younger writers, one of the crowd that Fanning privately called the Young Turks. The pink-skinned man was Danny Breen, the Nats' public relations officer. The kid he was talking to wrote a smart column for the *Daily News,* and showed up at the games in jeans and a flak jacket. Fanning had never seen him in a sport coat, and harbored a vague distaste for him. As for Breen, Fanning's distaste was not vague at all.

Breen had his back to Fanning, but Fanning could hear his voice.

". . . Most of the writers only make our task very difficult. I wouldn't want you to quote me on that."

"Yeah. Yeah-yeah." The kid was nodding his head vigorously, to show he was tuned in to Breen.

"Our task of, you know, *representing* the Nats baseball organization before the public. In the *totality* of its aims and objectives."

"Yeah." The kid was obviously thrilled at being the recipient of this kind of inside management thinking. He brought up a thumb and forefinger and stroked his chin, in a show of profound thought.

"Excuse me, Danny," said Fanning before he could think better of it. "Couldn't help overhear, old pardner. Maybe I'm out of touch, but I always thought the Nats' aims and objectives were to win the blamed pennant. And that's what the writers want too. I mean where does the difficulty come in?''

Breen spun on a polished heel. His slanted, city-wise blue eyes sparkled. The palms of his hands came up like a conjuror's. He appeared as delighted as if he had willed Fanning to appear out of thin air.

''Stop the music! It's the Voice himself! The cog! The 'Toot-toot' man! L.C., you god damned old immortal. How was the winter? You swing those blazing short irons?'' Breen turned his golden-topped head back over his shoulder. ''Chip Fensterwald of the *Daily News,* have you had the pleasure of meeting the immortal L. C. Fanning?''

The kid's glasses gleamed as he nodded in a grin that might have been satirical. Fanning ignored him. He stared at Breen. ''So where does the difficulty come in?'' he repeated.

Breen draped an arm around Fanning's shoulder. ''I'm going to let you have it from the top, L.C. What I'm saying is: what a lot of the press, and I'm talking writers, I'm talking *some* announcers, fail to understand is one simple concept: Winning a pennant—right?—is no longer the sole determinant of a major-league franchise's success. I'm saying these are the nineteen eighties. I'm saying we no longer live in a society that embraces the myth of all-out victory. Vietnam took care of that. Hey. Right, Chip? Chip'll tell you. I'm saying this is an era of *containment.* Of limited-objective goals. I wish I could get—well, *certain* guys to grasp that concept. Chip here. He's part of the new breed. They're overrunning us old farts, L.C. Chip doesn't have any trouble with that concept. What I mean is simply this: that the New York Nats, *qua* franchise, can enjoy a 'winning' season based upon a formula derived from personnel performance measured against career tendencies, from the relative strengths of opposing teams, even from the aesthetic enjoyments provided by the various attractions within Flushing Stadium itself. Our scoreboard, for instance. Victory as *cost-efficiency.* But it won't fly with certain guys, L.C. Ideologically, they are locked into an antediluvian set of expectations.''

Fanning stood speechless.

''The Nats as Policemen of the National League!'' chirped the kid.

''Exactly,'' said Breen.

A red-faced man wearing a sport coat that looked as though it had been sewn together from animal skins came sauntering by. He socked Breen in the shoulder.

"Don't let this asshole bullshit you," he told Fanning with a wink, and popped a handful of peanuts into his mouth.

Fanning looked down at the little public-information officer.

"That," he said, "is just about the screwiest line of bullcrap I've ever heard, Breen."

Breen raised his eyebrows. "*Language,*" he said. The kid snickered.

But Breen refused to take offense. "Guess I can't sell you, L.C. No hard feelings. World is changing, old man." Fanning saw that Breen had a carnation in his sober pin-striped suit. Leave it to Breen to wear a pin-striped suit to the ballpark on Opening Day. The little popinjay always looked like he was on his way to testify somewhere. The old ball-team public relations men Fanning had known had been part of the crowd, fans, easy to get along with. This one seemed to have crawled out of the package with the blue chemical grass.

Breen set his drink on the bar. "Come with me, L.C. We've added a bagatelle to your booth. I'd like to show it to you."

Entering the broadcast booth for the first time in the season accompanied by Danny Breen was not L. C. Fanning's idea of good rhythms. But something in the little man's smile made him apprehensive. He followed Breen out of the press lounge and into the curving concrete walkway that led down to the broadcast row.

Breen opened the door and gestured.

"Holy Christ, Breen!"

The booth was the same: three steps down into a compact cubicle, two Electro-Voice microphones angling upward from a plywood shelf, monitoring equipment in the corner, a fresh enameled scorecard in front of each microphone, several sharpened pencils. The work environment hadn't changed, in its essence, in forty-two years.

And yet changed utterly.

Fanning wheeled to face Breen.

A pane of glass now sealed the front of the booth from the stadium below.

"*Take it out!*" Fanning had to restrain himself from grabbing

Breen around the neck. "I want that god damn glass out of here by game time, Breen! Out! Or I swear to God I'm gonna throw a chair through it!"

Breen only smiled.

"Sorry, L.C. Out of my hands. Front office thinks it's a safety factor. Frankly, I agree." He gave Fanning an approximation of a playful punch on the shoulder. "We don't want to lose you reaching for a foul ball with that net of yours."

Fanning felt as though he were in the presence of a madman.

"Danny. For cripes sake. The net is part of my . . . it's what I *do*. The fans expect it. You can't just take that away from me."

Breen was waiting for that one. "We *haven't*, L.C." He rubbed his fingers together. "Wait'll you see this. You'll love it."

Breen took the wall telephone from its hook and dialed two numbers. "Eddie," he said, "punch up the net." He hung up the phone and gestured toward the scoreboard. "Watch."

The animation panel of the scoreboard suddenly burst into life with the image of a stick figure brandishing a giant net. Above the stick figure, the message board blazed the word, in alternating patches of black and white, "OLÉ!"

"It gives a nice feel, don't you think?" Breen held his hands up, framing the distant scoreboard between the filed nails of his fingers. "Don't you think it says *net*? I mean, now everybody can relate to the excitement of the whole net kind of experience you've created. Not just the customers sitting close by. What do you say, L.C.?"

Fanning lacked the strength to say anything. He sat down heavily in his chair.

"We've immortalized you, L.C. It's like part of you will be up there. Inside the message board. Forever."

Fanning winced.

"And we'll still have Nat Net Night," said Breen's voice behind him.

Fanning heard the door close. The booth was absolutely still. He sat there in his jaunty red sport coat. He could not hear the noise of the crowd. How the blazes do you broadcast a ball game without crowd noises? He could not hear the organ music—itself now a byproduct of the accursed scoreboard. He could not feel a breeze.

The broadcast booth suddenly felt like a tomb.

It was going to be a different kind of season. This season of his retirement. The thought sickened him. He was at the top of his craft. He was approaching artistry.

Mel Pelham's face came into his mind. . . .

But today there was a baseball game to announce. Opening Day for the Nats. And two hours later, when Bogart Humphries lined a forkball over the right-center field wall for his first home run as a New York Nat, L. C. Fanning was on his feet, screaming into the glass windowpane:

"Toot-toot-tootsie, *good-bye!*"

"Come in, Frankie. We're just finishing up here."

Jeffrey Spector perched on the top of his desk, his thin legs crossed like a yogi's. The four-thirty afternoon sunlight threw his reedy frame into silhouette. He looked to Frankie Wilde like a wilting house-plant.

"Platinum," the man in the green stovepipe hat was saying. "It's got platinum written on it, Jeffrey. It's got crossover written on it. It will puff up your head and turn your tongue green and put ants in your pants so you gotta dance."

"I'll think about it," Jeffrey Spector was saying. Frankie Wilde judged the man in the green stovepipe to be forty-five, minimum. He also had on yellow-tinted aviator glasses that wrapped around the sides of his head, and some kind of green cape. If Jeffrey was a wilting house-plant, this guy was a frog. Frankie Wilde almost snickered.

"Think about it, Jeffrey," said the frog. His companion, a fat man dressed in a designer suit fashioned after an Explorer Scout uniform, said: "Marvin is being totally upfront on this, Jeffrey. It's going to cross over and just crap all over the charts. It's *existential,* is the only way I can describe it."

A frog and a fag. Practically on their knees in front of this insufferable kid. Frankie wanted to vomit.

"I'll think about it," said Jeffrey.

Frankie Wilde sat down heavily in a chair opposite Jeffrey's desk. He took a handkerchief out of his inside pocket and mopped his face with it. He immediately felt self-conscious. That was another thing: none of these new people seemed to sweat. Wilde's shirt was soaked from his afternoon at the ballpark. Steam was oozing up from his ribcage. He could smell the ballpark beer on his own breath—an aroma that for some reason was mixed with the smell of bubblegum.

"Will you think about it?" asked Marvin the frog.

Jeffrey Spector fidgeted for a moment with the sleeve of his western-style shirt. He rolled it up another couple of folds past his knobby elbow.

"You know," he said finally, and his two visitors leaned forward like defendants at a sentencing. "I mean, I can conceptualize WERA *covering* this particular item after it's established in the market. What I can't flash on is us *breaking* this item into the market." He looked up from his elbow, a prophet emerging from his trance, and peered at the frog and the fag through his glasses.

"Dig it," he said, in his careful, scholarly voice. "A Metropolitan Opera contralto's first recording with Southside Johnny and the Asbury Jukes is not exactly mainstream."

Frankie Wilde, trying not to draw attention, put his fingers on his eyelids and rubbed hard.

"Flash on it," said the Explorer Scout. "It's the kind of funky crazy cockamamie concept that says Contemporary. Plus the fact that this lady says class. She'll bring the whole classical music demo group over with her."

"Plus the fact," said the frog, "she's got a pair of gazongas she oughta carry in a wheelbarrow. Wait till you experience her album cover. People are gonna tune in WERA hoping those headlights fall in their lap."

"I'll think about it," said Jeffrey Spector.

For no apparent reason the two men turned their heads in unison toward Frankie Wilde. Grins appeared like computer readouts on their faces.

The two men arose.

"It was a pleasure meeting you," said the frog, taking one of Frankie Wilde's hands.

"It was really a pleasure," said Explorer Scout in a hushed whisper, taking the hand after the frog had finished with it.

"Outasight. Overwhelming." Frankie Wilde felt like a world-class stiff. The way it worked on paper, these creeps should have been making their loathsome pitch to him. He, after all, was the program director.

"Well," said the frog, tipping his stovepipe. *"Adiós, muchachos."*

"Ciao," said the Explorer Scout.

"Geronimo," said Frankie Wilde.

The two men were gone.

Frankie Wilde couldn't bite his tongue.

"Is that what, uh, you're after, Jeffrey? You want your head puffed up? You want your tongue turned green? You want ants in your pants? Tell me. I oughta know. You may get sick someday and I'd have to program the music around here."

He stifled a beer belch and waited for Jeffrey Spector to knock over the wooden soldier that had "Frankie Wilde" on it.

But Jeffrey only gave him a rueful half-grin. "Record reps," he said, and shrugged. "Bandits." He seemed almost embarrassed. It struck Frankie that for all of Spector's high-handed ways, he seemed to care, on some level, about Frankie's opinion of him.

Maybe he was WERA's designated Gray Eminence. Who could figure it?

"They're out of touch, actually." Jeffrey nodded toward the closed office door. "They're operating on assumptions that were dead three years ago. They've never heard of perception studies. They don't even know we research our playlist. They think we still read *Billboard.*"

Frankie Wilde, who still read *Billboard,* managed a sickly grin.

Spector shrugged. "But we still have to deal with them. *Anyway.*" He waved a hand. "So what did Mr. Sonderling say?"

Frankie Wilde felt his shoulders bunch up. "It was a helluva game, thank you. Nats prevailed four to three, Fasano with relief help from McDoyle. Big blow, a circuit clout off the booming bat of Bogart Humphries. Maybe you heard it on the radio."

He cocked an eye at Jeffrey Spector, who wasn't smiling now.

"Sonderling?" Spector repeated softly.

Frankie Wilde rubbed the bridge of his nose.

"He laughed in my face, Jeffrey. Then he did an interesting thing with a clipboard. He snapped it in two with his bare hands. Then he pointed out to me that he had three years to go on a legally binding three-year contract with MetroCom and WERA and that if we so much as mentioned cancellation to him again he would drag said corporation through every court and front page on the Eastern Seaboard. Then he swore until his wife calmed him down. Then he personally threw me out of his private box, which is lovely, by the way. I'd say offhand that he's going to take a little more convincing.''

Frankie Wilde paused, puffed out his cheeks and waited for Jeffrey Spector to commiserate with him. After a minute it sunk in that he was waiting in vain.

"Jeffrey. Son. You gotta get this idea out of your head. Sonderling's not gonna budge. No other station is gonna take him and his white elephant. Christ, if I was in your shoes I don't know who I'd want to alienate less—MetroCom or Sonderling.'' Wilde recalled a newspaper photograph he had seen of the Nats' florid, granite-haired owner with an arm flung around Richard Nixon.

To Frankie Wilde's complete surprise, Jeffrey Spector said:

"You're absolutely right.''

"Hah?''

"No question about it. I was stupid. Of course Mr. Sonderling won't budge.''

"Then you're gonna forget this whole—''

"Right.''

"Jeffrey, that is a relief. Let me say that—''

"We'll begin my backup plan.'' Spector crossed to his desk, opened a drawer, and pulled out a magazine. On the cover of the magazine was the photograph of a beautiful blond woman. Frankie Wilde waited for Jeffrey Spector to explain further. But the young station manager simply stood, lost in thought, gazing at the photograph until Frankie realized that their conversation was over and he was free to leave the office.

THE WAY IT WAS

G OOD LORD,
         i'll never forget the first
football broadcast i ever
did from new york city
                    the polo grounds
                              cards–new york giants.
they put us
         in that scoreboard in left field. that overhangs the mezza-
nine there the thing we looked through was where
      during the Baseball season, they'd put the inning numbers. (you
      know, 1, 2, 3, or zero or whatever)
      and their idea of accommodations was a folding table a card
      table,
         and their idea of a comfort station was a bucket in the
      corner at the end of the thing.
      (and this *is new york city)*
      uh—i worked one of the most important assignments i've ever
had in my

life career-wise i've never had a disappointment like this one
now here we are
        i'm up here to do
               this is 'fifty-six
                    this is
the forty-seven–seven game where the giants killed 'em and gif-
ford had a big day
turtle teweles and i did this game for national television
   now,
        i knew more about these guys than their mothers
    knew about them
i never researched harder in my
life i looked at more damn film than
                 than
                    than the screen academy
for the
    for the oscars okay they put us
    in an overhang in a basket a photographer's basket
      overhanging the upper deck and right out where the bullpen is
    in order to get the time we had to
                phone
    to see how much time
    (we could not see the scoreboard.) our own hands were so
frozen that
      that
        that
    even my spotter
    it did no good for the kid with the pencil to point
    to who made the tackle because
    his hand was shaking so badly he ran upanddown the board and
covered four positions
    it was the only time in my
    life that i've ever had words
             absolutely
DRIVEN BACK DOWN MY THROAT
(because of the cold wind off the ocean.) new york city
that day
    this was their idea of how

to accommodate a
jillion-dollar telecast
and yet
　　　when you get down to the short strokes
　　　　　　　only one man
is gonna carry that ball for you
　　　　and that's
　　　　　your broadcaster

CHAPTER

4

So: IT WAS NOT AS THOUGH HER meteoric career in show business were finished. She still had that, at least. There were choices! Options! Concepts!

Five of them lay before her at this very moment, in the form of brochures, fanned out on the health-food emporium's natural-porcelain counter. Their enameled surfaces were drenched in California morning sunlight. In fact one of them—the Jungle Queen brochure—was drenched in a leftover ring of tiger's milk.

Brochures. When your agent sends you brochures, instead of scripts, it is time to think of leaving this business and marrying that man.

But after last night and the alligators, that was not exactly in the cards, was it?

Robyn turned the lurid Jungle Queen brochure over on its face, then covered its yellow-and-blue backside with a napkin. "Barbecue Ribs & Shrimp." Indeed. Celebrity hostess on a fake paddle-wheel steamer greasy with barbecue ribs? There were limits. She thought of Gloria Swanson in *Sunset Boulevard*—which she had watched through the *penseroso* hours on television that morning, after the wreck of a beach party. *Sunset Boulevard* had its messages. One is a star. One dictates one's working conditions to Mr. De Mille—never before ten in the morning and never after four-thirty in the afternoon—even when Mr. De Mille is not hiring.

That, thought Robyn, is more or less the old spirit. She pushed her sunglasses to the top of her blond mane with the tips of her red fingernails—cautiously, for some jerk is always watching—and arched her eyebrows to squint at the other golden opportunities arrayed before her. The bright healthy light in the place made her eyes throb, and she knew that they were red from her asinine weeping.

Only a nincompoop weeps for the love of a man who merits the nickname, however secretly applied, of Pinley Stripely.

Nevertheless . . .

To the order of business. Robyn took a final forkful of spinach from her mock tuna salad niçoise, pushed the natural wooden saucer away, and began to study the latest batch of personal-appearance opportunities assembled as if by magic by her superagent, Bobby Bilandic, the Croatian Comet.

There was the Jungle Queen. Gloria Swanson would not work the Jungle Queen. Robyn felt confident in that presumption.

What, then?

She could join the festivities for the grand opening of yet another Haunted Fun House ("A Whole Mansion-Full of Surprises") near Redondo Beach. That would be a morning's commute. If she were in the mood for travel she could lend her wholesome presence at a weekend prayer vigil and telethon at a Christian House of Prayer (franchise chain) near Palmetto, Florida. Something about her particular beauty title, Robyn noticed, seemed to make her acceptable for ecclesiastical functions throughout media-hip Protestantdom.

Hard to imagine a pouty sexpot deigning to be named Miss Yankeedoodle-doo, she supposed.

She placed the Christian House of Prayer brochure under the napkin, along with the Jungle Queen. Haunted Fun House she reluctantly left out on the table. What else? Oh, yes. The Cars and Melodies of Yesteryear exhibit in Lakewood needed a mistress of ceremonies. . . .

"Hey."

Cutoffs revealing the bronzed thighs of a running back. Budweiser T-shirt painted onto a muscular torso festooned with medallions. Shoulders like crystalline formations. California-golden hair over state trooper-style shades with surfaces like black eggshells—from behind which, Robyn somehow felt certain, two clear-blue eyes were fixed on the line dividing her silk running shorts from the tanned, silken expanse of thigh that curved like a length of polished sandalwood across her other leg, pressing against the counter. Robyn Quarrles owed much of her extraordinary height to two of the longest legs in southern California (a fact that only confused the natives when they learned she hailed from Missouri). These specimens—which she made the continual mistake of regarding as merely functional appendages—leaving them out in the open, as it were, for inspection by all and sundry—provoked an occasional breach even in the studied cool of Venice City Beach, a veritable Olympus of bodily perfection.

She trained her eyes on the cobalt eggshells. Immediately a faceful of white California teeth rewarded her glance. She remained silent.

"Heeeeeeey." So far the conversation was proceeding along lines she had come to regard as classical. She gave a brief shake of her head and turned back to her brochures. It did not escape her notice that adorning the rugged hunk's feet were a pair of fluorescent orange roller skates.

"The Insecurity Game." He named a daytime show where she had done a little time. Not surprisingly, his voice was California-flat, without inflection. Poor hunk didn't know it; he'd already shot himself dead. Voices were a big item on Robyn's attraction scale, one to ten.

She should have kept the glasses down.

Without raising her head, she muttered, "Strange time of day for a big strong man to be home watching television."

"That's a value judgment." Instead of taking offense, the hunk computed it as a conversation entree. He slid onto an adjoining stool, his knee brushing hers. She moved.

"No, hey," he went on when she didn't reply. "I respect video. I respect the whole matrix. I've *freed my head* from all those hangups about junk programming. It's a *false dichotomy*. It's part of the whole metaphor of the external culture we live in. I'm into nonstructured multivideo programming systems myself. My name's Brad. I relate to your body. What I was thinking, maybe we could do a number at my place. Like go for it.''

"Why don't you just buzz off and leave me the hell alone?'' Robyn didn't feel the energy to mock the silly bastard with his own idiot jargon. In fact she felt the shakiness of the horrible previous night well up in her, and in a minute, she knew, she could be bawling again.

"I *hear* you.'' Brad stretched both palms out to her. "No stress. No heavy manipulation trip. We're like *two beings*. We share the same consciousness. Let's start out mellow. I mean, *mi casa es su casa,* right? I mean our bodies have their own sexual *clock,* you know, and when it's the right time, right, this whole alarm is gonna just like *happen*. . . .''

She was off the stool, having laid down one of her last remaining five-dollar bills to cover the niçoise and her tea with honey, and now she was trying to walk calmly out of the place; but old Brad was right beside her, skating deftly along, even managing the two wooden steps down to the doorway without so much as a break in his patter. She could yell for help, but it wouldn't do any good—even in this muscle center of the world, her new friend was big enough to chop most men in half with the flat of his hand, and she had no particular reason to doubt that he would.

Oh, Jeezuz, her brochures—back on the counter! She needed them. She wouldn't dare turn around and go back now. She felt all white with panic. She just had to get away.

"What I'd dig,'' Brad was crooning, "would be to have my energy flow into your energy. . . .''

They were out on the board sidewalk now, in the bright sunlight. Up and down Cabrillo cascaded a blur of tanned humanity on wheels: skateboards, roller skates, bicycles. The whole stupid population of California, rolling itself into a soupy froth of self-erotic bliss.

Except for one man in wing tips. Who wouldn't let her love him.

God, did she suddenly detest California.

Meanwhile. There was one way to deal with a para-rapist on skates. Robyn stopped. She gazed steamily into Brad's eggshell shades—she was actually an inch taller than he—and slid one bare leg seductively between his.

Brad halted his monologue and grinned. It was the instant she needed. She hooked her foot around his calf and yanked, at the same time thrusting her red fingernails into his Budweiser pectorals.

Brad hung in midair for one exquisite moment—a human billboard for hot-dog skating. Almost before he had crashed to the boardwalk, Robyn had vaulted over the metal rail onto the hot sand of Venice City Beach. She darted among startled sunbathers until she reached the hard sand near the crashing ocean surf. Then Robyn Quarrles lowered her head and headed north, flashing along the sand with the fluid strides of a born distance runner.

It is very hard to roller-skate upon beach sand. That was one fact of California life that even a non-native could divine with careful reasoning—and Robyn held a Phi Beta Kappa key from UCLA. Nevertheless there was no telling whether the maniac would throw off his skates and pursue her barefoot—or even commandeer a bicycle and follow her along the main drag.

So she ran. She did not turn to look back. She didn't realize she was crying until the tears had all but stopped; then she reveled at the wind in her face and the flecks of spray that peppered her legs and arms. She ran, forcing all the frustration of the previous night, the sorry state of her career, her isolated life—all of it she funneled into her pumping legs. She ran the poisons of despair out through the pores of her skin.

Ocean Park. Santa Monica Beach, where Route 10 joined the Pacific Coast Highway. She had slowed now, breathing hard, coated with sweat, but measuring her stride—not really in fear of being pursued anymore, but using the fantasy to propel herself forward. The morning was white with glittering sand. She had lost her sunglasses somewhere, expensive pair, but she didn't stop. Will Rogers Beach was ahead—more than three miles, she knew—and beyond that, another three to Topanga Canyon Boulevard. Then on past Castle Rock Beach and Las Tunas Beach . . . all the beaches drilled into her brain now like street signs in south St. Louis . . . her own beach house lay nearly fifteen miles away. It had been a while since she had tried that distance. Far easier to hitch, as she had done on impulse to Venice City that morning. And she'd had only three hours' sleep. . . .

Like the man had said: Go for it.

*   *   *

It was nearly four-thirty in the afternoon before Robyn could get her eyes open. The bed sheet was still damp with her perspiration. She hadn't even pulled off her sand-filled running shoes before she'd dropped into a stupor. There were numb recollections, now, of dreams that seemed to involve telephones ringing.

She sat up and immediately touched her face, feeling the creases that the sheet folds had made. She probably looked like a zebra. If they could see her now in Palmetto . . . her legs were stiff; two dead weights below her waist. Stupid idea, to run more than fifteen miles.

Except that she felt prouder of herself than she had in weeks.

. . . *To have my energy flow into your energy.* That was a good one. Have to remember that . . .

Her small bedroom was dark with drawn curtains, but she knew that the living room facing the ocean would be a hot pool of angry light—the unlovely headachy light that precedes any regulation spectacular Malibu sunset. *Enjoy them while you can.* Rate things are going, this shack will be on the block by June. Real-estate ladies in frosted hair, squinting stockbrokers out to live life to the hilt . . .

Robyn stood, feeling slender ropes of pain, and made her way to the window. She ran her tongue around in her mouth to get some moisture circulating. When she pushed back the curtain, the light fell on a disorderly scene: suitcases and garment bags heaped in a corner of the hardwood floor. Three stacks of books without benefit of shelves. Jeans, draped across a chair, limp as clocks in a Dali painting. Her trusty teakettle, resting on a stool beside a honey jar. A bicycle that served as a clothesline for four bras. Some browning tulips in a green vase. A black-and-white portable TV set, supported by a stereo speaker that lacked wires. On her dresser top a collection of pastel-colored cosmetic vials, swept toward the edge to make room for three heavy volumes on the subject of case law: her cheerful genuflection toward Dunning Pinley's world. (Sweet, stuffy Pinley Stripely.) She had pored through those grim pages until her eyes spun: dutiful future lawyer's wife.

Now it seemed she might have spared herself the effort. Waited for the movie version, as they say. Last night's grotesque beach party had produced a denouement that, upon cold analysis, she had seen coming for months.

She gave a silent laugh and brushed a strand of hair away from her face, unslitting her eyes by degrees to the light. That's the kind of season she was having. As they say. Dunning Pinley: let's see. Was he another one of the Comet's finds?

Robyn snapped her fingers. *That's what you don't understand, Brad, old pal. We golden goddesses in swimsuits and crowns just ain't out there for plucking by you fine gorgeous hunks. We're programmed for long-term security. I ever tell you about Miriam? Give us a sweet-talkin' barrister with blazing briefcases any time. . . .*

Who, in turn, will not be programmed for a golden goddess in swimsuit and crown. Natural selection, Robyn decided, sucks.

Maybe she should have given old Brad a tumble. Sonofagun looked pretty good, she had to admit. . . . If only he'd had on wing-tip roller skates . . . they could have started the Master Race. . . .

She was standing beside her telephone, and she recalled the phone ringing in her afternoon dreams. Probably the real thing, she thought—even my dreams are low-budget documentaries these days. Bobby Bilandic, the Comet, calling with one multipackage concept after another. *No* doubt.

She plopped down upon a bean pillow beside the phone—a relic from a previous civilization—and activated her message machine.

The first voice was recognizably that of her orthodontist. Waxing wroth on the subject of a certain bill. The second was an inflectionless pitch for a Buddhist weekly newspaper.

The third voice was Dunning Pinley's. Quizzical. Hurt. "Why can't we at least keep the lines of communication op—" was the last thing he said before the beep. Robyn shut her eyes and bit her lip, but remained absolutely still.

The next message consisted as follows: "Hello *star*! Have I got a *concept* for you! I am talking *breakout*! I am talking big-time media unique guaranteed national publicity star-vehicle material! Love you! Get back to me!"

Funny, she mused. He didn't leave a name or a number. Who was that masked man?

On the merest of hunches, she dialed Bobby Bilandic.

Twenty minutes later the lanky form of Robyn Quarrles paced along the Malibu sand, at the rim of the heavy-crashing surf. Hands shoved deeply into the pockets of her white coveralls, chin buried in her throat, she collided with more than one late-afternoon stroller. She hardly noticed.

It was—easily—the screwiest proposal that Bilandic had ever unearthed. God knew, there had been some strong contenders.

This one made the Jungle Queen look mainstream.

It was absurd. She was utterly unqualified. She had exactly zero interest in the subject matter. She was not even totally sure that the whole proposal wasn't some elaborate practical joke. But Bobby, to give him his due, could usually smell that sort of thing out.

Why her?

Because this guy had seen her on the *Vita* cover? All right. Fine. But *this was radio*. Who sees faces on radio?

On the positive side (assuming the whole thing was legit): it would—as they say—pay the rent. And the orthodontist. And a couple of other things. It would get her the hell out of California, which was beginning to seem like a necessary condition for sanity.

And—ah—it would please Miriam. Any sort of gig would please her mother. Moreover (here was a sudden thought that seemed to swirl in on the wind) it would, in a curious and lovely way, square something with Everett, her father—something she could never square while he was alive.

God! She threw back her head and felt her hair trail out behind her in the wind. Was it possible?—she understood then that she was going to do it.

Robyn had walked more than a mile along the beach; and now, as she looked up, she realized with a little shock of sadness exactly where she had come. Not twenty-four hours ago her hopes for a graceful retreat from the world of bad movies and TV game shows and Jungle Queen appearances had come unraveled—fifty yards from where she now flopped, elbows behind her.

It was a lush curve of Malibu, where the waves rolled up into a crescent cup and dropped like liquid weights on clean sand. Cottages were all but invisible behind the dunes. Two immense ribbons of sand formed protective arms around a small hollow—she could see it now from the corner of her eye; there were children playing in it—and that was the site of Dunning's beach party.

Robyn lay back on the warm surface and stretched her arms behind her. She wanted to retrace the evening one more time in her mind, to search for nuances she might have misinterpreted, for things that might almost have been said.

Dunning.

With his silver-rimmed spectacles and his pipe, so orderly even at the beach. Squatting there on one knee to pour the last two ounces of banana daiquiri from his silver flask into the clear plastic cups held out by the others. Red sunset on the silver. Dunning, ever judicious, gripping his right wrist with his left hand to steady the pouring—it all must come out even.

She remembered, now, the almost giddy contentment she had felt. Their arguments, the doubts of the last months, seemed put to rest.

"All I am saying," Dunning said without looking up at his friend Worth, "is that you're saying gold is dead. And I'm saying gold is *not* dead."

"None for me." Robyn pulled back her cup at the last instant, causing Pinley to almost pour a drop of daiquiri onto the sand. He looked up sharply at her, frowning.

She shrugged her bare golden shoulders and smiled into the wind at him. "I just might want to go in again before it gets dark. I don't want to go in bombed."

"Gold is dead. Gold *isn't* dead. God, you men make it sound so *theological*." Kendall, Worth's wife, smoothed a damp strand of hair away from her forehead. She was the only one still wearing sunglasses. "Telespherically speaking, of course, you're both nowhere."

Dunning was still frowning at Robyn. "You haven't had a drop of anything all day, sweetheart."

"I get high on you, Dun."

He did not smile. Serious, scholarly, sweet Pinley Stripely. In his salmon-colored pullover. With the festive little alligator on the left breast. He had been wearing an alligator shirt on the day she met him. She would never dream of telling him that her private nickname for him was Pinley Stripely.

"I'm not denying that it's an investment." Worth grimaced with relief as he took his weight off his heavy haunches and sat ponderously back down in the sand, hairy toes splayed out like a child's.

His own alligator shirt was green. "I'm saying that anybody in this day and age who can maintain, with a straight face, that gold is an inflation hedge is—well . . ." Worth glanced, embarrassed, at Robyn, then let his eyes drop quickly to the backs of her glorious drawn-up thighs, where grains of golden sand clung. She was wearing what she'd thought was a relatively modest bikini; white, with brass rings holding the material together at either hip and between the cups. With these people, she was not at all sure what counted as modest.

Kendall, who had turned to study the sea, whipped her head around again at the tone in Dunning's voice. She appraised Dun, then Robyn, then the flask, from behind her sunglasses before she said:

"Well, my God, Dunning, what are you trying to do? Corrupt the morals of Miss Yankeedoodle-doo? Isn't that a federal offense or something?" Kendall's bathing suit was a one-piece, with the word Ahoy! printed on it several times. Kendall thrust her plastic cup out toward Dunning's flask. "I'll take that if Robyn doesn't want it."

"I didn't say it was an inflation hedge," said Dunning, without looking at Worth. "I said it was a *chaos* hedge. There is a significant difference."

"You are forgetting," said Worth, jabbing a thick finger into the sand, his back to the sunset, "that there are upward of one billion ounces of gold being hoarded by the governments of the Western world. If that isn't an ominous cloud over the market—"

"You're single-tracking, darling," said Kendall, and touched Worth's fluttering yellow hair with the tips of her fingers, tender as a mother.

Robyn wrapped her arms around her knees and tucked her chin down so that no one would see her grinning. The men had sworn not to talk shop on this day, and they were abiding by it. "Shop" was the practice of law. This day was a celebration. On this day Dunning had made good on his long-standing promise to introduce Robyn to Worth, his closest friend at the law firm, and Worth's wife, Kendall. Dun and Worth thought of themselves as the Young Turks of the firm.

They had spent the afternoon body-surfing on the beach commanded by Dunning's cottage. They had enjoyed what Dunning described as "an old-fashioned potluck slumgullion cookout": frozen mushroom quiche warmed to perfection over a butane heating unit, washed down with two bottles of ice-cold Montrachet, compliments of Worth and his portable Teflon wine-cooling system.

Kendall provided the dessert: chilled cherries and St. Maure cheese accompanied by a bottle of Dom Perignon. "It's part of this divine diet," she had explained in girl-to-girl tones to Robyn. "It's built around wines. It's called the Marvelous Melt-Away. You're supposed to lose five pounds in ten days on it."

"Sounds super," said Robyn. She shook her head, declining the cup of champagne that Kendall extended. Robyn had limited herself to only polite samples of the feast. She had brought her own food supply in a thermos—a mixture of wheat germ, raw egg, sunflower seeds, yogurt, and crushed ice. The others had turned down her offer to share.

Kendall withdrew the cup, glanced at Robyn's midriff, then looked away. "Not that I actually *believe* in diets," she had resumed in a slightly altered voice.

Over cappuccino Kendall revealed that her women's self-awareness group had launched upon a poetry-appreciation study. "Right now we're into prosody," she announced, wiping sand from her fingers with a linen napkin. She smiled at Robyn. "Prosodies, of course, are the systems of versification evolved in Europe and employed by her most eminent poets." Turning, Kendall continued in a coquettish tone, "You, Dun, you old closet literati—I suppose you know how intensely involved your man Nabokov was in prosody. We were reading in his wonderful *Eugene Onegin* last week—the passage that goes"—she adjusted her sunglasses and actually blushed—"let's see if I can get it right:

'Tak tochno dumal moy Eugeniy.

On v pervoy yunosti svoey

Bil zhertovoy burnih zabluzhdeniy

I neobuzdannih strastey.' "

Robyn clapped her hands. "Bravo!"

Kendall made a show of lowering her head. "Well, the point is, of course," she murmured, "Nabokov's wonderful use of the iambic tetrameter."

Worth had changed the subject slightly to reveal an eight-point plan, of his own concoction, "with follow-up possibilities," designed to minimize the risks of fixed-interest investments during inflationary times.

The wind cooled and the golden Pacific smashed upon the foaming sand. Robyn curled against Dunning and let the talk drift about her. She was the only one who had not drunk wine, and yet she felt as though she were the only intoxicated member of the party. She was aware that Dun's friends regarded her as exotic and possibly subversive: a celebrity, after all. There was nothing she could do about that. Her mind was involved with Dun's pipe. He had a way of hooking his forefinger and little finger over the stem. Everything that Dunning did had a sense of purpose about it; an intimation of deliberate planning and meditative forethought. It was a big reason why she loved him. She could never make him understand it. He always gave a short peremptory laugh and told her she only wanted him for his personal assets. In a way he seemed unable to comprehend, he was right. His personal assets were a large, scrumptious body (although it was softening already at the middle and in a descending dollop of flesh behind the magnificent chin; and although Dun's calves were never meant for public consumption, being virtually without definition, so that in bathing trunks he somehow gave the impression of a man who had forgotten to wear his trousers); a gentle, at times whimsical nature; and, at age thirty, a mind as penetrating and encyclopedic as any she had known. Years ago she had attended a party in the SoHo apartment of a New York rock critic. The apartment walls were entirely coated with long-playing albums, stacked edge to edge. Someone had said there were fifty thousand albums in the apartment. Many of them were rock albums, but most were classical, operatic, jazz. Dunning Pinley's mind was like that. The rock critic had employed a secretary, full-time, to do nothing but catalogue his albums and to play them, one by one, at the critic's parties. (The critic would not hear of turntables that employed automatic stacking spindles.) There were times when Robyn saw herself as performing a similar function for Dun. Dunning with a wall-to-wall mind, coated with the *Harvard Law Review* and old stacks of *Barron's*. Robyn rummaging around. "Don't mind me, dear . . ." Oh, God, she *loved it* . . . but, yes, *something* like that, after all. Dunning Pinley III was destined for politics. Already there was some talk about state treasurer. . . .

They had met when she was a senior at UCLA, already a beauty contest winner and on her way to academic honors. (Miriam had chosen well. Stage mothers had their points.) He was already established in his profession; law degree from Stanford, now an associate in one of Beverly Hills' blue-chip corporate law firms.

A friend of theirs had fixed them up. Classic. She'd broken a date to meet this ball of fire. There he had stood in the doorway of her apartment, in his steel-rimmed glasses, heels of his wing tips together, and oh, God, these half-dozen corny roses in his hand. He even had on one of his alligator shirts, under his blazer—a little tip-off that he was "laid-back," he'd admitted later.

Well. She had just melted. (Her broken date had been with the self-appointed "next Steven Spielberg.") Right there on the spot. It was ridiculous.

The first few months had been heaven. Like Robyn, Dunning was not a Californian—"like being a non-Catholic," they told one another. He had come west to flee an old-line Boston-Brahmin family. But he could never quite shake the family bearing or the destiny of the Pinley men: rich law. He admitted it, shrugging. Didn't matter, she told him. I can love you in spite of your past. God, but she was weary of junior movie moguls and linebackers.

They shared quiet restaurants, galleries, chamber music, and love-making at his Malibu beach house. She wanted to meet his friends. Absolutely no question, he told her. We'll get something organized. After her graduation she was always flying out of town on gigs—he hated the word—or filming at one of the TV studio lots somewhere. At first, the breaks and the money had been very, very good.

He didn't ask much about her career. She was glad of it. They talked law, politics, books, music.

After a while, though, Dunning had begun to show some doubts that she had not sensed in the early days of their affair. Did she think she could ever pull herself away from this—sort of thing? Was it absolutely necessary to have her picture on so many magazines? Did she feel that the summer TV series was—ah, exactly the thing for her image, long-term?

How could she answer him? Marry me? There had been long, searching talks. A couple of slammed telephones. Some raised voices. (He argued—infuriatingly—like a lawyer.) Tension, when she returned from an assignment. But never—or so she let herself believe—any serious doubt that their fundamental relationship was sound.

It had bumped along like that for these two years. Fragmented, off-and-on at times, but a consistent affair. Commitment. The total shot. And now, finally, Dunning had arranged this command performance, this little audition of a get-together with his friends.

Kendall said, "Worth, will you do something with that radio? I mean for *God's* sakes."

Worth had wedged it into the sand, where it now rested at an angle. Like all of Worth's possessions it was awesome: a black accretion of knobs, dials, antennae, two circular speakers, short-wave capability, cassette mode. Robyn had forgotten that it was on. A soft rattle of music issued from it; something that sounded like, *"Got*-cha, *got*-cha, *got*-cha, *got*-cha."

"Hey." Worth raised a cautioning hand, an unlit cigar between two fingers. "Objection." He was being droll. "This is the ball game station, lady. The pulse-quickening Los Angeles Dodgers will be on the air any minute."

"Worth believes himself to be a baseball fan," said Kendall. "There are few things more Wagnerian than Worth attempting to be a man of the people."

Dun regarded his colleague. "What is it, Worth—isn't it Opening Night or something? Dodgers in Pittsburgh?"

Worth was studying his wife; he didn't hear.

"By the way," Kendall said, turning. "It's not that I have anything against that sort of music, Robyn."

"Hey." Robyn shrugged. "You don't have to—"

"Ah . . . Robyn's not a part of that culture," Dun said quickly, and Robyn wished he hadn't. She felt him edge his body away from her an inch or so on the sand.

"Is there any of that champagne left, Worth? Robyn, tell me. Was winning that—*contest* a terrible thrill?"

Robyn didn't answer a moment. She found herself searching Kendall's face. It was hard to tell through the sunglasses that Kendall had worn all afternoon—even in the ocean, or so it had seemed—but

Robyn doubted that Kendall could be more than a year older than she.

"It's been more than two years ago now, Kendall. I honestly don't think much about it anymore. It's all in the past." (Like hell. A day didn't go by when it wasn't thrown back at her one way or another . . . smiling, she turned her face up to Dun to acknowledge this latest appearance of The Question, which they had agreed to tolerate good-naturedly. But Dun happened to be looking somewhere else, possibly out to sea.)

"I understand that the current Miss America is giving ten percent of her earnings to God." Worth snorted, lighting his cigar. It occurred to Robyn that this was the closest he had come to speaking to her all day.

"Oh, come on, Robyn." Kendall was boring in now. "Dun has told us all about your wonderful movie career and all the things you've done in television. Surely you're not telling us this didn't follow from Miss Yankeedoodle-doo. I mean, isn't that the thing, to go out and hustle that title into a big show-business career?"

The music went, *"Got*-cha, *got*-cha, *got*-cha, *got*-cha . . ."

Robyn waited, without looking up, for Dun to come to her rescue. When he didn't, she laughed lightly. "I wouldn't call one movie a career. Anybody want to hit the surf one more time? Sun's almost down."

No one moved. Kendall wasn't through. "I suppose you felt awfully exploited," she said, tracing patterns in the sand with her finger, "at having to subject yourself to all of that . . . exploitation. I mean, God, I've read about all those horrible fried-chicken people who run that contest."

"I didn't feel that I—"

"All those chaperones. Being dragged through a swimsuit competition, for Christ's sake, like so much meat on the hoof, although I gather that you did awfully well in the swimsuit." She lifted her plastic cup and swallowed the last sip of golden champagne. "I mean, is it all really as disgusting as everything I've read. . . ."

Robyn arose without using her arms and brushed the grains of sand from her legs.

"I don't know what you read, Kendall. But I'd go back and check some of my source material if I were you. Nabokov didn't write *Eugene Onegin*. He translated it from Pushkin. What you recited was Pushkin. The fried-chicken people happened to be quite civilized. There is nothing intrinsically wrong with being a fried-chicken executive. I don't know what you mean by 'exploited,' and neither, I suspect, do you. I'm going swimming. Dun, are you coming, sweetheart?''

Dun, as it turned out, wasn't. She ran to the ocean alone, conscious of the ruins behind her. She plunged at the booming curls of ocean again and again, until she was breathless. She found herself wishing to God that when she came out of the water they would all be gone.

They weren't gone. But the blankets, plates, bottles, and cooking equipment were packed away when she strode slowly back from the sea. The golden glow had faded from the world; in the dull twilight she could not tell the three figures apart until she was twenty paces from them.

It was as though nothing had happened. Kendall greeted her with a cheery flutter of the hand. "God, Robyn, you're an inspiration to us all. I'm going on the Scarsdale Diet first thing Monday." Dunning, his fingers clamped over and under his lighted pipe, favored her with a brief smile.

The lights of Santa Monica were winking on in a blue crescent to the south. The wind had turned cold. The four of them stood in the sand with their arms folded in front of them, all sporting congenial grins.

Worth offered her a ride back toward her own beach house. Without thinking, she blurted no thanks, she'd be staying with Dun.

"That's right," said Kendall, ever the model of enlightenment. "You guys are engaged, aren't you?"

"Well, not really." Dun left the pipe clamped in his mouth. "Not exactly, not yet. Not formally."

Robyn let her hand slide from Dunning's arm. To cover a wave of nausea in her stomach, she said in a too-loud voice, "I'm so glad to have finally met you, Worth. Kendall, I want to—"

Kendall stretched her lips in a wide smile and pressed Robyn's hand. "It was *delightful*. *Super*. We'll *all* be on the lookout for that movie of yours."

*   *   *

Now, sprawled on the beach, she recalled the scene that followed an hour later.

"Dun?"

"Mmmmmm."

"Can we talk?"

He marked the passage in his book and placed it on the reading table. He removed his glasses and set them on the book. He folded his hands in his lap.

They were slumped on canvas deck chairs in the living room of his beach cottage, their feet propped up on a small driftwood bench. Dun was wearing a tartan dressing gown. Besides the glow from the fireplace, the only light in the room came from a bulb in a stainless-steel shield above his left shoulder. The pool of light made his long serious face look like an oil painting, possibly of a Russian poet.

He was staring at her, the picture of the attentive counselor.

"Jesus, Dun, I'm sorry. Maybe I should make an appointment at your office."

"Robyn, let me begin with a caveat."

"Dun, don't use that goddamn courtroom jargon on me. Hey. It's your old friend Robyn Quarrles!" She wiggled her wineglass above her head. In this last silent hour she had suspended her own non-alcohol rule.

"All right. Then suppose you lay off the tough-sister dialogue. I for one don't find it all that evocative."

" 'Tough-sister dialogue.' Wait, let me guess. You're referring to the 'goddamn.' Oh, Dun."

After a minute he said, "You didn't do too bad a job on Kendall Hunter this evening."

"But that was—Dun, be fair! Now we're not talking *coarse*. We're talking *squelch*. I'm sorry I put her down. That's what I want to talk to you about. I'm sorry I'm sorry I'm sorry!" She set her wineglass down hard. "But she'd been on my case all afternoon. You saw it."

"I saw a very gracious and knowledgeable woman attempting to make conversation with you *on your ground*. You cut her to pieces. Hitting her with the Pushkin thing. That was so snotty. I could quote you a couple of your own missed references, if it came to that."

Robyn pulled her caftan more tightly around her. The room was ice-cold despite the fire. The wind from the ocean rattled the windowpanes. She gnawed at her lip and scowled into the dark reaches of Dun's living room for a long moment. When she faced him, her voice was light.

"You're right, Dun. I shouldn't have done that. I memorize things. It's my curse. I should've been a touring pro on the game shows. Look, I just wanted to prove to her I'm not some bubble-headed doxy you're dragging around town. I want your friends to *know* that, Dun."

"Maybe then you ought to wear your Phi Bete key around your neck. God knows it would've been in plain view this afternoon."

"What are you saying, Dun?"

"What are *you* saying? Do you think my friends are under the impression that I drag bubble-headed doxies around town? You leave that worry to me."

She could, if she wanted, extend one long leg and slip her bare foot between his. She wanted. He was wearing patent-leather slippers. Instead of doing it, she put both feet on the cold floor and leaned forward, hugging her elbows.

"Dun, this is savage. Let's not chew at each other like this. We never used to."

Instead of answering her, he began filling his pipe. She watched him methodically lift the tobacco from its tinfoil pouch and tamp it into the bowl. She thought of Worth staring transfixed as Dun poured the daiquiris on the beach.

"All right, Dunning. Let's drop the gloves. What is it you really want to say to me?"

"I don't really want to say anything. This is your conversation. Remember?"

"All right. I started by saying I was sorry that I was rude to your friend Kendall. I'd like to know how you think I should go about repairing that."

"I don't know that it's essential for you to go about repairing that."

She narrowed her eyes. "Will you please stop being so god damned . . . excuse me. So *terribly* cryptic, Dun. *What's the matter with you?*"

He lowered the pipe to his lap and watched it until the ember went out. He tilted his head back in the deck chair and gazed at the ceiling for a long time.

"Robyn, I don't think it's working."

"Why? How can you say that?"

Dunning Pinley closed his eyes and remained silent.

The image of Kendall Hunter came into her mind; Kendall, saying: *"Was winning that contest a terrible thrill?"*

She kicked at his shins.

"Look at me. Was I on exhibit this afternoon?"

"Robyn . . ."

"Is that what this little celebration was supposed to be about? Were you floating the beauty queen past a couple of key associates?"

"Robyn, that's not—"

" 'Not *really*. Not *exactly*. Not *yet*. Not *formally*.' God damn you. I memorize. Dun, you bastard, that's exactly the way you'd go about it!"

"Robyn, if we can't discuss this without you resorting to—"

"Oh, excuse me. That's right. Clean up my language and put my Phi Beta Kappa key between my boobs. Well, what do you think, Dun? Based on your friend Worth's not saying a word to me all afternoon and sneaking looks down my halter top, do you think I'd enhance the ticket or be a liability?"

"I'm not even going to dignify this conversation—"

"Well said. Spoken like a politician. I think maybe I'm getting the picture. As far as the god damned firm goes, I gather that *dating* a Miss Whatever is one thing . . . the senior partners lap it up . . . *marrying* the poor bitch is quite *another* thing. Am I right?"

"You're close."

"Ah. We're getting somewhere. Let me take it a step further. In California state politics it wouldn't look too bad for an Establishment type like yourself to have a show-biz wife. It might even help if I roller-skated. But let's take the long view. *Nationally,* the track record hasn't been too good for candidates with—"

"Robyn!"

He was on his feet, his dressing gown flying open. He grabbed her wrists, pulled her up to him. She smelled the Cherry Blend scent on his collar as she buried her face in his shoulder. He stroked her hair, and after a minute she pressed herself to him.

"You know," he was saying, deep in his throat, as his lips nuzzled her ear, "it's not as though we can't continue to *see* each other. . . ."

She took a step back and planted her foot to swing at him. When she saw his face, she stopped, her arm drawn back, and after a moment she began to laugh.

He looked puzzled, and then began to laugh too.

"Pinley Stripely," she gasped between convulsive bursts. "Did I ever tell you—that my very own private nickname for you was—*Pinley Stripely*?" She was laughing so hard she had to bend down and grip the caftan at her knees.

"No," he said, and chuckled. "I'd say that I deserve that one. It just about puts me in my place, doesn't it?"

Unable to speak, her head bowed, she nodded. When she was able to straighten up, she placed her hands on his cheeks and whispered:

"Give me fifteen minutes, Pinley Stripely. And then come into the bedroom."

"Oh, God."

"Don't peek. Fifteen minutes. Okay?"

"Christ Jesus okay. God I was afraid—"

"Hush. Go find something to do. Read your torts."

She crossed quickly to a small writing desk in a darkened corner of the living room and opened the middle drawer. The scissors were there. Tucking them inside the bodice of her caftan, she whisked inside the bedroom and closed the door, turning the knob to be sure that the latch held.

Now, sprawled on the beach nearly a day later, she smiled as she re-created the scene: Dun sweating out his fifteen minutes—probably timed it with a stopwatch—finally flinging open the door to the bedroom.

He would have found the overhead light on. The dresser drawers all opened. On the bed, his entire collection of pullover sport shirts—there must have been thirty of the damn things.

Each shirt with a jagged hole in the chest, on the left side. Where the little alligators had been.

The bedroom window open, the curtains whipping in the strong night wind.

He probably wouldn't have gotten it until his gaze settled on the little green alligators, all arranged on his dresser top.

In crude, but unmistakable UCLA halftime-show formation, spelling out:

STUFF IT

Cute. A lovely exit line. But now, as she picked herself up from the beach and dusted the sand from her white jeans, she understood for the first time how final it really was.

And she knew that she was going to march back to her trusty telephone and call up the Croatian Comet and tell him that she was accepting his guaranteed national publicity star-vehicle concept.

CHAPTER 5

SOMETIMES, LOOKING BACK ON it, he wondered if he ever existed in real space or in real time. He was, in the manner of speaking of such things, "on the radio." That was his job, his career, destiny's assignment. It was what the adult in him *did*. But the child in him was not so much *on* the radio as *in* it; in there, inside some eternal Emerson resting on a bedside table, while the night wind blew the distant vapors of Lake Michigan through white lace curtains and a boy, not himself but not someone else, lay listening. His soul, his essence, was an orange glow inside that small wooden cathedral, and his friends were the invisible voices that said, *"Good evening, Ladies and Gentlemen of the Radio Audience!"*

It was a wonderful phrase. It lay solid on the heart and spoke of a vast confederacy, perhaps secret—a network of citizens, indistinguishable enough (by day) from the common passerby, the gray wash of humanity; but at night a swift and alert cabal, elect recipients of an electric information as wonderful for its instant passage on the airwaves as for its cathartic effect on the brain's eye, but wonderful for that, too . . . the *Ladies and Gentlemen of the Radio Audience.*

(Years into his famous adulthood, when his voice was the voice of summer itself, he had heard someone's phonograph album of "Famous Radio Bloopers," in which an announcer was heard saying, "Good evening, Ladies and Gentlemen of the Audio Radiance," and it struck him that this was not necessarily inaccurate at all, that this described the situation as well as its reverse.)

Had he ever been a child? The records showed that there had been a childhood. For all that the present age had glorified something called the youth culture, he always felt that he had grown up in the Age of the Boy. Where he had lived, gin and jazz and roadsters were distant rumors. The pompadoured razorfaced men of the talking pictures, eternally lounging with hands in their tuxedo pockets in front of walls laced with the slant of venetian blinds, seemed irredeemably old and sad.

No, the abiding image of the 1920s in rural America, where he came from, was that of the Boy: the one surefire produce of the fragmenting family guaranteed not to slip, stall, wear out, or decrease in value. The Boy, supple, regenerative, the blood in his cheeks, haircombed and studious, bowtied and grinning, in control, the imitation uncorrupted adult: the twenties crackled with the legends of Boy Inventors and Boy Aviators and Boy Scientists and Boy Broadcasters. There were Boy Scouts and Boy Patrols; there were serials featuring Boy Detectives and Boy Pitchers and Boy Racers. Fanning was, in his mind, all of these.

And yet he was never purely a boy. Some distant thing in his face with its high, serious forehead, the eyes hidden by flashing spectacles, the thin mouth solemn, made the others leave him alone. He seemed born famous. He was never in a fistfight. He was in a baseball game once, an organized game, just one time, and the memory of it drove through the nightmares of his life.

What set him apart? Who knows the essence of the radio man? He was a receptor and a transmitter before America quite realized that something called radio existed. His father was the source of all his worldly information. His father was a traveling man, tall and with a high thrusting belly and cunning hazel eyes. A brush salesman, he worked the vast orchard country and the pinched Bohemian villages along the great eastern shore of Lake Michigan. Their own village, Three Pines, lay ten miles inland from the lake on a railroad line that ran from Chicago to Detroit. The boy's brain buzzed with the sounds of the names of the towns that his father traveled in: Cassopolis and Galien and Breedsville and Dowagiac and Kalamazoo. His father was at ease in these cities. He had dealt face to face with their Prominent Citizens. He had held conversations with Wealthy Lawyers and Well-to-do Doctors, many of whom had taken substantial orders for his brushes. He had seen the insides of their exclusive homes, had been invited in (through back doors, the boy later learned). Fanning's father could hold his own with any man. He was a talker, a Good Conversationalist, and his currency was baseball, the universal exchange. Fanning's father could talk baseball and break down a man's sales resistance. The child had seen him do it:

"Say, that Pants Rowland," his father would remark, looking a customer meaningfully in the eye.

There would be an expectant pause. A flicker of confusion would cross the customer's face. In the doubtful silence that followed, Fanning's father would hold the other's stare, one eyebrow cocked, a cut-rate cigar half out of its wrapper.

Something about the silence always made the boy want to turn his eyes away.

"Yes," the customer would say at last. "Quite a ballplayer."

"Say, I've got this vegetable brush that I'd like you to take a look at. . . ."

His father was an authority. His father had seen the sunlit stadiums in Chicago and Detroit. He spoke of the ballgames he had seen as though he were a runner returning from a distant battlefield, his eyes filled with flags and miracles. In this traveling man's scheme of values, baseball needed no reference to any higher sphere of activity. It was an absolute. The value of Pants Rowland was an article of faith. It required only acknowledgement, not analysis. Fanning's father knew all the names, all the averages. Fanning's mother was a thin pained woman who worked in Three Pines' only factory, fashioning corsets out of whalebone stays. She did not know the averages. This vacuum of piety affected her husband with an almost religious dismay.

So he would instruct his son, the receptor, in the catechisms. At the depot (now, in these lengthening shadows of the century, a "boutique") early on a Saturday morning:

"See them tracks. The *Detroit Tigers* will come right down them tracks in about twenty minutes. On their way to Chicago."

(A shudder between the small boy's shoulder blades. Prickles of delicious fear on the back of his neck. He could not possibly imagine the awesome thing he was about to witness—perhaps a boiling moiling blur of great men-beasts raging along the tracks, without need or benefit of train.)

"The White Sox come along these tracks. When you're sleepin'. You remember what I told you about the White Sox. Why, the Cubs come along these tracks in 1906 and 1907 when they beat the Tigers twice in the World Series. Cubs were also called the Spuds then. What's a Spud?"

"A potato." The child's eyes were fixed down the blazing tracks, alert for Tigers.

"The Cubs won one hunnert sixteen games in taking the National League flag." Again the pause, the arched eyebrow, the unlit cigar poised in midair. The child had felt (as had the father's customers) the overwhelming responsibility to say something. The Tigers were coming. He rummaged his mind for a baseball answer.

"Orval Overall," he said, and collapsed giggling. Orval Overall was a name his father mentioned often when talking about the Chicago Cubs.

His father hauled the child up from the platform by his suspenders and struck him across the face.

"Don't laugh at that name!" Through his terror the child saw something aggrieved, something haunted in his father's eyes, suddenly wet with tears. "Orval Overall! He led the Cubs in shutouts in 1907 and 1909!"

Perhaps it was out of some perverse obeisance to his father's obsession that he became a keeper of baseball statistics. A connoisseur of box scores (which he culled from his father's mail edition of the *Chicago Tribune*). The Boy Statistician. His schoolmates, hardheaded children of Michigan applegrowers, vaguely sensed that he was at once less worldly and more wise than they: naïve as to certain truths about human greed and aggression, oblivious to certain schoolyard secrets, unaware of the unfolding clues to adult lusts and secretions—too innocent even to bully or taunt, and excluded in sexual speculations. But wise . . . wise in other things. Major leagues fought for pennants in his head. Before sandlot games in Three Pines, the older boys lined up obediently to be handed identities by the child with the mind full of famous names—some of them obscured in history even in the 1920s.

"Thomas, you're Three-Finger Mordecai Brown [Thomas had lost a knuckle to his brother's woodchopping axe]. Frank, you're Rabbit Maranville, you got to hit down like this. Jimmy, you're Turkey Mike Donlin, you get to be married to Mabel Hite and you make six thousand a year. Winnie, you're Ray Chapman."

"No fair. He got killed."

"All right. You be Heinie Zimmerman."

Years later when they all read his name in *Look* and heard his voice on coast-to-coast hookups and saw his picture in the Chesterfield ads, they were not surprised. They had all assumed he would be famous, and he had, too. He had accepted his eventual fame as a consequence of living, like his apartness from childhood.

The first radio sound he ever heard came across a set that he had made when he was eleven years old. The year was 1928. Boy Mechanic. There were manuals, magazines. He wore grayish headphones around his solemn face—he felt himself connected to something terrible and bottomless, like the soul of America itself. The people of Three Pines came to look at his receiving set. There were few other sets in the town. The visitors were invited into the house by his mother, in the evenings, and were shown up to the boy's room. Staring through the doorway into his desk they beheld the child, the earphones crowning his unsmiling face, his eyes hidden by the flashing glasses, his thin mouth expressionless, and they scented a strange aroma, like hot metal. The visitors were struck silent with a kind of sheepish, fumbling respect, and they left quickly.

The boy did not notice. The earphones shrieked and wailed as he turned the tuning knob. He was awakening spirits on the air. The first voice he heard on the radio was borne across the lower lip of Lake Michigan from Chicago, eighty miles away, on a clear spring night in

1928; it was the spring after the Babe had swatted sixty. The voice was the falsetto voice of a man singing "Toot, Toot, Tootsie! Goodbye."

A year later his father brought home a secondhand Emerson from Detroit, where he had attended a brushmen's sales convention. The Emerson was a centerpiece in the family for a while, the three of them listening almost politely to orchestra music in the evenings. And then, without a word being exchanged, the boy moved the radio up into his bedroom. It was understood that the radio and the forces inside it were his.

His father took him to his first major-league game on a Sunday in June of 1930. It was a stately occasion. They had mailed in their orders for tickets months before, choosing the best dollar value—a doubleheader at Chicago's Wrigley Field between the Cubs (who were to finish second in the National League that year with a record of ninety wins and sixty-four defeats for a percentage of .584; he kept the statistic forever in his mind) and the St. Louis Cardinals (who were to win the pennant with a mark of ninety-two and sixty-two, a percentage of .597).

The boy had never seen Chicago, except as an infinitesimal speck on the far rim of Lake Michigan, eighty miles to the west, when, on certain late-August days, standing on a high bank in the Indiana Dunes, one could see the setting sun encompass the city.

Wrigley Field was a stadium of his mind. In that year five Chicago stations began broadcasting the Cubs' home games: he had his choice of listening to Bob Elson, Hal Totten, Pat Flanagan, Quin Ryan—or Mel Pelham, with his *"Heeeeeeee's out!"*

On that June Sunday his father woke him before dawn. The family lived in a small two-story shingled house near the edge of Three Pines; a house wedged between two others, and shaded by a single elm tree in the tiny front lawn. The two of them groped their way downstairs to the newly linoleumed kitchen—the alien scent of glue still hung in the room—where his father awkwardly attempted to cook breakfast. The child understood that on this day he and his father were to be "pals," and that baseball was to be the cementing bond between them.

"Say, that Hack Wilson," said his father in a low offhand voice, peering and jabbing at the gas stove. The orange morning light made unaccustomed shadows on the kitchen walls. "Now *they's* one of the best dam' ballplayers ever lived."

He wheeled to face the son, fixing him with the raised-eyebrow look that he used on his brush customers. The boy sensed for the first time the full impact of the desperate urgency behind his father's baseball small-talk—a longing to invest the words with a meaning that he could not quite summon. The boy realized that the use of "dam'," forbidden by his mother, was in this case ceremonial: a further signal. So was the scent of forbidden sour mash on the highbellied salesman's breath. The awareness of it all descended over the boy and suffused his early-morning exhilaration with sadness.

"I guess I'm not too hungry," he said from the table. His father had failed to solve the lighting of the gas stove.

"Now you'll hear some people *say*, " his father muttered on, looking around for something to wipe his hands on, "that Mr. Wilson is a *saloon man*. You know what that means?" Again, the look—intended to be conspiratorial this time, two men of the world sharing their amusement at the foibles of the mighty.

The child forced himself to say it, feeling miserable.

"It means he likes to take a drink."

"Tha-ha-ha-ha-hat's right." His father's glance invited him to share the mirth. But the face contorted into seriousness again. "But I want to tell you something . . . when that old bird steps up to the plate . . . why . . ." His hand traced a vague arc. Words failed him. It was too big.

They left the cold kitchen in silent failure and went upstairs to dress for the doubleheader. The boy put on a starched white shirt and his best pair of breeches, which were woolen—buckled at the knees, they resembled baseball breeches—polished his spectacles, and descended to the small parlor to await his father. The Sunday paper had not arrived yet, so in the dim morning light he reread Saturday's account of the big day at the plate by Rogers Hornsby, the vivid phrases evoking an almost Grecian grandeur. On that very afternoon he was to set eyes on Hornsby. He spread the sports pages out on the parlor floor and lay on his stomach, rereading the exalted prose, constructing from it the fantasy of gallant athletes leaping and diving about on an endless meadow of a diamond, their spikes flashing in the basepath dust. He recalled the unearthly sough of the crowd from the radio broadcasts he had heard, and tried to imagine himself inside the stadium.

Forty-five minutes later he heard his father's slow step on the stairs. The salesman had put on his best suit, a three-piece number in chocolate brown with subtle chalk-stripes (which he had bought secondhand from a Prominent Banker in Cassopolis), a cellophane collar, and a bow tie. There was clove on his breath and Brylcreem on his sandy hair and his hands were unsteady. They were going to a ballgame, pals for a day embarked on a festive occasion, but his father's manner suggested an event infinitely more somber. It was as though he were taking the boy to his first brothel.

They drove mostly in silence the twenty-three miles to Michigan City, across a dirt road through sun-crowned wheat fields in his father's used Model T (which he had bought, cut-rate, from "this old fella I know" in Niles, and which had spent most of its time inside Three Pines Motors). His father drove slowly, because two of the tires were patched. His father offered him a "cake" of Wrigley's Spearmint gum, tore off half a "cake" for himself, and informed the boy casually that he had once seen Mr. P. K. Wrigley's summer mansion while on an excursion around Lake Geneva.

At Michigan City they parked the Model T and boarded a train on the South Shore Line for the two-hour trip into Chicago. His father attempted to rekindle the insouciant holiday spirit by purchasing a Sunday *Chicago Tribune* at the depot, even though there would be one in the house when they got back, already paid for by subscription.

The two of them sat in the smoke-filled coach, his father with the sports page opened on his knee. The father essayed, in a dutiful way, to impart some of his experience in baseball-attendance matters to his son.

"Don't buy nothin' off them vendors. They's just out to soak you. The red-hots ain't worth half what they charge. They's pickpockets so keep your hand in your pocket where your money's at. Don't pester me for one of those flags they sell. If you get separated from me in the crowd go find a policeman and tell him who you are. You

better watch it too''—sly smile, a poke in the ribs—''because Al
Capone and his boys are big Cub fans. All those big hoodlums go out
to those games, they got box seats. I know 'em when I see 'em. You
watch it 'cause you ain't but knee-high to a Navajo.''

The boy rode into Chicago conceiving of Wrigley Field as a char-
nel house.

He had never been so conscious of his own smallness. Streaming
with the crowd along Addison Street, he beheld the astonishing triumphant structure that flung itself skyward like a jolly king's crown:
Wrigley Field. A strong breeze was blowing in from Lake Michigan
and the pennants on the stadium rim crackled like cannon. He
thought he could hear them above the streetclamor of the crowd,
above the great echoing growl that boiled up like steam from inside
the park, from the fans already in the stands.

He had never seen so many people together at one time in his life,
and the sight filled him with an intolerable sense of insignificance.
These people do not know I'm destined to become famous! Stepping
along Addison in the clutch of his sweatsoaked father, on the lookout
for trolleys, he let his nostrils fill with the collection of aromas that
teased him with the hint of an exotic society (*Good evening, Ladies
and Gentlemen of the Radio Audience!*) and left him dizzy with longing: the strong gasoline fumes from the excursion buses, the cheap
perfume steaming off women's bare arms, the pungent tobacco aroma
from wet unlit cigars held in hands, the warm smell of Polish sau-
sages rolling out the dark open doorways of lunchrooms. (''Don't go
in there,'' his father warned as he stopped to peer inside. ''They's a
place I know we'll go to after the game.'')

Once through the ticket turnstile the boy spied a man in a straw hat
hawking souvenir scorecards. The sheets, fanned out in the man's
hand like giant playing cards, looked crisp and white and efficient;
there were sharpened pencils in the man's apron, the points up. The
child longed for one, longed to mark it with the evidence of his having been there, but he knew better than to ask. (Years later, when he
returned to Wrigley Field as the Voice of the Giants, the memory of
the forbidden scorecards seared into him, and when he entered his
broadcast booth and found one placed beside his microphone, free of

charge, courtesy of the Chicago Cubs National League Baseball Club, Inc., the import of his privileged status hit him for the first time, and he wept.)

Approaching the stadium, his father had begun muttering beneath his breath, in a nervous incantatory way, about the heroic qualities of the Cubs' outfield: "I don't give a rat's ass what anybody says, that Hack Wilson is the best gaht-dam' hitter that's ever wore a Cub uniform. Now you take your Frank Chance. Okay. I seen him too. But Hack Wilson could of wore a *blindfold* . . ."

For the first time in his life, the boy saw his father as a small man, no larger, no grander than anyone else in the crowd, a scuttling atom in the swarm, paying his way. The urge to detach himself grew in his chest; he wanted to float above these people and commingle with the essence of the ballpark, to partake of its majesty. The longing gripped him and he felt as though he were suffocating.

Their seats were in the bleachers. Cut-rate. Upon walking up the concrete ramp and into the sunlight, the boy stopped and stared.

The ballpark was both greater and lesser than he had imagined it to be. The precision of its lines held him in fascination. The green horizontal sweep of the far grandstand seats, alive with the flow of white-shirted men; the upright intersections of supporting steel beams suggesting a permanence and a purpose ordained by God. The white-chalked foul lines splayed away from home plate in unerring lines of absolute judgment, all the way to the ivy-covered outfield wall. The outfield grass was a fulgent green, richer than Michigan alfalfa fields under the cobalt sky (Sunday doubleheader skies were forever to be a pleasure to him; they touched a chord like a high saxophone note). The geometric shapes of the dugouts—he could see shadowy men moving, men wearing small-billed caps; he knew that he knew their names, and he sucked in his breath. The raised lump of the pitcher's mound—it suggested an artillery emplacement, aimed at a target. And crowning the tableau, dominating the stadium, soaring not fifty feet from where he stood, the enormous black scoreboard, infallible as one of Moses' tablets.

In that stunned moment the boy understood the absolute authority of major-league baseball; understood its wordless suzerainty over American life.

But there was something else.

"What is it?" asked his father, for the boy was motionless, his thin mouth open.

"It isn't as big as I thought it'd be."

"I'll big *you* if you don't siddown. Come along."

It was true. He realized his astonishment that the park was finite. And he realized why he was astonished. The radio men had made it *sound* bigger. The radio men had created a stadium of the mind, boundless, of which the real thing could be only a shabby imitation.

They watched the doubleheader over Hack Wilson's shoulder that day. The boy's gaze kept drifting up from the playing field to the radio booths, where the dreambuilders dwelt.

CHAPTER

ELVIN RAY TEWELES. HEIGHT: 5-10. Weight: 195. Bats: Left. Throws: Right.

Maj. Lea. Totals:

G	AB	R	H	2B	3B	HR	RBI	AVG.
642	2022	205	535	88	12	67	283	.265

As a Brooklyn Dodger [the yellowed captionlines said].
With the St. Louis Browns.
Catching for the Redlegs.
Wearing a Giants uniform.
A left-handed swinger, Teweles gets a quick start toward first on a hit.

Off-season hobbies: hunting, fishing. [You expected something else?]

"Turtle" married a Fayette girl, Helen Lovenvirth, while still a minor-league player.

Taxpayer. Baptist. Private first-class. Abstainer from alcohol, chewer of Mail Pouch tobacco. A face on the team bus, an oval of blurred white in the team photograph. Anonymous traveler in the big cold cities that made him famous. Hater of conversation in big-city taxicabs, aware of the wise driver's eyes; distruster of his own voice in confined spaces, better not to talk, not to think of anything beyond getting his wrists out in front of the breaking pitches and beyond the remember smell of cooling tar paper on summer nights in Arkansas; porch swings after a day's work chopping cotton; the biblesmell and the cicadasound and the skies full of stars. Locomotive whistles. Memories Turtle Teweles could not explain; memories that embarrassed him, made him spit; memories that he knew were his future: the dull yellow cloud that settles into dust over a plain man's brief bodyfame and returns him to a life that he might once have found acceptable . . . but the big leagues get into your blood, he couldn't explain it, not even to Helen, and facing the end of your career is like facing the end of who you are; the number taken off your back ("They'll have to tear this uniform off-a me") leaves a naked spot on the soul.

L. C. Fanning saved his soul.

It was Fanning who had talked Teweles up into the broadcast booth when the catcher retired in 1954. Teweles was transported by the unexpected reprieve. (Helen left him.) Perched in the pressboxes with Fanning, high above the home plates where he had for so long squatted, Teweles at first could do little more than sit blinking like a large old turtle indeed. His gaze tended to stray upward from the action on the diamond, up toward the light towers and the pennants fluttering on the rims of the stadiums, and outward toward the rooftops and the baked hotels and the distant factory smokestacks beyond—toward the industrial sunsets and the chilling urban moons. It was as if for the first time in his life Turtle was comprehending that the ballparks of his manhood were not self-contained universes, suspended in time and space, but only small and fragile preserves, artifacts, existing at the mercy of the heavy and indifferent cities that pressed in on them.

Fanning taught him everything he knew. At first, Turtle had little to add to the broadcasts. He sat in cowed silence, his iridescent seersucker sports jacket bunching up on his shoulders, the haircut line showing on the back of his neck.

But Fanning helped him along. Fanning told his listeners what a character the Turtle was. Fanning eased the time through lopsided games and rain delays and pitching changes by recounting comic escapades from Teweles's playing days—"Why, Turtle, you were ready to pop that big lummox then and there, and I guess if Durocher hadn't stepped in . . ."

Fanning had a wonderful gift for telling tales, and he wanted desperately for Teweles to succeed. The Turtle was one of Fanning's all-time heroes. And as that first season wore on, young Willie Mays belting 'em out for the Giants, Teweles hunched in a paralysis of silence, Fanning reached further and further into his imagination: he told of the Tortoise's boyhood on an Arkansas farm, a farm that somehow existed purely in the metaphor of baseball: he told how the young boy Turtle perfected his technique for snagging foul pop-ups by catching hailstones bare-handed during a summer storm; how he learned his overhand snap-throw to second base by grabbing rattlesnakes by the tail and popping their heads to smithereens with a whiplike motion—how, in fact, the stalwart lad had received his original inspiration to enter the brotherhood of catchers on the night he watched his daddy, the legendary Slewfoot Teweles, literally defend "home plate" by standing in the doorway of the family tar-paper cabin, thick legs planted wide, and cut down a raiding party of onrushing Indians (who, through reasons unexplained, had not received word that the Arkansas frontier had been tamed).

Fanning realized that his tall tales were having an effect on the imagination of his idol when, one August night in Philadelphia, during a station break, the Turtle leaned over and whispered diffidently into Fanning's ear:

"How'd I learn to hit?"

He began, shyly at first, this leathered profane old Baptist stoic, to affirm Fanning's tall tales—"That's righter'n rain, L.C., that's jist the way it happened." Later, Turtle was emboldened to venture embellishments on his own, and before the season was over he was matching Fanning lie for lie in his Arkansas twang, spinning stories each more outrageous than the last, and somehow, by a subtle and half-realized implication, beginning to draw Fanning into the lore, until, in the minds of the regular radio listeners of Giants baseball, the careers of L. C. Fanning and Turtle Teweles became intertwined, historic, epic.

For Fanning the intertwinement had a spiritual dimension. He *entered* Turtle Teweles; passed through a chamber of the athlete's consciousness, sojourned in the catcher's hypostasis (this big sedentary man, wearer of two-tone shoes); slapped his own chest and crouched in space and felt himself a man of action, at least in his mind. Thus the surrogate eye for the radio millions had found his surrogate self. Teweles, understanding dimly, welcomed him inside. It was a chamber that few men who are not ballplayers are privileged to explore.

As for Turtle, he was at large in a bequeathal even more precious and ineffable: a personality. In his exhaustive campaign to make Teweles interesting to his listeners, Fanning had succeeded—quite by accident—in making the Turtle interesting to himself.

Thus Elvin Ray Teweles, the son of dim lost parents and the Arkansas soil, workaday athlete in the yellowing dust of home plate, man of few words (and master of none), ginrummy player on ten thousand forgotten train rides, hunter and fisherman in the off-season, a man unprepared for the cool hotel sheets and the high glory his brutish skills had brought him (but a man resigned to give it all back without a whimper when the shadows grew long) was miraculously spared the need to face the deferred truth of his ordinariness.

Thanks to L. C. Fanning, Turtle Teweles was, in 1954, at age thirty-five, a man in chrysalis. He wore the personality that Fanning had created for him like a new suit. (He even began to wear new suits, to fit the personality.)

The pair was a smash radio hit for the last half of the 1950s. Although the radio station people were doubtful at first that Fanning and Teweles's cornpone act would rest well on the cosmopolitan East Coast ear, it quickly became apparent that New York fans doted on the routine. This was, after all, the heyday of Herb Shriner and Tennessee Ernie Ford and Dizzy Dean; of lovable plain-speaking American voices that calmed a national psyche made frantic by the fear of Reds.

CHAPTER 7

BY THE END OF APRIL, L. C. Fanning could say that the New York Nats—in a certain sense—were leading the National League.

"You can say that we are seven *components* ahead of the second-place Pittsburgh Pirates," Danny Breen told Fanning and Turtle in the press lounge before a night game against Montreal. Breen compressed his lips and looked from one man to the other—an indulgent father waiting for the children to guess the riddle.

"Components," repeated Turtle. He squinted at the foam on his Heine Meine beer. "You know you're one sorry pissant, you little whistle-britches."

"Now, Turtle," said Fanning, who thought so too.

"Turtle, I can see you haven't caught the Nat spirit yet." Breen sighed and withdrew a notepad in a silver case from the pocket of his linen suit. "Let me explain it to you, and I'm sure you'll be as excited as everyone else in the Nat family." He produced a silver ballpoint pen and flipped open the notepad.

"He's gonna draw pictures," groaned Turtle. "I can't stand to see a grown-up man draw pictures."

"The Pirates are widely celebrated for their nine basic uniform combinations. Right? Black. Gold. White with a stripe. Or any combination of two colors. I say 'basic,' because I'm not counting sleeve changes. Black or gold."

Breen frowned over his notepad until he had finished scrawling a column of words on the page. "There." He held the pad up for the two of them to see. "Have I covered the total range of Pirate uniform options?"

"You're not only a pissant," said Teweles. "Your brains is all melted and run down your tail bone."

Breen drew a crisp blue line down the middle of the page.

"Here's us," he said, starting a new column of words. "This hasn't been generally announced yet. I'm going to distribute a press release tonight. Beginning this home stand the Nats will add a *fourth* basic color motif to their uniform wardrobe: Navy field with a white stripe. That gives us white, navy powder-blue, navy-blue and navy-with-stripe. Total up the components, you get sixteen. A major league record." Breen fell silent again as he became absorbed in completing his new list.

"There oughta be a special place where the fans can come see you, Breen," said Turtle. "Charge admission. 'See the Crazy Freaken Flack, Twenty-five Cents.' "

"You're underselling," muttered Breen, still scowling at his pad. "Nobody pays a quarter for anything anymore, Turtle. That's your problem. You guys don't think progressively. Now: Have I got sixteen? Let's see. White. Navy. Powder. Stripe. White-navy. White-powder. White-stripe—"

Turtle scraped his chair back and lunged away from the table. His face was dark.

"I ain't foolin', man. Sometimes you get right on my edge."

Breen turned his official smile on Fanning.

"L.C.? What say, old fellow? I mean, there's your opening line tonight: 'The New York Nats are in *first place* in the National League!' "

"No thanks." Fanning pushed his chair back. "We'll think of some way to start out, I guess. We generally do."

"I already gave it to the television side," Breen called to Fanning's back as the tall old broadcaster ambled away. "The television side *loved it!*"

Fanning caught up with Turtle in the radio booth. For a few minutes both men stared in silence through the glass pane, down toward the artificial surface of the playing field. The Nats were wheeling through their infield practice in a uniform combination that consisted of dark trousers and powder-blue jerseys. To Fanning's eye they looked less like a major-league baseball team than a collection of European acrobats without their trapezes and trampolines.

Turtle touched a match to a Marlboro and pinched the flame out. A couple of flecks of ash immediately settled on his polyester sport coat.

"You know the shit part," Turtle said finally. He nudged an elbow into Fanning's ribs. "The shit part of it is they can put on new uniforms every god damned night of the year. And people'd still recognize the sons of bitches."

They brayed into each other's faces.

But it was true: With the season barely a month old, the Nats were playing a style of baseball that had scholars reaching, for comparisons, into antiquity.

"They are keeping pace with the 1916 Athletics of Philly," the man from the *Post* announced to the pressbox at large one night. "The 1916 Athletics of Philly, as you all are cognizant, copped thirty-six triumphs while tasting the bitter wine of defeat on one hundred seventeen occasions. Of course with the expanded schedule and night baseball and all, it would be premature at this point for us to create a groundswell of enthusiasm. There is always the danger they could fall into a late-season winning streak."

A wire-service man roared: "Not to take anything from the Nats. Right, Joseph?"

A harbinger of what was to come occurred in the very next game after Opening Day. The Nats, wearing white tops and navy bottoms, lay down before the Cubs (powder-blue field, white stripes) by a score of 9 to 3.

In the Nat clubhouse following the loss, a newly acquired second baseman named Richie ("Pig") Shoat (late of the Houston Astros) complained loudly and in the presence of the press corps that he was not accustomed to wasting his talents "on five-hundred ball clubs."

"I have wonderful news for you," said the man from the *Post*, whose name was Dorton. "You are not playing for a five-hundred ball club. Believe me."

Ballplayer oughtn't be popping off that way, thought Fanning, who stood nearby. He waited for a Nats veteran to take the malcontent aside and set him straight on the question of team spirit.

But no head turned. No blow drier was so much as lowered.

Apparently Shoat spoke for the entire team.

One week later the losing streak reached six games. "These young Nats are strugglin' to find themselves," Turtle Teweles offered as the fourth unearned San Francisco Giant run crossed the plate in the seventh inning. "They're a scrappy bunch of gamers."

But as soon as the mike was clear for a station break, he added:

"They're poorer than skimmed piss."

Turtle took that loss hard. He took them all hard.

"Post mortem's at DiMaggio's tonight." Downing, the play-by-play man from the TV side stuck his blond head into the booth. In his fitted navy blazer and his television makeup smoothing all wrinkles, Downing projected the striking effect of an elegant corpse that refused to stay laid out.

"I'll be there," said Fanning. "You in, Turtle?"

"Naw."

The hell of it was that Turtle Teweles had never played a game in his life for the New York Nats. The New York Nats hadn't even been formed when Teweles got out of baseball.

Turtle was the scrappiest gamer of them all.

By the first week in May the Nats' record stood at six and sixteen. Humphries was tagging the ball with all the authority he had shown in the American League. Sorrowful Sam Fasano had twirled a pair of complete games—one win, one loss. Other than that there wasn't much to cheer up the WERA listening audience.

"I told you, you should've used the Nats-are-in-first-place line when you had the chance," Breen told Fanning. Downing, the TV man, had used it. Often.

"I got an idea for the next wardrobe components," Turtle told Breen. "Masks."

The Nats won a couple back-to-back in St. Louis. And then came Philadelphia.

The Blueclads stormed into the City of Brotherly Love and rang the welkin for twenty-three runs against a parade of Phillie hurlers in the series opener. The catch was that the Phils accounted for twenty-eight, in a rare daytime game that took five hours and twenty minutes to complete.

"But if there was a ray of hope this afternoon, Turtle," a hoarse Fanning rasped into the microphone on the wrapup, "it was the gutsy determination of these kids to show they could battle back, time and again, and match these power-hitting Phils almost blow for blow. I wouldn't be surprised if this game turned out to be the turning point that brought this talented collection of youngsters together and molded it into a team, a unit that will stand up to the very best the National League has to offer, and maybe even surprise a lot of the so-called 'experts' as this season rolls along."

"Not to take anythin' away," said Turtle, "from the National League."

After the wrapup Fanning headed for the Nats' locker room to see how the players were taking it.

"I wouldn't go in there," smirked the *Daily News* kid, whose by-line read, " 'Chip' Fensterwald." Fensterwald had just emerged from the locker room, and was pulling the door shut behind him. "They're having meditation."

"Meditation!" Fanning scowled. *Now* what kind of crazy fad were the players into?

Fensterwald released a snicker. "Yeah. With their pocket calculators. You oughta see 'em, Fanning. They're all figuring out what the game did to their averages."

Fanning wished to blazes he hadn't paid any attention to the brash little son-of-a-biscuit-eater in the first place. He tightened his mouth and reached past Fensterwald for the doorknob.

"I guess you heard the rumor about the franchise shift," came Fensterwald's voice behind him.

Fanning's hand on the doorknob froze.

He turned back to face the kid. "*What* franchise shift?" His tone was grudging.

"They're gonna move this team to Dallas. Call 'em the Texas Instruments." Fensterwald giggled and did a buck-and-wing down the corridor.

Inside the locker room, Fanning could see that the Nats had in fact recovered from their disappointing loss. A black reserve catcher and a white outfielder had pinioned a young Mexican relief pitcher to the concrete floor. All three were naked. The reserve catcher was goosing the Mexican relief pitcher with his free hand. The pitcher's eyes were tightly shut and his teeth were clenched.

"One finger, fastball, two fingers, curve," the catcher chanted.

The outfielder spotted Fanning and inclined his head toward the catcher. "You can see why we call Goose 'the Goose,' Voice," he said.

A bearded pitcher was standing before what appeared to be a birthday cake, sent by a fan, extinguishing its lighted candles with a serious expression on his open, handsome face. He was extinguishing the candles in a disgusting manner.

Only the Nats manager, Tommy Pachelbel, seemed to be taking the situation seriously. Pachelbel sat on a stool in front of his locker, the sweat still glistening on his expressive, heavy face. It was a face that had grimaced and sagged under a thousand humiliations, and the wear of seven seasons at the Nats' helm was showing around Pachelbel's hooded eyes, where the skin was as dark as if fists had pummeled him there.

Pachelbel sat with his uniform pants still on. He had stripped off his jersey almost before the team was through the runway. A man in his fifties, Tommy Pachelbel looked about as natural in the new baseball uniform as one of those grandmotherly airport cocktail-lounge waitresses looked in her above-the-knee skirt, low-cut bodice, and milkmaid's bonnet. Fanning felt a twinge for Pachelbel. The manager sat there talking to two men in business suits, his shoelaces undone, his belly spilling over his elastic waistband. At least Pachelbel wore his stirrups low, the way they were meant to be worn, showing the stripe on the sox. That was the kind of guy Pachelbel was.

Fanning waited until Pachelbel had finished his low-key conversation with the two men, each of whom had his feet planted wide apart, each of whom kept stealing sidelong glances at the ballplayers around the locker room. If they were reporters, Fanning didn't recognize them. Philly writers, maybe.

Finally Pachelbel looked up and beckoned Fanning over. His heavy face was more serious than Fanning could remember seeing it.

Pachelbel stood up as Fanning approached. He put a sweaty paw on each of Fanning's shoulders, the way he did with his ballplayers, and looked the Nats announcer right in the eyes.

"I don't know, Voice, I don't know," Pachelbel growled.

Fanning was embarrassed and touched. He gave a shrug. "Aw, Skip. It's early. Anything can happen."

"I don't know, Voice. Talk to me, Voice. Tell Tommy Pachelbel what he oughta do."

"Skip, you know I never second-guess—"

"I ain't got but the rest of this year left on my contract. Those fellas"—Pachelbel's expressive eyes shifted over Fanning's shoulder to denote the departing men in business suits—"tell me I might not get renewed. You been watching, Voice. Tell me what I'm doin' wrong."

Pachelbel was almost wheedling. Fanning had the clammy notion that the whole team was watching their exchange. He felt the embarrassment deepen. "Skip, I can't tell you how to—hey, wait a minute. Your contract with the Nats has *two* years to run. Criminy, the crumb-bums can fire you just like that if they want to, but what the heck, Skip, you've only played twenty-five games. . . ."

"No, Voice. No, Voice. I ain't talkin' about that contract. I'm talking to you about the TV commercial I do. My Husky pants commercial, where I model all the different kinds of Husky pants. These guys are sayin' to me I haven't got it anymore, Voice. They're sayin' Tommy Pachelbel might not come back next year for Husky pants. You been watchin' those commercials, haven't you, Voice? Tell me what I'm doin' wrong."

Fanning's throat felt as if he had had a yoke around it, a yoke by which he had tugged and pulled the New York Nats baseball team for five hours twenty minutes. He stared back at Tommy Pachelbel.

"Husky pants," he heard himself repeat absurdly.

The words seemed to invest Tommy Pachelbel with a new resolve. The two paws on Fanning's shoulders tightened.

"I'll tell you what, Voice." Pachelbel's voice had risen to a brittle rasp. "They'll have to tear the Husky pants off of me. That's what.

They'll have to tear the Husky pants off of Tommy Pachelbel. And you can quote me on that, Voice.''

"Five hours and twenty minutes, Frankie.''

Wilde stood in front of Jeffrey Spector's desk, trying his best not to look hangdog. He felt as though he were on the carpet. As though a five-hour, twenty-minute ball game had been *his* idea.

"Hey. Fifty-one runs, Jeffrey. Lot of action. Seesaw ball game.''

To judge from Spector's expression, Frankie Wilde might have just remarked that tithing might be great for the soul.

"We . . . lost . . . our . . . bloody . . . *asses.*'' The little silver airplanes on Spector's desk began to jiggle and move as if by their own accord. "By the end of that game I don't think our *engineers* were listening to us. And we didn't recover for the rest of the day.''

The child-face was white.

From God knew where inside him, Frankie Wilde summoned a paternal impulse.

"Jeffrey, those things happen, that's all. I've been in this business for almost thirty years, and—''

"You're the program director. What do you think we should do about it?'' Spector's voice hinted at contempt.

Frankie Wilde's paternal impulse went up in smoke. "How the hell do I know what to do about it? We're stuck with the Nat games. What do you want, Jeffrey—a virgin sacrifice, for chrissake?'' In his mind's eye Frankie Wilde could see a little toy soldier toppling over, one that had on a natty brown blazer. *The hell with it. Life's too short for this crap.*

Frankie Wilde was not going to be this snotnose's whipping boy. He had just about worked himself up to open his mouth and say so when Jeffrey Spector's child-face lost its fury and turned cunning.

"Well, I have an idea what to do about it, Frankie. Do you know this woman?''

Frankie Wilde gazed down at the photograph on the magazine cover that Spector had plucked from his desk drawer. He recognized the cover as the one that Spector had stared at on Opening Day.

"*Sure* I know her. I mean I know *of* her.''

Who the hell didn't?

"Well, I have some news that you might enjoy, Frankie. In three days you're going to get to hire her. She's joining our staff."

"That's great, Jeffrey. In what capacity?"

"As a member of the WERA Nats' baseball play-by-play team."

CHAPTER

T HE RHYTHMS WERE WORKING.
There was so much to say.
The cities of the National League rushed up to meet his plane, and
parted their expressways for him like lonely women. His aluminum
net identified him in hotel lobbies (for there were still stadiums where
he could use the net) and his attaché case was full of stories, full of
dreams. There were memories in the stopwatch, anecdotes in the felt-
tip pens; in the scorebooks and the statistic sheets (brought up to date
each night in the hotel room, Fanning under the yellow light, tran-
scribing) there was the very stuff of the country, the secret tale of
America rendered in figures and decimals, awaiting his translation
every evening on the air.

People came up to him in coffee shops and shook his hand. (Turtle
at his side.) The two of them stood out in a crowd in their fearless
sport coats and their white shoes, and daddies brought their children
for a quick look-see. ("Used to follow you on the *Game of the Week*
when I was a kid, L.C. These new fellas they just don't give it the
same oomph that you did.")

The *Game of the Week*—now that was a painful memory to him, although he never let on to the public who came up to shake his hand. He'd done three seasons of it on television in the late fifties. Heine Meine beer was his sponsor. They wanted him and not Barber, not Allen, not anybody else. He had taken Turtle with him—insisted. And it had made his national reputation. But after three years he had to give it up. In television sportscasting the art was to keep your mouth shut. Let the camera do the talking. The blazes with *that*. L. C. Fanning wasn't built to keep his mouth shut. He went back to radio, where the art was. Turtle came along.

They had their good times. . . .

An inning ends with a bang-bang double play and Fanning sends it back to the station. Balmy weeknight at Dodger Stadium, temperature in the eighties, low-scoring battle of two control artists. Fanning stretches his arms in the air and yawns.

"Sixty seconds, gentlemen," calls Joey the engineer. Joey is a dark-haired little man with skin like cocoa butter who smokes Camels out of the side of his mouth. He has been their engineer, home and away, since Fanning can't remember how long.

"Hooooooo-*weeeee*! Come a-*runnin'*!" Turtle has the binoculars up.

"Where?" Fanning's chair legs slam down. "Gimme those."
"Foller down from aisle double-E. Fifth row up, third seat in."

Fanning pushes his regular glasses up on his forehead and twists the focusing rim.

"Holy Amos."

"Whatta you think about *them* apples, scale of one to ten."

"*Momma, buy me one of those!*" Fanning has never quite mastered the profanity of the veteran ballplayer, but he loves to try his hand.

"I'd like to slide into *her* base. Whatta you think, L.C.? You like to slide into her base?"

Behind them, Joey is starting to snicker. He knows what's coming.

"I'd like to rub *her* rosin bag."

"I'd like to bunt *her* around."

"Thirty seconds, fellas." There is glee in Joey's voice.

"I'd like to squeeze *her* home."

"I'd like to swing at *her* curve."

"I'd like to steal *her* signs."

"I'd like to muff *her* grounder."

"I'd like to . . . *ground her muff*!" That does it. Fanning is horse-laughing so hard he can hardly breathe. He has to stop and cough.

"I'd like to . . . I'd like to go into the bottom of *her* ninth."

Now the L.A. crew in the adjoining booth are up with their own glasses, trying to pinpoint the target that Fanning and Turtle have spotted.

"Ten sec—" Joey can't finish, he's so broken up.

It's a game they play. Pussy roulette. See who can get the last line in before live air. And not get caught on-mike.

"I'd like to win *her* pennant."

"I'd like to dig into *her* box."

That finishes Fanning. Face beet-colored, he fishes his handkerchief out of his pocket and wipes the tears away. He turns around and gives Joey the fish-eye. Shaking his head in a you-guys-are-nuts gesture, Joey gives the "air" sign with his finger.

Muffled silence. Five seconds. Ten.

Turtle is the first to recover his voice.

"Yessir . . . fans . . . they's been a *lot of action* thus far tonight." Fresh fit of convulsions for Fanning. "You talk about your great defensive plays . . . we've seen a couple o' *big ones* here tonight . . . haven't we, L.C.? . . . Folks, I think L.C.'s got sump'n the matter with his tongue . . . 'cause it's a-hangin' out. Well, meanwhile, down at the old ball game . . ."

They were famous for scenes like this. The radio audience always knew it when Turtle had L.C. going. The fans looked forward to it. A trademark. What Fanning thought of as the Human Element.

Like the Tru-Form lingerie commercials. It was an unspoken tradition that Turtle always got to read them. Why the Tru-Form people ever thought to buy time on the Nats' radio broadcasts, Fanning would never know. But the account had run for years, and Fanning had always read the spots just as routinely as if they'd been for Heine Meine beer or Chesterfields—this is back, now, when you could still advertise tobacco on the air.

But then Turtle joined the broadcast team, and the first time it comes his turn to read the Tru-Form spot—well, they still talk about it, Fanning supposes, in the advertising world. If you were listening that day, you just had to buy yourself a paper the next morning to find out whether the Giants had won or not (this was back before the Nats were formed, you see. It had to be prior to 1960).

Because when Turtle, who at that point still had not totally mastered the English language, gets to the part about "these luxurious wisps of satin elegance, designed to create a more streamlined You"—in that Arkansas dung-kicker twang of his—well, cripes. School is out, that's all. There must have been five solid minutes when the radio audience doesn't hear anything more than *crowd* noise, punctuated by the occasional slap of a bat on a ball followed by a roar.

Fanning is on the floor. Quite literally squirming around on his back, mind you—and Turtle is staggering about the booth with the script in one hand and the other making a boob out of his shirt front. Well, of course the Tru-Form people are going to have Turtle Teweles's everlasting family jewels in a glass jar, and Fanning's too, for that matter . . . that is, until the *mail* starts coming in. Well. That's when they change their minds. Now you see the Tru-Form people are sponsors of Nat ball games *to this day* . . . and it's a tradition now for Turtle to bust a gut every now and then while he's reading one of their spots. Of course it isn't as spontaneous today as it was back then, heck, it must have been over twenty years ago now . . . but a couple of times every season, why, Turtle cranks himself up, and L.C. too, and they pretend to have a good old-fashioned case of the giggles. The Human Element.

The Human Element. Like Fanning's identifying cry, "Light up a Chesterfield!" that he would use in a tense moment, back in the old days. It pleased the sponsor, and the fans liked it. The cry got to be almost as famous as his "Toot-toot-tootsie, good-bye!"

And the heck of it was, they got paid for this sort of thing.

Now in this secret season he felt like an ambassador making a final tour of a beloved country. He found himself drawn to the old restaurants and the old bars in the central cities, neon-sign restaurants and peanut-shell bars that still survived near the rims of the scars of stadiums that had seemed as though they would outlive the earth. He was delighted to find waitresses still working whom he used to know when railroads connected the cities of the National League. Some of them hadn't changed much. Hell, nothing changed, really. People looked for the same things in life as they always had. To bring it down to Fanning's bailiwick, they wanted a good story, filled with adventure and drama and crisis and courage and romance, a story peopled with characters, some of them romantic, some of them comic, some of them villains, some of them pure. They wanted to hear the sounds and see the colors and have the smells in their nostrils. And they wanted to take something away with them, something to think about, a little moral or a lesson that they could apply to their own lives.

They wanted what L. C. Fanning brought them every night of the summer, in the baseball games on the radio.

He could give them colors unimagined by television. He could zoom in closer than the closest zoom lens; he could zoom inside the pores in a player's skin and report the secret language of the player's heart. He could fill up the boundless spaces of a mind with fantastic stadiums that laughed at the constipated tight small screens. . . .

He would miss it. God, it was a pity, this pressure on the nerve, this slow fading of the orange glow . . . Fanning held a private belief that the greatest days of the radiomen were still to come, that the future *was* radio, that television would soon be discarded by the American people for the fraud and the pinched humbug that it was . . . and, God, he'd love to be a part of it . . . but this pressure on the nerve . . .

The thing was to keep the rhythms working. Purify the art.

Tell the stories to the people.

The stories were thick as pears in a Michigan orchard, waiting to be harvested.

Even the 28 to 23 loss to Philadelphia yielded its treasure.

In the second inning, a Phillie batter had lifted a foul pop-up that bounced high off the top of a seat behind first base and landed in the flailing hands of a woman in a red hat. In the brief scuffle for the ball, Fanning thought he saw a whalebellied man slosh beer on the woman's festive dress.

"*Now* that lady has herself a nice souvenir of the *ball* game. . . ." Fanning, half-turned in his seat, arching an eyebrow at Turtle. "She has herself a two-dollar ninety-five baseball. . . . And do you

know what that two-ninety-five souvenir cost her, Turtle? It cost her
the cleaning bill for a three-hundred-dollar dress that she just bought
yesterday at Wanamaker's. . . . It cost her a brand-new pair of
*panty*hose that she snagged on the top of that *seat* in front of her.
. . . It cost her a broken *finger*nail, as Simms takes low . . . so now
she can't go home and cook that *pot* roast she was planning on fixing
for Dad and Junior . . . so now *Dad* is gonna have to take the whole
*fam*ily out to *Bookbinder's* tonight and lay down, I don't know,
twenty–thirty bucks for a *meal*. . . .''

To Fanning's right, Turtle Teweles was swiveling his stare between Fanning and the box seats behind first base.

Fanning knew that if Turtle was hooked, the audience was hooked.
Turning to glance behind him, he caught a rapturous grin, the grin on
the engineer's face.

"So I don't know, folks, *you* tell *me*. Is a three-dollar baseball
worth all that trouble?"

As the marathon game stretched through the afternoon into the
twilight hours, Fanning returned again and again to the Lady in the
Red Hat. What must she be thinking of all this hitting, all these home
runs? Was she bored? Enthralled? Was she here on her own accord,
or as a deference to some husband, boyfriend, favored child? What
had she done with the baseball—put it in her purse, given it to some
boy in a Shakey's T-shirt, had it snatched from her hands by a beer-
maddened male?

These questions exploded in salvos in Fanning's mind. He told his
audience that the Lady in the Red Hat was without any possible question a forty-five-year-old English teacher from a high school in Roanoke, Virginia, and that she was here attending the Phillies game by
virtue of having won the ticket . . . here's Edwards lifting a high
lazy pop fly out into short-right field, McBride coming on, and
there's two away . . . won the ticket in a PTA raffle. Never been to a
ball game before in her life. That'll bring up Carty who's one-for-one
in this game. Got here on a Trailways bus, by golly. Packed herself a
good lunch, tuna fish salad sandwiches on whole wheat bread, none
of your hot-dog nonsense for Mildred—her name, it was clear to
Fanning, was Mildred Fennewig, "that's two *n*'s"—and a thermos
full of . . . Carty drills a *shot* past third base and the Nats have

something going here—full of, what would you say, Turtle, I'd say grapefruit juice.

"You know, Turtle, Mildred Fennewig didn't know thing one about this game of baseball when she arrived here at Veterans Stadium this afternoon," said Fanning in the fifth inning when the game was nearly three hours old with the score Nats 15, Phillies 13. "But ever since she made that outstanding barehanded catch back in the second inning, why the fans around here have sort of taken her to their bosom, as it were. And of course Mildred, being a high school English teacher and all, is a *very* fast study. And I'd imagine that by now . . . Evans takes a cut at a *fast*ball and gets nothing but air . . . I'd imagine, wouldn't you, Turtle, that she's seen just about every kind of situation that you could *see* in a baseball game . . . I wouldn't be surprised if Mildred's down there *formulating strategy* for these Phils. . . . In fact I think I see her flashing signals to the Phillies dugout . . . so for the rest of this game we'll just try to match our thinking with Mildred Fennewig's. Now Evans lines a clean single to left. And Turtle, with nobody out and hard-hitting Gary Purcell due up next, I wonder if Mildred will have Gary swinging away trying to break this game *wide* open?"

"I donno," said Turtle.

But after the game Fanning had found that he could not stop the fantasy; could not bring it under control. A dark underside had edged its way into his imagination, like a pressure on a nerve, even as he spun out his lighthearted improvisations on "Mildred" for his audience on the WERA airwaves. "Mildred" in her red hat grew real for him. He imagined terrible disasters that awaited her when she left the enveloping confines, the known universe, of the stadium.

She had bone cancer and would shortly die. Teen-age thugs, having marked her where she sat enjoying the game, would set upon her and cut her throat for the baseball in her purse. (A new stain on the three-hundred-dollar dress from Wanamaker's.) Her Trailways bus back to Roanoke would end up in a fiery turnpike crash.

It was happening again to Fanning, the thing his mind did sometimes, cutting his imaginary palette to ribbons, smearing it with imaginary blood. It happened most often when he singled out a fan from the mass of humanity in the stadium, concentrated his fantasy upon one soul. A sleepless night was inevitably part of the bargain. He should never let himself concentrate upon a single fan. The concept of a crowd was something that his mind could handle. But let him begin to atomize the crowd—even to the tune of just one person within it—and the panic set in, the feverish imaginings.

"What the *hail's* the matter 'thew? You ain't had but three of them now." Turtle Teweles eyed Fanning's double scotch. They were in the lounge of the team's hotel. "You know it don't only take but two of them to get you actin' silly as a loon."

For an ex-catcher Turtle could be an interminable old lady at times.

"I don't know. Five-hour game. My goshdanged tongue's hangin' out."

How could he explain to Turtle about Tommy Pachelbel and the Husky pants commercial? How could he explain that just now he could clearly see "Mildred Fennewig" lying dead in her own blood, his blood? Toot-toot-tootsie, good-bye.

Part of the price you pay in this business.

Behind the darkside fantasies lay an ancient burdening idea. He'd had it since he was the Boy Announcer; maybe since he was a boy, since that first day he'd ever set foot in a stadium, in Chicago, with his father. The idea was at once a source of curious comfort and the wellspring of his most savage torments. To even begin to admit it to another human being, even somebody professionally trained, would cause him so much mortification that the idea's recurring pain seemed preferable.

The idea was that the ballpark—any ballpark—was a sanctuary. Once inside it, people were safe. Time stood still. The rules didn't change, like they did on the outside. There were no surprises. There was no death. Fanning liked to think that if somebody who had lived and died, say, in the 1920s or 1930s or 1940s could return to earth and walk inside a major-league baseball park, they would feel immediately at home, and have the comforting assurance that a continuity had been upheld since their passing.

The idea also stipulated—and here was the mortifying part—that, as the announcer in the radio booth, Fanning was somehow *in charge* of the people. He was the shepherd of all the people whom his voice reached on the radio airwaves.

This was one reason that, as the years went on, L. C. Fanning reached further and further to make the broadcasts compelling. As long as he had the listeners in his thrall, nothing could happen to them. Who had ever heard of anyone dying while listening to a ball-game on the radio?

It was after the game was over, the broadcast finally wrapped up, that the world outside the stadium took over. Then the great impregnable unity that was the crowd started to dissolve, to bleed out from the stadium's portals into God knew what individual tragedies and griefs. (His father, oozing out of Wrigley Field that day, an atom in the stream, to be dead of a stroke before World Series time.) Fanning to this day could not keep his eyes on the crowd after the final out had been made.

Fanning's sleep in the endless hotel nights following these confrontations with his nether spirit was ravaged by nightmares. The worst of these was a recurring dream: Thomson's home-run ball dropping into Pafko's glove. This most sublime moment in the history of baseball—this seminal moment in American time—reduced to a cosmic practical joke. The illusion of baseball's connection to the great circling energies of man's triumphant will—exposed as a fraud. The comet faltering, falling aimlessly, an ash. Towing in its wake the empty shell that was once thought to be L. C. Fanning, the voice of America's soul.

You had to put that kind of foolishness out of your mind. It didn't do you any good. L. C. Fanning abruptly plunged his finger into his Scotch glass and extracted the lemon peel. Look at the bright side. Bogart Humphries was hitting a ton. Couple of long ones today. Real toot-toot jobs. Best deal the Nats had swung in years.

Fanning bit into the lemon peel. It made him think of St. Petersburg, Florida. Spring training. Happy days. "Mildred Fennewig" made him grin now. He had done a bang-up broadcast this afternoon. Gave his audience their money's worth. Now it was time to howl at the moon.

He looked over at Turtle, who was sitting patiently in the booth, waiting for his partner to finish his drink. It was nine o'clock at night. Turtle was dressed to kill in a snappy new pink plaid blazer over a yellow shirt. Damn ballplayers. They really knew how to put on the threads. L. C. Fanning had on a plaid blazer too. The night was young. The season was young. It was spring.

"You ready?" Fanning asked Turtle.

"I been ready for a hour. You drunk?"

"Nossir. Let's go raise us some dickens."

"Hot dam'. I'll go call the Trotter sisters, I told 'em we'd be in."

The Trotter sisters were a couple of unmarried schoolteachers, real lookers (retired now) whom Fanning and Turtle "saw" when they were in Philadelphia.

The Trotter sisters knew how to have a good time.

The Trotter sisters weren't at home. What Fanning and Turtle ended up doing, when the smoke had cleared away, was take in an old Joel McCrea western that, lord, they'd first seen when Turtle was still an active player.

CHAPTER

TIME GETS AWAY BEFORE you know it.

The orange face of the clock radio beside the bed said it was ten o'clock in the morning. What morning? What city were they in? The dark room offered no clues. The radio promised the CBS *News on the Hour* after this word about Aamco transmissions. The CBS *News on the Hour* was everywhere. Fanning reached over and shut the radio off. He lugged the thing around with him from city to city; it took up space and meant setting the clock every time he checked into a hotel, but he liked to wake up to a clock radio. He always had. A clock and a radio. They seemed like a natural combination in Fanning's life. Besides, he'd always gotten a kick out of listening to the different voices in the different towns. They all had their special rhythms, their quirks, their giveaway mannerisms.

Or they used to. Until every jerkwater station on earth started carrying the CBS *News on the Hour*.

Not to take anything away from the CBS *News on the Hour*.

Texas.

It seemed to him that they'd been in Texas the last thing he knew.

About twenty-five minutes ago, it felt like. He took a thumb and finger and rubbed the sleep out of his eyes. His breath stank. He must have been eating chili in Texas with Turtle. *Get naked and eat chili.* That's what Turtle always said he wanted to do whenever they went to Texas. *Texas,* for criminy sake. Texas with its two teams in the major leagues. If God had meant for Texas to be in the majors, he wouldn't have bothered to create the Texas League. Man was never meant to play major-league baseball in Texas, and the Astrodome was there to prove it. God's punishment. Without the Astrodome they never would have figured out a way to build a monstrosity like Flushing Stadium. Or any of the rest of them where you could dribble a hardball around the bases and they had professional chickens to lead the cheers. Thinking about the Astrodome made Fanning's bowels hurt.

He decided he might as well get up and figure out what town he was in. There must have been a good reason why he woke himself at ten o'clock in the morning. A golf game, maybe.

He put his palms down flat on the mattress to raise himself up, and the mattress had a familiar feel to it. His mattress. Ah, yes. They were in New York. Fanning had slept in his own bed last night.

He swung his feet down onto the floor, yawned, and reached a hand under himself to let out the twist in his silk pyjamas. He worked up saliva to dull the ache in his throat. It wasn't unusual that he didn't recognize his own digs. He wanted it that way. When Eleanor had passed from his life, he dismantled their home in Connecticut. Put it up for sale, lock, stock, and barrel. Except for the souvenirs and the sentimental caboodle. He had all that boxed and stored. He wasn't going to end up a pathetic old vegetable like Mel Pelham, drooling on his framed telegrams and newspaper clippings. He'd got rid of everything except his clothes, and he'd come to live in this little apartment on Fifty-seventh Street near Seventh Avenue.

The apartment looked like a hotel suite. He had chosen it for that reason. He liked hotel rooms. He liked smelling the same disinfected air; liked the same location of the dresser drawers—where he could find them in the dark—liked the standard blankness of the walls, the constant telephone that hooked into a central switchboard. He liked the brochures you found on top of the color TV, the ones with the "Welcome, Traveler" message from the hotel chain's president, who was always a young fellow going bald. Yes. He liked his apartment to resemble a hotel. It helped reinforce his notion that his real home was not in any fixed earthly location, but on the airwaves themselves.

He liked his curtains, the opaque industrial curtains of hotel rooms everywhere, curtains that held back the morning light until a radioman could get rid of last night's game that lay in bed with him like a faceless whore. Sour as breath, but compelling a kind of love: a fading remnant of half-forgotten shouting.

What were the line scores; hits, runs, and errors? Who boosted his record? How many games off the pace? Who led the hitting attack? Who broke the contest wide open? Who the blazes won? Who did we play?

All the games looked the same the morning after, in a darkened hotel room, faded recipients of the radioman's ardor and shouts of ecstasy. A radioman needed several dark private minutes to disengage the receding memory of the game from the orbital fantasies of the late-night dreams that followed, the radioman's dreams that propelled him out there on the cold airwave bands to the edges of space where his voice plummeted, lost in an eternal present where all is immediate—where the white comet of Thomson's ball is still rising and Eleanor is at home in Connecticut listening on the radio. Nothing is lost in the radioman's dreams. Time stands still. His voice, charged with the power of the air itself, is the force that binds past and present together.

He had to see a man about a horse.

He groped his way to the bathroom and flipped on the light. It would be a heckuva nice thing if he could coax the bowels to work too, but he doubted he could get anything going in under an hour. Not after that chili.

And then, pausing, with his hand on the light switch, Fanning remembered why he had set his alarm: there was to be a meeting this morning at eleven. At the radio station. Frankie Wilde had notified them while they were in Houston. Some confab with this young fellow who'd taken it over. Get-acquainted session, he imagined.

He'd rather play golf. Or see a movie. Or buy himself a sport jacket. The normal kind of day.

Standing at a sixty-degree angle above the bowl, his left hand flattened against the tile wall like a traffic cop's, Fanning told himself that he was being selfish. He couldn't blame a new young fellow for wanting to say hello to a major talent. When you're a top personality, the way Fanning and Turtle were, it's only right to maintain good bridges back to management. Who knows, maybe the kid even needed a bit of advice, or a little reassurance from some of the older hands?

Fanning made a mental note to maintain good eye contact with the young man, act interested. Hand of fellowship. If they zipped right through, he and Turtle could still get in eighteen holes in plenty of time.

L. C. Fanning stood in front of his mirror—a shiny and unspotted mirror that ran the length of the dresser top, in the style of the better hotels—and ran the knot on his orange silk tie right up to the throat. He fastened a gold tie bar under the knot. He had on his most elegant sport coat, a subdued brown-and-orange windowpane plaid. Gold slacks. It was what he wore for formal business occasions. He hoped to God that Turtle would think to put on something halfway sedate. He found himself wondering whether a certain twinkle-eyed receptionist was still employed in the WERA offices.

It had been a while, now that he thought about it, since he had last set foot inside the station. Time gets away from you. He couldn't remember the exact date. But for some reason he recalled that Sonny Liston had been heavyweight champion of the world.

Fanning understood, without even having to turn his head and look, that Turtle Teweles was wiggling his ears.

"Cut it out, now." He released the words from the right corner of his mouth, keeping his eyes straight ahead. The two of them were seated side by side on a cushioned bench outside Jeffrey Spector's office. Fanning knew what Turtle was up to from the expressions on the faces of women who sat at nearby desks.

"Cut what out?"

"You know doggone well cut what out." Fanning folded his arms across his middle. Then he checked his wristwatch. They had been sitting there like two birds on a rail for the better part of an hour now. Spector's office door had remained closed the entire time.

This was not at all the type of reception that Fanning had anticipated. He thought again of the days when he didn't even need an invite—when he could breeze right past everybody to the big boss's wigwam. The secretaries all knew him then. But not these tomatoes. Not these new solemn-faced bits of business all in blue jeans, mostly teen-agers to judge by appearances, one of whom would now and then lift her face to steal a glance at Turtle and then exchange a series of top-secret looks with her sisters. Fanning didn't need to be hit over the head. He could tell that Turtle's act was not going over very well.

He tilted his body an inch to the right. For some reason the climate of the place discouraged movement, or conversation above a whisper.

"You are making," he informed Turtle, "a blamefool monkey out of yourself." He noted that Turtle's face was adorned with a grin. For the benefit of the womanhood at large, he well knew.

"Why? Feller's got to have somep'n to do as long as he can't smoke a butt."

"Read a magazine."

"They don't seem to have any of my particular favorites."

"They don't display any of your particular favorites north of Forty-second Street."

"Well, besides, now, this is scientific, L.C. I done already explained that to you oncet."

Fanning felt the old mischievous impulse to guffaw starting to boil up inside him. Turtle. God. If he carried this line of thought a step or two farther they'd both be snorting and gurgling like schoolboys in a minute. The crazy old bald jockstrap *believed it* . . . believed the theory. Turtle had a string of theories as long as a man's arm. To compensate for his lack of any formal learning, Fanning supposed. Par for the course among them was the notion that a man who could wiggle his ears commanded extraordinary sexual power over women.

"I got it off a harelip third baseman for the Mattoon Phillies of the Three-Eye League," he had confided to Fanning years ago. "Sumbitch never did make it to the big leagues even though he had the sweetest natural swing I ever saw. Why, he just got pussied out after a while. You see he could wiggle his ears, and that works on a woman like Spanish fly. They connect it in their minds to how good you can wiggle your whatnot around inside. Well, I want you to know this boy was *pussied out*. And him a harelip."

There were people who considered Turtle eccentric. Quaint.

Heck—face it—*rustic*. Fanning knew it. Himself, he relished Turtle as an American original.

"Lookit that one over there, the stout old girl. I think she's already got a wide-on."

Despite his resolve to set a dignified example, Fanning could not help himself. He leaned his bulk another inch toward Turtle.

"I'd, uh—I'd like to punctuate *her* form letter."

"I'd like for her to take *my* dic-tation."

Red mirth was creeping up his neck again. Oh, the Turtle. One thing about him. He did make the time go by.

At that moment a small, boyish-looking figure came hurrying down the corridor. He had on thick glasses and bluejeans. He paused at the door to Spector's office, shot a sharp and questioning glance at Fanning and Turtle, and then slipped inside.

"Looks like even the stock boys are pullin' rank on us," Fanning remarked.

Turtle grunted. He hadn't seen the kid. He was busy checking inside his worn briefcase—for about the twelfth time—to make sure the Gift was safely inside. Turtle brought the Gift whenever he was to meet someone of consequence. He presented it to toastmasters at Rotary luncheons, slipped it into the purses of new women friends. The Gift was a copy of a slim book that had been out of print since the Eisenhower administration. The title on its chocolate-and-tan cover read, *Destiny Was My Strike Zone*. The slim young ballplayer, face grinning out from the cover, was that of Turtle Teweles. The author of the book was L. C. Fanning.

He checked his watch again. Noon.

"L.C., Turtle! How long have you boys been sitting here?"

It was Frankie Wilde, all sweating around the forehead, hands outstretched.

"Come on in. Jeffrey has been dying to meet you."

Frankie Wilde never used to say things like "dying to meet you," Fanning reflected.

The first thing Fanning noticed once they were inside was how the old wigwam had changed. No more oak cabinets. No more expensive draperies. Just white walls, bare mostly—a couple of posters with hippie designs. And a big sign that read:

REALITY IS ONLY WHAT
YOU PERCEIVE IT TO BE.

The second thing he noticed was that the stock boy had seated himself behind Jeffrey Spector's desk.

And was talking on Jeffrey Spector's telephone.

"Jeffrey—L. C. Fanning and Turtle Teweles."

Fanning wheeled around, thinking the new boss had walked in behind him.

"Hey." A young voice murmured.

He wheeled back to see the stock boy half-rising out of the chair. The boy threw up his unoccupied hand in a limp motion. Turtle, grinning, grabbed it as though it were a high-bouncing ball in front of home plate. He pumped it so hard that he nearly detached the kid from the telephone.

Fanning felt poleaxed. Before he quite realized what he was doing, he lifted a finger toward the kid and turned back toward Wilde.

"Is this—?"

"I'm Spector," said the kid. He pried his hand from Turtle's and examined it. "Why don't you guys have a seat. I'll be finished here in a sec."

Frankie Wilde and Fanning and Turtle Teweles sat. No one spoke. Fanning put a hand to the pocket where he kept his White Owls, and then took it away again. He felt like somebody who'd barged into the wrong building by mistake. This office room, where he had sat with other station managers, coats off, ties loosened, an open bottle of bourbon on the desk, yawping about this and that—about Durocher, say; the time Leo ordered Kirby Higbe to throw a curveball to Johnny Mize at the Polo Grounds.

"Kirby tells Leo," Fanning would say, "he says, 'Leo, this man's the best golblamed curveball hitter in baseball. You want me to throw him the curve?' And Leo says, 'Right.' You know how Leo talks."

(And the slick-haired station manager sitting forward with his elbows on his knees, eating it all up, grinning like a son-of-a-biscuit-eater and nodding his head—he's never heard Leo talk in his life.)

"Well. Leo goes back to the bench, and poor Kirby . . . Kirby throws Johnny the curve, you see, and of course Johnny hits one past Kirby's ear . . . it sounds like a *bee* going by . . . I mean he *brands* one, see . . . and it sails over those right-field stands clean out of the ballpark. So now Higbe's back in the clubhouse and Leo comes up to him. 'Hig,' he says, 'I lost this one. Not you.' And you know what Higbe says?''

(The station manager's pink mouth hanging open, awaiting the "kicker." . . .)

"He says: 'Oh yeah? You look in the papers tomorrow and see who's the losing pitcher, Durocher or Higbe!' ''

But here. Now. With this chrome furniture. This music coming out of some hidden speaker, out of the very walls it seemed; music that sounded like "*Got*-cha, *got*-cha, *got*-cha, *got*-cha . . ." a man couldn't even think straight. And this boy behind the desk. A whelp.
. . . Fanning could see that he even brought his toys to work with him. Some kind of airplane contraption on the desk, that kept wiggling, almost in time to the music. What the devil was the station coming to?

Spector hung up the telephone. Immediately Turtle was on his feet, the copy of *Destiny Was My Strike Zone* in his fist. Too late, Fanning put up a hand to stop him.

"Here you are, chief. Comp'ments L. C. Fanning and the Turtle. Little keepsake there. No charge.''

Fanning squeezed his eyes shut. When he opened them a moment later, the boy was turning the book over in his white hands as though it were a piece of plaster that had fallen from the ceiling.

"Hell, don't even mention it,'' drawled Turtle. He returned to the chair next to Fanning, and L.C. noticed that his grin was gone.

Already Spector seemed to have forgotten that the exchange took place. He was leafing through some papers on his desk. His child's face was absorbed in the task. He might have been alone in the room.

No one spoke. Frankie Wilde was trying not to look at anyone or anything.

This was easily the strangest meeting that L. C. Fanning had ever attended. It occurred to him now for the first time that this confab with the new top kick might be something other than social. Considerations of protocol began to churn in his mind. But before he could come up with an appropriate ice-breaking pleasantry, Turtle was off to the races again.

"Say, guv'nor. I bet you never knew the best way to get the ladies to rustle up their twitchets? Looky here."

Oh, cripes. If he didn't jump in, Turtle was going to get them both carted out of here in straitjackets.

He cleared his throat.

"So you're the top dog at this outfit now, Jeff?"

Jeffrey Spector lifted his eyes from his papers and fixed Fanning with a quizzical stare through his thick glasses. He shifted his gaze to Frankie Wilde, as if awaiting a translation.

Fanning hurried on.

"I imagine they probably call you the Boy Broadcaster around here. You know, that's what they used to call me when I was comin' up, about your age. I was known as the Boy Broadcaster."

"That's right, Jeffrey," said Frankie Wilde in a strained tenor. "He was the Boy Broadcaster."

In the silence that followed, Fanning heard Turtle Teweles expel a pellet of air between his teeth.

"The Boy Broadcaster." Jeffrey Spector murmured it as though to himself; as though he were in a private conversation that the rest of them weren't supposed to hear. Spector stared at his silver airplane arrangement, then gave it a thump, launching the planes along their bobbing orbit.

"The Boy Broadcaster," he murmured again. "I wonder if that's promotable."

There was a knock on Spector's door and the young secretary opened it enough to crane her head through.

"They're here," she said.

Jeffrey Spector circled a finger in the air and pointed it back toward the room. A moment later the door opened wide.

A tall young woman of stunning beauty strode into the room.

"King Jesus jump down," Fanning heard Turtle breathe.

In age and in clothing style she was interchangeable with the half-dozen young girls Fanning had observed bustling about the WERA corridors: a blonde in her mid-twenties, wearing jeans. But even L. C. Fanning (rising hastily with the rest of them and fumbling with his coat button) could see that this number had nothing more in common with the office girls than a Broadway musical star had with the chorus line.

She glowed. Her thick shags of hair and her tanned skin gave off a luminescence that reminded Fanning of wheat in the light of afternoon sun. It might have been her slim body or the way she carried herself, the head thrust back and elbows near her sides, but she had an effortless way of making her simple dark jeans and silk violet blouse appear more expensive, more *correct,* than anything the rest of them were wearing. The rich hues seemed to catch the reflection of her hair. She carried a leather bag and wore a large pair of rose-tinted sunglasses.

"Gentlemen, may I present Miss Robyn Quarrles."

Fanning hadn't even noticed the small man who had entered behind the vision and was now darting from person to person, offering tight little handshakes. He was dressed in a loose-fitting khaki jacket with a belt and epaulets. There was perspiration beneath his wiry curls of black hair. His sunglasses were dark rakish ovals that somehow suggested the wearer was familiar with hand-to-hand combat on burning sands. He had two chins.

"Name's Bobby Bilandic," the little man was saying to each of them. "I'm Miss Quarrles's manager."

Turtle Teweles emitted a low whistle. "What do you do, honey? You play basketball?" He turned to Bilandic. "She's gotta go six foot, stockin' feet."

Bilandic looked curiously at Teweles, then seemed to decide he had heard a joke. He gave a sickly grin that vanished immediately. "We don't *promote* her as six feet," he said. "Robyn's not comfortable with the six-foot image. The language in her contract calls specifically for five feet eleven and one-half inches."

Bilandic turned briskly away, leaving Turtle with his mouth open.

Bilandic finally ran out of hands to shake. "Uh—which one of you guys is Jeffrey Spector?"

"That's me." Fanning realized that Spector alone had not arisen; that in fact he had scarcely looked up from his papers when the two visitors entered. Now, however, he made the same halfhearted gesture of a raised hand, which Bilandic seized as though it might contain a ring to kiss.

The young woman removed her sunglasses. Fanning was confronted with a pair of blue eyes that were at once humorous and penetrating. The woman met the stare of each man before turning to her manager with a questioning smile.

Bilandic, in turn, was staring down at Spector, a convivial grin frozen on his face. Spector had turned coolly back to his papers.

"With you in a second," he mumbled without looking up.

The piped-in music filled the silent room with its beat of *"Got*-cha, *got*-cha, *got*-cha, *got*-cha."

Fanning decided he had never seen a fellow quite the measure of this Spector for all-around snootiness. He wondered if the kid considered what kind of a public relations effect his behavior had on the station. He wondered what the MetroCom people had been thinking about, putting a wet-behind-the-ears schoolboy in this kind of a job. Boy Broadcaster or no.

To his right Turtle Teweles stood with his neck slowly sinking into his bulky suit.

Frankie Wilde rocked on his heels next to Turtle. He was acting like the cat had his tongue.

Again, it seemed left to Fanning to try and rescue the situation. Get some kind of a conversation going.

"And who," he asked in his most fulsome voice, "might this very lovely young lady be?"

Apparently it was the wrong question.

Bobby Bilandic whipped off his own dark glasses and shot Fanning a questioning scowl. Frankie Wilde finally found his voice.

"Robyn Quarrles, L.C. The former Miss Yankeedoodle-doo. You know her. I'm sure you've seen her on TV."

"I mean which the hell Robyn Quarrles did you *think* it was?" Bilandic had his fists on his hips.

"Why, *sure!*" Fanning nodded his head, more out of a desire to spare the girl embarrassment than to placate her manager. For the second time in this office he felt knocked off balance by his own good intentions. He searched his memory for the name "Robyn Quarrles," and realized he hadn't paid any attention to the Miss Yankeedoodle-doo contest since . . . well, hell, he didn't exactly know there *was* a Miss Yankeedoodle-doo.

"I sure as hell never heard of no Robyn Quarrles." Turtle was coming to his rescue. Fanning appreciated that, but he didn't like the menace he heard in his partner's quiet voice.

Bilandic opened his mouth to reply to the ex-ballplayer, thought better of it, and instead turned to face the girl.

"I don't believe this," he said to her. "Do you believe this?"

The girl named Robyn waved her hand in a sort of shrug. "Hey," she said, in a breathy voice. "It's no problem. Hey, I'm really looking forward to working with you guys."

"*Working* with us?" Fanning gaped.

"I think we all need coffee." Frankie Wilde jerked the office door open. "How do you folks take your coffee?"

"Thank you," said Robyn, "I'm a tea person. Actually, a tea and *honey* person."

"A tea and honey person," muttered Turtle, still looking at Bilandic. "Imagine that."

Bilandic replaced his dark glasses with a violent motion.

"What way are you going to be working with us, sweetheart?" asked Fanning. The girl smiled uncertainly.

"Uh—however we set it up, I guess." She brushed a strand of hair back and shot another glance at her manager. "Wow," she breathed.

Wilde had his head out the door. With his jumping shoulder muscles he resembled a man newly guillotined. "Janie, bring us six coffees—no, make that *one* tea and *five* coffees," his muffled voice said. "Cream and sugar. Lots of cream and sugar."

"No sugar for me," called Robyn.

"She's a *honey person,*" trilled Turtle in a falsetto.

"I don't *believe* this." Bilandic had finally found what it took to face Turtle. "You guys act like you've never heard of Robyn Quarrles before."

"Come to that," Turtle said evenly, "I never heard of you either, Sky King."

Frankie Wilde held up his hands. "Guys. If we can just be patient for another minute, I think Jeffrey will explain everything."

Fanning had forgotten that the kid was even in the room. Evidently the feeling was mutual. Upon hearing his name, Spector looked up again from his papers and arose from his chair. All eyes were on him.

"I gather you people got acquainted." He raised one pipestem leg above the desktop and climbed atop it like a skinny grasshopper, plopping down cross-legged on the surface.

"Make yourselves comfortable," he said. No one did.

"Frankie," Spector continued, "does everybody here understand what the deal is?"

Frankie Wilde coughed into his fist. "Ah—I thought it might be better if L.C. and Turtle heard it directly from top management."

"Jesus Christ." Bilandic let his hands fall on his lap. "You're telling me they don't *know*?"

Something tightened in Fanning's chest. He turned to stare at the girl, lifting a hand dreamily to his face like a man attempting, too late, to ward off a blow.

In the instant of perception allowed him, he could see that the girl was looking back at him from a corner of her eyes, behind her rose-tinted glasses. Was there a smile? He was conscious of red fingernails.

"Gentlemen, say hello to your new partner." Spector's voice came from somewhere inside the walls. It mingled with the hard music's pulse. "Robyn Quarrles will be the third member of the Nats' play-by-play team for the duration of this season. She will do color and her own commentary from a woman's perspective. Home and away. Starting tonight."

The music in the room went, "*Got*-cha, *got*-cha, *got*-cha, *got*-cha."

"Now just a minute." For the first time in his life, Fanning had lost control of his voice. The words crackled from his throat like dry static.

Spector gave no sign of hearing. "I expect you guys to treat Robyn as a professional and allow her a fair share of mike time. How you divide it up is your decision. What Robyn has to say is up to her. I'm giving her absolute and total artistic discretion."

"Just hold on a minute here!" Fanning was on his feet. He felt unsure of his balance. Below him, as far as he could see, were the stripes on his sport coat.

"If you have any questions," Spector recited, touching an experimental finger to the fuselage of a tiny silver airplane.

"You're goddamn right I have a question!" The shout took Fanning's voice away, and he stood there feeling the way he had felt that night in front of Tommy Eagle's—jumped, ambushed, *violated*—sucking air and fighting off shock.

He had talked his way out of it that night: the Voice. Now he had to do it again.

He turned to the girl and made a stiff bow.

He saw the man called Bilandic reach under his dark glasses to rub his eyes. "Christ Almighty," he heard Bilandic hiss. "I don't believe any of this."

Fanning faced Spector.

"*Chemistry.*" The word spilled as if by accident from his lips.

"*What?*" Spector leaned forward.

"*Chemistry!* You can't just come in here and tamper with the whole *chemistry* of our broadcasts. You see"—he glanced at Turtle Teweles, who stared back at him with eyes as opaque as an Indian's—"I don't know how much you understand baseball announcing, son . . . but Turtle Teweles and I have worked about twenty years to develop . . . a *chemistry* between us. We . . . we have a whole . . . we've worked up a certain . . . *method* between us where you just can't tear it down by saying you want to add a—" He felt the gaze of the woman on his neck, like heat. He lurched about to face her again.

"This is not to take anything away from you, ma'am—" He saw red fingernails. He turned back in confusion. "But . . . and I'm not anti-women's lib. . . . But I mean for chrissake, you don't break up a *winning combination.*"

" 'A winning combination.' " Spector was looking at his own fingernails.

"That's *right!* Now I can see you're the new fellow here. And I can see where you want to hit the ground running and make a splash. But let me give you a little free advice about WERA Radio. Son, this is a *personality* station. Our listeners build up loyalty. They don't like to have things changed around. Hell, it's not just us. It's people like Parks Madison in the morning and Whispering DeWitt late at night. You start to tinker around with those people . . . why, and pretty soon you've destroyed everything that WERA stands for."

Fanning paused, groping for more arguments. He reached a finger inside his sleeve to tug the cuff out.

"Not," he repeated, "to take anything away—"

"I guess you listen to WERA a lot." Spector's tone was mild. It was almost as if the kid had pitched in the towel and was now changing the subject.

Fanning shrugged. "Why, sure."

"Then I guess you know that Madison hasn't worked here since February. Neither has DeWitt."

The room felt cold and hot at the same time. Fanning wanted to put his hand somewhere solid. He looked at Spector in the idiotic hope that the kid was joking; that his lean child's face would crack into a grin.

After a very long moment Spector's mild voice resumed:

"As I was saying a minute ago. If you have any questions, I'd appreciate it if you took them up with Frankie Wilde."

Fanning pointed a finger at Spector. The finger tembled. "Now *look!* I've known Jake Purcell at MetroCom for *thirty years!* All I have to do is *pick up that phone,* son." But even as he said it, Fanning knew that a test of wills had been waged, and he had lost. Something shifted in the room. So palpable was the shift that Spector's next words came almost as a kindness, a formality that the kid needn't necessarily have observed.

"Mr. Purcell has given me absolute authority on decisions regarding this station."

"Why are you doing this?" It came out almost as a whine. He steadied his voice. "You're tampering with the most respected play-by-play setup in the country."

Spector pursed his lips. He regarded his silver airplane ensemble. Then he shrugged and looked back up at Fanning.

"You really want the total shot?"

"Well I sure as hell think that Turtle Teweles and I are entitled to some kind of an—"

"Your numbers are crap, man."

It took a minute for Fanning to fully comprehend what he had just heard.

The piped-in music went, "*Got*-cha, *got*-cha, *got*-cha, *got*-cha."

He stood in the center of the room, a big full-faced man, the Voice of the Nats, hair combed back, shoes shined—and tried not to feel like a clown who'd just been smeared with a custard pie.

"Now wait a second, Jeffrey." It was Frankie Wilde. "I don't think that's exactly a fair description of—"

"They're crap. Look, I'm sorry to be the one to lay it out for you, man. Check out the books. The baseball games on WERA are room-emptiers. I'm sorry to put it to you like that. You come on, we lose our eighteen-to-thirty-fours cold. They just abandon ship, man. Like that."

"But just to put it in perspective, Jeffrey," came Frankie Wilde's voice, "we are showing strength in the forty-nine-and-over—"

"You and I have had this conversation, Frankie. The forty-nines don't buy Bubble Yum. Look. Mr. Fanning. Nothing personal. That's the way life is. I've made a business decision. My thinking is that Robyn Quarrles can create a 'chemistry,' as you call it, that might bring back some of the younger demos. Do you understand what I'm saying?"

"I understand that Turtle and I could walk out of this office right now and leave you with the biggest can of worms in New York City radio. And a helluva lot of explaining to do to Jake Purcell."

It was a last-ditch attempt to throw a scare into the kid. Call his bluff. But Jeffrey Spector's child-face merely widened in a little smile, and Spector's watery eyes shifted to a point behind Fanning—the door.

Fanning's eyes darted, met Turtle's. Teweles raised his eyebrows and jerked his head ever so slightly.

The old catcher was giving Fanning the signal. If Fanning started for the door, his partner would follow.

And so would the legendary career of L. C. Fanning. The Dean of American sportscasters. The radio Voice of the Giants and the Nats for two generations.

Oh, the accolades. . . .

The Day.

If he walked out of here, there would never be a Day. On the other side of that door he would become just a man in a sport coat, a citizen in the swarm.

He needed time.

He wanted the Day. . . .

He stood there staring at Jeffrey Spector in a kind of paralyzed confusion, while the piped-in music went, "*Got*-cha, *got*-cha, *got*-cha, *got*-cha."

It was Robyn Quarrles who broke the silence.

"Look. I'd like to say something," she said.

"Keep out of this," muttered Bilandic.

The girl got up and crossed to Fanning in two feathery strides.

"Mr. Fanning—please believe me. I didn't have any idea this whole thing was going to be such a *problem*. . . ."

"It's no goddamn *problem*," came Bilandic's voice. "Siddown, Robyn. For Christ's sake."

Fanning turned to her. He made his voice sound businesslike.

"Now how much baseball have you done, Robyn?"

"I—well. None."

"None." He turned back to face Spector.

"She's a quick study," came Bilandic's nasal whine. "She's been readin' all kinds of stuff on baseball. She's up to her kishkies in baseball statistics. She watches the *Game of the Week*. Tapes the announcers. Does her own practice tapes. For chrissake. How much experience do you *need* to call a ballgame?"

"I'm sorry," said Turtle Teweles pleasantly. "Would you mind repeatin' that again, chief?" He scooted forward on his chair.

"Hey." Bilandic shrugged. "I only meant she's takin' it *seriously*. She's getting into the whole baseball *gestalt*. Robyn! Say something in baseball." Bilandic mopped his brow with a pocket handkerchief, folded it, mopped again. He refolded the handkerchief.

"Hey, people." Jeffrey Spector's quiet voice brought everyone back to attention. "I don't mean to run a number. But, uh, time flies. So if everybody's cool . . . ?"

In the pause that followed, Fanning realized that the next move was his. He thought one more time about the other side of Jeffrey Spector's office door.

Then he extended his hand and took Robyn's. Her palm was smooth and warm, and it hit Fanning how much time had passed since he had last touched a woman's hand.

"Welcome aboard, Robyn," L. C. Fanning said.

CHAPTER 10

"THAT WAS GRUESOME."

Bobby Bilandic shrugged.

"Couple of rough spots. I thought everything was copacetic by the time it was over with."

They were sitting under the striped canopy of a sidewalk café on Central Park South. A block away was the hotel where WERA had provided Robyn with a suite for the duration of the baseball season.

Robyn said: "I understood that everything was copacetic going in. You didn't tell me I had to emasculate anybody to get this job."

Bilandic shrugged again. He had shrugged a lot that day. Just to vary the pace, he picked up a swizzle stick and stirred his vodka gimlet.

"Hey, it's done. *Fini*. Plus the fact that I thought you handled yourself with a great deal of poise."

"I thought we agreed never to use that word again."

Poise. The word had attached itself to her like a leech ever since Columbus, Ohio. Columbus was the historic site of the annual Miss Yankeedoodle-doo Beauty Classic—a "classic" that stretched back all of five years into American history.

"Miss Yankeedoodle-doo" had been the brainstorm of a Columbus frying-chicken magnate and sometime cable-television evangelist. The poultry potentate had founded the pageant with the declaration that in these Bicentennial times it was appropriate for a man like himself to step forward and pay respect to some of the *good* things about America—namely, its exalted business and religious ideals and the high quality of its wholesome feminine pulchritude.

(This high standard was never clearly spelled out. But it seemed to involve massive traces of "Poise.")

"Miss Yankeedoodle-doo" seemed to tie in all these values nicely—and despite a rash of feminist backlash ("It's the old 'woman-as-chick' syndrome all over again," fumed one angry magazine publisher) and a little less-than-highbrow japing, in the men's mags, about saluting America's finest breasts and thighs, the contest became something of a middle-American institution. When the poultry king was sentenced to two years in federal prison and fined $100,000 on an antitrust and price-fixing conviction, "Miss Yankeedoodle-doo" even took on a kind of cachet.

Its promoters, in fact, aspired to place the pageant in the same pantheon as Miss America. But even in an era of overnight traditions, dosed up with heavy television exposure in much the same manner that the poultry king's chickens were dosed up on chemicals and animal fats—"Miss Yankeedoodle-doo" never quite managed to scale that height.

Despite the glitter, the heavy-duty celebrity "guest hosts," the state-of-the-art lighting effects, and the camera filters that made each grinning contestant's mouth seem electronically wired—despite, even, the presence of top-rank college contestants such as UCLA's Robyn Quarrles, a Phi Beta Kappa from St. Louis, Missouri—despite all this, "Miss Yankeedoodle-doo" remained a middle-echelon media event, mired somewhere in the public consciousness amidst the Macy's Thanksgiving Day Parade and the Liberty Bowl and the *Celebrity Challenge of the Sexes*.

Miriam had thought that "Miss Yankeedoodle-doo" would be ideal for Robyn. Darling mother, patroness of "Poise." Some are born with poise. Some achieve it. Robyn had had "Poise" thrust upon her.

"I don't want to talk about 'Poise,' " she said, as though to herself. Then: "For that matter, I'd be just as happy if you'd stop saying *fini*. Nobody says *fini*. Except on every bad TV drama."

"You should know," said Bilandic.

She halfway felt like throwing something at him for that. If she had done some bad TV drama, Bilandic had found her the roles. But this was not the time. She made herself grin.

"Hey. I just got a plan. *I'll* fly back to L.A. and get people booked in show business. *You* stay here and broadcast the ball games. End of the season, we'll see if anybody figured out the difference."

"You kidding? That other guy, the one that drags his knuckles—he was already measuring me for a pelt."

"Well, thanks a fat lot for leaving *me* with him."

"I've seen you with worse."

She thought for just a fleeting second of Pinley Stripely, and then pushed all such thoughts far from her mind. Poise.

"I did feel sorry for the other guy, though." Her voice was serious. "I don't think he likes this idea very much."

"What tipped you off, exactly?" Bilandic jiggled his ice. "I couldn't believe any of 'em. A zoo." He drained off his gimlet and glanced at his watch. "Holy Christ. I gotta hump."

"You really have a wonderful gift for words. Do you know that, Bobby?" She placed one red fingernail on his sleeve. "Hey. Before you fly away. Tell me one more time. Why am I doing this?"

Bilandic was craning his neck for a waitress. His black glasses flashed.

"I already told you. One word. *Track record.* Just—"

"That's two—"

"Just keep that concept in mind. We're building you a track record. I want you to think *track record,* I want you to think *multimedia exposure.*" He was thumping his fingertips on the table to emphasize each key syllable—another trait that Robyn did not adore. "We are positioning you for a run at some opportunities that I happen to think are very unique and which I cannot elaborate with you just at the moment. I am talking *major network.* I don't have to tell you that sports are a major concept at the network level these days. In my opinion, what you have got here is an incredible opportunity to establish an image for yourself in the sports milieu in a major—''

She held up a hand. "I think I've got it."

Why did she never give up the hope that Bobby Bilandic would someday speak a straight sentence to her? She knew the drill. The truth was, she could feel the onset of an awful loneliness, and she didn't want to let go of Bilandic just yet. Dear blundering Bobby Bilandic. The Croatian Comet.

"Hey. I gotta hump." He was gathering things into his arms. "You gonna be okay now?"

"Unless the guy called Turtle turns me into a pelt, yes, I guess."

A waitress squeezed through the tables with a check on a tray. Bilandic set down his armload of folders and flight bags to search himself for a credit card.

"You just sit here and eat your sunflower seeds. Get yourself psyched up for tonight. My understanding is the guy from the Nats' front office will call you this afternoon. Breen. He's got all the stuff you need. My understanding is they're gonna walk through everything with you a couple hours before game time. It's gonna be a piece of cake. Meanwhile you sit here and relax. They try to hustle your seat, you tell 'em it's taken care of by Bobby Bilandic.''

There was a stupid wetness at the corner of her eye, beneath the rose-tinted glasses.

"Right, chief."

"Hey." His face was suddenly close to hers and for a moment she thought he might kiss her. "Do me one favor before I split."

"Name it."

"Talk a little baseball to me."

She lowered her head and gave it a shake; came up grinning. "He's got *good velocity* and he's *locating well!*"

"*Outasight!*" He grabbed her hand in a thumbs-up shake. Then he swooped in and pecked her once on the cheek, knocking her glasses aside.

"*Ciao*. I'll tell Miriam everything's copacetic."

"You do that."

Robyn sat alone at her table, under its bright-colored umbrella. She watched Bobby Bilandic scurry into the pedestrian swarm along Central Park South. She'd have to give Bilandic one thing: he knew how to scurry. He hadn't quite mastered the hustle, but scurrying he could handle. He had been scurrying the first time she met him—hours after some curly-haired talk show perennial had placed the Miss Yankee-doodle-do crown on her head in Columbus, lo these three years gone.

"It's a quality agency," Miriam had kept shouting into her ear after Bilandic had scurried up to them at the formal ball—how he had broken through pageant security was a secret Bobby had never disclosed—and presented himself.

"The best," Miriam had shouted over the crash of the band. Miriam prided herself on knowing her Postimpressionists and her agencies.

As for Bilandic, he knew his mothers. "I see singer, I see dancer, I see actress, I see nutbar comedienne," he told Miriam, who was nodding so hard her facelift started to settle. "Face it, Mrs. Quarrles. Your girl has bankable potential in so many areas that I am going to develop *colitis* deciding where to begin. She's a goddamn talent *vending machine,* Mrs. Quarrles."

"Well, she does have a certain poise," said her mother. "I wish you'd call me Miriam."

"We'll build her a track record," Bilandic had shouted. "My concept is to develop a multimedia exposure."

Now, three years later, Bobby Bilandic was still talking track record. He was still talking multimedia exposure.

Here. In New York, a city that intimidated her. A continent away from everything she knew and understood.

She was here because there was nowhere else to go. She knew it. She supposed that even Bobby Bilandic knew it. Poor Bilandic. The Comet. Possibly the only agent in the country with the subtle blend of skills necessary to take an awesome new talent on the American pop cultural horizon—that's what *Variety* had actually called her once—and transform her, by meticulous stages, into a starlet begging for scraps on a radio sports-announcing gig.

"Multimedia exposure."

That's what Bobby had shouted at her when she had laughed in his face upon first hearing the scheme. That had been in her Malibu cottage six weeks ago.

"You're not looking at it long-term," he had continued in that whine only she and certain dogs could hear, following her out to the surf where she knew he hated to walk because his stubby little Beverly Hills legs got bogged in the sand. "Let me tick it off for you. Print. Video. Variety-musical. Theatrical release. And *now,* you've got your audio in the news/sports matrix. God dammit, Robyn, my shoes! Look, it's all part of this whole total package that we are creating for you."

His voice had faded then. She knew that he was trying to run while rolling his pink cotton carpenter casuals up to his knees. ". . . total spectrum of the entertainment/media mix," she heard him say. "It's *scientific,* for chrissake. We run *market research!"*

When she finally shut her eyes and told Bilandic to close the deal with WERA, it was only because her resume was starting to read like a suicide note. That, and Dun. Dear Pinley Stripely. She didn't particularly care to hang around L.A., scrounging auditions and replaying all the nice interludes she'd had with Dun. Before his white-knuckled friends convinced him that a beauty queen wife would not look good on his resume. *Plaything,* okay. In Dun's circles, squiring a beauty queen around was considered a sign of a healthy libido, like wearing paisley pants to the firm's golf outing. Approved: up to A Point. But after a while the tribal elders would appear bearing some Bel Air virgin breeding stock so woozy with lineage that they'd have to wheel her down the aisle on a pulley. Some Lord and Taylor spitfire like the redoubtable Kendall. (Robyn recalled Kendall's "prosody" lecture, and smiled. Robyn had been routed, but not before she'd drawn a little blue blood.)

Yes, that was the kind of woman that fate had in store for Pinley Stripely. Robyn tried to envision the Bel Air virgin in a wedding gown with a little alligator on the bodice, and for a moment the blues lifted.

"Something else, miss?" The waitress tapped her pencil significantly against her pad.

"I'm fine. Thanks."

There had been a time, not long ago, when waitresses genuflected to her despite her glasses. It was amazing how many waitresses were students of cigar commercials. As Miss Moravia Cigars, Robyn had cast a greater shadow on the culture than she had as Miss Yankee-doodle-doo. The Miss Moravia Cigars title had represented Bobby

Bilandic's high-water mark as a manager. The coup endeared Bobby to Miriam and sealed his position of influence on her destiny.

It was probably a coincidence that cigars made Robyn nauseous.

"Miss Moravia will do for her what Ivory Snow did for Marilyn Chambers," Bobby informed Miriam in pressing his request to enter Robyn in the annual Miss Moravia auditions.

Miriam took instant offense, as Robyn expected from her mother.

"That was a case," she said acidly, "of Marilyn Chambers doing for Ivory Snow."

Robyn—fresh from her demure reign as Miss Yankeedoodle-doo—torched and kicked and pouted and slinked like a trouper until she had landed in the Miss Moravia final three. As was customary, the Moravia Cigar Company sent its final three on a nationwide press tour, affording talk-show audiences and gossip column readers across the land an opportunity to compare the contestants' views on how to check the flow of foreign oil imports and how to create a travel wardrobe around synthetic washables.

Fortunately, no one thought to probe Robyn Quarrles concerning her views on cigars.

There followed a nationwide balloting, in which more American men wrote Robyn's name on Moravia cigar wrappers than had voted in the last aggregate municipal elections.

Her "election" had touched off the first serious riff with Dun.

"You're going to be seen on national television, kicking up your legs in a slinky gown?" he had asked her, dismayed.

"The people have spoken," she answered him. She did not realize at the time how shocked Dunning Pinley really was.

As Miss Moravia Cigars, she haunted the prime-time television airwaves. The slogan for the current campaign happened to be, "I wanna see Moravia." Robyn's performances consisted of variations on that theme: Robyn undulating into some unlikely all-male enclave (a locker room, a poker game) to the accompaniment of a big-band beat and singing to each man, "I wanna see more of-a-ya," while peeking down his shirt collar, inside his jacket, and so forth—until she "found" a package of the sponsor's product.

She was famous.

Dunning Pinley called less frequently.

It seemed a logical step in the game plan when Bobby Bilandic announced that he would not push to have Robyn's quite generous one-year contract with Moravia renewed. "Hit the ground running," he counseled Miriam. "Our game plan is to let no dust settle. We have a very good shot at a summer miniseries on ABC; I personally creative-managed the concept; it has 'pilot' written all over it."

The summer miniseries—*Presenting Miss Robyn Quarrles,* a phrase that apparently rang in Bobby Bilandic's ear—did nicely. Robyn danced, sang, and engaged in what ABC was pleased to call "off-the-wall comic sketches" with guest stars. A typical sketch involved Robyn in a tank top roller-skating after a famous songwriter, who was dressed in a purple bunny suit.

When ABC smiled politely at Bobby Bilandic's suggestion of further pilot development, it did not seem to matter. "Summer series are like found money," he explained. "They come, they go. The important thing is, we are establishing Robyn a track record."

She was piling up the TV credits now—an *All-Star Secrets.* A *Password Plus.* A *Card Sharks.* A shot on Merv Griffin (in which she was poised, witty, and profound on the subject of What Men Really Want). A stint on CBS's *Celebrity Challenge of the Sexes.* (She had punted. Attached to her lengthening resume was a glossy photograph of Robyn Quarrles in full punt. Newspaper photo editors around the country reached a grass-roots consensus that Robyn Quarrles was about the last word on punting.)

By this time the creative people at Bobby's agency had negotiated a major movie package.

Dun was not calling at all.

"The public is very athletics-conscious," Bobby reported to Robyn and Miriam. "The whole goddamn country is a locker room. This is our opportunity to move Robyn into another media facet as well as exploit her own inherent God-given gifts as a female jock."

Bilandic showed them a treatment about a girl who recovered from polio to become an Olympic diving champion secretly programmed by Strother Martin as a nuclear spy.

"You'll be essentially playing yourself," he told Robyn. "The movie is a vehicle to showcase Robyn Quarrles the athelete and basically pro-American girl. The public is ready for a sports vehicle that says honest, that says overcoming big odds, that says here is Robyn Quarrles essentially playing herself."

"I've never been on a diving board in my life," said Robyn. "I get vertigo."

"We'll use a double in the medium and long shots," said Bobby.

"Shut up, Robyn," said Miriam pleasantly.

The movie opened after an advance campaign that featured a poster of Robyn bending forward as though from a diving board, clad in a "U.S.A." swimsuit that might have been designed by Frederick's of Hollywood. It played the drive-in and suburban shopping-mall circuit of America, behind a feature titled *Gland Hotel*.

"So we got edged off the main track," said Bobby, shrugging. "How are we to know we're competing with a tennis movie, a bowling movie, a squash movie, a stock car movie and a goddamn Frisbee movie? Anyway, I think I'm close to a deal to get this property on a video cassette."

"Don't you think that by now Robyn should be positioning herself for her own, ah, series?" Miriam had begun a barely perceptible retreat from unconditional trust in Bilandic's acumen.

"Oh, and I didn't tell you another cookie I've got in the oven," Bilandic replied, squeezing a lime rind into his vodka-and-Perrier. "We may have Proctor and Gamble interested in a celebrity detergent spot. You know what I mean; the kind where the announcer can't tell the famous actress from her mother."

"How interesting," Miriam had purred.

Robyn left the café and walked the two blocks to her hotel.

Her suite commanded a view of Central Park. Dense green trees were still a novelty to her after the seasons in the California palms. Opened bags lay on and near her bed, bearing airport tags from Los Angeles International.

She ran her fingers through her thick hair. She felt the perspiration on her neck. She was tired.

Her suite felt enormous and empty. On a small table by the window, she saw that room service had left a bowl of fresh fruit and a bottle of iced champagne. There was also a telegram. The champagne made her feel unaccountably blue.

She opened the telegram. It was from Jeffrey Spector.

It read:

REALITY IS ONLY WHAT
YOU PERCEIVE IT TO BE.
BEST WISHES.

She looked again at her wristwatch. It was one o'clock. Six and a half hours until game time.

She removed her coral sunglasses. She undressed and weighed herself in the bathroom. She lifted her garment bag and hung its hook over the top of the closet door. She removed the blouses and skirts that were susceptible to wrinkles and shook them out. She placed them on hangers, taking care to allow plenty of space between each garment.

She returned to the bathroom and turned the shower on, letting the hot-water spigot run to heat up.

She walked to the dresser, picked up a nylon brush, and began to run it through her hair. . . .

She crossed to the bed, lay face down across it, and wept until she fell asleep.

CHAPTER 11

THE TELEPHONE AWAKENED her at ten minutes past four o'clock.

"Hi, Robyn Quarrles, Danny Breen. Welcome to the New York Nats family! Listen. I've got your press credentials, your timetable, hotel information for the road trips, airline tickets—the total package. I, ah . . . I assume that L.C. or Turtle has contacted you by now to go over the whole broadcast scenario for tonight."

Robyn had lifted the telephone still groggy from her nap. But at the mention of the two men she had confronted earlier in the day, she came fully awake.

"Mr. Breen, not only have they not called. Judging by Mr. Fanning's performance at the radio station this morning, I'm not going to be surprised if I'm locked out of the booth tonight."

There was a pause on the other end. "I was afraid of something like that," said Breen. Then, louder: "Lissen. L. C. Fanning is a sweetheart, Robyn. Believe me, he's a pussycat. He is one of the great towering personalities in this business. He's a pro. He's a—''

"Mr. Breen." Robyn's voice had assumed a different tone. "Shall you and I play straight with one another?"

"He's an idiot," said Breen, as though completing an interrupted sentence. "But he can be dealt with. You won't have any trouble with Fanning long-term."

"And his partner?"

"Don't walk past his kennel carrying red meat. Lissen. I think maybe you and I ought to sit down as soon as possible and block out some kind of game plan for you tonight."

"You don't know how relieved I am to hear you say that."

"I'm sort of in the neighborhood. Your hotel has a soda fountain off the lobby. I'll meet you there in let's say thirty minutes from woof."

The soda fountain was filled with rich, pale vanilla children clutching mothers' hands. They seemed to Robyn like miniature versions of the sleek people who had surrounded her and Bobby at the sidewalk café. The children looked at once more fragile and more resourceful than the tanned, bland California children she was accustomed to.

"Let me tell you straight out front that I think that hiring you was an absolutely brilliant stroke on the part of WERA," said Danny Breen.

"Would you mind not smoking?"

Breen, who had been fumbling with a crumpled pack, looked up in surprise. She didn't care. His remark had annoyed her almost more than the prospect of cigarette fumes.

"You must think I'm a bigger idiot than Fanning. Look. I saw what those guys thought of me this morning. Nobody bothered to be subtle. I feel like I'm about to walk straight into a massacre, Mr. Breen. I don't need your flattery. I need your help. That means concrete, specific ideas on what to do in that booth tonight."

Lifting the little finger of each hand, Breen tore open a pink package of artificial sweetener for his coffee.

"As a matter of fact," he said, "I wasn't flattering you. I was quite in earnest. If you want to hear my reasons I'll get to them in a while. First let me ask you a question. Why are you here? I would think the natural placement for someone with your . . . image . . . would be television.''

She indulged a sardonic half-smile.

''If you want to hear *those* reasons I'll tell you—in a while. It would probably explain a lot if you could meet my manager. Suffice for now that I believe this is the first stage of a master plan to, uh— what's the word—''

'' 'Position'?''

''That's right. God, I'll never get this language right. Yes. 'Position' me for some kind of move into television in the fall. There's another expression Bobby used. . . .''

'' 'Paying your dues.' ''

''You really have to meet Bobby, Mr. Breen. You two could talk for hours.''

''Anyway. I'm relieved to hear you're not doing this out of some unquenched love for baseball or something.''

She straightened. ''Now that's a weird remark, coming from a baseball public relations man.''

Breen winced. '' 'Image consultant' is the term I prefer. 'Public relations'—it makes you think of bodies heaving away in some shopping mall.''

Despite herself, Robyn giggled. ''I've thought that too.''

''I should be shot for desecrating the ears of a Miss Yankee doodle-doo with such vulgar thoughts.''

''Do you think you can forget for about a minute that I am a Miss Yankeedoodle-doo?''

''No. And I wouldn't advise you to. You're going to need every prop you can get here. That funnels into what I was saying about your not loving baseball. Let me be absolutely clear on this. You *don't* have any romantic notions about, God help us, the National Pastime, do you?''

''Well, I—no. But please understand something, Mr. Breen. I am a professional. In whatever I do. And I intend to do a professional job broadcasting Nats baseball.''

''That would be a serious mistake.''

''You are wonderfully cryptic.''

''Then let me be blunt. Jeffrey Spector didn't hire you because you're a baseball expert. Surely you can appreciate that.''

She stiffened. "Maybe he didn't. But it so happens that I have a degree in fine arts from the University of California at Los Angeles. I have done a good deal of work in television—"

"Modeling, acting—"

"All right, modeling and acting. *Using my voice.* I'm not another cute dumb beauty queen, Mr. Breen. We may as well have this out right now. For the last month, ever since my agent notified me about this job, I have been watching every baseball game on television that I could find. I have tape-recorded the announcers. I have even done my own play-by-plays into a tape recorder. I have crammed my head full of statistics. It would scare you, Mr Breen, to realize how much information I can store away. *I am a competent announcer.*"

"Then I'd advise you to do everything you can to disguise that fact."

"Oh! You're just like the rest of them! I don't know why I'm sitting here listening to you!"

"Because I can help you. Let me talk bluntly again. Because I gather Jeffrey Spector hasn't spelled any of this out for you. He doesn't project toward women. But I think I know how his mind works. He's a genius. He doesn't want you to out-Fanning Fanning, Robyn. You couldn't do it anyway. The old coot's got a certain native aptitude for what he does. You try to compete with him and Turtle, they're just going to have you for lunch."

"Well, then, what is it you suggest I do?"

"Counterprogram."

"Counter*program.*"

"You're here to add a dimension to the broadcast that is missing. I don't know if Jeffrey went into the numbers this morning, but it's no secret—the Nat games are going down the toilet and sucking the rest of the station along with them. Conclusion: people aren't very interested in listening to baseball on the radio anymore. Not surprising. It matches my own perception that people aren't very interested in baseball anymore, period."

"How can you say that? I happen to know that baseball attendance has been going up for the last several years."

Breen leaned across the table and pointed a finger at Robyn.

"That is *right.* Thanks in great measure, if I may be immodest, to me. And to professionals like me."

"You mean publ—"

"*Image* consultants. We don't just spend our days translating some subliterate knuckleballer's quaint patois into human language for the sporting press, Robyn. Those days are over. Take my range of responsibilities. I do conceptual planning. I do socioeconomic constructs that break the median Flushing Stadium crowd down into fine-tuned demographic units. I am bringing modern marketing science into a vestigial industry, Robyn. Do you follow me? I and some others have been keeping this sport breathing by artificial life-support systems for about the last fifteen years. Ever since Mantle retired. If it hadn't been for us, for God's sake, the National Football League would be playing in July."

Robyn sat watching Breen, bewildered.

"You still don't get it. All right. When you get out to Flushing tonight, I'll give you the grand tour. The whole damned zoo is my private lab. The scoreboard: mine. I designed it. I chose the carpeting—the artificial grass. I selected the themes for the theme restaurants. I program the Muzak, I dream up the promotion nights. I decide on the exact calibration of the amount of ass the usherettes will show—my apologies, Robyn. You know who auditioned Bavarian dwarves for the role of the Nat mascot? Me. You know who hired the Fire Island drag queen who conceived the wardrobe that our heroes dip into after dark all summer in strange cities? Me. What I am doing, Robyn—what others in the field have been doing—is keep pace with the state of the art in *leisure-time attractions,* for God's sake. The teams that can afford it draw customers. The teams that can't afford it go hungry. Check your figures. Attendance growth is not a universal phenomenon. I can name you major-league teams that are eating at Burger Kings on the road."

"You make it all sound like Disneyland."

"Disneyland. Now there is a concept. There is my idea of the ultimate stadium." Breen put down his coffee cup.

"It's all very fascinating. But what does it have to do with baseball?"

"Baseball!" Breen spat the word so that a child standing near him flinched. "What does *anything* have to do with baseball? What does baseball have to do with anything? That's the point, Robyn. Surely you don't think today's fan is coming out to the ballpark to see *base-*

ball. Not at the prices we charge. Not for the product we put out. Don't tell anybody, but baseball went out with the Cuban Missile Crisis. Or was it Vista-Vision. Anyway, my job as I see it—although I doubt that it has dawned on the Nat management in exactly these terms—is to persuade people to come to Flushing Stadium *in spite of the fact* that there is a baseball game being committed while they're present.''

"I see. And you think Spector hired me—"

"To help WERA listeners forget the fact that they are tuned in to a baseball game on the radio. If that is possible.''

"I could regard that as an extremely cutting insult if I wanted to.''

"I don't intend it as an insult. I wish you'd pay attention to what I'm saying. I think it is a marvelous opportunity for you. As someone who has an interest in generating publicity for the Nats, I am thrilled and delighted for us.''

"But you haven't even heard me broadcast.''

"Let's say I have certain instincts about chemistry.''

Chemistry. She recalled Fanning in Spector's office, looking toward his partner, and felt a twinge.

She conquered it. "Well, what is it you envision me doing? I mean, I just don't understand what it is you see me doing.''

Breen's eyes dropped to his coffee cup. He smiled a private smile.

"I can't tell you in so many words. Let's say that I am confident that your persona will manifest itself, ah, organically, out of the situation. I mean, you can do as you please. You can try to be a female Fanning if you want to, although as I say I wouldn't recommend it. But while you're feeling your way, I am going to try and help you along. I've put together a little package of notes''—Breen reached down inside an attaché case at his feet—"that deal with various human-interest aspects of Nat baseball. Notes on the stadium, the players and their families, some anecdotes, biographical sketches— that sort of thing. You can just about read it verbatim and I think it'll sound natural and spontaneous. That is how I skewed it: natural and spontaneous.''

CHAPTER 12

" **B**LAZING FASTBALL NIPS THE
. . . outside corner of the plate
. . . and now Nervous Mike Purviss is ahead of Randolph oh-and-
two . . ."

Fanning felt the woman behind him in the broadcast booth. Her
presence lay across his and Turtle's shoulders like chains. It filled the
tiny cubicle with a kind of silent sound: a feedback that got into the
microphones and warped the purity of what it was that he and Turtle
sent out onto the airwaves, that indefinable delicate pitch of
rhythms—there was static in the air tonight, and Fanning felt sure
that the fans must hear it.

". . . Randolph steps out . . . takes a *look* at Purviss . . . one
away . . . and Randolph says, '*Hey,* Nervous, *gimme* somethin' I
can *see* . . .' "

She was perched on a metal stool, back alongside the engineer—
her with her fancy gabardine pants and her shoulder bag and her
armload of looseleaf binders stuffed with notes that he guessed Breen
had supplied to her . . . that whole eager-beaver first-day-on-the-job

attitude that filled him with a damp horror and that had driven Turtle inside his shell, his on-air voice only a thin echo of its old raw bombast. . . .

It was the sixth inning and she hadn't coughed up a damn syllable yet. That was her problem. If Her Majesty had anything to add to the description and account of this game, she knew where the microphone was. See if she wanted the job bad enough to endure a little bit of the old Treatment. Same thing any rookie could expect. Likely as not, she'd had enough already. Likely she'd be on the first plane to the West Coast tomorrow morning, crying to that little whelp of a manager of hers that this job wasn't as much fun as she thought it'd be. Well, fine.

He recalled that she had said something about cigar smoke before the game. He touched the flame of a match to another White Owl. Watched the blue smoke billow out and flatten against the glass pane.

The goddamn glass pane.

Turtle, hoarsely:

"Nervous Mike . . . the rookie . . . tryin' to pitch his way out of a jam, L.C. . . . Tobias the runner at first leans away . . . Price dances off third . . . two runs in . . . Manager Tommy Pachelbel with that foot on the top step of the dugout . . . Purviss might be one bingle away from an early trip to the showers . . . and you *know* the kid is thinkin' *I got my smoke but where oh where'd I leave that hook tonight? . . .*"

"Kid's just grabbin' that pill, now, Turtle, sayin' *'Come* on, fellas, let's play *hard*ball. . . .'"

At the same time, now, he had to admit he kind of enjoyed it. Being aware of this girl behind him was almost a way of watching himself in action at the mike. He tried to picture himself and Turtle from her vantage point. The effect pleased L. C. Fanning. An old exhilaration, long banked but always smoldering, blazed to light inside him: the exhilaration of being *at the controls*—of being *in the cockpit* of a great craft that was the stadium and yet more than the stadium: some light-bathed capsule of baseball that arced across the airwaves at the speed of time, propelled by the fuel of their voices, his and his copilot's, Turtle Teweles's. . . .

"Nervous backs off the hill . . . cool summer breeze tonight but

Purviss has sweated an ocean already . . . now into that routine of his . . . fingers to the bill of his cap, now to his belt, now to his knees . . . rubs up that baseball . . . does this kid remind you of anybody in particular, Turtle?''

"All the listeners know who you mean, L.C. . . . you look at this boy out there, you see the great Robin Roberts in those Phillie candy-stripes of his . . . Robin drives you crazy out there, that baby poker face . . . fixin' his cap, belt, pants . . . next thing you know the umpire'd be yellin' 'Steeee-rike!' . . .''

He marveled through her eyes at the sweeps of physical motion expended in a baseball broadcast. He admired the constant turns that he and Turtle made toward one another. It violated the rules, pulling the mouth away from the mike to aim a remark at your partner. But the effect (painstakingly crafted, over many seasons) was that of two regular guys gassing about baseball. *Ha-ha. Let her try to break in on that.* He became aware, again, of the touching that took place between himself and Turtle: the gestures, taps, nudges . . . their eyes and hands in a perpetual Morse code of alerts, signals.

(Turtle's hand sudden on his shoulder; Turtle's finger pointed to third base. And Fanning: *"Here's Carty* moving in for a *pickoff play at third*—Purviss *throws* but Price is *back in time,* and Carty *alertly* bluffs the throw back to first base to keep Mr. Tobias *honest. . . .''*)

He saw how the stadium light must have danced about their heads as they snapped back and forth on every accented syllable. He saw his own left hand, cupped to his ear with the fingers pressed in, forming a natural earphone, a hollow for his voice. He saw how the light picked up the finish on their fine sport coats as both men hunched forward, tilting their metal chairs to the last tolerances of balance, their left legs jiggling in cadence.

"Roberts of course was one of the Whiz Kids. Plus Purviss with that great overhand smoke that put Robbie in the Hall of Fame. But has this rookie got the *intangibles* that made Roberts an all-time all-timer? . . . Let's see, as he hesitates at the belt . . . *brings* it home, and the Atlanta captain *spins* away from a little love note right under his chin.''

"That's of course the one thing Robbie never learned how to do, L.C. He'd never throw that intimidation pitch. Hitters knew that.

Cost him a lot more home runs than if he'd had that mean streak like Early Wynn used to have.''

"Old Early used to say: 'Them hitters are tryin' to take the bread out of my children's mouths.' ''

"He'd say: 'That space between the white lines, that's my office. That's where I conduct my bidniss.' ''

How had this happened? What was she doing here?

She had never felt more foreign in her life. If she had stepped off a bamboo barge into a West African village to find herself surrounded by *kankurang* dancers wearing bark masks, she might, after prolonged thinking, have thought of something appropriate to say. Not here.

"*Two*-and-one the count on Randolph. *In*field back, *hop*ing for the old six-to-four-to-three and out! *Hop*ing for the double dip! *Purviss* takes off his cap. *Glances* over at Price who's been bluffing a start for the plate. Now *you're* the catcher, Turtle Teweles. What are you gonna be sayin' to this big hard-throwing rookie?''

Here was a ceremony as esoteric to her as the Latin mass. From her vantage point she could see men playing baseball on the harshly lit cone of the stadium floor. She could follow the conversation of the men who were now her colleagues—a reasonable, if piquant approximation of English.

"I'm sayin' don't pay any 'tention to them ducks on the pond, Nervous, I'm tellin' him *rare* back for that somethin' extra and bring that heat home to Daddy. 'Cause here's where you know if a youngster's got that quality you was talkin' about, L.C., the *intangible*.''

The enigma lay in connecting what she heard with what she saw.

There was the field: a cold geometrical fact. There were the athletes in their uniforms, tangible beings enacting the precise choreography of a game she understood—or understood as well as any sentient American of the late twentieth century. There in the stands were her fellow citizens: thousands of presumably stolid men and women and kids, absorbing the game's progression, commenting on its yield in their great collective seismic roar—the yield ratified by the great scoreboard's tabulating lights, as infallible-seeming as the red figures in a calculator. Runs, hits, errors. The inning-by-inning score. The pitching changes. The batter's uniform number. All of it there, on the record, available of proof, a mathematician's blackboard.

"Purviss *deals* to Randolph . . . breaking ball down *low* into the *dirt* . . . Mike Russo blocks it and *saves* a run as Price was *half*way down the line. *Count* two-two now. And Manager Tommy Pachelbel is trying to decide whether to pick up that *tele*phone and call in the *Fire* Chief . . . Lloyd *Hew*itt loosening up *quick*ly down in the Nat *bull*pen."

"Russo reminded you of ole Roy Campanella on that play, L.C., gettin' his body in front of that ball . . . now he strolls out to the hill just the way Campy would . . . just to say, 'Remember this fella's a low-ball hitter, so let's keep it waist-high on 'im' . . . and Nervous Purviss is sweatin' now like a hog come butcher time."

But up here! This broadcast booth commanded other planes. What action did they see that she could not? Were they part of this night, this park, this game? True, their physical dimensions swelled the small chamber. They were so close to her that she inhaled the cologne on their necks. . . .

"Ready to go again now . . . *ball* game on the line . . . maybe this promising young hurler's *career* is in the balance as well . . . what a *spot* . . . *crowd* silent . . . *Price* gives it that false *motion* off third . . . Tob*ias* edges off first . . . *game situation!* What's Nervous Purviss gonna show Randolph in *this* spot, Turtle?"

"He's got to prove he can come home with the breakin' pitch in a spot like this, L.C. . . ."

Yet she felt as though she were observing them secretly, from a distance, as though she had crept through darkness in strange country and had come upon two primitive shapes before a bonfire, weaving in a trance, invoking spirits from another plane for the benefit of invisible worshipers out in the night air beyond the flames.

Only the spectral engineer, skinny and grinning, shared her perspective of real time and place; and even he seemed struck by the spell.

They conjured the shapes of other ballplayers from other times, vanished games—it was like gazing upon old confetti, or hearing a march recorded by musicians now dead. But their throbbing cadences made the phantom players dance on this diamond beside the real ones, separating the lit night air under the moon: a resonance of images.

Their incantation summoned the distant living players before her senses; and she heard the hard voices of the playing field, the grunted challenges, the taunts, the manic chatter. She smelled the tobacco and the sweat and the dust on catchers' hands; she saw the raw faces glisten and saw the whites of eyes; and she felt the terror and the hope that rode every pitch that caught the edge. . . .

"Purviss from the belt again . . . checks the runner . . . *here* it is . . . *and a ground ball out towards second, Pig* Shoat up with it, steps on the bag for *one,* the throw to *first*— and the *Nats* are *out of the inning*! *Bang-bang*! Maybe the *big*gest double play of Mike Purviss's *young career*! Two runs on four hits, no errors, *two* Atlanta ducks left on the pond! And Turtle, you talk about your *pressure pitching* . . . maybe at *some* point we'll look *back* on that double play as a *turning* point in this season. . . ."

And a memory awakened from a place inside her that she had forgotten was there.

From a province of her childhood, buried until this hour under the silt of time.

It was a province that had not belonged to her. Not even to Miriam, who owned so much: but to her father, Everett, and to Denny, her younger brother. . . .

With the city-flavored breeze blowing hot and sulphurous through the open car windows; odors of a working city at orange dusk; black water-towers silhouetted against the hot orange behind them, the urban sky before them already dropping down dusk over East St. Louis and the Mississippi River—in the direction of the strange blazing cylinder where the St. Louis Cardinals were playing baseball. Where the voices were.

"Wouldn't it be lovely to be sitting out at the Muny Opera tonight?" Miriam had slung the red point of her left elbow over the front seat and was talking to Robyn, enunciating with exaggerated clarity over the staccato rhythms of Harry Caray's voice floating up from the dashboard between her and Everett.

It was a province entered at twilight on summer days, the four of them arranged inside her father's Studebaker ("I was brought up with a respect for Oldsmobiles,'' Miriam had liked to lament, ''and I married a Studebaker'') on their way to some Knights of Columbus hall or public school stage: a recital night for Robyn.

With the baseball game on the car radio.

Aromas and colors filtered back into her memory now, stirred by the vibrations of the baseball voice: the baked smell from her father's attaché case of imitation leather as it lay on the seat between Robyn and Denny, the case still warm to the touch from a day in the sun-baked car. The glitter of the aluminum star on the wooden stick that she would hold while she danced. The blend of hair oil and Life Savers that seemed always to hang faintly about her salesman father, like a beloved old coat.

Her father: now she recalled—across a gulf of years—the delight she had felt as a tiny girl when Everett would brace her over his head, her little belly safe in his hands, and demand:

"What is it Harry Caray says?"

Harry Caray was the Voice of the Cardinals.

And she would recite, the blood in her face, giggling:

"It might be it could be it *is* a home run!"

"Put her down, Everett, before you drop her and cripple her.' From Miriam.

It might be it could be it is a home run. She had made it sound like a nursery rhyme. But the voice on the radio (she now recalled, dimly) had invested the words with majesty.

Everett was a ball fan. Everett knew all the statistics, all the averages. And knowing that Everett knew somehow had made the small girl glad.

Yes, the baseball voices were in the car with them on those dance-recital nights in the car, the four of them.

Robyn bobbed her twelve-year-old head. *"Showboat*'s opening to-night. Parnell Roberts! Oh, *God,* Mom! Can we go? I wanna *go.*" The Muny was the large open-air amphitheater in Forest Park.

Denny stuck two fingers in her ribs. "Quiet, Worm, Brock's gonna steal second. I wanna hear it."

Robyn pushed Denny's fingers away and made a face. At the same time Everett, slowing for a red light at South Jefferson, reached down to turn the volume up. Harry Caray's high-pitched tenor flooded the warm Studebaker.

". . . Brock, now, a long lead off first base . . . Niekro, into the stretch . . . at the belt . . . now, the throw over there . . . Brock back easily! Once again, that long lead. . . . This is where a Lou Brock, Jack, can upset a pitcher's rhythm and change the whole tempo of the ball game. . . . Niekro looks down . . . has his sign . . . now he's ready . . . checks the runner, here's the pitch now to Cepeda, *there goes Brock* . . ."

Click.

Miriam had switched the radio off.

". . . *Fouled* back and out of play. Cepeda had a good cut at a fast ball."

They were hearing the radio from the car idling next to them at the traffic light.

"Hey, god dammit, Miriam."

"Come on, *Mom!*"

Everett looked at his wife a long time before he switched the radio back on. Robyn saw sweat in Everett's thin curly hair. Her eyes welled with tears, but she pushed them away.

"Talk to your father about the Muny Opera." Miriam's eyes were concealed by sunglasses that swept upward like wings.

They began moving along Gravois again. The hot wind blew in on Robyn's face. "Your father isn't interested in the Muny Opera. Your father is interested in bowling and the Cardinals and Denny's Little League. As for your interests, your father doesn't give a good sweet—"

"Miriam, *for chrissake!*"

In the backseat thin Denny in his Cardinal cap began to cry.

"You see what you do." Miriam turned to Robyn: "You see what your father thinks about your dancing career."

From the dashboard, unsuspecting Harry Caray cried: ". . . There's the throoooooooow, it sails off to the left, and Brock is in there with a stolen base. That's number twenty-four on the season for Lou. . . ."

"Robyn, honey, Christ, I'll get us some tickets to the Muny. Whaddaya say, sweetheart? Let's see, don't they still have those seats where we can all get in for a buck apiece, I'll bring along a bag of peanuts. What the hell. . . ."

Robyn was staring out the open window at the orange St. Louis twilight, the sun on old red bricks. "Never mind," she said in a small voice. "It's not important."

"Sure it is—"

"I don't want to go."

"Let's pause quickly . . ." said Harry Caray.

One year later Robyn was dancing at the Muny, in the chorus of *Oklahoma!* Everett was dead of his heart attack. Miriam was in complete charge of the family, orchestrating Robyn's career out of her own shrewdness and her husband's substantial life-insurance policy. It was the one thing, she observed to Robyn—after the mourning period was over, of course—that her husband's job had been good for.

Robyn remembered, now, how she had stared at her father's body at the funeral and wondered what would happen to all the things that were in his head—all the statistics and averages. All the stories he knew about the Cardinals.

She had found it strange that no Cardinals had come to the funeral. Nor Harry and Jack: the voices.

If Everett could see his daughter now. . . .

Good God! Her head cleared. The wash of the crowd was suddenly real in her ears. She was a part of this broadcast, not an observer. And it was the sixth inning and nobody had as much as turned around to look at her. And if she were not to be buried by these two Prince Charmings, she would have to make her own move. Thank heaven for this P.R. man. Danny Breen. She drew in a long breath and ran a last quick survey of the blue index cards in the binder that he had given her.

She raised her hand, hesitated, and tapped L. C. Fanning on the shoulder.

She felt his flesh contract. He wheeled around, words of play-by-play still spewing from his mouth. His glasses glinted against the white stadium light. There was a terrible frozen second. Then Fanning gave a slight nod and turned his face back toward the microphone, still talking play-by-play.

". . . There's ball *four* to Carver . . . Nervous Purviss has issued his *fifth* walk of this game . . . two away, and who's digging in at home plate now but *Mr. Long Ball* himself . . . Earl 'Sweet Potato' Waddell . . . Waddell at thirty-nine years old, *still* tomahawking that ball like he did back in 1963 when he first came up to the majors, Turtle.''

"L.C., you take a natural hitter like a Sweet Potato Waddell . . . I don't care if you have to *push* 'em up to home plate in a *wheelchair,* they're gonna get that bat on that ball.''

"And Turtle . . . I don't know if we've mentioned it yet . . . we're fortunate to have some *feminine pulchritude* in the booth with us tonight . . . a very lovely young lady from the world of show business . . . I'm sure our listeners will recognize the name of Miss Robyn Quarrles, who they tell me is a former Miss Yankee Doodle Dandy . . . and we're gonna see if we can't get her in front of these microphones to say a very few words before this ball game is over.''

At the mention of her name her abdomen went numb. But at the same time she caught the nuance of Fanning's remark: He had not introduced her as a member of the broadcast team. So that was his game. *"Who they tell me . . ."* botching her title. The son of a bitch. All right. If those were the rules, she would play. Her anger, slow to build through this evening of insults overt and implied, was at a flash point now. Her romantic absorption in the broadcast—that was gone. And with it her stage fright.

The blue index card she held in front of her contained some "human interest" data that Breen had assembled. On the subject of team mascots.

Despite her feeling of clearheaded resolve, she could not stop her hands from trembling as she slid off the metal stool. She smoothed the wrinkles from her jeans and advanced a step until she stood between Fanning and Teweles.

Without bothering to look back at her, Fanning held up a cautionary hand.

She froze. She felt lightheaded with anger and anxiety. There she was. Standing like an obedient child in the middle of this smoky, butt-strewn broadcast booth. Waiting for an obstreperous middle-aged stranger to give her permission to lean over and speak words that probably would stamp her immediately as a babbling idiot.

Why had she let this happen to her? She thought of Dunning, old Pinley Stripely, and the surrealistic course her life had taken since she fled from him that night in Malibu.

She felt as though she had come to the brink of a cliff. There was nowhere else to go. Nothing to do but take the next step.

She stood as straight as she could. She filled her lungs with the cigar-stale air to calm the pounding of her heart.

She heard Fanning's excited voice: "Waddell *swings* and chops a one-hopper down to Steve Carty at third . . . the loooooong throw . . . and once again young Purviss has pitched his way out of a jam. *No* runs, *one* hit, *no* errors, *two* men left on . . . as we go now into the top of the *sixth* inning with the Atlanta Braves *on top* by a score of *six* to *two*."

She took a last wild look at Breen's index card. Like a woman plunging from a height, she closed her eyes and opened her mouth.

"L.C., many of baseball's most popular stars are folks you'll never find in the starting lineups or the box scores."

Fanning's head snapped around as Robyn commenced to read verbatim from Breen's blue card. "They're folks with names like 'the Chicken,' and 'the Pirate Parrot,' and 'Chester Charge,' and 'Krazy George.' [She heard her own voice as from a distance, too strident, cracking at the top registers, droning on without inflection,—no stopping, dammit, go on with it!] It's all part of base—of *major-league* baseball's newest and wackiest crowd-pleasing fad . . . the human cartoon characters who lead the cheers and moti—helps, *help* motivate the home team to victory. [The eyes of both men were boring into her now; both of them, half swiveled around, their breath in her face. God the whole stadium listening to her, the whole *world*, what had she done, don't stop, finish it.] And of course here tonight at Flushing Stadium, we're enjoying the antics of 'the Nat Gnat,' who sticks out his hot-pink tongue at opposing players and generally brings lots of good, G-rated laughs from young and old alike."

End of card.

She straightened up, breathing rapidly.

Fanning turned offhandedly back toward his microphone.

"I personally think these 'human cartoon characters,' as you call them, Robyn, are a desecration of the game of baseball."

Turtle said, "I think they're about as necessary as tits on a boar."

Fanning said, "I hear the guys who wear those costumes are a little, you know, this way, Turtle."

Turtle said, "Some pansy in a chicken suit come up to me between those white lines, I'd take his feathers an' stick 'em where the sun don't shine."

Fanning said, "You mean up his—uh—ass, Turtle?"

Turtle said, "I mean right up the ole choc'late freeway."

Robyn Quarrles stood looking from one face to the other. Trying to process it. Trying to make it fit with her understanding of reality.

She had entered a nightmare room, she thought, where the walls pitched and yawed and became the ceiling and floor. Where the voices of unseen people laughed at her. The sound of her own hideously strained voice still echoed in her mind. Now these grotesque men were mocking her, profanely, on the airwaves.

From beside her came the voice of the engineer, calm and drawling, as though nothing at all out of the unusual were happening:

"Okay, you two wise birds. Back on the air in fifteen seconds."

She shut her eyes. Understanding dawned.

She had made her broadcasting debut during the commercial break.

Fanning and Teweles thumped each other and whooped.

"Welcome to radio, honey." Fanning daubed at the corner of his eye with his handkerchief. "Oh, lordy." Turtle gave her a salute and a wink.

"Stand by," said the engineer.

Robyn felt the blood drain from her face.

She heard Fanning:

"Bottom of the seventh . . . Nats will send up Carty, Russo, and Shoat . . . if anybody gets *on,* maybe a pinch hitter for Mike *Purviss.* Chester *Harper* on the hill for Atlanta has shown no signs of weakening."

By God . . .

She dipped her shoulder between them. She pushed until her mouth was inches from Fanning's—inches from the mike.

"Harper continues to have good velocity out there, L.C.—and he's *locating well.*"

She breathed tobacco air. To her right Turtle Teweles recoiled.

But it was Fanning who unnerved her. He smiled.

"We want to welcome now . . . the newest member of the Nats baseball radio broadcast team . . . the former Miss Yankee Whatsher-doodle we spoke of a minute ago . . . *Robyn Quarrles . . .* as

Steve *Carty* steps in, Carty batting at two twenty-seven . . . *no* homers, *twelve* runs batted in . . . Robyn, let me *translate* what you just said for our fans, because I don't believe any of them are familiar with those newfangled terms, '*good velocity*' and '*locating well.*' Harper's first pitch is a slider inside . . . I think that by '*good velocity*,' Robyn meant that Mr. Harper is *throwin' strawberries through locomotives*, Turtle . . . and by '*locating well*,' it's just possible she was saying he can shave the hide off a buffalo nickel and give you *four cents change.* It's obvious to me that Miss Quarrles learned her baseball watching television . . . and I imagine she's gonna give us old-timers some lessons in grammar as this season goes along. Welcome to Nats baseball, Miss Doodle-doo!''

CHAPTER 13

During the drive back into Midtown in Turtle's Continental, L. C. Fanning did not bring up the subject of Robyn Quarrles. Neither did Turtle. That left them very little to talk about.

"Could still use us some left-handed power," Fanning ventured as they ascended the approach to the Fifty-ninth Street Bridge.

The city on the other side looked as though someone had switched it off.

"On the other hand," replied Turtle, "it appears like we got more than our share of right-handed twat. Right-handed twat, we're leadin' the league."

That was as close as either one of them came. Fanning left it alone, and they drove into dark Manhattan in silence.

"Come to Tommy's for a nightcap," said Fanning when they reached Third Avenue.

"You help yourself." Fanning knew that his partner had darker enclaves in which to shrink from this night.

"You keep your nose clean, you hear, tonight," Fanning said, when he had lifted his big frame out the door. "You don't get too far into the bag, Catch."

"You pick a sorry dam' time for tellin' other folks how to behave." A car behind them honked and Turtle screeched away so suddenly that the door jerked out of Fanning's hand. Fanning stood on the warm Third Avenue pavement, his jacket lapels billowing in a late-night wind. He watched Turtle's taillights shudder away, red as fingernails.

"What the hell was I supposed to do," he said aloud, "overrule that kid? I didn't hear you speaking up when the smoke cleared, you old sack of . . ."

And yet he knew what Turtle meant. It had been up to him to put a halt to all this nonsense right there in Spector's office. Yes, he had registered a protest. But it was probably true he could have nipped this color-woman mischief right in the bud by offering his resignation on the spot.

But then of course you have to consider the feelings of the young woman involved. Fanning was not so insensitive as to . . .

Feelings, hell. Face the blasted truth. He had crucified the poor skirt on the air tonight. He hadn't played the resignation card because he'd been scared of the slight chance that this Spector would call the bluff. *Accept* his gesture, heaven forbid (even now the thought made him shiver). And put the kibosh on any possibilities for Fanning's Day.

He needed a drink. Buttoning the middle button of his sport coat, he hurried along Third Avenue toward Tommy Eagle's.

You wouldn't know the place was open for business if you didn't try the door. There were no lights out front. Tommy's green canopy over the entrance could use some repairs. Inside, Tommy Eagle himself sat on a stool behind the bar, totaling receipts on an adding machine. There weren't more than six or seven customers in the place. Fanning remembered when you could come in here after a night game at the Polo Grounds or the fights at the Garden and have to squeeze through the white-on-white shirts just to get standing room at the bar.

"Break up the Nats," Tommy Eagle intoned when Fanning came

in. He looked back at his receipts. "Ain't no one team deserves to have all that talent. Bad for baseball."

One of the people at the bar was Dorton, the *Post*'s man.

Fanning made his voice boom.

"Tommy Eagle. Tommy, fix me a Chivas on the rocks, a double, and put it on Joe Dorton's tab here. And remember, Joe, write Tommy a big tip. I have a reputation to consider." He laughed his big broadcaster's guffaw, the famous laugh that never failed to turn heads his way in a crowded restaurant or nightclub.

Joe Dorton jerked his bald head upward.

"Hell, look who's here. Christ, Fanning, if I had what you had stashed away up there tonight, I wouldn't be down out of that broadcast booth yet."

Dorton was the chief needle among the press-box regulars. A Joe Dorton victim on Monday was fair game for everybody on Tuesday.

Fanning decided not to give him the satisfaction. He took a stool as far away from Dorton as he could, over on the short leg of the polished bar's L.

"Just out of curiosity," called Dorton. "How do you put that on your expense account? You think the station'll buy 'room service' during the course of regulation play?"

That one would be public domain by tomorrow. Fanning looked at Tommy Eagle. "We get the bats," he said. "We don't get the arm. We get the arm, we don't get the bats. What are you going to do?"

"It's like everything else," said Tommy Eagle. He was searching for the Chivas on the whiskey shelf. Fanning saw the lines under Tommy's eyes as they reflected in the mirror. Tommy Eagle was getting old. How old he couldn't tell. It was hard to tell with Koreans. When the likes of Jimmy Cannon and Dorothy Kilgallen used to come in here, Tommy never had any trouble locating the Chivas. Tommy was a bright young restaurateur for the sporting element once not long ago.

Something was wrong with the place. Fanning tried to put his finger on it. It hit him that this was the first time he had visited Tommy Eagle's since the season started. Time gets away. There were the same photos on the wall of the coat-check alcove—autographed glossies of fighters and the old Giants, mostly. Thomson, Mueller.

There were the same little green lampshades on the tables. One or two waiters he recognized from over the years. But something new was in this place. Something that Fanning had seen out of the corner of his eye. Something he didn't like. Something that lay bad on him like Joe Dorton's wisecrack. It would come to him.

"I'll tell you what it is." Tommy Eagle set the Chivas in front of him. Fanning looked up with a hard scowl.

"It's left-handed power," said Tommy Eagle. "That's what you're *cryin'* f'r. This Bogart Humphries. Okay he's startin' out hittin' a freakin' ton. But what about the second time around when the pitchers get the book on him? I saw him look bad a coupla times tonight. Breakin' pitch low and away."

Saw him? *Look* bad?

"Besides," said Tommy Eagle, "one guy can't carry a ball club on 'is shoulders. Look at the 'seventy-nine Cubbies an' Kingman. It's like everything else."

Fanning tipped the shot glass to his lips. The golden liquor burned Fanning's throat, and for an instant he saw the young doctor turning the gold Eversharp over and over in his fingers. He oughtn't to be touching this stuff.

He wiped his mouth and said carefully:

"They jumped on young Purviss pretty good. I don't imagine it was much fun listening after, oh, about the seventh."

He was trying to draw Tommy out on the Robyn Quarrles episode. See whether it had sounded as bad on the air as it had in the booth.

Tommy was busy with some glasses and a towel. He shrugged.

"Cum si cum sa. You know. I thought the kid looked okay in spots. It's all the same."

Looked okay.

Down the bar Fanning could see that Joe Dorton was listening to their conversation while pretending not to.

Loudly enough so that Dorton was sure to hear it, Fanning said: "What's happened to your clientele, Tommy? Fer cripes sake. You used to get a crowd in this joint. Guys with babes. Now whaddya got, a couple of drunk writers. What's the story, Tommy? Where're all the dolls?"

Joe Dorton's voice came from down the bar:

"Where are all the *dolls?* Christ, Fanning. Don't you ever get enough? Most guys at least have the decency to leave it alone when they come to work."

Fanning eyed Dorton. From inside the writer's polyester sport jacket he could see a spiral notebook bulging from a pocket. That was the thing about writers. They always had papers and notebooks slopping out of their pockets. And they wore cheap sport coats. Fanning couldn't understand how a guy in the public eye like that could be so careless about his appearance.

He said to Dorton, "Dorton, if you ever got lucky you'd prob'ly spoil it by putting a pencil where your business was supposed to be."

"A broad in the broadcast booth." Dorton's tone had flattened. "Come on, Fanning. What was the story in there tonight?"

He really wanted to know. That was fine. Fanning ignored him.

Tommy Eagle was gazing off into the darkness at the rear of his place, where the empty dinner tables were.

"So come on, Tommy. What about that clientele?"

"Don't talk to me about clientele," Tommy Eagle said moodily. "Freakin' ghosts. It's like everything else. It all changed ever since the war."

Fanning knew Tommy Eagle well enough to understand that Tommy meant World War II.

He turned his gaze to the wall of the coat-check alcove. Bobby Thomson grinned back at him from 1951.

"You're getting a diff'rent class of customer," Tommy Eagle was saying. "All up along Third Avenue and everywhere else. These people never heard of a necktie. Never heard of earrings."

Without looking up at it, L. C. Fanning suddenly knew what the problem was. The source of his bad feelings about the place was behind him and over his head, in the corner by the window.

"Except some of the guys," Tommy Eagle was saying. "Some of the guys heard about earrings."

He could actually feel the cursed thing behind him. Its presence lay heavy on his shoulders. He swiveled his torso back the other way from Bobby Thomson's photograph so that his belly brushed across the rim of the bar as he turned. And Fanning looked behind him and up.

"Oh, for cripes sake, Tommy."

Tommy Eagle, back at his adding machine now, followed Fanning's gaze.

"Hey. What am I gonna do? You didn't think I was gonna realistically hold out forever."

"You swore to me, Tommy. You swore you'd never put one of those god damn things in this place."

"Hey." Tommy Eagle's palms were out to the side. "You want to subsidize Tommy, L.C.? You want to underwrite this place? Keep Tommy Eagle's open as a freakin' charitable institution? Hey, all right. I made a mistake. I shoulda put one in here twenty-five years ago like everybody else."

"You stood right over there, Tommy, you little skeezicks, right over there where that Jim Beam bottle is right now, and you swore to me and everybody in his joint that as long as you drew a living breath—"

"What a memory," intoned Dorton's voice. "What a grasp of history, sports fans. Who was on the hill for the locals that day, L.C.? Who toed the slab for the hostiles? Was it that day or the next one that Bobby Thomson broke his immortal shoelace rounding second base?"

Fanning ignored Dorton.

"For cripes sake, Tommy."

Tommy Eagle shrugged. "Doesn't bother you I got a *radio* in here."

"Well for cripes sakes that's a different matter entirely."

"God damn right it is, Tommy," came Dorton's voice. "Fanning's *on* the radio to name just one difference."

"That's not the point, Joe." But for the moment he couldn't think what the point was.

"You shoulda seen the crowds here last fall. I opened up for them whaddaya call 'em, the football brunches."

"Oh, criminy. Not the football brunches too, Tommy."

Fanning wanted to take another drink of his Chivas, but there was nothing left in his glass but ice cubes. "Bring me another one, Tommy. See what Dorton needs over there."

"I'm okay," said Dorton without looking up.

"So anyway," said Fanning in a lowered voice when Tommy

Eagle brought his drink, "I mean, the point is, I guess you *watched* the game tonight."

"Most of it." Tommy Eagle glanced away. "I mean I wanted to see what that new kid Purviss looked like." He shrugged, trying to make it sound offhand. "I normally lissen to you and Turtle, you know, movin' around the bar, pourin' drinks and whatnot. Radio's better." He shrugged again. "I seen 'em flash the Net on the scoreboard tonight. They got a camera shot of it."

"Wonderful." Fanning's stomach felt sour and he knew he ought to be home in his bed asleep. Tomorrow was a getaway day. Instead he took another drink.

Tommy Eagle stood in front of him on the other side of the dark bar. There was a sad expression on his lined face. It was as if he were waiting for L. C. Fanning to release him from an apology.

Fanning remembered when the crowd used to kid Tommy Eagle about being more of a Yank than Rocky Marciano. Tommy used to love that. The joke didn't seem funny anymore. Tommy Eagle was like everyone else.

Fanning wanted to say something light and good-natured to Tommy. But the Chivas burned in his throat and instead he said, more loudly than he meant to:

"May I make a strange observation? You would have seen that kid Purviss better, Tommy, if you had been listening to me. What the hey, Tommy, did you see on that television boob tube tonight that I couldn't have told you about so you'd see it better?"

"He didn't see no toot-toot-tootsie," muttered Joe Dorton, and snickered into his drink.

"Who asked you, Joe," said Fanning. "Tommy. Answer me, chum. What did you see up there on that idiot boob tube tonight? Tell me what you saw. Give me a capsule description of Purviss, now, based on your own eyewitness experience."

Tommy Eagle, defensive and anxious now, stopped clicking the adding machine keys.

"Purviss," he said. "Shit, L.C., I donno. Christ, it looked to me like the kid was locatin' well. Good velocity."

Fanning slammed his fist on the bar.

"Tell me in English, Tommy. For cripes sake. Tell me in your own words. Don't give me Jack Downing's description. Jack Down-

ing, for cripes sake, sits there in the booth and looks at the game on
the *monitor*. He sees the same thing you do, Tommy. Jack
Downing—he does *airline commercials*! Don't give me any of that
synthetic TV crap about good velocity and locating well!''

Now Tommy got up and came over to Fanning again.

"Maybe you better go home, L.C. You guys gotta fly outa here tomorrow, don't ya?"

"Guys?" came Joe Dorton's falsetto voice down the bar.

"Just tell me one thing," said Fanning. "Was Nervous Purviss
sweating? Now you saw him. On the television screen. I mean if you
had to bet your life on it, Tommy, would you say that Purviss was really *leaking* out there tonight or was he dry? Just tell me that,
Tommy."

Tommy Eagle shrugged. "Jesus, L.C. Everybody sweats. Show
me a pitcher that doesn't sweat, I'll show you a freakin' freak
pitcher."

"Tommy. That's not the point, chum. I mean the kid's out there
on the hill, now, he's a rookie, the Braves're roughing him up, he's
always one pitch away from getting yanked, he knows Pachelbel's
gotta trim the roster, he doesn't know if he's gonna stick with this
club. . . . *Now all I wanna know is, did Jack Downing tell you
Purviss sweats?"*

From down the bar, Joe Dorton called:

"You after a piece of Jack Downing, L.C.?"

"You writing a column, Joe?"

Dorton's eyes were hard and searching. "No, L.C. I was just
curious what it is you got against the TV side."

"He didn't say anything about sweat," Tommy Eagle said. "He
said he had good efficiency against right-hand hitters. What the hell.
I don't watch a game to see if a guy sweats. Go home, L.C. Drinks
are on Tommy Eagle tonight."

Fanning looked at Dorton.

"I got nothing against the TV side," he said. "I'm not takin' anything away from the TV side. I think Jack Downing is one of the
premiere sportscasters of this or any other era. For the record."

"Because," said Joe Dorton, "you say what you want about Jack
Downing. I'll tell you one thing I've never seen Jack Downing do.
I've never seen Jack Downing do a ball game with a broad."

Fanning had an impulse to climb over the bar and go for Dorton's throat. If Tommy Eagle hadn't been a pal of his, maybe he would have.

"That's out of line, Joe. She wasn't my idea. Cripes sakes, it's some wildhair the station has. This new guy—"

"This isn't just my thinking, L.C. Word to the wise. Lot of the guys were a little put off at what they saw tonight."

"I'm telling you, Joe, it isn't my—"

"I'm closin' up early tonight, gents. Whaddaya say." Tommy Eagle's worried eyes darted.

Fanning felt exhausted. Long, hard day. Meatgrinder of a day. The confrontation in Spector's office. This new Robyn Quarrles. Now this bar, the changes, the emptiness. The idiot boob tube television set. Tommy Eagle getting old. What Joe Dorton was saying. He remembered the way the Manhattan skyline appeared, coming over the Fifty-ninth Street Bridge. As though it had been switched off. Everybody left. It always looked that way, late, of course, but tonight . . .

Tonight something had changed. Something important, it seemed, had left. Gone away.

What was it the doctor had said—pressure on the nerve?

He looked at his wristwatch.

Criminy. Was it that late?

CHAPTER 14

SHE WAS NOT ABOARD THE charter flight to Pittsburgh the next day. Her absence seemed to him a reprieve. Maybe the old Treatment had worked better than he had dared hope.

"Maybe she had her fill last night," Fanning remarked to Turtle when the aircraft, full of Nats, finally began its backward roll out of the LaGuardia gate and Robyn Quarrles's absence was assured.

"Maybe she got all the sports announcing she wanted for a while," Fanning went on, settling his frame in the seat—because Turtle had not answered. Turtle's long face was red and ravaged. The old catcher had taken himself to some other country last night, Fanning gathered. Teweles had a look on his face that frightened even L.C., who knew him best: an uncivilized look that reached back to his playing days and discouraged small talk.

"Yessir. I imagine she decided she was in the wrong line of business." Fanning flipped the in-flight magazine to an article on rediscovering America's inland waterways. But it bothered him, at the back of his mind, that Danny Breen wasn't on the flight either.

Sure enough, there she sat in the visitor's radio booth at Three Rivers Stadium when Fanning and Turtle strolled in from their customary pregame visit with the managers.

Breen, dapper in seersucker, lurked near her. Also present was a tangle-haired woman with a tape recorder. Fanning could not help but notice once again that Robyn was some looker. She had on tight-fitting jeans that made a fellow think about long lean young legs, and over them she wore a western-style blouse. There was a little red bandana tied around her neck. Her blond hair wisped about her face like a fashion model's. It seemed to play with the stadium light, sending up coronas in the air. Fanning almost forgot himself and grinned. But when she saw him, her face, which had been bright and open with conversation, froze into a wary gaze.

"Join the party," piped Danny Breen. "Robyn's giving an interview."

Fanning felt something rise in his throat.

"I'm Madeline Crane from the *Pittsburgh Post*'s Living and Style Section." The woman with the tape recorder made a show of toothy affability. "Robyn was just saying what a challenge she thought it was to work with a couple of 'old pros' like you fellows. Now I wonder if you fellas would tell how it feels to work with a contemporary-oriented *color person* like—"

"Madeline, sweetheart, excuse me just a minute," Fanning said pleasantly. He laid a hand on the seersucker shoulder of Breen's suit and bunched the material into a ball. "We have to talk to Mr. Breen here about an urgent matter outside."

Several paces down the corridor, Fanning and Teweles pressed Breen against a slate-colored wall.

"I should warn you that my hands are registered as lethal weapons," began Breen.

"Good. Maybe they'll go off when I stuff 'em up your asshole." Turtle's dark face was even with Breen's. Fanning pushed his partner away like a manager separating his player from an umpire.

"Breen, who gave you permission to hold a tea party in our booth."

"Take your hands off me. Stop touching me."

Fanning removed his hand from Breen's seersucker shoulder.

"You guys aren't dealing with reality. For chrissake, *I* didn't hire the lady. Your own station did. I'm just trying to facilitate things—"

"Sneaking her on a separate plane flight. Keeping her supplied with all kinds of background and notes—"

"*Somebody's* got to. Do you guys realize you've got her scared to death of you? I mean, what kind of macho-tripping scene is this? L.C., frankly I'm very disappointed in you."

Fanning felt embarrassment. He had never expected to hear a sensible word out of Danny Breen's head, but he had to admit to himself that the little son-of-a-biscuit-eater had a point here. Fanning believed in fair play. He glanced at Teweles and saw his partner's jaw grinding. It was clear that Turtle wasn't being ripped apart by any doubts.

Fanning knew where his duty lay. You back your partner. You dance with the guy that brung ya.

"Who set her up with the *Pittsburgh Post*?" His tone was gruff.

"The *Post* wanted *her*." The facetious edge was gone from Breen's voice. "I'm just doing what I'm paid to do. Listen, L.C. You and Turtle may as well get used to it. Robyn's a hot item. The press is going to want her every time we come into a new city. TV too, I would imagine. Now it would be in the best interest of both you guys to close ranks. Present a unified image to the media, regardless of your personal feelings. That's just my own personal opinion, for what it's worth."

"You mean play kissy-ass," said Turtle.

"I mean explore your options carefully, Turtle. Don't give the media a chance to—"

"Bugger the media."

"Whatever turns you on. Believe me, Turtle. This is the best advice you'll ever get from me."

Fanning reached a decision.

"Oh, the blazes with both of you. Come on, Turtle, we're ten minutes behind." He turned and marched back to the broadcast booth.

When he shouldered through the doorway the *Pittsburgh Post* was still there. And even though he knew that Turtle was seething behind him, L. C. Fanning wrapped a smile on his kisser and declared to the *Pittsburgh Post* that Robyn Quarrles was "an unexpected delight to have with us here on the WERA play-by-play team as well as a fine young talent."

Robyn shot him a look that had roses in it. But the sound that came from between Turtle Teweles's lips was unreproduceable in the *Post*'s Living and Style Section.

It was the last sound Turtle was to make during the course of the evening.

The next several days were as strange as any that L. C. Fanning had ever lived.

Robyn Quarrles existed only in the nighttime broadcast booth, where she haunted Fanning and Teweles like a reproachful wraith. (Who among them was about to die?)

They never saw her at the hotel where the team stayed. Where she slept, where she ate, how she reached the ballpark, they didn't know and didn't want to know. Once the game was over, she left the booth before the postgame wrap-up and melted into the general press crowd that funneled into the elevator, leaving a shard of perfume in the air to cut through the stale tobacco musk.

In the moments before air time each night, there existed only the most strained and perfunctory courtesies between Robyn and Fanning. Turtle remained aloof, indifferent to it all. They left him alone.

They did not discuss a division of announcing duties. If Fanning had ideas about Robyn's "style," such as it was, he kept them to himself and she did not dare ask. Tacitly they arrived at an "arrangement": Robyn would venture a few comments somewhere within the first few innings of a game, then perhaps speak up again in the eighth or ninth inning. Fanning would force out a civil reply. Fanning recognized some of her commentary as stock material; general stuff about a player's wife's charitable interests or an amusing "foible," clearly supplied by Breen.

But some of it was her own. As the first week or so wore on, Robyn began to venture a modest analysis of the game's progress. She struggled through a few amateurish clichés the first couple of nights. But she became perceptibly smoother, more focused, after that. Fanning couldn't decide which he resented most: her ineptitude or her incipient flashes of skill.

Whatever she had to say, however, was in a weird way essential to the broadcast. For Turtle Teweles had virtually stopped speaking into the microphone at all. And L. C. Fanning was discovering that his throat could not meet the stressful demands of a nine-inning baseball game as it could even a few years ago—when he had called every play, in the days before Turtle had joined him in the booth.

The furtive strangeness of this new situation began to oppress him. Meeting this girl each hot night in the broadcast booth, the closest thing to a home for him, closer even than the fine blank hotel rooms—meeting her with eyes averted, as it were; with nothing said, nothing acknowledged, just *getting it over with.* Christ, it was like the thing Dorton joked about at Tommy Eagle's. Except the hell of it was that *she* was the customer! He, Fanning, didn't want any of it. He felt mortified. Soiled. Watching her lower her head into that Electro-Voice—god damn it, it violated something. "Made a mockery of one of life's most beautiful moments." Who'd said that? Eleanor had. Some time ago. What was she talking about? He couldn't remember. But looking at this girl, here where she shouldn't be, doing something she ought not to do—well, it made him crazy with a sense that the universe was being rifled of all the things that stood in their proper places. He couldn't explain it. But it made his throat ache to think about it.

And Turtle. Sitting there with his yap shut. Watching them.

The Nats dropped two out of three to the Pirates and moved on to Cincinnati. Humphries alone continued to hit with power and consistency. When he belted one out in the third inning of the second game and L.C. went into his "Toot-toot-tootsie" routine, Robyn had turned to stare at him as though Fanning's next remark might be in a Pentecostal tongue.

Again, she found other means to fly than with the Nats. By now the players were on to the fact that a smashing blond beauty queen was upstairs in the booth with the radio team. The *Post* article had appeared on the last day in Pittsburgh, along with a three-column photograph of Robyn.

The scent was in the air.

"When you bring her down for *postgame interview,* man?" Chavez, the utility infielder, placed a jeweled hand on Fanning's armrest. Fanning looked up into a cascade of satin lapels and neck chains. When Chavez smiled, a gold tooth showed.

"Hello, Cha-Cha. How's that bone spur? You feel it when you swing?"

"Hah? When you introduce her to the lovers on thees team, Fannin'?"

Carty, the third baseman, bumped Chavez from behind. "You lay off Fanning's quail, Cha-Cha," he boomed in a mock-authoritative voice. "See, in the U.S. of A. it's the announcers gets all the snatch and the players, hell, they just gotta hump ass. That's the reason why so many players turn into announcers, ain't it right, Turtle. It oughta be a incentive for you t' learn the English language, you expansion Latin hot-dog."

"Carty, Pachy says he's thinking of moving you up in front of Humphries. Bat you third. What do you say about that?"

"Weemin's *leeb*!" Chavez continued to grin at Fanning. "Bring her to the *lockers*, show her what is made of the players!" Chavez had a refreshing sense of humor, Fanning thought. So did Carty for that matter.

"Hey." The deep voice of Pig Shoat came from the seat behind Fanning. "You ain't been in this league very long, Chavez. You wanna stay clear of the broads that come in the locker rooms. They got bigger balls than you have."

Fanning noticed that his little group had an audience. Bogart Humphries was facing them. The outfielder lounged in the aisle several rows forward, just out of their conversation range, leaning his weight against Nervous Purviss's seatback. Fanning could not tell which way Humphries' eyes were fixed behind the dark glasses. He could have been gazing around the plane, or at a stewardess, or at his own peculiar patterns and spaces. But Fanning had the notion that Humphries was studying him. It gave him the heebie-jeebies. Like being in the cross-hairs of a rifle sight.

What was it about Humphries? Something in the man made Fanning conscious of the hairs on the back of his own neck. (*And of the absence of hair on top of his head,* he now thought.) Resentment. Fear, even. He'd never feared any ballplayer before, not even the mean ones, the savage drinkers. Was it the man's color? Hell, Fanning was color-blind. All for equality. Blue, green, polka-dot . . . why, Willie Mays had been like a *son* to him . . .

No, it was more than that. (Well, it was that. But more.) Somehow there didn't seem to be room in Fanning's head for thoughts of Turtle Teweles when the thought of Bogart Humphries intruded. They were like contradictory arguments. They couldn't exist in the same universe. When Humphries appeared in Fanning's line of sight, Turtle evaporated. The sensation tempted panic. Humphries, with his maddening efficiency on the field, his endless aloof posturings off it—he was a machine, something from another time. A time that canceled the other time that Fanning nurtured inside him; the time of the orange glow.

He tired of thinking about the problem. He drifted to sleep, and lost track of time.

It was in Cincinnati that Fanning began to detect a palpable distance among the writers and the other announcers. It seemed that the afternoon golf foursomes were chosen up by the time L.C. and Turtle arrived in the lobby. Dorton and some Cincinnati writers happened to be just leaving the coffee shop when Fanning strolled in. Nobody thought to mention dinner plans for after the games. In the press lounge at Riverfront Stadium, the writers nodded to him over their wax beer cups and their ham sandwiches, but nobody could think of too much to say.

He cut her dead on the air the first night in Cincinnati.

In the bottom of the fifth inning a left-handed slugger for the Reds named Thorn slashed a wicked low line drive into left-center field. With the Nats overshifted to the right, it seemed certain that the ball would bounce into the gap for an extra-base hit.

Bogart Humphries somehow caught up with the ball. He left his feet, plunged and trapped it in the tip of his glove's webbing just inches from the top of the field. His momentum carried him several yards skidding on his chest.

"DID HE—YES HE DID, A TREMENDOUS DIVING CATCH BY BOGART HUMPHRIES! WHO GOT ON HIS HORSE AND GALLOPED ALL THE WAY OVER FROM RIGHT-CENTER FIELD . . . AND CHARLIE THORN SAYS, 'HOLY COW, BOGART . . . WHILE YOU'RE AT IT YOU MIGHT AS WELL TAKE MY WALLET AND KEYS!' "

The Cincinnati fans booed and tossed paper cups onto the field.

Fanning made no mention of that. He signaled to the engineer to pick up the crowd noise.

And then Humphries did an odd thing: Instead of firing the ball back to the infield, he held it aloft for a moment, waving it at the crowd in the outfield stands. Then Humphries let his hips undulate— once, twice, three times—before he finally flipped the ball under-handed, in an exaggerated arc.

Fanning remained silent.

"And look at Bogart Humphries out there," he suddenly heard Robyn cry. "He's giving these Cincinnati fans something extra for their money! A little disco action out there in the field, with the ball held high!"

Fanning said nothing. He snapped his pencil between his fingers.

He saw Robyn stare at him for a second. Then she whipped her gaze back toward the playing field.

"I like that, L.C.! Where I come from we call that 'giving atti-tude.' Bogart Humphries is telling those fans out there, 'Hey! Look at me! I'm here, I'm now, I'm beautiful, and I'm just as groovy as your hometown boy Charlie Thorn!' "

Fanning tossed a handful of statistics sheets into the air. One of them floated out into the stands below. He shoved his glasses high on his head, rubbed his eyes.

"Let's save the fan-club gush till after the game, Robyn," he said into the mike.

She recoiled as though he had slapped her. The blood rose in her face.

His eyes fixed on the playing field. "Now, I think you'd be doing our listeners more of a service by pointing out, as I'll now do *for* you as Mike McGregor, the next batter, takes a low overhanded curve ball . . . that the interesting thing about that play was this: Bogart Humphries was signed on by these Nats mainly for his *bat*. His *off*en-sive capabilities. And with a sparkling play like that in the outfield, why, he's already paying dividends with his glove."

"That is gibberish," he heard her say.

"Well . . ." Fanning uttered a cold laugh. He did not deign to face her. "Well, *you* may think it's gibberish, Robyn, but those of us who follow the *game* of *baseball* probably aren't really too concerned with *what* you think. Let's get back to business. Folks, please pardon us. There's a ball and a strike now, the count on Mike Mc-Gregor . . ."

At the end of the inning he snatched his headset off and fumbled in his coat pocket for his package of White Owls. To his right Turtle Teweles scraped his chair back, lurched to his feet, and slammed his way out of the booth.

Fanning struck a match. Contemplating the flame, he said, "In forty-two years in this business I have never had words on the air with another announcer."

"Would you mind not smoking, please?"

He turned to stare at her. His hands remained cupped.

"Oh, now the smoke bothers you." He aimed the cigar tip at the flame. He worked his cheeks over it and released a stream of blue smoke—not directly at Robyn Quarrles, but not exactly away from her, either.

"Maybe," he said, "you can find work in a place where you like the conditions better." He raised an eyebrow. "Whenever you decide you've proved your point."

"What makes you think I'm proving a point?" He could see that she was trembling faintly. There was a tremble in her voice, too, but she met his gaze. Again he felt a stab; her expression made him think of a child that has been unfairly punished and knows it.

"What was all that business about Bogart Humphries doing the disco?"

"Thirty seconds," came the voice of the engineer.

"Mr. Fanning, I mean it. Cigar smoke nauseates me—"

"Then get a job in a beauty shop. You've proved your point." He noticed that she'd waited until Turtle was gone to speak up about the cigar smoke. "Where do you get off telling me what I say is gibberish?"

"I . . . apologize for that. You put me down, Mr. Fanning. How do you think I felt—"

"And what the blazes is all this hoo-ha about Bogart Humphries? Doing the disco?"

"What *hoo-ha*? I'm an *announcer*! He did this *great thing* out there—"

"*He's a showboat! He's a hot-dog!* He's bad for this *game! He's*—"

"Black?"

"Ten seconds to air."

Fanning noticed that Turtle had not returned to his seat.

"Look, you know I'd *like* to be friends—"

He held up a magisterial hand for silence. But something told him that he'd have to finish this conversation sooner or later. Humphries. Why did the guy make him so sore?

It was four days later, in St. Louis, that Turtle disappeared.

Fanning's first hint came in the late morning, when he awoke and tried Turtle's room on the phone. There was no answer. This was strange. It was their custom for Fanning to make the first contact of the day. On the rare occasions when Turtle had awakened first and left the room, he would leave a message of his whereabouts at the desk. On this day there was no message.

The team hotel was at the intersection of two great boulevards. It overlooked a vast park preserved since the World's Fair of 1904. Of an afternoon before night ball games in St. Louis in June, Fanning liked to put on a linen suit and walk along streets of maple trees and ivy and wrought-iron fences. Something about this town had not let go of its past. It kept an affinity with barber shops and streetcar lines and with baseball itself—the way baseball was before the fancy boys got hold of it.

At noon Fanning dressed and left the hotel. He would kill a few hours. Maybe Turtle had made a connection last night and hadn't made it back yet. Maybe by midafternoon Fanning would find him slouched in the lobby, same as ever. The idea was to kill a few hours.

He walked east on Lindell Boulevard. In the old days Lindell had been one of America's great avenues for strolling—a wide old thoroughfare straight as a rule, bordered by shade trees and marble cathedrals. And fine old St. Louis homes. The sun warmed his freckled head. He thought to touch up the tan he had cultivated in spring training. He thought of Robyn.

He thought again of that day in Jeffrey Spector's office.

It was not possible, what that boy had said about his and Turtle's ratings. Fanning had never paid any attention to the ratings. He took his audience as an unquestioned fact, absolute as his own soul. The idea that his followers were not listening . . . *and to think that if it was so, the problem could somehow be solved by hiring a girl!* That proved the madness. This kid was working on some kind of grand design. Had just taken the place over. He didn't see how a reputable organization like MetroCom could let a thing like that happen. . . .

He was walking past a boarded-up A&P store. He had to stop for a moment and get his bearings, make sure he hadn't wandered off onto some side street. No, the sign said Lindell. He couldn't remember there ever being an A&P store on Lindell Boulevard, much less a vacant one. The June sun was bringing up a band of sweat on his forehead. He glanced at his wristwatch, and then realized he'd meant only to check the direction in which he was heading.

The sidewalks along Lindell were mostly empty, even in daylight. The boulevard itself overflowed with fast traffic, changing lanes in dangerous braiding patterns. A lumpish blue bus, its bulk listing to the right, began to pull away from a stop several feet from where he stood. Its tires scraped along the cement curb. The bus released a brackish plume of exhaust, and Fanning feared for his clothes.

A lone pedestrian now approached him on the glittering pavement. Fanning heard the boy before he saw him: an ebony sylph of a black teen-ager, all gym shoes and bluejean cuffs. The kid supported on his shoulder a radio the size of a tombstone. From inside the radio came the sounds of metallic riot—a crashing of steel plates, a pulverizing of glass. The riot sounds followed a cadence that sounded like "*Got*-cha, *got*-cha, *got*-cha, *got*-cha."

The boy drew near. He grinned at Fanning. Half-moon whites of his eyes eclipsed under a dark brow. Fanning thought of the night at Tommy Eagle's. His right hand slid into his pocket where the money clip was.

The kid passed. The "*got*-cha" noise evaporated into the traffic sounds.

Fanning realized that his chest was heaving and his shirt was damp. Was it the kid that set him off so—or the radio? Or something else. He needed to be sitting down someplace.

There was a place he knew. A dinette on Grand Boulevard near where the old ballpark had been. Sportsman's Park, later called Busch Stadium. Grand and Dodier. Near the streetcar line. One of the most beautiful ballparks in the country, green and geometrical, trees in the centerfield stands. Before they tore it down and built that other place, big concrete salad bowl down near the river.

The dinette was a long way off. A good three-quarters of a mile. Down Lindell to Grand, then all that way north on Grand . . . his legs were a little shaky. He hadn't put anything inside him all day. (No bowel movement this morning, he couldn't get it working after Turtle failed to answer his phone.) And he didn't know what kind of shape the neighborhood would be in down there now, with the ball-park gone.

But he remembered how he'd used to enjoy the little place. The name escaped him. He had a recollection now of grilled ham with applesauce. Strip sirloin. Lemon Bavarian. Ice Cream Bell. Congo Square. Bottomless Cup of Coffee. He recalled the satisfaction he used to feel, the satisfaction of a traveling man who knows where to eat on the road. All the good out-of-the-way places in all the cities. There was a certain waitress in that dinette, in the old days . . . and the place had air conditioning.

He set off again down Lindell for Grand.

And to pass the time, and to keep his mind off Turtle, he let his thoughts return, as he sometimes did, to October of 1951.

It had been an early autumn that year. In the New York suburbs (he could recall reading in the papers the next day), the leaf-rakers had put their radios in the open kitchen windows and turned up the volume to listen to the games. . . .

A radio resting on a kitchen window ledge. Something about that image always hurled itself at his senses. It seemed to say so much about the fixed rightness of things. Eleanor, of course, had the radio going on that day. . . .

The day his voice joined with all the voices and all the minds of all the people everywhere; the day he called Bobby Thomson's home run.

The dinette was called the Grand. (How could he forget?) And her name was Ceceline. Both still remained, with changes. In the old days the place had throbbed with a sense of busy whiteness: bright artificial light gleaming on polished surfaces. Waitresses in starched white dresses scribbling orders. Ball fans and businessmen from the neighborhood in white shirtsleeves. Now the place had darkened into gray, as if all the cigarette smoke from all the years had been allowed to coat the walls and ceiling and the vinyl booths. A doorway that once had led into a table area had been plastered over, leaving a dark rectangular smudge. The mimeographed menus were gone (he remembered that the prices never came out even; a dish always cost ninety-two cents or sixty-seven, or a dollar fourteen). In their place were torn, colored cardboard ones that offered "broasted" chicken and deluxe club sandwiches. These prices came out even.

The only fresh-looking object in the place was a large businesslike clock that someone had installed over the dirty plastic-covered shelves where the Jell-O and cantaloupes were displayed. Fanning took a seat on a stool whose vinyl cover had been ripped in small recurring patterns, as with the point of a knive. He found himself following the sweep of the red second hand. It was seventeen minutes to two.

"Hello, L.C." Ceceline pulled a pencil from her hair. She acted as if Fanning hadn't been in since sometime last week. He didn't know whether her nonchalance was real or affected. In an odd way he felt a blow to his pride. He shivered once. It might have been the air conditioning. At any rate, it felt good to sit down.

Ceceline: they'd had a little hanky-panky thing together back in the fifties, one of the little flings he'd never told Eleanor about. It happened in the best of times that L. C. Fanning had ever known, the crest of his early radio fame. Green grass in the outfields, eight teams in the National League. A time of great teams. Legendary teams. Ceceline was a sassy young waitress up to the city from Tennessee. With padding in her shoulders and her curls up like Ginger Rogers, she'd ignored all the businessmen and ballplayers and had given Fanning the once-over. He'd been flattered as much as gaga, he guessed. He took her to the Fox, up on Grand near Lindell, one of the great movie cathedrals of the land, giant organ that rose out of the floor and scalloped tiers that rose to heaven like a stadium wall.

And so they had their hanky-panky, in the fine hotel by the park that she'd never thought she'd see the inside of. Afterward L.C. took her downstairs to a fancy cocktail lounge where he was the guest on a local late-night radio interview show. She watched from the table. How she glowed! (Orange hair in the dim cocktail light.)

And then he had watched her age. He came to the dinette all the years the Cardinals played their games at Grand and Dodier. They remained on friendly terms. She never left the place. She'd had some kids and got blue lumps around her ankles and now she was as much a part of the dinette as the fossilized jukebox selection terminals on the counter. Then in 1967 the Cardinals had moved away and he hadn't been back since.

God, it had been that long.

"Here you are, L.C." He had ordered Special K with sliced bananas, for even though it was well past noon, he didn't feel up to challenging his bowels with anything else on the menu.

He watched her amble to an unused booth—the place was nearly empty—squeeze back into her seat, pick up the newspaper to scan it through slanted glasses on a chain, tamp the ash from her Lucky, idly scratch what once had been a pinup leg.

He turned his gaze back toward the cereal bowl. It had a brown stripe around the rim like they all used to have.

What else, now, could he remember about October 1951?

He thought of Jack Dempsey's Restaurant on Broadway. The famous Jack Dempsey's. "A Must for Out-of-Towners." (He recalled the pride on the day he read that ad and realized that he, himself, was no longer an "out-of-towner.") Special luncheons from seventy-five cents. Broadway at Fiftieth, yes.

Craven "A" cigarettes. Ha-ha.

Cripes, who was on Broadway then? He could almost remember the marquees. Shirley Booth and Johnny Johnston in *A Tree Grows in Brooklyn*; that was at the Alvin. Ethel Merman in *Call Me Madam* at the Imperial. *Guys and Dolls,* he thought, would have been at the Forty-sixth Street. *South Pacific* was playing somewhere; that would be the Majestic. Martha Wright. Why aren't they naming girls Martha anymore? *Mostly Martha,* he thought. *Mo-hostly Martha. What has she got? She's got the most!*

Let's see. *South Pacific.* All right. *The King and I* at the St. James. Gertrude Lawrence. *Two on the Aisle,* with Bert Lahr, somewhere. *Stalag 17.* Criminy, what a year for Broadway! (And you, Fanning, you old coon dog—who in blazes are you trying to kid? You never got inside half of those Broadway shows. A *tenth.* What kind of a dried-up old con artist are you to sit there and make believe that you were a connoisseur of the Great White Way?)

It was pride, he told himself. It was a swelling, delirious pride that made him stare at those marquees in that city in that laughing season and let the titles blaze their way forever into his memory. It was a pride similar to the pride he'd felt ten years before, in 1941, when he had heard that President Roosevelt was going to allow baseball to continue through the war years because America needed it as recreation and diversion. It was a proprietary pride, a pride at once self-glorifying and selfless, the consummation of that distant desire he had felt on that long-ago day on Addison Street in Chicago, outside Wrigley Field, with his father; the consummation of his wish to be *detached* from the crowd, *above* it, yet *connecting* it with his voice . . . to be a conduit of vital things. A unifier, a participant in something as grand and tangible as the theater buildings themselves: the Voice of the Giants—an institution among institutions. The Broadway theaters were his peers.

Connoisseur of the Great White Way, his ass. On the night before The Game, he recalled, he'd gotten on the subway and ridden all the way up to the Fairmount in the Bronx to see a double feature . . . what was it, now . . . oh, cripes. *Sleeping City* with Richard Conte, and *City Across the River* with Stephen McNally. "All-Thrill Program," he remembered the sign proclaiming outside the theater. Eleanor had said no thank you; he had gone alone.

Thomson hit .289 before the playoffs that year. It seemed important for someone to remember. Fanning remembered.

He encircled the bowl of Special K with his hands. He studied the backs of them. The brown liver spots hadn't been there five years ago, two years ago . . . how long? He hated to see the brown spots come.

Anger overwhelmed.

"Cripe sakes, Ceceline."

"What's your problem, L.C.?" Her voice was as familiar as yesterday.

"Come over here and feel this bowl." A sleepy-lidded customer glanced up, ran his eyes up and down Fanning's sport coat, smiled. Ceceline's glasses glinted; she arose and squared her shoulders. She took the rim of Fanning's cereal bowl between a thumb and forefinger. The red polish on her nails was cracked.

"I don't feel nothin' wrong with it."

"It's *hot,* Ceceline."

Ceceline reflected.

"Well it just come out of the dishwasher."

"Well dad-blessit, that's the *point*. It just came out of the dishwasher and it's curdling my milk."

"I just washed it," said Ceceline, ambling away. "It just come out of the dishwasher. That's why it's hot."

Jack Dempsey's. Toots Shor's. Stan and Biggie's. The Dutchman. Eli's. Forty-two years, the vagabond diner, taking his pick of the best, never bothering to total up the bill (*Write yourself a good tip, Marie*) . . . why could he never remember that it always came down to something like this. The hair in the coffee cup. The stack of hotcakes that soaked up the allotted syrup from the tinfoil packets and didn't leave a trace. The check that never arrived. *Her fingernails were bright red.* He remembered staring at them in the Cincinnati booth. Ten bloodsoaked claws. Now he wondered if it was Turtle's blood.

Fanning placed two quarters on top of a dollar bill and slid them under the rim of his dish. Bracing his fingertips against the edge of the counter, he pushed himself off the stool. He stood, feet apart, until he felt the damp insides of his cotton slacks pull free from his legs and settle, the crease lines straight. He hadn't finished his bananas. He walked out of the dinette. He did not say good-bye to Ceceline. He did not suppose that he would ever see her again. He looked at his wristwatch. Still more than four hours to game time.

And not a decent burlesque show in town.

Turtle wasn't there.

It was the first hot night of June. An ice cream night, a night of Daylight Savings Time. The concrete causeways around the stadium still held the baked warmth of the sun. It was one of those nights when the composition of a ballpark crowd is tangibly different from the crowd the night before. The stadium was filling up with children and elegant grandparents, wearing pastels.

And Turtle wasn't there.

A Dixieland band, trombones and straw hats, made tinny music on the first-base dugout roof. Mosquitoes and moths blazed in the incandescent air, which tasted of mustard. The pitchers in the bullpens had shed their bright warmup jackets for the first time on an outdoor night.

And Turtle Teweles was gone.

Fanning watched the crowd take shape from behind the batting cage. He had never quite grown oblivious to a gathering baseball crowd. Down among the players, hearing their accents, hearing the metronomic crack of bat against ball, the angry snap of thrown ball against glove leather, he felt that he heard, more than he saw, the distant genesis of the encircling crowd. Piped into the stadium, it seemed, by the magnetizing conjurations of the organ music, they—it—trickled with the hypnotic inevitability of water along timeless arterial ducts, first vertical, then horizontal, until the trickles joined and became unified energy. There was always a certain moment each day or night when the thousands of individual wills inside a stadium coalesced into a single thing, a crowd, and after all the years in all the ballparks, Fanning thought he could hear the moment when it happened. The notion filled him with the same dull, happy terror that he sensed when he tried to imagine his listening audience (of which the crowds, in New York at least, were a continuing reaffirmation, the Word made flesh).

But tonight Fanning was not thinking of any of that as he watched the crowd take shape. A vein throbbed in his forehead, and he found himself lost in the absorption of contemplating individual faces. People with festive terry-cloth hats, with large Go! Cardinals buttons fastened to their shirt collars, with scorecards and beers in their fists, with wicker handbags dangling from their meaty freckled forearms. People whose foreheads gave off the same white glow from the stadium lights that danced on the fierce polished batting helmets of National League players.

They were strangers. He had never quite thought of them in that way before.

Turtle had not been at the hotel when Fanning returned. The desk clerk could find no record of his checking out, and Fanning had retained a faint hope that his sidekick was simply on some private excursion—until he reached the park.

Turtle was not there for the nightly visit to the teams' locker rooms, the ritual pregame conversations with the managers. This was a part of the broadcast routine that the old catcher had enjoyed above all else—the last tangential link with his environment as a player.

No one had seen him upstairs in the press lounge. Back at the press gate, Fanning had found that Turtle's name had not been checked off the list. He was vanished. Fanning knew it. And now he stood with his back to the batting cage, the blood pounding through the veins in his temples, his aluminum net and his attaché case forgotten in his hands, watching the strangers in the crowd and trying not to feel as he had felt on the night that Eleanor had passed from his life. Trying not to feel bereaved.

And yet, an hour later, in the fifth inning, Robyn perched like a vulture on his left and a hole in his life where Turtle had been, L. C. Fanning was on his feet and screaming in the lost language of a time that even now was slipping back from the present:

"TOOT-TOOT-TOOTSIE, *GOOD-BYE*!"

CHAPTER 15

FANNING'S TELEPHONE RANG and rang.

She had been afraid of that.

There was no question of waiting in the hotel room until she got through to someone. Too good a chance that her nerve would fail; that she would change her mind. Give in to her sense of duty. She had Miriam to thank for her sense of duty. All those years marching in the ranks, twirling that baton, grabbing those accolades . . . Phi Beta Kappa key, Miss Yankeedoodle-doo, whatever they threw at her next. Front and center, smile and salute, then back to active duty. It was the least she could do. All of it.

Fanning's telephone rang and rang, and she finally replaced the receiver on its ivory-colored cradle. She did not exactly regret it that no one had answered. She had left the hot-water spigot on in the shower, and now the mirror in front of her was turning opaque with steam. She felt that she was behaving foolishly. It took a minute to realize that there was no one present to watch her and make a judgment. For a change. She checked her watch, and then examined her fingernails.

She got up from the bed and began to search absently for her scale. It seemed a good idea to weigh herself, although she was already dressed and had her bracelets on. She remembered that she had packed the scale the previous night, along with the rest of her travel paraphernalia. The first flight to the West Coast would not leave St. Louis until midafternoon, but there was no way she was going to be around the hotel a minute longer than was necessary.

She took a seat on the chair beside the bed and considered her reflection in the mirror.

It was going to be hard enough killing half a day in St. Louis, with all the memories this town held for her. If she didn't watch it, she was going to bawl. Just seeing the ballpark last night had filled her up with thoughts of her father. And that Studebaker and those games on the radio, oh God. There it was again, of course—that chalky-flavored sense of duty, filtered now through Everett's memory. *Don't do it—think how proud your father would be.* She thought she recognized Miriam's voice.

A sweet and worthy and noble thought, counterbalanced only by the simplicity of the fact that she couldn't take it anymore.

The steam from the shower was thickening on the mirror, causing her reflection to fade like a memory of childhood. In a minute or so the steam would ruin her hair. But she did not get up. She found herself fascinated, almost hypnotized, by her disappearing reflection. She was glad to see it go. There had been too many mirrors. Everett had died never knowing a child of his would be a guest in a room in this fanciest of hotels in his hometown; never dreaming his baby's face would peer out of Chase-Park Plaza vanity glass. Oh, the things Everett never dreamed about his baby's face. The things Everett never dreamed.

It was curious, her dialing Fanning's room at this critical moment in her life. What did she owe him? Fanning was the reason she was about to go through with this—and suffer the inevitable harvest of ridicule, public and private. Fanning and his cretinous partner, who had been mercifully absent from the booth last night.

She told herself that there was simply no one else to call. Breen would probably talk her out of it. The West Coast wasn't up yet; no use (she told herself) throwing Miriam or Bobby into ulcerous fits before breakfast. She supposed that she owed her employer in New York an explanation, but the very image of Jeffrey Spector gave her a scaly feeling. At some point, of course, she would need to return to New York and claim her belongings from the hotel suite. The logistics of this little abdication were more than she wanted to even think about.

There was not a single girlfriend she felt right about telephoning— God knew, she had rehearsed the list enough times in enough cities the past few weeks. It was astonishing how many good friendships one beauty contest title could kill. The myth about all the "close ties" that were "fostered" during the pageant. They forgot to mention what winning did to those "ties."

And then, of course, there was Dunning.

Sweet Pinley.

Out of the question to telephone Dun. She had made her break from Dunning and his censorious friends. Better to proceed in an orderly way, with her plan.

She arose, finally, from the chair beside the bed and advanced through the billowing steam toward the shower spigot.

And tried to avoid answering her own question: Why, if not for Dun, was she flying to California?

Hot bricks in Fanning's bowels.

Turtle had left him. Slipped away into—where? Into the weather itself, it seemed. Into the great river that rolled south past the city; into the green; into the June. No ripples, not a trace. (He hadn't even checked out of the hotel.) Fanning thought he could imagine how it had been, although it wasn't a thing he could see in his mind's eye. More like a sound; brief, rustling, disturbed water; then silence. An absence. A vacancy. While the uncomprehending world hummed on. Ballplayers circling the bases, getting good wood on the ball, hitting the cutoff man. The great sucking nighttime roar of the crowd, not comprehending what had been lost. Something not explainable on scoreboards, through circuitry.

The full impact of it hadn't struck Fanning until the broadcast was over. (Cardinals 7, Nats 3; home runs Cruz, Humphries.)

He had come back to the hotel and gotten on the phone. Calling up people all over the country who might have heard where Turtle had gone to. Retired ballplayers. Former sportscasters "taking it easy" in Florida, New Mexico. All who remained in the old network of their friends and acquaintances from the good years, the Thomson years.

Nobody had the slightest notion. Holding the hotel telephone receiver in one hand, flipping through notebook pages of faded numbers with the other, Fanning could almost feel the machinery's resistance; it was as if Turtle's departure was a thing that could not be expressed or resolved through electronic means.

Arkansas lay to the south of Missouri.

Long past the time when he should have been asleep, L. C. Fanning dialed the telephone number of the Bowl-A-Wile lanes in the small Arkansas town where Turtle lived in the off-season. Turtle was a part owner of the Bowl-A-Wile. Fanning could see the town in his head while the telephone rang and rang. He'd never visited there, but Turtle had described it: One sorry lonesome winking caution light that throbbed yellow over the business-route intersection outside of town, the only thing alive by this hour, turning the sumac leaves on and off. An Esso truck stop. A convenience grocery store. A grain elevator. A brick post office. A boarding house. A few fatigued houses, and the Bowl-A-Wile, a Quonset hut that housed six lanes and a kitchen where barbecue ribs were cooked to order. No one answered at the Bowl-A-Wile and finally Fanning hung up, waited a minute for the line to clear, and dialed Frankie Wilde's home number in New York.

It was after four A.M. when he drifted off to sleep, lulled by a vision that turned into a dream, of something at the corner of his eye flashing in a fast-washing stream and then lost, forever indistinguishable from the shadows and the smooth stones.

The hotel coffee shop was four-fifths empty. Thank God. People recognized her in this town. In this town her saucer-size sunglasses were hardly an adequate disguise. In this town saucer-size sunglasses only drew attention.

She wore them anyway.

She prayed that none of the ballplayers would be in the shop. A few of them knew who she was by now. This morning a ballplayer was the last thing she wanted to look at. A ballplayer or Danny

Breen. At nine-thirty in the morning, her chances were good. She needed a cup of tea, a chance to sit and analyze in a calm way the decision she had made. To think of the consequences, the most important of which was, clearly, an end to what she laughingly thought of as her "career" . . .

An unforgivably dreadful sport jacket caught her eye from across the room.

Her first impulse was to turn her back. But he was sitting alone, and she had, after all, tried to reach him on the phone.

It wouldn't kill her to say good-bye. She had caused him as much anguish, inadvertent though it had been, as he had caused her.

And besides, in a curious sort of way, she had never exactly met him.

She shifted her shoulder bag and slid into the seat opposite him in the booth.

"Good morning, Mr. Fanning. I have some really terrific news for you. . . ."

She paused when she saw his eyes. They were focused somewhere beyond her. Even through her sunglasses she could make out the shadows. She was struck by the rumples in his jacket—she had never seen him in less than razor-sharp lapels. But in one eyelet he had fastened an absurdly festive boutonniere.

Fanning did not react immediately. A beat passed before the big head snapped back an inch or so, and the lips compressed.

"Good news," she repeated. "As of today I'm no longer in your hair. Gone. Know when I'm licked. End of experiment."

Still he continued to gaze beyond her. He brought up one large hand in a sudden motion, as if too smooth back his hair, but instead he examined his wristwatch. When he finally shifted his attention to her, it was as though he had been awaiting her arrival, as though this meeting had been planned.

"One of the things I deplore about today's broadcaster," he announced abruptly, "is his lack of responsibility when a microphone is on." He pushed his glasses down toward the tip of his nose and gave her a significant glance over the top of the frame.

She stiffened. The distaste she had always felt in his presence returned.

"Mr. Fanning, I, uh, didn't come down here to discuss broadcasting styles. I just told you I'm leaving. I—"

"You want some coffee, sweetheart? Warm it up for you, L.C.?"
The waitress's attention was all on Fanning.

"Uh—tea and honey, if you have any," she said, irritated beyond
all proportion now. Why didn't the goddamn waitress look at *her*?

"This is the tea and honey person, Madeline," Fanning told the
woman, who now stole an appraising glance at Robyn. "Remember
I told you about the new partner we have with us, the tea and honey
person."

"*Oh* yes." Madeline nodded, a dark rumor confirmed. "The tea
and *honey* person."

"Look, I don't appreciate your sarcasm," Robyn spat when the
waitress had gone. "Look, can't you understand what I'm telling
you? I'm *quitting*. I thought that maybe we could at least part on
friendly—"

"Some of us may be so old-fashioned"—Fanning gave no sign of
having heard her; he was preoccupied now in rummaging through
some sort of small valise at his side—"old-fashioned that we lean too
far toward being cautious and conservative about what we say on the
air. And for that reason we perhaps don't say enough."

It sounded rehearsed. Robyn had an inkling that in some indirect
way he was referring to their clash over the Bogart Humphries incident in Cincinnati. Now her irritation softened. It amazed her the
way this absurd old man yanked her emotions this way and that.

"But today," continued Fanning, his chin folded on his chest, his
hands still groping in his case, "I suppose we may as well accept that
thanks to Mr. Cosell we are in the era of the so-called tell-it-like-it-is
type of guy—"

"*Person*," hissed Robyn before she remembered it didn't matter
anymore.

"—who just feels that he has to find some kind of a sociological
peg for everything that happens down on the field. Now I'm a man
who believes in keeping up with the times. So I'm not going to butt
in anymore when you put your liberal slant on some stunt that a black
player pulls, not that I have anything but the highest—"

"ARE YOU DEAF? I TOLD YOU I'M QUITTING!"

Somewhere behind her a busboy ceased clattering dishes.
Waitresses turned their heads. The entire coffee shop came to a dead
silence.

Fanning regarded her directly for the first time. His fist came up to the tabletop and there were three plastic pens in it, each a different color. She saw that the fist was trembling.

"I heard you loud and clear. Now I'm going to teach you how to be as good an announcer as you want to make yourself. I taught a half-ignorant broken-down catcher and I imagine I can teach a woman too. You see these pens. . . ."

She was shaking her head so violently that her hair whipped about her. She dug the heels of her hands into her temples.

"Good, you taught Turtles Teweles. It's perfect. You two are made for each other, and I've got the message. I'm gone, Mr. Fanning. I'm out of here."

"Miss Quarrles, you can't do that. Turtle quit on us last night and I'm asking you to stay. I can't handle these broadcasts alone."

"Oh, shit," was all she could think to say.

An hour later they were still in the booth. Brown bracelets of coffee stains decorated the surface on Fanning's side. His ashtray spilled over with the cellophane from cigar wrappers. Robyn's fourth refill of tea sat cold and untouched in her cup. Upon the remaining space on the table was scattered an astonishing selection of items: a pair of binoculars, several spiral-bound booklets, colored pens, a stopwatch, an egg timer. Props, all, for an L. C. Fanning lecture on the art of baseball announcing.

"An ordinary fifty-to-sixty-cent egg timer." Fanning plucked the gadget up and rolled it in his fingers. "Get one at any hardware store. Keep two or three of them in your pocketbook, Robyn—they break."

Wearily she lifted her cheek from her cupped hand; she felt the imprint of her fingers linger.

"Let's sort of keep this on a theoretical plane, Mr. Fanning. I haven't said I'm going to stay yet."

"Every baseball game"—Fanning's voice rose to a lecturer's pitch—"is played by the score. You forget to give the score, you've lost your audience. So!" Fanning brought the egg timer down on the tabletop with a sharp thump, salt side up. "You give the score. You turn your egg timer *up* . . . and, why, you go right on ahead with your business. Now, you look . . . you see the sand has about run out . . . why, you give the score again, turn the thing *up* . . ."

Robyn waved a languid hand. "Correct me if I'm wrong, but I think maybe I've got it," she drawled. "And when the sand runs down, you *give the score again*. Am I right or what?"

"I never seen the like." Madeline, the waitress, stood beside Fanning, transfixed, her coffee pot forgotten in her hand. "L.C., you never told me that was how you done it."

The old man looked up and smiled for the first time that morning— the first time, in fact, that Robyn could recall.

"One inexpensive device," he said with a wink, "one less worry. I learned it from Red Barber."

"Red Barber," Robyn repeated. "Red Barber." She shrugged.

Fanning's expression changed. "Red *Barber*. Pardon my French, miss, but for cripes sake you're not going to tell me you never heard of Red Barber."

"I never heard of Red Barber. God dammit. And if you don't stop saying things like 'Pardon my French,' I'm leaving. In fact I am leaving. I don't know why I've wasted your time and mine sitting here listening to this nonsense. I'm sorry your partner left. But I'm sure there are *thousands* of men who'd gladly give their left—" She stopped herself short of the vulgarism that would only shock the old man. She checked her watch and reached for the strap of her shoulder bag.

"Miss Quarrles."

Something in his voice brought her back to attention. She looked up to see Fanning's head bowed. Little white ridges of flesh formed above his knotted brows. His large hands were interlocked around the egg timer.

"Just let me say this before you leave. Just sit still a minute."

She relaxed and waited.

Fanning's throat worked several times before he spoke.

"There was a ball game in 1951. . . ."

Robyn sat silently, but if the old man had a thought connected to that remark, he didn't finish it.

Instead, he looked up at her after a minute and began again:

"You see, what I love about this game of baseball is the, is the human element of it; the stories that come out of . . . now, you take a fellow like Casey Stengel. I don't suppose you ever heard of Casey Stengel. . . ."

"Charles Dillon Stengel. The Old Professor. Manager of the Yankees, 1949 through 1960. Played for Brooklyn, Philadelphia, Pittsburgh, New York, Boston, through 1925. Lifetime batting, two eighty-four." She blurted the statistics, pleased for the chance to drive home to the old guy, however belatedly, that she was not the hopeless dilettante that everyone had taken her for.

But instead of appearing impressed, Fanning only seemed more distracted.

"Well . . . you see I'm not dead sure of those figures, but Stengel, now, you see he had this wonderful way of talking. . . ."

"Stengelese."

Fanning's attention seemed diverted off to the side. He brought his clasped hands up to his face and rubbed his thumbs absently against his mouth.

There was another uncomfortable silence. She was suddenly conscious of her own perfume. Then Fanning cleared his throat and spoke again.

"I look upon this job, you see, as more than a line of work. I guess you might say that I see it as a calling, an opportunity to practice a certain kind of—not to get too fancy about it now—but almost what you would call an art. . . . It's a kind of thing you build up over the years . . . it's like the colors, you see, that you mix. . . . That's why when you lose a fellow like Turtle . . ."

But she was already blurting, "It's just a shame they never discovered you for television!"

She intended it as a supportive remark, but once again the old man's reaction seemed inexplicable. He shuddered like a man emerging from sleep. His eyes widened. He fixed Robyn with a hard, penetrating gaze that frightened her with its intensity.

Now when Fanning spoke, it was in a voice she hadn't heard before.

"I want to tell you something! You're talking about things you don't know anything about! You come into our profession all made up like a Tijuana tart with a smart boy out front clearing the way for you and hell, missy, you don't even intend to last long enough to match the names up with the uniform numbers, you're going to get your puss in the papers and get yourself discovered by some talent scout for the Hollywood movies or a Broadway show! Now don't tell

me that isn't so! You don't think you've been shown the proper respect! Pardon my French! It took me eight damn dog-day years riding
Trailways buses around the Southern Association and glad of it before I got my chance at the big leagues and the boys gave me the
silent treatment for the first six weeks I was up here and every day I
wanted to get down and kiss the earth I stood on! You never heard of
Red Barber! I expect you never saw a corrugated aluminum radio
shack on top of the grandstand where you had to climb up a step-
ladder, and the red dust in your mouth and horseflies on your arm!
Give a colored boy a nickel for a bottle of ice-cold orange soda pop
and throw a carton of Luckies down to the kid who hit a home run!
You never took a room at the YMCA in Nashville nor broadcast a
game from the Sulphur Dell! Oh, you quote me your record-book statistics! Lady, what record books are gonna tell you that the right-field
wall at the Sulphur Dell in Nashville Tennessee sat on a steep bank
two hundred thirty-five feet from home plate? How many of your
record books can tell you about a catcher for the New Orleans Peli-
cans by the name of Del Ballinger? Hah? Who I swear to God nearly
drowned himself in the visitors dugout one day after he caught a pop
foul, the dugout flooded with water from the Cumberland River? My
God, *Stengelese* you tell me! If you knew the stories, the humanity! I
was there and I saw it and I put it on the air! And now you sitting
there with your makeup and your airline ticket in your pocket and
you can't hightail it out of here fast enough, and you have the *temer-
ity,* mind you, to talk about it's a shame they never discovered me for
television! Why, *television killed the Sulphur Dell!* Television killed
the Southern Association! It killed Allen's Alley which was something else I guess you never heard of! And now it's killing the big
leagues! It's where you belong! Sitting on a television show in your
hairdo talking about *Stengelese* and good velocity and locating well!
You don't know the chance you're being offered! To learn something
that's not being taught anymore! To learn how to talk to people in a
way that makes them see all the things they can't see on a television
screen! There are maybe half a dozen men still working this business
who can do the things I can do with a microphone! The television
people are *crazy* to learn how it's done, you see, but what they'll
never understand is . . .''

Fanning's eyes suddenly filled with tears and his face went red; his voice broke off into a violent spasm of coughs. His hand fought its way inside his coat pocket and he brought out a handkerchief. He put the handkerchief to his mouth and coughed deeply into it, his shoulders hunched forward. He was helpless in a breathless series of deep moist racking coughs.

Robyn did not dare move. She sat rigid, her eyes beneath the sunglasses as wide and fixed as the eyes of a woman in a trance.

After what seemed like minutes, L. C. Fanning managed to draw in a long gasping breath. His face was the color of brick on an old building. His wet eyes found Robyn's and his brows drew together again.

"Locating well . . . criminy . . . the person who coined that . . . ought to be shot. . . ."

Still she didn't dare move or speak.

"You've done . . . bad damage. You've done damage you . . . don't even know you've done. You've turned things upside down . . . that you didn't even know were there. . . ."

He reddened and coughed again.

There were a thousand thoughts exploding in Robyn's mind. Part of her wanted to laugh at this preposterous old man and his semi-coherent tirade. A Hollywood movie! Where in the world was he coming from?

But another part of her mind had been mesmerized by the words. She had the eerie notion that they had come gusting out of a dark place on a cold wind.

She had an intimation of a chamber all but closed. An urgency grew in her.

"Why did Turtle leave?" She asked the question before she knew she was going to.

"Because you drove him away, I would imagine." Fanning's eyes danced with a luminous intensity.

"He's only missed one game so far. I mean, how do you know he's really—*gone*?"

"Because I . . . know him. I wouldn't expect you to understand anything about it."

"You say all these things—you make all these assumptions about me without bothering to understand *my* position—"

"Missy, I understand your position—"

"—and yet you want me to stay on?" She ignored the interruption.

"No." Fanning leaned in toward her and lowered his voice. "Let's get that cleared up right now, once and for all. I sure wouldn't want any confusion on that score. I don't want you to stay on."

"Well, good. That puts us back to square one—"

"I'm *asking* you to stay on."

She simply looked at him.

"I can't handle these broadcasts all by myself. I have a —it'd just be too much strain on my voice. You stay on, I guarantee you'll get three to four innings a game, play-by-play. I'll teach you things that'll help you in broadcasting no matter where you go."

"Well, I mean, look, aren't you being a little . . . surely the station will hire somebody else. I'm sure there are thousands of men who'd gladly—"

"They're not going to hire anyone else." There was a cold hatred in his voice now, and as soon as she heard the words she knew he was right. "You got a look at this Spector the same time I did. You know what he's trying to do with these broadcasts, Robyn."

She found herself nodding.

"In fact you're part of his strategy. If you didn't know it then, you know it now. He'd let me hang out there on the air until I couldn't talk above a croak, and he'd use that to drive the ballgames off his station. I know what he's up to."

"If you believe that, why don't you quit?"

Fanning did not show any sign of having heard the question. Instead, he said:

"There will be times I imagine you'll cuss me. I'm not saying I'll be the easiest fellow you ever worked with. It's a matter of you take from it what you need, I take what I need. Nowhere does it say we have to be friends."

Again Robyn found herself bemused. Strange, troubled man in his absurd clothes, half lucid, half deluded, redolent of another time. A piece of outdated merchandise layered with dust. She felt repelled by him. His past and his obsessions clung to him like cigar smoke. They were all in his clothing, on his face. And yet she no longer feared him. He had opened something of himself to her, something of a musty chamber; a compartment where the workmanship still showed;

precision integers no longer understood. He had hinted of a mystical skill he was willing to share—she had glimpsed it already . . . and he needed her. At this point, and although the thought seemed unworthy of her mature consideration, he was the only person in the world who did.

Teweles was the character she feared. His dark presence had been like a threat personified in these last bewildering days. And if it was true that she had, after all, driven him out of the broadcast booth. . . .

"What does your wife think about this calling of yours?" Again, the question leapt from her with no advance warning.

"Eleanor? Eleanor has passed along . . . God rest her soul. . . ."

Already she could see that his intensity was ebbing. The opaqueness returned to his eyes; his voice was lapsing back into its curious distracted tone. She doubted that she would soon see this side of L. C. Fanning again. How strange it was to discover that she had already resolved to stay. . . .

CHAPTER 16

THE SLENDER SILVER ROD WAS vibrating when Frankie Wilde approached Jeffrey Spector's office. The little silver airplanes bobbed and dipped in the invisible turbulence that seemed to be a permanent weather condition around Jeffrey Spector's desk—an eternal hazardous flight plan from nowhere to nowhere.

Spector's child-face followed the bobbing silver planes from the chair behind the desk. His lips were moist and parted. What universes did Spector see that Frankie Wilde missed? Where were those planes flying, what evil cargoes did they carry?

Frankie Wilde's shoulder blades began to bunch at the thought. To cover, he essayed a bit of humor.

"Ground Control to Silver Eagle One," Frankie barked into his fist. "Ground Control to Silver Eagle! You read me, Silver Eagle? Lissen, kid, I'm gonna *talk you down*! You see the stick in front of you? Pull up on it, kid! *Pull up on the stick. . . ."*

Now Spector's mild eyes were focused on him, and Frankie Wilde's shoulder blades were doing a furious rhumba.

"It's an old movie line," he mumbled after a minute, to break the horrible silence.

Spector said nothing. He continued to stare at Frankie Wilde with the mild attention of a circling bird.

"Listen, we got grief on our hands this morning." Wilde prepared to do business. It was ten minutes after nine A.M., and the only other people at the station were invisible; the studio engineers and the on-air morning man. The secretarial staff wouldn't be in for nearly an hour. Best to get the ugly part over with now, and if the laser beam was going to come out of Spector's forehead, at least there wouldn't be any witnesses.

"Turtle Teweles quit." Wilde paused a beat for Spector's reaction. When there was none, he went ahead. "Disappeared yesterday in St. Louis. Fanning called me at home. I called all over hell last night. Nobody knows where he went. You know the poor bastard doesn't even have a family. Fanning thinks he went back to Arkansas. He thinks Turtle was upset over Robyn Quarrles. He says he doesn't know whether it's permanent or whether Turtle will—"

"What else is new?"

Every muscle in Frankie Wilde's body went rigid. This was not the voice of a station manager. This was not even the voice of a socialized human being. This was the voice of a punk who stood over you and went through your pockets while you lay bleeding on the sidewalk. This was the voice of a scavenger, a looter.

"You're destroying this station." Wilde could feel no need to conceal his disgust for Spector any further.

"In order to save it."

Frankie Wilde felt that at any minute, he might start swinging his big arms. There was a trembling anger in his chest. He wanted to reach out and club Jeffrey Spector senseless, smash the silver airplane construction into his skull; leave him steaming and sparking on the rug, a bloodless jumble of transistors and tape. What held him back was not compassion and not decency. What held him back was the almost religious desire to keep working. If he left this job, Frankie Wilde knew, there wouldn't be any others for him. Not in radio. Frankie Wildes were getting to be almost extinct.

So he stood there helpless in front of Jeffrey Spector and went right on being the program director of Radio Station WERA.

"About Turtle Teweles," he said.

"What about him."

"We'll need an explanation. Something to put out . . . a press release—"

"Why?"

"Why? Because he's been with the station for over twenty years and now suddenly he's *gone,* that's why. Vanished. Don't you think people will want some kind of—"

"Not the people I'm aiming at, man."

"Well, for chrissake, Jeffrey, you could at least give him . . ."

"A decent burial" was what Frankie Wilde almost said.

"He's a nonperson, Frankie." There was a gentle quality in Spector's voice now—almost fatherly, in a grotesque sort of way. "Hey. Guys who leave the business never get press releases. You know that, man. That's a custom your generation invented. That's one practice you can't hang on bad Jeffrey Spector, dad."

In the outside corridor someone switched on the antiquated intercom system that piped the WERA on-air sound through the station's business offices. Once again Frankie Wilde's nervous system tightened, by reflex, to the alien, pulsating beat: *"Got-*cha, *got-*cha, *got-*cha, *got-*cha."

Jeffrey Spector abruptly arose from his seat and walked around his desk toward Frankie. He perched his thin frame on the edge of it and clasped his hands in his lap. Frankie sensed that it was some kind of attempt at camaraderie. He recoiled.

"You know something, Frankie?" Jeffrey Spector studied Wilde. "I know right where I'm at in your head. I know where you think I'm coming from. And man, you're wrong."

Frankie Wilde didn't say anything.

"You think I program this station the way I like it. My tastes. Right. Hey, Jeffrey Spector and his buddies *run* it. We blow in and there goes the neighborhood."

Because that was exactly what Frankie Wilde thought, he didn't say anything.

"See, man, that isn't the way it works. I don't have that power. It's the numbers, Frankie. The numbers have the power. My only thing, my only talent, is that *I know the numbers.* I know how to get them. I know how to read them. I know research. I believe in the numbers, Frankie. They're beautiful. Someday if you're interested I'd like to . . ."

Wilde was listening for the concealed put-down, waiting for the sarcastic twist—Spector's trademark. He could detect nothing of the kind in Spector's voice. It made him wary. He didn't say anything.

Jeffrey Spector lifted his pale hands and dropped them again in his lap.

"I mean here it is. This is like the bottom line. If I thought—if the numbers told me—that ballgames were what turned everybody's crank—Jesus, man, I'd do *ballgames*. You wouldn't believe how many ballgames there'd be coming out of this station. Christ, man, I don't control what people want to hear—"

"That's bullshit. You do control it," Frankie Wilde blurted. And then, because he was more disturbed by this side of Jeffrey Spector than by anything else he'd seen of the kid, he spun around and walked out of the office. "I got work to do," was the only amenity he offered the kid.

Behind him, he heard the mild voice:

"You want to know what music I *like,* Frankie? I like—"

He didn't want to hear what music Spector liked, and he rounded the corner, leaving the monster intact, alone in his cave.

CHAPTER 17

THE HOMEWORK GOT HER through the nighttime hours after a game. Got her so sleepy the depression didn't matter anymore. Hotel room, draperies drawn, FM radio tuned to whatever all-night jazz station she could find, room-service tea cooling at her elbow, she stared at the enameled pages of baseball yearbooks and the New York Nats Official Handbook until the names of shortstops merged in her memory with the lineage of Tudor kings. She copied pertinent statistics into the spiral binder that she took with her to the games, an improvised but roughly efficient catalogue of self-reminders.

It was the capsule biographies in the Handbook that usually did it: put her out of her misery, acting like Valium on her freshly wounded sensibilities each night. The bios were litanies of straws in the wind, the eternally hopeful scraps of evidence that some kid might have the magic: . . . "despite 2-4 record, he still had a good '79 season" . . . "had 8.2 inning scoreless streak over next five games" . . . "forced to leave game early after pulling adductor muscle in his leg and exited triumphantly to cheers of the crowd" . . . "raises champion Great Danes which he shows" . . . "selected American Asso-

ciation's best defensive outfielder in a poll of league managers" . . .
"underwent surgery September 2 to repair cartilage damaged in his
left knee" . . . "likes to play cards and listen to music" . . .

God, she thought. And these are men the whole country wor-
ships. . . .

In the mornings there were her exercises, aerobics, to occupy her
first hour. A confirmed early riser, she hated the necessity to fall
asleep late and arise late. She also disliked the regimen of unfamiliar
beds. It all prompted a kind of lethargy, so that she had to will herself into the exercise routine. But she sensed that if she stopped,
something besides muscle tone would slip away from her. Discipline
was a defense against chaos.

After her workout, her shower, her weigh-in (despite her virtual
self-starvation, she had gained a pound and a half since taking this
job; the sedentary life was ruining her) came the grimmest part of her
routine: the soul-baring confrontation with the Sony TC-92.

Robyn brought the tape recorder to each broadcast. She noted the
numbers on the spool digits that bracketed her air time. Each morning
she rewound the tape to those numbers and listened to her voice again
and again, analyzing her tone, her choice of words, her reactions to
Fanning, her overall authority. In another section of the spiral binder
she kept a chart of her progress.

The session with the Sony TC-92 was often the low point of her
day. (Except, of course, for the broadcasts themselves.) Aware of
some approaching malapropism, some break in her voice, some hostile rebuke from the old play-by-play man, she would press the heels
of her hands against her temples, squeeze her eyes shut, and brace
her body. But when the moment had passed, she would hit the re-
wind button and hear it again. And again. Until she had memorized
it, or satisfied herself that she would not fall into a similar trap again.

She hated her voice on the tape. It sounded tinny, pinched, strident. Pushed to its limit.

But even Robyn Quarrles, in the throes of each morning's confrontation with her radio persona, knew that she was improving.

The final obligation of the morning was reading the paper. Robyn
made herself a student of the sports page in all the cities—gaining a
feel for the image of the Nats around the country as well as for the individual characteristics of other National League teams, their stars,

their managers. When a newspaper feature article about her appeared, she read it with interest and mild astonishment, as if the article were about a distant friend. The articles usually described her in some variation of the term "perky." The interviewer usually cited her single status and raised the "controversial issue" of whether Robyn would insist on "equal rights" to the Nats locker room. Invariably, Robyn would answer no.

She wondered whether L.C. Fanning read her press notices. She wondered when the last newspaper feature about L. C. Fanning had been published.

After the morning papers, the day generally stretched like pavement ahead of her. She talked frequently on the telephone with Bobby Bilandic; less frequently with Miriam, who unwaveringly wanted to know when Robyn was to make her "television debut." Other than that, she wandered. Of the twelve National League cities, she was knowledgeable in perhaps four: St. Louis, Los Angeles, San Francisco and—to a lesser extent—New York. For the first few weeks, strolling in strange cities was a source of delight. She made a systematic inspection of museums, galleries, parks. She shopped for shoes, blouses, handbags, suits, scarves . . . shopping, she realized, was an unavoidable affliction of the road.

She sat on sunlit park benches and composed letters to Dunning Pinley—some acerbic, some impersonally "cordial," some tender—and mailed none of them. She took in movie matinees and dance matinees in the cities that offered them.

And always, it seemed, there were three hours until game time.

After a while, wandering in strange cities lost some of its charm.

"Don't talk to me about men," she told Miriam on the telephone. "Don't even ask. No, your daughter is not having herself a high old time. No. Oh, God no, Miriam. Most of them are married, and besides, I couldn't even begin to tell you—no, I haven't. I haven't tried. And neither has he, as far as I—well, I *told* you that whole story, Mother. So don't even—okay?"

It wasn't just that she lacked the time or the connections to date. What distressed Robyn the most (aside from L. C. Fanning's generally dark attitude toward her) was the opaque behavior of the other announcers and writers who formed the Nats' traveling entourage.

They were not so much hostile as oblivious—deliberately so, as was plain to her. They had a way of turning slightly when she approached them in a press box or in a hotel lobby, so that she was unseen, rather than ignored. If she stopped and waited to join the conversation, the voices became a wall, unbroken by pauses long enough for her to join in.

Individually, the members of the baseball press were a mixed bag—from sloppy, cigar-chewing troglodytes whose bellies spilled over their trousers to young, almost intellectual men just a year or so out of college. One member of the latter group, a kid named Fensterwald who always wore a sly grin on his blemished face, gave her the shudders. But the rest seemed decent enough. And in isolated moments several of the men from all age groups managed a sentence or two of pleasantries toward her. The trouble was, these people seldom allowed themselves isolated moments. As a group they were cold, clannish—she was being hazed for breaking some idiot masculine code that was ancient history in the rest of America.

Only Danny Breen treated her with open friendliness.

Well all right. She could endure it for the rest of the summer. If Bilandic parlayed this gig into Miriam's dream of a "television debut," she supposed, the torture might be justified. If he didn't . . . she refused to think about that possibility.

It was the ballplayers themselves who truly intimidated Robyn.

As a beauty contestant and an actress she had spent her share of time in the company of ego-driven men. The Nat players fit no established category. Fanning had not yet invited her to accompany him on his pregame rounds, so she had not yet seen them at close quarters in their battle dress. But she was flying on the Nats plane now. Separate flights, she realized, would only reinforce the aura of division between her and everyone else. Breen was her constant seat companion. The Nat P.R. man seemed always to act as a buffer or a liaison as the circumstances demanded. The players had become aware of her. She was appraised, challenged with looks. She found the looks unnerving. It was not the sexual implications that bothered her. In a peculiar sense the stares were not even personal. What disturbed Robyn was a certain transfixed quality contained in the stares. She had seen it in Vietnam veterans: a stare at once voracious and detached, a wide-eyed look on the faces of men whose interior clocks ticked out a faster time. These were restless, haunted young men whose features were as jutting and extreme as their bodies—flared nostrils and warrior cheekbones; renegade moustaches spilling under patrician noses. Their thick hands, encrusted with rings, drummed the armrests. They smoked savagely and made a feverish kind of small talk in syllables like bullets—except for the silent ones whose heads snapped back and forth to private, earphones rhapsodies.

In their sharply tailored dress-up traveling clothes (jackets were a Tommy Pachelbel rule, though only he wore Husky pants), big shoulders rubbing in the small 707 seats, the Nats players gave the aura of commuters stripped of several civilizing layers. She had always accepted as a truism that athletes were competitive by nature. What she saw here was that the competition was perpetual; infinite. The vulgar camaraderie masked a continuing war of all against all. Here was a planeload of straining stars, gods under pressure, poster boys agonizing at .220; toothy bubblegum-card righthanders obsessed with two losses and three no-decisions in five starts . . . men clinging to the fast track. And the restless eyes missed nothing. Robyn felt no emotion toward these men other than a vague sympathy. For all their bravura and posturing, they seemed as pressured and driven as any stockbroker. But there was a hard, secretive quality about them, and on the flights she kept her distance.

"I want to get to know some of them," she informed Breen at last, during a flight from Atlanta to New York.

The little public relations man was measuring gin into a plastic cup. He held the miniature airline bottle motionless for a moment before he said:

"Well? The plane is your oyster. Go mingle."

"Thanks. I don't think this is the right setting, somehow." In the aisle two gigantic outfielders and a relief pitcher were auctioning off a brassiere purportedly owned by a network situation comedy star.

"Then get Fanning to take you along on his rounds."

"Oh, come on, Breen. You know better than that." She glanced across the aisle and three rows forward where the crown of Fanning's bald head was visible next to a vacant seat. "Since his friend disappeared he's barely spoken to me." She thought immediately of the coffee-shop conversation, but held back from mentioning it.

"I've noticed that. And I've noticed that the rest of the troops haven't exactly snatched you to their bosoms. I am frankly damned,

Robyn, if I understand why you're putting up with all of it. Although I continue to feel that it's an admirable coup, from the station's point of view.''

She didn't answer his question. Instead, she said, ''So. Will you help me?''

''What exactly did you have in mind me doing?''

''Your job. As a public relations man. Get me some interviews.''

''Oh, God. Robyn, you're not going to storm the locker-room doors after all. Consummate all those smoldering fantasies out there in Cincinnati and St. Louis.''

She ran a hand impatiently through her golden hair. ''Come *on!*'' Why was he fencing with her? ''You know I don't mean *that.* Get me—get me some lunch appointments with some of these guys.''

''Lunch appointments.'' Breen rolled his eyes. ''That will be a new experience for many of our stalwarts. The lunch appointment.''

''Oh, look. Everybody's on me about my dumb usage. I don't need your contribution. You know what I mean. I need contacts if I'm going to have any credibility as an announcer.''

''Robyn, if it's *credibility* you're after, let me—''

''I don't want to hear it, Breen.''

''All right. Who would you like to start with?''

She puffed her cheeks. ''Well. Might as well get over the scariest hurdle first. Can you get me Bogart Humphries?''

At the sound of the name Breen winced and cast an apprehensive glance around, as though to make sure the enigmatic slugger were not within hearing.

''God, Robyn. Can't you start with somebody easy? Bogart hates the press. He hates to give interviews. How about Pig Shoat? He's a veteran, been around, he'll give you some good quotes.''

''I don't want *good quotes.* I want to know what makes the Nats tick, and my hunch is that Bogart Humphries has better insights into the team than anybody else. Anyway, he's certainly the biggest star. He's the guy people want to know about.''

''He's not the guy your colleague wants to know about. Judging from past exchanges on the air.''

''That's L.C.'s problem. Try to get him for me, Breen. You can at least ask.''

* * *

There were more sirens than there used to be. Fanning noticed that. A man could get his throat cut walking three blocks from his hotel. And his broadcaster's voice wouldn't save him, either. There were new people on the streets nowadays, and the radios they clutched seemed to be tuned in to alien stations. Turtle had had a funny line to say about that once; he struggled to recall what it was.

Trying to hit the hay long past midnight in a hotel bed, he was conscious now of the sound of radios in other rooms. He couldn't quite make out what the voices were saying (even when he cupped a hand to his ear in the dark, in the way old broadcasters do, to hear their own voices as they might if they were standing outside their bodies); yet he could hear the rhythms, or rather feel them in his forehead, and the rhythms were unlike any that he was used to. He wondered whether the radios were tuned to stations that spoke different languages. He got into the habit of turning on the color television set in his hotel room, even when he got in past midnight. He would sit watching the program with a dull fascination, the screen throwing colors onto his big blank face.

Then he would lie back on the unmade bed with the lights off and try to recall what it was like, coming into a National League city before air travel . . . how many years was it now? Ten? Christ, *twenty-five*?

Oh, God. *Well, you know something, Robyn, you can't be as close to the ballplayers in these days of air travel as you used to. Can I make a real strange observation? Trains. Criminy, in the old days, if Turtle and I are gonna travel with the ball club, we get on that train . . . now, we'd sit in the diner, we'd sit in the bar car, we'd sit in the lounge. We'd sit in the men's room for cripes sake. And where did I learn my baseball? I learned my baseball sitting on trains, with guys like Jimmy Dykes or Leo Durocher or Charlie Grimm, and I'd listen to the newspaper talk, and now, you've got yourself—if you're smart enough to listen, young lady—some very, very fine professors teaching you this game.*

But she knew the game. She was learning to broadcast play-by-play faster than he had ever dreamed possible. That was what tied him up in knots whenever he thought about it. That was what got his bowels to heating up until he thought he'd have to have somebody cut him open. He never learned announcing as fast as she did. It took him years. And when he finally made the big leagues, he was *still* called the Boy Announcer. But the thing that got him the craziest whenever he thought about it, was that *she didn't give a damn.* She didn't care two hoots for the history of the game. Didn't matter to her. She got what she needed to know out of some book, memorized the statistics and went right to work. She sat there in the booth and watched him work and *memorized his style*! Like a vampire! Sat there and sucked the style out of him. And he had to give her a few innings now and then. He didn't have any choice. The voice was beginning to go. He could hear it rasp and fade in his throat now, in the late innings, in the second games of doubleheaders, fading in and out on him like an old tube; so faint now that only he could detect it—the doctor said the pain wouldn't start in till later—but he wanted to have something left by the end of the season. He wanted his Day. So he had to let her have her innings.

Danny Breen stole into the broadcast booth.

"Everything all right, L.C.? Beautiful night. Can I get you anything?"

"You can get the hell out of my sight." Fanning spoke without looking up from his notebook. He was compiling his own broadcast notes from an eclectic stack of magazines, newspapers and box scores. The palette. It was an hour before game time in Atlanta. He had come into the booth to get a little work done in privacy. The girl, he knew, wouldn't show up until right before game time.

"*Language,*" said Breen in mock horror. "Here are tonight's stat sheets."

"Little early, aren't they?"

"We try to do our best. We want to keep you happy, L.C."

"Get lost, Breen."

"Oh, and here's another little cookie I didn't think you'd seen." Breen dropped a copy of the New York *Daily News* in front of Fanning from over his shoulder. The newspaper sent pages of notes and clips scattering.

"You're getting to be a superstar back home, L.C. You're getting more ink than some of our ballplayers. I love it. Gotta scamper. Everything all right?"

Fanning looked at the headline in front of him, boxed in by

Breen's red ball-point pen. Then he pushed his glasses up on his forehead and rubbed his eyes.

The headline read:

FEUDIN', FUSSIN' AND A-FIGHTIN'

The story carried the by-line of Chip Fensterwald. It described, in a tongue-in-cheek style, the on-air squabbling between Fanning and Robyn Quarrles. "Not since the golden age of radio comedy," Fensterwald wrote, "has there been an act to equal the nightly dustups performed by veteran play-by-play man Fanning, who plays George Burns to ex-beauty queen Quarrles's Gracie Allen. 'The Bickersons live' is the motto of some radio cognoscenti who are not normally baseball fans, but who would not miss an episode of 'The Fanning and Quarrles Show.' "

Fensterwald's story then provided a "typical exchange":

Fanning: One out . . . Pendleton on at first . . . Braves' infield in now, looking for Chavez to bunt. . . .

Quarrles: The Braves are taking a big gamble. . . .

Fanning: Oh, the Braves are taking a big gamble. Why are the Braves taking a big gamble? Listen close, now, fans, Robyn's going to explain to us. . . .

Quarrles: Well, it's a big gamble because Chavez can handle that bat. He's been known to swing away in this situation. . . .

Fanning: Swing away?

Quarrles: Yes. Fake the bunt. He's done it before.

Fanning: . . . Miller from the belt, the glance over, and the first pitch to Chavez, he squares around, but it's low for a ball. Robyn, why don't you go check the ticker for the other scores?

Quarrles: You don't think he'll fake the bunt, L.C.?

Fanning: Stay with us, folks, we have a little lesson in fundamental baseball coming up. Here's a quick throw to first, but Pendleton is back in plenty of time. Miller with that good motion. Robyn, I don't know how they play it in the Miss Beauty Queen Puff Softball Game, but in the big leagues you go by percentages. With one man out, score tied, why you want to move that runner over and give your big power man a chance to drive him home. As every baseball fan knows.

Quarrles: Yes, but today I was checking—

Fanning: Excuse me, Robyn, here's Miller into the stretch, he deals, and . . . well, I'll be a son-of-a-biscuit-eater.

Quarrles: Base hit! Chavez at the last minute brought his bat around and fooled everybody! Even L. C. Fanning! Right, L.C.?

Fanning: That'll bring up Shoat.

Quarrles: Should have listened, L.C. I was going through the Nats Official Program Guide today . . . Chavez used the fake bunt three times last year in the minors! Way to go, José!

Fanning: We don't normally cheer up here in the broadcast booth, Robyn.

Damn her.

Breen called Robyn at her hotel suite in New York.

"Don't ask me how I did it, but Humphries says yes."

"Terrific. I'm glad." But she was immediately uncertain.

"There are conditions. He won't talk to you about his relationship with Pachelbel. Or his contract. Or his extracurricular life."

"All right. What else?"

"Well . . . when I mentioned you wanted to have lunch with him, he wanted to know what the word meant."

"I'm not sure I understand."

"Bogart's a night person. He said after the game or not at all."

Robyn thought she knew what that meant. So did Breen, judging from his voice.

"Look, I hope he realizes that this is a—"

"This is your idea, whatever it is. You know his reputation. I can only wish you luck. At least he didn't stipulate his penthouse."

Breen gave her the address of a Second Avenue steakhouse. She had heard of it: overdecorated, overpriced, a hangout for athletes and the people who like to follow athletes. "He said for you to meet him there an hour and a half after the game. Just ask for his table."

"I gather you didn't tell him I'm a vegetarian."

"Somehow, I don't think it would have gotten through."

*   *   *

That night Robyn wore a pastel linen suit, high heels, and a color-ful scarf to the broadcast booth—an ensemble several notches more festive than the jeans or pantsuits she had become accustomed to wearing. Despite her trepidation over how the encounter with Humphries might go, Robyn's spirits were lighter than they had been in weeks. This night was to be an adventure—a chance to at least play at the social whirl. Better than a hotel room and the spiral binder.

For the occasion she had also taken down her golden hair (she had been pinning it up in a practical bun) and combed it out so that it lay about her shoulders. Fanning gave her a startled up-and-down when she walked into the booth. But as usual, the old announcer offered no commentary on her appearance.

Humphries managed only one hit in the game, but it was a two-out triple off the center-field wall in the sixth inning that drove home two runs. Humphries scored on a Carty single that followed, thus ac-counting for all the Nat runs in a 3–2 victory over San Francisco.

Two and one-half hours after the game Robyn reclined with her arms folded in Humphries's booth at the steakhouse, a dim, tun-nellike establishment where tablecloths, shirt cuffs, and chrome gleamed under unseen light. She nursed a weak rum drink through a straw and concentrated on the muffled thuds of the background music, keeping her eyes deliberately random.

Everyone was looking at her. Women as well as men. For once, she knew, it was not because her sensational looks singled her out. Every woman in this place could have been a beauty contest winner. Probably many were. No, this time she was under scrutiny because she was sitting at Bogart Humphries's table. The regulars were sizing her up. Trying to figure where she fit in Bogart's constellation.

She had feared trouble only once in the forty-five minutes since she had arrived, punctual to the Great Man's specifications. A ball of fire had moved in on her as soon as she had sat down—clearly the only customer in the place not wise to the significance of where she sat.

The guy wore a white stetson pushed forward on his nose and a cowboy shirt opened halfway down the front, and he introduced him-self as "Wild Dave Chabak, scrappy second-sacker for the Giants?"

"Oh, yes," she had replied in a neutral voice, against the possibility that his approach might be in the line of player to announcer.

"And I led all Western Division infielders in extra-base hits last season? Four years over three hundred? Led the league in assists? You ever make whoopee with a league leader, sugar?"

She had folded her red fingernails under her chin and smiled up at him sweetly. Conversation in the vicinity ebbed.

Robyn was satisfied that this was not a professional approach. At least not in the profession she worked.

"I've read about you, Dave. I think you also led the league in strikeouts, didn't you?" Her voice was sibilant, husky.

The cheesy grin on the athlete's face flickered a bit. "Got to strike out some when you aim for downtown, darlin'."

"Well, I'd work on cutting down on your swing, Dave. Because you just struck out again."

It got an *"Olé!"* of a laugh from the people standing within ear-shot, and Dave decided not to pursue the subject. To Robyn's relief. Had Bogart Humphries happened upon their little tête-à-tête, she was pretty sure he would have thrown Wild Davey Chabak and all his statistics through the restaurant window.

She was just starting to count the various aromas of after-shave when a beringed hand the size of an overshoe descended with a slap upon the tabletop before her. An instant later the entire booth shuddered under the impact of Bogart Humphries's bulk. He came to rest beside her.

"All *right*," said Bogart Humphries.

At least thirty pairs of female eyes had turned upon the booth now, like searchlights.

"Hello, I'm Robyn Quarrles," Robyn began, sounding asinine to herself, but the Nats outfielder was already engaged in a ceremony of palm slaps and cheek kisses with the stylish patrons who pressed in from the surrounding dimness.

"My main *man*," Humphries said a number of times.

He was a famous dresser. Tonight he had chosen a gray silk suit with chalk stripes, an effect almost prim had it not been offset by a black shirt and white necktie.

His head swiveled about between his shoulders without visible benefit of a neck—an extraordinary piece of workmanship, Robyn thought, like a heavy block of sculpted wood, the face broad-featured but delicate. A trimmed moustache sat correctly above his lips. Humphries's eyes were free from the hunted quality that Robyn had seen in his teammates. Heavy-lidded, they seemed sly in a sleepy sort of way.

Now those eyes were on her.

"What yo' want from this nigger, girl?"

She froze, even as she realized this was exactly the effect he wanted. The slurred country-boy syllables, the impassive stare—Humphries was probing her tolerances, establishing a quick fix as to whether she was worth his time. Would people in this self-important business ever stop testing her? A wave of anger rose up and dispelled her confusion. With the anger came inspiration.

She drew in a breath to keep her voice under control and said through a fixed smile:

"That depends, Mr. Humphries, on whether you are a *regular* nigger or a jive-ass nigger."

In her ensuing flash of panic, Robyn's mind backpedaled all the way to childhood; to a movie cartoon she had seen in which the woodpecker wound his arm to propeller velocity and fetched the bulldog a mighty blow across the chops—only to watch in horror as his own arm began to vibrate like a gong, the bulldog unfazed.

Bogart Humphries slowly turned to ice. For several seconds he sat as motionless as a granite statue, hunched forward ever so slightly, his brown eyes studying her as though to be absolutely certain she had said what he'd heard. Her own skin grew numb. She wondered which of his hands would come up to sweep her away from the booth like a stray crouton—the right or the left.

Then Bogart Humphries laughed.

He threw back the massive head and Robyn caught a glint of a gold tooth as Humphries hurled a guffaw, rich and deep as a note from a French horn, at the ceiling. He stopped, sobered, looked at Robyn, and roared again.

"Son of a *bitch*!" he bellowed. "*Reg*ular nigger or a . . ."

His howls cascaded throughout the steakhouse. Soon the people standing near the booth were laughing along—bending at the waist, clutching their guts, stamping their feet. None of them could possibly have heard the cause of Humphries's convulsions—but Robyn didn't consider that, because now she was laughing, too.

The tension of the last weeks welled between her temples and spilled out of her with the force of a flood. Giggling, she started to fish in her shoulder bag for a handkerchief, then gave up. Head back, her arms crossed at the wrists in her lap, she welcomed the release of the laughter. Her cheeks were hot and wet. Soon she felt herself gasping for breath.

She realized that she was sobbing.

She seized her napkin and mopped her eyes, gulping air, hoping that Humphries wouldn't notice in the dim light. But Bogart was having his own problems getting under control.

"Sweet Jesus," he gasped, mopping one eye with the corner of a monogrammed handkerchief. His shoulders convulsed once more. "You hit my funny bone," he said offhandedly, in a low drawl. "I'd soon kick the ass of any man and most women said 'jive-ass nigger' to my face."

"Oh, that's me. Miss Hilarity. Stick around, I've got a million of 'em." She had rested her head against the cushion of the booth. Her better judgment told her to be on her guard with this mercurial man, lest her next remark hit a bone not quite so funny. But the laughing bout, so near to hysteria, had produced in her an afterglow. She had desperately needed the release. Now she felt in harmony with the world. Yet, strangely, she sensed that she could burst into tears at any moment. Her breath was still shaky.

Above and around them, the musical beat went, "*Got*-cha, *got*-cha, *got*-cha, *got*-cha."

"So, uh"—Humphries folded his large hands together on the table and cocked his head—"what was it you wanted with me, now that you done crapped on the color of my skin. Honey, bring old Bogart Humphries about two fingers of Johnny Walker Red neat, and bring a split of champagne for the lady here." This last without bothering to look at a mesh-stockinged waitress who had hovered respectfully at Humphries's shoulder through the major part of his laughing fit.

Despite herself, Robyn was flattered. In fact, she feared that her eyes would brim again. Who else in the baseball fraternity had so much as offered her a cup of coffee since she arrived?

"Look, I don't really—I mean, this is probably a stupid idea. I don't have a list of *questions* to ask you or anything"— she took another gulp of air, and again her breath caught—"it's just that I've been on the announcing team for more than a month now, and I don't seem to be making any headway with anybody . . . I just thought it would be a good idea if I got to know some of the players; sort of opened up the lines of communication. . . ." Her voice trailed away under his opaque stare. She shrugged one shoulder and waited for what she was pretty sure would be a miserable silence.

Bogart Humphries reached inside his silk jacket and withdrew a pair of silver spectacles. When he put them on, their effect changed his entire face. The stolid features became almost owlish.

"Damn, woman, your eyes look like a pair of ice cubes in a bloody mary," he remarked, gripping the silver frame with a thumb and finger.

"I'm sorry, I've got some sunglasses somewhere. . . ." She turned toward her purse.

"Hey. Cool *that*." She felt the light pressure of his fingers on her arm. "That was just me agitatin' you a little bit. That was just *jive-ass*." They both laughed again.

"Naw." Bogart Humphries's voice was couldn't-care-less casual as his eyes roamed the establishment. "Some of the guys on the club think you doin' a helluva job."

That did it. In an instant she was bawling like a schoolgirl.

"Now. Hey. Shit. Here." A heavy arm coiled about her shoulders, drawing her in. She turned her face toward the warm hollow formed by his arm and chest, grateful to hide her face from the attention of the crowd.

From inside the cove she blubbered:

"Oh, God . . . I'm a mess . . . your friends . . . 'll think I'm drunk . . . I've got to get out of here. . . ."

"Bull *shit* on that noise. First you call me a jive-ass nigger. Then you go messin' my fine clothes. Now you say you gone walk out the do'. What kind of number you tryin' to run on the Hump here?"

With her free hand she groped for her bag, found the flap, rummaged for her sunglasses. She slid them on and then withdrew from Humphries's light embrace. She filled her lungs with air and ran her fingers back through her hair several times. Poise, she thought. And: dignity.

"I know you think you're dealing with a crazy woman, Mr. Humphries. I know I've embarrassed you in front of your friends—"

"Don't pay no 'tention to them. Bunch of chumps." Humphries shot a preemptive glance about the booth; quite suddenly, no one was staring.

"—but I can assure you I have been under a tremendous amount of pressure these last few weeks. And it's like . . . when I heard you say that about the guys on the club . . . I mean, nobody, but *nobody,* has so much as—"

"I didn't *say* the guys on the club." Humphries was talking casually again, hooded eyes scanning the room at large. "I said *some* of the guys on the club. Some other ones think you're messin' with the *natural order,* you understand what I'm sayin'."

"Well, the point is, it's just awfully difficult to do my job in this . . . climate, and I thought I might help myself if I got acquainted with some of the players."

The waitress placed a champagne glass and a silver bucket in front of her. Inside was a small bottle of Mumm's on a bed of ice.

"Mmmmmm." Humphries reached across his drink, extracted the bottle and pulled the cork as though it were a size too small. The champagne foamed into her glass. "Old Fuddy-duddy ain't cuttin' you in on the action."

"If you mean Fanning . . ." she laughed again. "Well, I mean after all, he is the Dean, isn't he? I guess I can't really expect him to get used to the situation overnight."

Humphries grimaced. "Fanning. Let me tell you something about Fanning. He doesn't know squat about the game of baseball. He's as bad as the rest of 'em. They all sit up there like the King of Siam every night with nuthin' between them and the ballgame, and the load of bull crap they lay down . . . they don't know what they're lookin' at! They don't know nothin' about a game's *rhythms!* They don't know every game's got its own special moment, dig, that *defines* all that's happened before it and all that's gonna happen after it. A ballgame, shit, you gotta feel the rhythms workin'. I move two steps this way and one thing might happen. Everything you do affects the ballgame's *chain,* you understand. Knowing the right dam *instant* to step out of the batter's box. Knowing right when to jive with the fans. Knowing when *not* to throw on a man, set the dude up. Whole thing about *base* stealing. It's like a dance. Hell, it's *beautiful* what goes on . . . nobody talks about that. Bunch of chumps."

Humphries fell silent abruptly and took a quick sip of his drink. He seemed embarrassed about having made a speech.

"Bunch of chumps," he said again.

Robyn was mesmerized. She had never heard anyone describe baseball in such rhapsodic terms. Part of her mind was aware that as Humphries talked, some of the country-boy affectations fell away from his speech, until the deep rich voice assumed a cadence of its own. Nothing she had ever read about the man had prepared her for this depth of intelligence or feeling.

Nevertheless, her sense of loyalty (ah, Miriam!) tugged at her.

"Now wait a minute. That's all very lovely. But I've heard L. C. Fanning talk about rhythms. It seems to me he tries for something extra in his descriptions. . . ."

"You're defendin' the man that's messin' you over."

"Well, I'm trying to be fair."

He pursed his lips. "Fair. Well, I'll say this for old Fuddy-duddy. Least he doesn't go on about how much money the players are makin'. Least he doesn't throw down on the guys that ain't pro-ducin'. Hell, some of these announcers, you'd think they didn't know the ballplayers had radios in the dugout."

"So what is it—"

"What it is, the dude don't know *when to shut his mouth*. Hell, half the time I can't tell whether he's callin' the game I'm playin' in or one that got played twenty-five years ago. He's off in his own world, see. He hasn't moved with the times. 'Course most of these guys haven't. That's why I don't fool with interviews anymore; all these writers want to do is talk money or gossip. Or else they want to tell the colored boys how to behave. You understand. That's one reason a lot of the players were happy to hear you replaced that other guy, *Frog* or whoever he is."

"I didn't replace—"

" 'Cause, yeah, he knew his baseball, but the sucker was still fightin' the Civil War, man. Now I'll tell you how it is with you. Your strong suit is that you try to *understand the game*. Players can get behind that. Don't let them fool you, but they know who you are and what your rap is. They don't miss nothin'."

"What's my weak suit?"

Humphries gave a cynical snort.

"That you're *stuff*. It's not just like you're a woman. Hell, you're A-number-one choice. You're a god dam' prize-winnin' piece of goods, see. And that cuts a lot of ice with the troops. They're just not gonna *deal* with you the same as if you had tobacco juice comin' down your shirt."

She smiled and sipped her champagne. For the first time in weeks she felt beautiful. The bobbing, laughing people around her were beautiful. Bogart Humphries—*surprise*—was beautiful. The music—"*Got*-cha, *got*-cha, *got*-cha, *got*-cha"—made her want to dance. Dunning would never have brought her to a place like this. But she belonged here, among good bodies in good clothes. Perfume and wristwatches. She was among the *elect* and the exhilaration lifted her. L. C. Fanning and his cigars, the dirty little press booths and the flaccid hostile men who haunted them—all receded back into the night.

She had earned this evening. She was making contact after all. She had partly won a battle she didn't even know she was fighting—a battle for the respect of the *players*. Suddenly her future did not seem so hopeless. She could see herself on network television in a year. . . .

She raised her glass to Humphries, who was studying her. In her euphoria she convinced herself that her earlier flood of emotions had drawn the two of them together as kindred spirits. Created a bond. After all, Bogart Humphries was a loner, the same as she—a man just as misunderstood by the sportswriting crowd; a man who battled his own private demons. That much had been evident in his own flood tide of laughter.

Feeling safe in her presumptions, she cocked an eyebrow at Humphries. "And what about you, Bogart? Does that cut a lot of ice with you?"

Immediately she knew she had stepped in a forbidden place. Humphries's expression went opaque. She sensed curtains closing.

When Humphries spoke again, his voice was back in its country-boy accents that now seemed even more remote to her than ever.

"Shee-it, girl. I'm just a jive-ass nigger dumb-chump ballplayer. Now'f this here interview is over with, I got to keep an appointment with a certain friend of mine."

Leaving the steakhouse, Robyn tried to convince herself that the meeting with Humphries had been a success. He had been open with her, even sympathetic. He had brought her welcome news—that her efforts were being taken seriously by at least some people on the outside, people whose opinions counted. And she had gained entry, however peripheral, to an attractive crowd of people. On her next visit she wouldn't be a total stranger.

Still, she couldn't suppress a wince when she turned back, at the door, and saw that Bogart Humphries's "certain friend" was a blonde every bit as beautiful as herself.

CHAPTER 18

THIS TIME WHEN FRANKIE Wilde walked into Jeffrey Spector's office, his shoulder blades weren't dancing. This time, Frankie Wilde felt pretty good.

The kid was perched behind his desk as usual, dabbing at the tiny silver airplanes. Making them bob along on their shuddering little arcs from nowhere to nowhere.

This morning the airplanes looked to Frankie Wilde like 747s.

"Talk of the town, Jeff," he sang out. The boy behind the desk lifted his face and held it for an instant, an animal testing a new scent in the wind.

Then Jeffrey Spector's pale lips stretched in a grin.

"Talk of the town," he repeated.

Frankie Wilde helped himself to a chair. He opened a button on his new navy-blue designer blazer—the narrow-lapel look was back; he never thought he'd live to see that again—and swung a leg over the chair's arm. The leg was encased in denim. Frankie had caved in and bought himself a couple pairs of jeans. They took off years. They made him feel mellow.

Spector wasn't wearing jeans today, he noticed. Ah, well. To each his own.

"Blitzkrieg, is what I'd call it," he continued. There was warm coffee in his belly and there were ratings figures in on his desk, figures he knew Spector had seen. There was no harm in showing a little humility. A man is never too old to learn in this business.

"Yes," said Spector's voice. "We are doing well, Frankie. We are ahead of my timetable, if you want to know the truth."

"Great." Frankie Wilde reached over and slapped his palm down on Spector's desk. The impact made the silver planes vibrate. He allowed a warm smile to cross his big puss.

"You showed me something, Jeff. You brainy bastard. I'll admit it. I wasn't hot about the Quarrles bit at the beginning. But, Christ, these numbers . . ."

The numbers showed that audiences were starting to flock to the Nat baseball broadcasts on WERA.

And the beauty part was the demographics. A close examination of the rating charts indicated that it wasn't the old forty-nine-plus listeners, the "core" group for radio baseball, that was on the rise. These people seemed to have been driven away by the new announcing format.

No, these new hordes were kids. The prime buying group. Eighteen-to-twenty-fours, with a healthy sprinkling of twenty-five-to-thirty-fours. Clearly, they weren't tuning in to hear baseball. They were tuning in to enjoy the nightly warfare between Robyn Quarrles and L. C. Fanning.

In actual share points, WERA had not yet drawn close to its targeted rivals. But the July figures indicated a recognizable upward curve. Everyone in town knew that the momentum was with WERA. And best of all, the increases were rippling backward, into the station's drive-time music programming.

"The numbers are encouraging, Frankie. But we have to keep the momentum going. I thought you might like to see phase two."

Spector reached below his desk and drew up an elegant zippered folder made of soft leather. He placed it flat on his desk and, as Wilde arose to get a better look, ran the gold zipper in three satisfying *rorrrrrrp*'s.

When he opened the folder, Frankie Wilde whistled through his teeth.

"Jesus, Jeff. Those have to cost a bundle."

Frankie recognized the bold cartoonish sketches for what they were: full-page newspaper ad layouts.

As Spector silently peeled the sheets aside, Frankie saw that the campaign had a common motif: Fanning and Quarrles, their faces in photograph and their bodies in cartoon, engaged in a series of comic confrontations.

The sheet on top of the stack showed the two of them facing each other in sitting positions, roller skates on their feet, each with a microphone in one hand and the other hand held to the head, as though they had just collided. The second sheet depicted Fanning in an umpire's garb chin-to-chin with Quarrles in a baseball cap, Nat jersey, and short shorts. The third sheet portrayed the two of them in Kentucky moonshiner dress, aiming their mikes at one another like long rifles. And so on.

Wilde could see the blue-pencil outlines of the campaign's unifying headline slogan, drawn lightly onto each sheet:

FEUDIN', FUSSIN' AND A-FIGHTIN'

And, under it, a paste-up of the copy text:

> The hottest scrap in baseball is not taking place on the field. It's up in our WERA broadcast booth, where each night the wackiest, sassiest, most unlikely play-by-play combo in the major leagues is knocking the sox off Nat fans and nonfans alike. (Not to mention each other.) Spend a couple of hours with L. C. Fanning as the Veteran and beauteous Robyn Quarrles as the Newcomer as they bring you their freestyle play-by-play of Nats Baseball, on New-Era WERA.

That seemed a little potent even for Frankie Wilde in his new hip mood. He raised an eyebrow at Spector.

"Kind of hitting 'em over the head with the controversy aspect, aren't we? I mean, it's *great,*" he hastened to add when Spector's eyes went cold. "Just the ticket. Great way to sell the new image. By the way," he went on quickly, still trying to get rid of the ice that had formed on Spector's expression, "what kind of loot will a campaign like this cost? It looks to me like you're really gonna saturate the market."

Spector zipped up the soft-leather folder. *Rorrrrp. Rorrrrrp. Rorrrrrp.*

"It will cost," he said, bending to arrange the folder once again beneath his desk, "a little more than we are paying you a year, Frankie."

Frankie Wilde's shoulder blades were already starting to do their ass thing again when Spector's right hand reemerged over the top of the desk. In the hand was a small wooden soldier.

"That's the reason I wanted you to drop in this morning, Frankie," Jeffrey Spector said in an abstracted sort of way. He placed the small wooden soldier on the desk top. Frankie Wilde found himself short of breath.

"I'm a bottom-line man, Frankie. And frankly I think this ad campaign is going to produce more tangible results for this station than you will produce in your capacity as program director. I mean, there aren't really any programs left to direct, are there?"

Frankie Wilde did not wait to watch the wooden soldier topple. He heard its body strike the desk as he was halfway through the door. The tears in his eyes were not so much for himself as for a kind of country he knew, one that had been conquered by wooden soldiers and tiny silver airplanes.

Bogart Humphries restored a measure of laughter and delight to Robyn Quarrles's life.

The morning after their meeting at the steakhouse, he surprised her with a gift of a dozen yellow roses delivered to her hotel suite. The accompanying note waxed self-critical, in a humorous way, of his manners the previous night—terminating their conversation so abruptly. Robyn placed the roses in a vase and deposited the note in a wastebasket. The encounter had been lovely for her, regardless of Humphries's subsequent romantic obligations. She did not wish to dwell on the way it had ended.

A couple of hours later the telephone call came.

It was Humphries. Speaking in his most urbane accents, he wanted to know whether Robyn would be interested in attending (of all things) an auction of stained glass at a gallery that afternoon on the Upper East Side.

"That," she blurted, with delight in her voice, "is the *last* thing I'd expect—" she stopped, aware of the ugly presumption.

Humphries finished the thought for her. "—a country nigger to be interested in?"

Robyn clenched her teeth, but managed to keep her voice light.

"Well, actually I was thinking of *ballplayer*."

There was a silence. Then came Humphries's rich laughter. "Shee-it! I'm two strikes in the hole and I ain't even lifted the bat off my shoulder."

The early afternoon was lovely; cool under a thunderhead that was making its way up over Manhattan from the southwest—the World Trade towers were in shadow but the Chrysler Building still glinted in sunlight. The day carried the first redolence of autumn, and Robyn was pleased that Humphries (again, contrary to his public image as an addict of fast expensive cars) suggested that they walk. He turned up in a sober dark business suit, cut with far less flamboyance than his silken costume of the previous night. He actually wore a homburg.

Humphries's subtle disguise deflected recognition as they strolled Fifth Avenue on the Central Park side, although several people turned to stare admiringly at the splendid couple—the tall, lean, fashionable woman and the imposing, clearly athletic man.

As they walked, Humphries—with an air of casually remarking on weather, the front page, the stock market—displayed a strain of intellectual curiosity and uninflected speech. For some reason, the South Bronx happened to be on his mind, and he constructed, with half-facetious disclaimers, a thread of metaphor that linked the years of speculation, capricious highway construction, decline of building stock, and cynical real estate exploitation in that gruesome wasteland of rubble with a more generalized tendency to dismantle, plough over, repave, or replace (all in the name of "expansion" or "renewal") an entire cultural arsenal of edifices that had come to represent, in the mass consciousness, continuity and order.

Among these edifices, Humphries named Ebbets Field and the Polo Grounds.

"I was just a scrawny little shirttail growing up in Georgia when they took out the Polo Grounds," he said, grasping her hand lightly as they crossed Seventy-ninth Street, "but I'll tell you something: it *hurt*. Hell, the Polo Grounds *meant* something, even to an ignorant colored kid in the Deep South. It was a people's park. You could tell that by lookin' at a photograph of it in a magazine. The way the stands crowded right up on top of the field, like you could get to *know* the players if you came out every day. That's the way we thought about it. Well, I never played in any Polo Grounds. Never played on a team that gave much of a god damn about the fans, and a lot of times I suspected it was vice versa. It's almost like the fans are out there to get into their particular number, and the ballplayers are there to do their thing, and if any of 'em happens to notice the other side, why, that's nice, too." The disclaiming jauntiness had left Humphries's voice now, supplanted by a bitter tone.

"I could almost close my eyes," said Robyn, her head bent forward in amused thought, "and make believe I was listening to L. C. Fanning."

"What? Old Fuddy-duddy?" Humphries squeezed air between his teeth. "No, Robyn, I'll tell you the difference between me and old Fuddy-duddy. The difference is, Fuddy-duddy *thinks the Polo Grounds is still standin'*." His sudden application of a comic twang made her laugh, although she felt disloyal. "Fuddy-duddy, see, nobody ever *told* him it done changed. Now me"—and, just as abruptly, Humphries's voice was devoid of accent—"I'm a realist. I may think about the past, but I don't dwell on it. I make a helluva good buck based on the fact that they tore down those little old parks and put up a god damn file cabinet to store people in and changed the game around to where every team's a damn corporation. Flushing Stadium is my *office,* you see; it's where I do my thing. Folks want to pay the price of admission, I don't care whether they boo, cheer, get drunk, freak out on the crazy scoreboard, or fall in love with the rubber chicken."

The disturbing edge had returned to his voice, and so she did not dwell for longer than a second on the curious phrase of his— "Flushing Stadium is my *office*"—she thought fleetingly that she'd heard it before, in another context . . . but now they were crossing Fifth Avenue at Eighty-second, and she lost all thought of baseball parks and the South Bronx. For a few hours at least, New York was a city and not just an abstraction, a point on an itinerary, a necessary construct of taxi routes and broadcast "facilities," and she was in the company of a magnetic and provocative male. She meant to enjoy herself.

Humphries bid with understated good judgment at the auction, managing not once to draw the small, elegant gathering's attention to himself. They left with the ballplayer in possession of two matching miniature Tiffany lamps in an emerald and gold motif.

In the ensuing weeks they saw one another often. They dined together after some games (but by no means all; Humphries maintained an active social file in each National League city). More often, Robyn accompanied him on his daytime sojourns through out-of-the-way pockets of the various towns as he indulged his passion for antiques. Sometimes they saw a movie or even escaped to a local sports center for tennis—despite Robyn's calisthenics program, she could feel her body softening, and the fast exercise was a godsend.

Always, by tacit agreement, they took care to keep their relationship out of the public eye. They avoided the mainstream jock bars and restaurants, seldom traveled together to a rendezvous site. The last thing Robyn wanted was publicity over an "affair" with Bogart Humphries. Besides, although he never mentioned the fact, she was aware that he had a wife and children living somewhere—California, if memory served. If Humphries wanted to play the bachelor game on the road, that was entirely his business, but she was not about to become a part of the Humphries legend.

She found him a witty and agreeable companion, if bewildering sometimes in his rapid changes of mood and syntax—a far more complex man than the stolid, vaguely sullen and threatening superstar that the sportswriters knew.

In fact, their only serious disagreements came over the subject of what Humphries called "the chumps with the typewriters," a category that included L. C. Fanning.

"The man has practically told the world on the air that he thinks you are a clown," he told her, leveling a ringed finger in front of her eyes. "That plus the fact that he's losing whatever grip he had on the games. I can't tell you about your business, understand. But if it was me, I'd put the dude down once and for all. Then I'd take the mike and never let the som'bitch have it back again. That's how you get ahead in the broadcast world, the way I understand."

"You're right," she answered. "You can't tell me about my business." Some lingering instinct for affection, or tolerance, or perhaps even pity prevented her from feeling real anger toward Fanning—especially now that, through Humphries, she had a social valve.

But the disagreement seemed minor in light of their overall friendship—a friendship that deepened by such imperceptible degrees, and through such mellifluous, summery nuances, that she was hardly aware of a contradiction in her own definition of the relationship when one evening he tendered, and she unhesitatingly accepted, an invitation to share his bed.

CHAPTER 19

TIME BROKE DOWN, STALLED. July lay on the earth, a damp thickness of steam. Doubleheader days, those high orange saxophone Sundays he had once loved, now inched into headachy twilight as the curved black blade of the grandstand shadow edged across home plate toward the pitcher's mound. On doubleheader Sundays the waxed litter piled up in the outfields until the players sloughed through it, hot dog wrappers in their spikes. He was aware of fist-fights in the stands; of glazed fans peering through slit eyes over slick bellies. While the scoreboards, flashing manic streaks and colors, lost their minds in a blowout of preprogrammed circuitry.

Fanning had thought that Turtle might appear again. For weeks following Teweles's disappearance in St. Louis he had instructed the engineer to keep active a third microphone in the booth. Turtle was AWOL. Turtle was thinking it over. Turtle had simply wandered away for a while, to take stock and purge the demons. It was happening all the time now with the athletes themselves. You'd hear of this or that fellow jumping the team . . . in the old days it would have been a scandal, instant suspension from the league. Now, the man-

agers more or less accepted it, only grateful that the hiatusing superstar hadn't cracked in the clubhouse, smashing a teammate's sound
system, shredding comic books, breaking toys. Turtle would be back.
In time for Fanning's Day.

Meanwhile, the season pushed its way toward that climactic moment, an inchworm sliding toward the horizon. His throat was giving
him hell.

An afternoon game in Chicago. Robyn Quarrles working the middle innings:

"A base hit here would score one run and possibly two . . .
Bogart looking for his first hit of the day; he's been bamboozled
twice by that sharp-breaking Snyder fork ball . . . and *here's* Bogie
lining the two-two pitch over the second baseman's head—and it *falls*
for a single, *Shoat* coming in to score, Carty *wisely* holding at third
as Crowell *rockets* a one-hop throw into the infield. So, L.C., the
Nats have *one* of those runs back . . . and Humphries is doing what
he knows he *has* to now . . . *short*ening his stroke on a two-strike
count and just *going with the pitch* instead of trying to *golf* it over the
wall."

Fanning with a jerk of the head, bestirring himself from what
might have been sleep:

"That's wonderful, Robyn. I didn't know that mind-reading was
one of the things you did now."

Robyn: "*Mind*-read—"

Fanning: "How do you know, not to take anything away from
your style, Robyn, what exactly it is that Bogart Humphries knows
he has to do?"

Robyn: "He *told* me, L.C. Bogart said he had to work on cutting
down his strike zone on a two-strike pitch. . . ."

Fanning didn't pursue the question any further, but gave Robyn a
long, penetrating look. At the end of the inning, back in the press
lounge getting a beer, he spotted the kid Fensterwald from the *Daily
News* and recalled a remark that Fensterwald had passed along to him
a couple of nights ago:

"Better watch your new sidekick, L.C. She's gettin' to know some
of the players better'n you are."

A wave of nausea hit him with such force that he almost took a
step forward and cried out. He put his hand out to a chair back and

steadied himself, breathing in short bursts through the mouth. His hand was shaking so that he had to set the beer cup down.

In a sudden burst of vision, Fanning had seen himself for what he truly was: an old and foolish man in a world being taken over by the young.

He told her. Bogart said he had to work on cutting down his strike zone. . . .

Fanning had never taken her down on the field with him. Never exposed her to any of the players. But of course she couldn't keep away. Probably a hot-to-trot number who'd slept with half the team by now. Laughing at him, as likely as not, along with them—behind his back.

He put his wrist up to his mouth to hold down something on the verge of spilling out. It didn't, but he had to keep his fingertips against the wall going back to the booth. Things were coming together in his mind. Falling into place. Certain pieces. Evidence adding up. He was a man awakening from a long and dangerous dream.

That night Fanning stood in front of the bathroom mirror in his hotel room, a glass of room-service Scotch in his hand. His pants down around his ankles; he'd been fighting constipation through the late afternoon.

His foul breath wheezed out in gasps, fogging the mirror glass. Through the fog he could behold, with the clarity of dark loathing, just what he had become: the face that Robyn saw.

The yellow teeth. The latticework of red veins in the nose. The splotchy brown freckles high on the forehead where the blond forelock had once dropped. The crescent moon of soft fat now, under his chin, the pouches under the eyes. Fanning: a big swollen Stromberg-Carlson console radio set with the tubes wearing out. Ready to be unplugged and thrown away for scrap.

Robyn had come into his life like a judgment. She mocked him with her youth. She forced him to confront the widening distance between himself and the players he covered.

There had not been that great a distance the last time he looked. The last time he looked had been a long time ago.

*   *   *

"Hi."

It was a blistering afternoon at Wrigley Field, the very wind hot off Lake Michigan, the stands two-thirds empty. He sat as usual, an hour before game time, alone in the broadcast booth. His back to her, he was copying figures into a thick spiral notebook. He jerked at the sound of her voice, swinging around enough to glimpse her out of the corner of his eye. He turned immediately back to his work.

He had on a plaid sport jacket of almost belligerent yellow design. Electric-blue slacks. His customary white loafers. Beside him, against the wall, rested his aluminum net.

"I brought you a beer. Heine Meine? Isn't that what you drink?" Robyn peered down at the steep incline below her. She pointed one leather-booted toe at the lower concrete step. A shopping bag dangled from her left wrist. On the floor between her and Fanning she noticed several wads of Western Union ticker and a tipped-over Styrofoam cup with cigarette butts in it.

Instantly, Fanning was on his guard. She seldom if ever dared to address him off the air. But he did not seem to notice as she set the fresh cup down beside his arm.

"I really shouldn't be encouraging you to drink this stuff. It's *awful* for your system. Someday I'll bring you a thermos of yogurt and banana and crushed ice. You'll love it."

Her voice was light, almost festive. Fanning rolled his eyes about, a man expecting an ambush.

He glared for a moment at the frothing wax cup. He could use an ice-cold brew. He lifted a hand to pick it up; brought the hand instead to the rim of his glasses. Then he resumed his copying.

"You're welcome," she said.

He turned a page. There was a silence. "You're up here early," the low voice finally rumbled. "I thought you'd still be asleep or out havin' your hair done or somethin'."

"Nope. I've been shopping."

"Or shopping." He gave a nod, as if something had been confirmed.

She reached into the bag and withdrew a bouquet of daffodils, wrapped in tissue and secured with a rubber band. "I found these outside the ballpark. I thought we could stand a little interior decoration. God, this booth is even worse than all the others." Her eyes were running a quick inspection of the narrow little cubicle, with its tangle of wires, its exposed sockets, the inevitable gray stack of engineering consoles glutting the corner.

She saw that he had turned to stare at the flowers, his body drawn back as though she were holding a handful of snakes.

"Can you think of something to put these in?"

"Yeah, I can think of something to put those in." The voice was toneless and dry; the growl of a dog that meant business.

She was ready for that. "Look. If you don't like them you don't have to look at them. Half this booth is my space, Fanning. I'll damn well fix it up the way I please."

The "Fanning" was new. So was her cussing, which shocked him. He watched as she found an empty popcorn box under the shelf and propped the flowers inside it. "This will do for the time being."

"What are you up to? What do you want?"

"Oh, come on, Fanning. This is so crazy. Look. We've been working together for two months now and we don't know anything about each other. Let's be friends."

He continued to stare at her. Evidently Robyn took this for acquiescence, for she sat suddenly on the metal chair next to him, placed her hands on her knees and returned his gaze, her perfect face intent on him, a face as fresh and untroubled as the flowers she brought. For a moment he ached.

"So. Look. Tell me about your wife. Eleanor? How long ago did she die?"

Not a hundred feet below them the Nats were taking batting practice in their blue-tinted uniforms. Infielders whistled and talked it up. Balls arced and dropped above the Wrigley Field ivy. But up here, now, a dark presence swam between Fanning's eyes and the day.

"Die?" He was half out of his chair. "What do you mean, *die?*"

Now it was Robyn's turn to feel a shock of unreality. She opened the fingers of her hand. "But—I've heard you talk about her like . . . I mean, you say things like, 'After Eleanor passed along.' . . ."

"That's what she did, she passed along. She passed out of my life. She left me, god dammit. She walked out on me ten years ago. Now what the hell else is it you wanted to know?"

He could tell that he had stunned her. There was genuine anguish in her face. But it was clear from her posture, from the set of her mouth, that she had come to have a conversation with him, hell or high water. So it didn't really surprise Fanning when Robyn drew a breath and said:

"Well—I guess I'd like to know why she left you."

He was ready for that one. *"Turtle Teweles,"* he almost cackled at her. "She got so she couldn't stand him. Couldn't stand all the time I spent running with him, the times I had him over to dinner at the house. Couldn't stand Turtle." There was a malevolent gleam in Fanning's eye. "Now *there* was a case," he said, with a thickness in his voice like suppressed laughter, "where the woman walked out."

This time the look on her face was so wide-eyed, so nakedly injured, that Fanning relented a bit. "Maybe I shouldn't blame Eleanor," he said in a lower tone. "She put up with a lot. Criminy, I suppose she never got over the time I invited old Turtle along on our honeymoon."

Robyn's jaw dropped.

"You took Turtle along . . . on your *honeymoon?*"

Fanning nodded. "Nineteen forty-nine. Turtle was still an active player then. Cripes, I thought it would impress her. Me having a major-league player as a buddy, you see. We went to Hot Springs, Arkansas. Where the mineral baths are. Turtle is from Arkansas, you see, so we . . ."

Fanning's voice trailed off; he appeared to be struck with a sudden, secret thought.

Robyn shifted on her metal chair. She rubbed her hands together and then examined her red fingernails.

"Well, um—so Eleanor left you. Were there any children?"

"A boy, yes." Fanning's voice was distant.

"Grown?"

"Yes."

"What does he do?"

"He's a bull masturbator."

"I'm sorry?"

Damn it! He hadn't meant for this to spill out. Most embarrassing secret he had. This was how quickly they got it out of you. You had to be on guard every minute.

"He, uh—he works for an agricultural extension laboratory for

Michigan State University. He specializes in animal husbandry. That's the technical term for it, I guess." Fanning slapped his breast pockets for a White Owl.

"You must be very"—why did she pass her hand over her mouth?—"*proud* of him."

"We're not close." Matthew, the last wounding remnant of his former life. The last tangible evidence that Fanning the pure airwave Voice had been anchored in an earthbound identity. God, but he hadn't always wanted to put Matthew behind him. He'd had high hopes. There was a time when he'd hoped the boy would join him in the broadcast booth one day—a father-and-son play-by-play duo. A radio "family," dear to the hearts of Americans. The former Boy Broadcaster with his own boy broadcaster—it had seemed too right to be true. And so it proved. Early on, Matthew had indicated he had no intentions of ever joining his father, in a broadcast booth or anywhere else. College degree, high and mighty attitude. His own notions of what was important and what wasn't. And out of all the possible careers under God's good golden sun, he had to choose this . . . *bull* business . . . it made Fanning sick with shame every time he thought about it. (And a sockdolager voice, too. What a tragic waste.)

Fanning had had to invent Turtle Teweles instead. He never mentioned Matthew to anyone. People who knew him well didn't even know he had a son. It was astonishing how easily this woman had yanked the information out of him. It was a warning signal.

He held a match to a White Owl. "Why do you want to know anyway?"

She shrugged and looked away.

"Look, there's just something I—you remember when I was just getting started here, and there was all this big question about how much baseball I knew? Whether I even listened to ball games?"

When he remained silent she went on, her eyes lowered.

"Well, the point is, I never got a chance to actually elaborate on it, but . . . I *had* heard of you. Before I got here, I mean. My father was a great baseball fan. We lived in St. Louis. So it wasn't like we could tune you in or anything. But . . . well, your name was practically synonymous with baseball. When I was a little girl."

He nodded, a sickened expression on his face. What was she trying to tell him? That he was like a goddamn granddaddy to her? This, after hearing about her escapades with the likes of Bogart Humphries and all the rest . . . or was she making some kind of advance? He gazed at her, speechless, a ruin of a grin on his mouth. His clothes felt like ancient rags.

"And"—she looked up at him and almost winced at his expression—"well, I mean I just never got around to telling you what an"—she closed her eyes—"*honor* it is to work with you. If my father were alive he'd be the proudest man in the world." She ran the palms of her hands rapidly up and down the sides of her slacks. "That's all."

Not knowing exactly what else to do, Fanning arose and stood heavily before her. He had a wild, confused impulse to offer to take her to dinner. In the silence, both of them could hear the laughter of men's voices farther down the press row.

Fanning abruptly turned his head to stare down at the playing field. A Nats coach was hitting ground balls to infielders.

"The very first big-league game I ever saw was right here in this park," he said softly.

Robyn waited.

After a long pause Fanning said, "With my father."

She waited again. Then she asked him when, what year. But a hot wind blew through the booth just then, fluttering papers, and she had to reach out to catch the daffodils, and it seemed as though he hadn't heard her. And then she remembered the other thing she had to say. She set her mouth and opened the strap to her shoulder bag and fished out a folded sheet of newsprint.

"There's this, Fanning," she said. "I don't know if you've seen this."

Fanning took the sheet of paper. He stared at his own face, the photographed head and the cartoon body. Fanning in an umpire's suit, chin to chin with the cartoon Robyn Quarrles.

"What the devil is this?"

"That," said Robyn, "is the ad campaign for us. WERA is running it in the New York papers."

Fanning regarded the sheet of newsprint for such a long time that Robyn began to think he had fallen into some kind of trance. Then he slowly crumpled it into a tight ball. He flipped it with his thumb out the window of the booth, where it unfurled a little on the hot breeze, tumbled, wafted, and bounced off the shoulder of an arriving fan, a fleshy teen-ager in a sleeveless polo shirt and wraparound sunglasses. The kid had a transistor radio in his ear and never noticed the impact of the paper ball.

"Now what you need for those daffodils," Fanning said to Robyn, "is some kind of a tall glass vase that will hold the stems together." And the next day he bought one.

In the weeks that followed, L. C. Fanning never again contradicted Robyn on the air. He became her most attentive listener, encouraging her opinions on the games' progress, grunting agreement, piping up with a "You can say that again!" as she described some particularly scintillating play.

Gradually he allowed her middle-inning play-by-play stint to expand: first by a half inning, then an inning, then two—until he himself was doing little more than a ceremonial inning or two at the top of the broadcast and the final six outs or so for each side.

He worked her into some of the pregame interview assignments, which meant escorting her down onto the field, introducing her to that day's player-guest, even suggesting an outline of questions until she began to insist on creating her own.

He pronounced himself impressed, even astonished at the accuracy of her insights. During his late-inning turns, he got into the habit of prefacing his own comments with, "As Robyn Quarrles was saying earlier in this ball game . . ."

Still, he managed not to be accessible to her away from the ball parks. On the airplane flights he tended to sit in rows otherwise filled with members of the Nats front office. On the occasions when they sat together, he would envelop himself in the in-flight magazine, or sleep.

But when the two of them were visible to a crowd—when a fan called their names during a pregame interview, or when they happened to meet at the press elevator—Fanning would grab Robyn around the waist and wave an expansive hello to all and sundry.

Robyn was at a loss to explain his sudden change of behavior. Fanning's fellow pressbox regulars, aware of it, merely shrugged and gave him a wider berth than usual. To allow a woman the privilege of the microphone, even under duress, was contemptible enough in their eyes. To openly embrace her was a form of sickness.

Only Danny Breen understood.

"L.C.'s a desperate man," Breen confided to Fensterwald one night in the San Diego press lounge. "Ask me a year ago if he'd treat his station like this—undermine the promotion campaign—I'd say, *no way, José.* Bastard's falling to pieces. You hate to see them go, the great ones. Call me sentimental. I say it's sad-making."

But not even Breen understood all of it.

L. C. Fanning followed up his new attitude toward Robyn with an amazing transformation in his behavior at large. He reemerged from his brooding withdrawal and seemed to rejoin the world. The booming laughter came back into his voice. Color returned to his face. His pace quickened. He winked at people. He swept through the hotels and the bars and the good restaurants and the golf courses of the National League like the greatest celebrity of all the summer, a man at the peak of his time.

During a late-July homestand he retrieved the ancient Ambassador from its box of mothballs—he normally retrieved it only for Opening Day—and jammed it square on the top of his head. Its two-and-three-quarter-inch brim flopped rakishly about his ears. Its peaked crown towered above his skull like a pyramid. He wore it at all times—in the booth, in the dugout, on the field, on the plane, to movies, to dinner, to the tobacco stand in a hotel lobby.

He began sporting an ever more lurid array of jackets—shimmering lime and lemon pastels, sassy pearl grays with western stitching and trim, drop-dead orange-and-yellow hound's-tooth, a Miami Beach number in snowy white that he wore over a silk shirt of bold geometric design. It was as though in every city he made straight for the most garish pick-'em-off-the-rack warehouse he could find and walked out with as much as he could carry in his arms. He seldom wore the same jacket twice.

In Houston he bought himself a pair of cowboy boots.

He smoked one White Owl after another, thrusting his jaw out so that the cigar pointed into the air like a howitzer, the ember threatening the Ambassador brim. He reemerged along press row in the various stadiums around the league, slapping shoulders with the old authority, a joke or a piece of information for his contemporaries, an encouraging word for the younger fellows on the beat. Even Fensterwald got the Fanning glad hand. Yes, and even Danny Breen.

Danny Breen watched, and had to admit to himself that he admired Fanning's tactics.

But not even Danny Breen fathomed all of it.

Fanning had come to understand what Robyn was after.

When he had understood it, a calm had descended on him. And he was able to concentrate more fully upon an idea that had taken root in him: an idea that, with refinements and modifications, and particularly with a growing sense of justice, had come to be identified in his mind as the Plan.

The first days after Turtle left had been the worst for Fanning. He had begun to see his once familiar environment through a sort of prism created by Robyn's presence. The prism cast a harsh distorting light on things. It drew the ballplayers up into a horrible immediacy, intensifying their youth, their animal leanness, their sexuality. That was no doubt the way Robyn saw the players. Particularly Bogart Humphries. The thought made it hard for Fanning to breathe.

At the same time, the prism acted as a mirror upon Fanning. He saw, as he had that night in the hotel bathroom, the ravages of all the years in his face and on his belly. (His throat, the inside, didn't reflect in the mirror, but the throat was ensnaring him with an awareness of its own.)

The image tore at him. Wouldn't let him alone.

The day she had handed him the sheet of newsprint with that mockery of his image on it—that had nearly killed him. But at the same instant, in a kind of revelation of the same nature that had allowed him to see Thomson's ball actually leap upward in mid-flight, Fanning had divined what it was that Robyn was after. And the knowledge had allowed him to at last arm himself, turn in the direction of the enemy. His mind was calm before that wadded newsprint had hit the grandstand concrete.

The knowledge he held was not specific at first, not explainable in words. It had the nature of something silver, which flashed brilliantly in his mind's eye and then vanished.

But as he developed it, the answer came to be this:

Robyn was here to *pillage his brain*.

And knowing that, he could loathe her. With a clear conscience. The knowledge had this quality for him:

It had the sense of a stadium door flung open onto a twilight universe, and Robyn striding in out of a slate-gray sky on a cold wind, like hotel air conditioning, the metallic dullness behind her contrasting with the warm enveloping stadium lights, the cold wind stirring up scraps of paper yellowing at the edges, and rattling things long left unexamined; the cold wind raising a damp musty smell from inside, and the sportswriters and the other denizens of the stadium averting their eyes, like monks, from the open doorway through which Robyn had entered, as if not wanting to gaze upon the knowledge contained in the iridescence of her skin, the hot light in her eyes.

The face of a vampire.

That was it. That was the quality which Fanning recognized in Robyn Quarrles. She had strode into his world from a slate-colored realm that Fanning understood only dimly. A realm in which things were prized for being not what they seemed to be. A realm that fit in the palm of your hand but had not learned how to duplicate human emotion. A realm that had produced artificial turf and giant scoreboards that, in turn, could artificially produce Fanning's net. A realm of Danny Breens and Jeffrey Spectors. Fanning's bowels flamed anew. In his agony he understood what it was that Robyn Quarrles wanted from him: what it was that would help occupy the vacant spaces behind her beautiful face.

He understood why Turtle had fled.

She was an agent working for his enemies—not only his enemies, but the enemies of the America that had not changed despite everything you read in the papers, despite the pornography and the new music and the slick styles and the homosexuals and the stadiums that had been torn down: an America that resisted the surface changes and remained intact, its values still derived from the great era when radio voices spoke the common, linking incantations of the human soul.

But the art was all gone out of the radio now. Except for a few of the old tribe who remained, people like L. C. Fanning. And *that's* what Robyn Quarrles was after.

"*Got*-cha, *got*-cha, *got*-cha, *got*-cha."

She wanted to plunder his brain and find out the secret that made him so magical on the airwaves. That was the one thing her generation of big-deal wizards and fast-money operators hadn't been able to figure out.

They'd invented television and made billions off of it, but they never had figured out a way to make it magical. People watched it but they hated it. Fanning had always believed that the end of the television era was soon at hand, and now the money wizards knew it too, because *it couldn't satisfy the soul*.

And neither could radio, after what they'd done with it.

So they wanted to probe his brain. And Robyn was their instrument.

Knowing it at last made him feel better. *Fat chance she had*. Let her sit there next to him till kingdom come, spying on him, making notes, tape-recording him as he'd seen her do. She'd never get the answer.

Because the answer was not inside Fanning. The answer *was* Fanning. It was him growing up in Michigan with the lace curtains blowing and the orange dial glowing late into the night; him not knowing for certain whether he had ever existed in real space and time; him hearing that crooner's voice that night as it floated out of Chicago over the lake and into his darkened bedroom: *"Toot, toot, tootsie! Good-bye . . ."*

It was him on the day he had sat in the Polo Grounds in weather so cold the spotter's hand couldn't grip the pencil, him *naming* Turtle Teweles (and thus creating him) on that day Turtle spun in the home-plate dust, him seeing Thomson's home run ball actually rise in flight. . . .

Let her spy. He'd confound her and her bosses with his cruel kindness, and humor her along. In so doing, he'd save his voice until the closing of this last season, when he'd have his Day, and get out of it gracefully, taking his secret, which was him, with him, and leave the rest of them high and dry.

As for the Day—well, he had the Plan.

And so L. C. Fanning waited for August.

CHAPTER

Y ELLOW SUNLIGHT FLOODED
into the little rent-a-car of-
fice, and the morning felt like Sunday. Fanning drummed his fingers
on the counter top and whistled a fragment from an old tune. His
nails were newly manicured; smooth and round as pennies. The
morning was too fast for a Sunday; Sunday mornings were lone high
saxophone notes, austere preludes to the variations of the doubleheader afternoons. The traffic that thrust and pounded behind his
back, along the service road near Lambert-St. Louis International
Airport, was fast workaday traffic. But Fanning stood outside all that.
For him it was a Sunday. The fragment he was whistling was from
"Toot, Toot, Tootsie! Good-bye."

"May I see your driver's license and a major credit card." The
gum-chewing girl behind the counter might well have been speaking
to the computerized typewriter at her red fingertips. She wore a
yellow uniform dress and a matching yellow scarf, but the scarf had a
penny-size brown coffee stain down near the tip, and to Fanning that
was wrong. He grimaced. The brown coffee stain spoiled something
that might have been perfect, for the colors of the rent-a-car office

were white and yellow, and the ashtrays were clean, and the morning light bathed the yellow and rendered everything in a clear light that left no shadows, no possibility of doubt. Everything stood certain: the ashtrays gleamed empty and waiting. The counter top ended at a point just so, and there was the window and that was the floor, and Fanning's decision was illuminated by a universe of summer-colored truth. Except for the little penny-size coffee stain on the reservationist's scarf.

Fanning studied the girl's thin chewing face as he brought his wallet out of his hip pocket. He remembered her from other times, when he and Turtle had come in here to pick up a car for a day of helling around before a night game. But she didn't give any sign of recognizing him. This, too, annoyed Fanning. As he slid out his license and credit card—the one with the intersecting orange-and-yellow circles, his name in proud relief like the tooling on an emperor's seal—he pressed his thumb against one of his gold-embossed business cards, as if by accident, and dropped it on the counter so the lettering faced her. It said:

L. C. FANNING
VOICE OF THE NATS

She glanced at it, chewing her gum, then raised her brown eyes to his smiling face.

"I won't be needing any additional identification," she said.

The car awaited him at the side of the entrance, a small mustard-colored compact, still dripping water from the automatic wash. Fanning got his suitcase squared away in the trunk. Then he took off the ash-gray cashmere cardigan he had brought along for the trip. Even in August heat Fanning never felt completely dressed in just shirt-sleeves. He arranged the sweater on a wooden hanger. This he fitted over the hook above the rear window. He had brought his Ambassador, with its peaked crown and two-and-three-quarter-inch brim. Now he removed it from his head and placed it on the front seat. He smoothed a hand back over his high forehead to set the hair in place.

He took two state road maps out of his attaché case and arranged them, folded to his route, on the seat beside the hat. He rummaged in the attaché case again until his fist was full of Life Saver packages. These he placed gently on the seat so that they wouldn't slip down the crack. On second thought, he picked up one of the Life Saver packages, a butterscotch, and got it started, pulling the small tab ribbon away until the waxed paper unfolded, exposing the first crescent of candy. He looked around until he spotted a trash barrel for the scrap. Fanning did not normally allow himself the luxury of Life Saver candy on doctor's orders. Today was an exception.

Finally, he withdrew from the attaché case a fresh package of White Owls. He wedged these over the sun visor on the driver's side. He closed the attaché case and flipped it over the seat into the back of the car. Then he rubbed his nose several times, took a width of his limecolored checked trouserlegs between each thumb and forefinger, and pulled until they rode high and free on his shins. He settled himself behind the wheel. The pants were loose around his waist and hips now. They'd fit snug when he'd bought them just a few weeks ago. Time gets away. But the shoes on his feet felt just right. They were a new pair of tassled white loafers, the kind he and Turtle liked to wear, their hard rubber soles as fierce and inviolate as the walls of unconquered cities.

The attendant had left the engine running and the radio on. The radio was tuned to some Negro rock 'n' roll station up at the end of the dial. *Got*-cha, *got*-cha. As Fanning eased the car out into the traffic, his nostrils full of the warm molded-metal aroma of the dashboard, the syrupy vinyl of the seatcovers, he twisted the dial back down toward the fat part of the spectrum. Toward the big old standard middle-of-the-road stations that he'd known about for years, the ones that covered the ball games. He tuned into a lively morning call-in show on the issues of the day. He thought he recognized the announcer's voice. He couldn't think of the name right off hand, but the voice was one of the good ones, one of the old standard voices, deep and rich as liquid gold. The voice of the eternal announcer. And he lit up his first White Owl and settled back behind the wheel to drive and listen. He wished he could think of the name.

He headed the little car south on Interstate 270, the expressway that formed an outer belt around the St. Louis metropolitan area on the western rim. As he drove, the orange morning sunlight shimmering on his windshield, it occurred to him how little of any given metropolitan area a radio announcer got to see over the course of a season. You slipped into grooves. You didn't take advantage. You stay at the same hotel, you eat at the same restaurants, you play golf at the same links. All the while, the metropolitan area around you is constantly changing, expanding and you're not even aware of it; you might as well be a thousand miles away, or on the moon. A caller's voice came on the radio to wonder why it was that there were so few movies nowadays you could take your whole family to see. Fanning made himself keep a lookout for all the new developments along Interstate 270: the lowslung chrome-and-glass company headquarters that flashed by at extravagant intervals of open space, terraced and landscaped with sculpted fir trees and artificial lakes, mute architectural rebukes to the jagged upthrusting coziness of the central cities he knew. Well, you adapt with the times. He passed a valley on his left that contained a corporate headquarters set in a sumptuous verdancy of shrubbery and lawn. He glimpsed the corporate logo, a giant scarlet letter of the alphabet that seemed to rise like an iris from the land itself, and he realized that he was looking at the company that invented artificial turf for baseball diamonds.

Just south of the city of Kirkwood, he left 270 and got on Interstate 44, which knifed south and west through Missouri. Immediately the vestiges of metropolis dropped away behind him, and Fanning knew that he was in the country. On the rim of the horizon was a tree line: oak and maple and ash. The pavement under him was old now; great jagged chunks of ancient cement held together by ridges of tar. He whisked past a couple of truckers' cafés, the pennants of an amusement park, and a vast automobile manufacturing plant—white glass windshields in infinite rows—and then L. C. Fanning was in the bosom of the Ozarks.

It shocked him, at first, how the great boiling hills of the Ozarks rolled up to the very rim of St. Louis and then stopped, as if held at bay by the flimsy band of landscaped office buildings he had been observing; the "metropolitan area" now, in retrospect, an unconvincing shred. In all his trips into St. Louis over the years, Fanning had never realized the immediacy of the surrounding wilderness.

But as he rolled deeper into Missouri—skirting little towns named

Eureka and Pacific and St. Clair, towns that sprang up like berries on a bush and then vanished—Fanning gave up his resistance to the boiling hills. The warm yellow light of morning had burned off into a whitish blue haze now. The world and all its possibilities opened to him. He put a match to another White Owl. He relaxed his grip on the wheel and settled his weight back into the seat. He leaned over and switched the radio dial away from the big station's call-in show; that was now a part of the world he'd left behind. He twisted through bursts of static until he located the flat voice of a middle-aged man reading the midday market reports. The man's accent was like an old tune played on a stringed instrument. It pleased Fanning. It was like a memory. It reminded him of Turtle Teweles. Fanning felt a brotherhood with the nameless announcer. He pictured the man in his cramped little studio somewhere, a fatbellied local boy with pink skin and a string tie, perched on a stool and surrounded by crumpled cigarette packages and thick sheafs of work schedules thumbtacked to the bulletin board and banks of ancient gray audio dials and a stopwatch somewhere in the mess of his desk and a girlie calendar taped up on the glass to the engineer's booth. He tried to picture how it would be if the man had any inkling he was being listened to by a famous broadcaster from the East—by L. C. Fanning himself. And he had to laugh out loud, a laugh that had been building in his belly since he left St. Louis. It was crazy, but he almost wished he had time to find the town the man was announcing from—it couldn't be far—and just pop into the station unexpected, and introduce himself and see the expression on everybody's face. The idea being that they were all fellow journeymen, all humble equals in the great brotherhood of the airwaves. Like the great Arthur Godfrey turning up in a small station somewhere, sending all the secretaries into a tizzy. Of course the local man would want to get him on the air for a few minutes, pump him about the Nats, about the tight Eastern Division race, get him on the record about his pennant picks—a real scoop for the local fans. And Fanning would have to oblige, of course. You never got so big that you couldn't take the time to give a boost to the little man in your profession, and if you ever thought you had gotten that big, God help you. Then it was time to get out.

And so he drove his mustard-colored rent-a-car with both hands firmly on the wheel (the way they used to make catches in the outfield, even the great ones; everybody had to do it the one-handed showboat way nowadays; you had television to thank for that trend); a fifty-five-mile-an-hour fleck in the rushing stream of eight-wheel rigs and flatbed pickup trucks with hard sunburned faces at the wheel, and the wild flickering motorcycle riders that were his new companions on this strange and lonely interstate slashing south and west through Missouri. Sometime after one o'clock in the afternoon the market-report announcer faded into static. Fanning's hand went to the dial automatically; he'd forgotten about the man before the needle reached the next clear station, which was playing a country and western ballad.

Near Rolla the landscape changed. The boiling hills deepened into abrupt peaks cut through with gullies and ravines. The Ozark forest crowded in on the highway's edge now. Birds with great black motionless wings circled in the blue-white sky, and once, coming out of a wide sweeping curve, Fanning caught sight of a roadside diner on the crest of a hill, beetle-shaped and silver-plated, in the style of the old cafeterias you used to find in the 1940s. He had a sudden inner vision of round gas pumps and a rainbow-colored jukebox inside. He couldn't tell for sure in the second or two that he had to glimpse it, but the place looked deserted, its curved art-deco lines oddly irrelevant to the eternal forest that pressed upon it, like a home run baseball lying abandoned in the outfield bleacher seats. Toot-toot-tootsie, good-bye.

Strangely, the image didn't depress him. (Nothing could dampen his spirits on this sunlit day.) On the contrary: the old diner reinforced a notion that had taken root in him: that on this expedition he had blundered upon the essential America that he had always believed existed, in spite of the evidence offered by the cities. (Perhaps the diner wasn't closed after all; it may just have been the time of day, getting on toward two in the afternoon, well after country people were used to taking their dinner.) These were the Ozarks: where people still worked the land and read the Bible and ate fried chicken on Sunday and listened to the radio. The cities give you a false impression of things. He smoked his cigar, tamping the ash into the tray, with an imperious flick of his finger, like a general riding through captured territory. At Rolla he turned off Interstate 44 and headed due south on a two-lane highway, Route 63. For a while there was a national forest on his right. He could see blue and white tents that people had pitched. Families. He passed through towns named Yancy Mills and Edgar Springs; feed mills and stores with signs that said Bait; and running the radio dial along the band, he heard a man's voice say, "All righty, it's ninety-two degrees under Great God Almighty's fair skies."

He would say to Turtle: Why you old owlhoot.

And Turtle would say: You ole hound dog.

And he would say: Why I was in the neighborhood, I thought I'd come around and see how the other half lived.

And Turtle would say: You crazy ole porkypine. You sumbitch.

And he would say: Where can a man find himself a cold bottle of Heine Meine beer in these parts?

And Turtle would say: Boys I want you all to shake hands with the greatest god damn sports announcer ever lived, L. C. Fanning, the Voice of the New York Nats. L.C. and me used to work together.

And the boys would say: *L. C. Fanning.*

And: *Toot-toot-tootsie, good-bye.* Ain't that right, L.C.?

And: *Mister* L. C. Fanning. Why I lissened to you do the 'fifty-one World Series. That's the one where Thomson hit the home run in the playoff to get 'em in.

And: Off of Ralph Branca. He th'owed the pitch. Old Number Thirteen.

And: Why it's a pleasure, L.C. Heine Meine beer! Hot damn!

And he would say to Turtle: Now I have a bidniss proposition for you, if you don't think you've lost your touch. I know of a certain radio team where there might be a vacancy. Certain team looking to sign on an old pro, help carry 'em into the stretch drive.

And Turtle would say: I don't know. [Playing hard to get.] I done packed it in, L.C. Got my Bowl-A-Wile to look out for. Got my pals here. [That would hurt.] I don't need that aggervation anymore.

And Fanning (Turtle's biggest pal of all, after all) would say: Turtle, not to change the subject, but did I ever tell you the story about the time I got stuck up at the point of a gun outside Tommy Eagle's?

And Turtle would say: Boys, Tommy Eagle's is a famous honky-tonk right in the middle of New York City. It's where all the big-name ballplayers hang out, and all the writers and the sports announcers. Me and Fanning we used to drink there all the time. Ain't it the truth, L.C.?

He was coasting along the main street now of a small town whose name he had not noticed. There were sunburned squinting people lined up at a frozen-custard stand. A small movie marquee, jutting out over the sidewalk like a rowboat's prow, advertised: *Saratoga Trunk*. Fanning was so bemused with *Saratoga Trunk* that he barely had time to hit the brakes before his car clattered over a thuddle of railroad tracks that split the middle of town. *Saratoga Trunk!* He'd seen it he didn't know how many years ago. With Eleanor. He passed gas stations, blue pennants shimmering in the hot sunlight, and then the main street ran through a brief neighborhood of white frame houses, their roofs nestled in shade trees, before the road opened up into the country again.

Front porches! In spite of the air conditioning there was perspiration on Fanning's forehead. He wiped it off with his handkerchief and helped himself to a Life Saver. The ashtray was growing thick with cigar butts; he would have to empty it soon. He fiddled with the radio dial until he found what sounded like another country station, a chorus of untrained women's voices singing "The Good Reuben James." He was going to need a beer or a Coca-Cola before long. But he felt good. In the clarity of the afternoon sunlight—blazing down just now on a barn roof, making the Mail Pouch lettering dance—Fanning could see the truth as clearly as he had seen Thomson's home run ball rise in flight: The great bedrock republic of his imaginings was still intact. It hadn't evaporated. It hadn't been paved over, spoiled, transistorized, turned into shopping centers, whatever the modern commentators were saying about it. Hadn't been taken over by the smart boys, the advertising hotshots, the modernistic kind of crowd that Robyn Quarrles came from. The blazes with them. The land that lay beneath the airwaves, the decent hardworking family people he broadcast to—they had never gone away after all. His eyes were wet, and a sudden memory from childhood sprang into his mind: He had drifted asleep one summer night, in his bedroom, with the radio on, the orange dial still glowing, the faraway voices still murmuring in his ear; and beyond them, the voices of his parents talking quietly downstairs. And he had awakened again, he did not know how much later, but the radio was hissing static, and in his confusion he thought he might have slept for hours—and then a dreamy panic had seized him: how much time *had* washed by in the darkness? Had he been asleep for years? The radio seemed dead; was he the only one left in time? Trembling with fear, he had thrown the sheet off and felt his way across his darkened bedroom to the door. But when he opened it, he saw the light from the downstairs lamp still glowing on the stairwell; and when he listened, he heard the soft voices of his parents, talking still. The relief he had felt then had almost made him sob. Time hadn't washed by. It was as though he had been rescued from eternity. Lord, it must have been over fifty years ago that had happened. He'd forgotten it—but still, he'd never wanted to be around a stadium at night when they finally turned the arc lights out. And the old memory flooded back on him, fresh as yesterday, as he headed south.

Turtle would say: What about that new snatch sidekick of your'n?
And he would say: You mean that gash neophyte they sent us.
And Turtle would say: I mean that highheeled lipstick blond-haired little piece of Hollywood tail that come in there an' taken my job away.
And he would say: You mean Miss Yankeedoodle Poontang.
And Turtle would say: I mean Miss All-America Makes-My-Ass-Crave-Cold-Buttermilk. It's me or her. There ain't any other way I'm gonna do it. Them's my terms, L.C., and you can take it or leave it.
And he would say: Don't you worry about her, Turtle. You let me take care of Miss Robyn Quarrles.

Because he had a plan. Every contingency, every corner of L. C. Fanning's master scheme was as bright and clear as this sunlit summer day.
Yes sir. This was the Ozarks. This was the eternal heartland. The kind of country where most of the great ones came from. The Dean brothers, Paul and Dizzy, cotton-pickers from Mississippi. (Doctor to Dizzy, after examining the toe hit by that line drive in 1938, in the All-Star Game in Chicago, that ruined Diz's career: "This toe's frac-

tured, Diz." Dean: "Fractured, hell. It's *broken*.") Ha-ha. He still had to laugh, thinking of that one. Pepper Martin, the Wild Horse of the Osage, who ran out of the dugout and kissed the soil at home plate before a World Series. Vinegar Bend Mizell. Turtle Teweles. Decent, clean-cut, salt-of-the-earth boys, who represented the values of their families and their fans, of that great grandstand full of people called the United States of America. God rest her soul.

And putting it out for free for a buck nigger outfielder probably wasn't Mr. and Mrs. Average Taxpayer's idea of wholesome.

Ha-ha.

Fanning hated to use that kind of pressure. He was after all a respecter of the fair sex. But Robyn had made her own bed, so to speak. And while Fanning wasn't perhaps on the best of terms lately with the press corps (thanks mostly to Miss Robyn Quarrles), he still had one or two key contacts who'd be only too happy to play around with that little tidbit of information.

Christ, he'd go to Fensterwald himself if he had to.

Getting on toward four o'clock in the afternoon, not twenty miles from the Arkansas state line, Fanning realized that his neck was sore and his pants were sticking to the seat from perspiration. This despite the air conditioning. Plus the fact that he had to see a man about a horse. He'd been holding it in for several hours now. The last radio station he'd tuned to had long since gone to static. He had been gripping the wheel with both hands since before noon, and he hadn't had anything to eat if you didn't count the Life Savers. The gas dial was wobbling near Empty. In his determination to get to Arkansas, Fanning had not taken stock of how the time had slipped away.

There was a combination diner and Texaco filling station off to the right. It sat on a harsh little island of white asphalt. Behind it was a scraggly cornfield dropping off into an indeterminate forest of scrub oak. The owner's name was painted onto a board above the filling-station door, and the diner section had been joined to the original cement structure like a tool shed. A torn screen door yawned open like a tired dog's jaw; it had the remnants of an Orange Crush sign on it. Behind the station somebody's gray sheets hung limp on a clothes-line.

In the lengthening shadows of late afternoon, the place had a pinched, forbidding air about it. But Fanning had to see a man about a horse.

A lone automobile commanded the lot by the diner: a long, pearl-gray Bonneville 500. One of the last of the full-size luxury cars. It was a few years old, but Fanning could see that the chrome gleamed to a high polish in the sun, despite the dust-choked roads the car must have traveled to get here. On the shining rear bumper was pasted a decal: an American flag.

Fanning guided his own compact to the Unleaded pump, feeling, as the car rolled to a stop, the exaggerated sense of stillness that envelops one who has been traveling at highway speeds for several hours. His muscles ached. A teen-age boy with long, caked hair and a goatee came ambling out of the station, sucking the dregs of a grape Popsicle.

The heat of the afternoon hit Fanning like a physical blow when he got out of the car. For a moment the world went purple. Then he was conscious of long shadows. He felt the hot asphalt under his shoes. He put a hand on the door to steady himself and the metal burned his hand. Damn the afternoon games to hell anyway. The kid was staring at him, the gas pump motionless in one fist. "Where's Turtle?" Fanning demanded of the parking-lot attendant. "Where's who?" said the kid. "Did he bring the net?" Fanning asked, and he could hear that his voice was loud. His throat hurt. "The *which*?" bleated the kid. The purple cleared from Fanning's eyes. He blinked. The kid retreated a step. Fanning remembered that he was in southern Missouri, not far from the Arkansas state line. "Fill 'er up," he said to the kid, who was now regarding him with chin tucked into skinny neck, as though gauging which way Fanning might jump. "I got to see a man about a horse," Fanning explained to the kid. "Which way?" The kid looked at him for a long time before he said, "Straight on th'ough 'at door."

Trudging across the hot asphalt toward the filling station men's room, Fanning noticed that the Bonneville 500 had a New York license plate. Fans of his, probably. He'd have to pay them a little surprise visit before he hit the road again.

He finished up in the men's room, which didn't have a light. On his way back to the pump he sneaked a glance inside the diner. Through the screen door he could make out two hazy figures seated at the counter. A man and a woman. Plump through their middles; middle-aged. The kind of people he had seen by the tens of thousands passing through the turnstiles at Flushing Stadium, the Polo Grounds. Solid-looking. Fanning's kind of people.

Yes. He really ought to stop in and say hello to these people before he got back on the road. The thought of it made him almost want to laugh, with a feeling like love.

He paid the boy in bills from his money clip. He got back inside the rented car and eased it away from the pump, over to the other side of the Bonneville. He transferred the White Owls from the sun visor to his shirt pocket. Stepping back into the glare of the sun, he thought about donning the ash-gray cardigan. He didn't want to. It was hot. But he hated to go sleeveless. When you're in the public eye, you have a certain image to maintain. He pulled on the cardigan. Then he picked the Ambassador off the seat, placed it atop his head, and strode into the diner.

The man and woman sat on counter stools, sipping cola through straws. On the other side of the counter a fat waitress fanned herself with a cardboard fan that had Jesus' picture and the name of a funeral home on it.

The man wore a western-style shirt and squared-toed cowboy boots. His silver hair was combed back in waves.

The woman had on a white blouse with embroidered figuring around the shoulders. At her throat was a ribboned bow tie with the ends dangling down.

The two looked up at Fanning when he entered, but no one spoke. From somewhere out of sight came the sound of religious music on a radio.

The only counter stools left vacant were in a pool of slanting sunlight, so Fanning took a seat on one. From this vantage point the place and the people in it looked dim, indistinct.

"I guess I'll have a large Coke with plenty of ice," Fanning announced to the woman behind the counter, although she hadn't asked him. He tried to roll his eyes to the left, to see whether the couple showed signs of recognizing his voice, but looking out of the glare into the dim light, he couldn't tell.

The woman behind the counter slowly got to her feet.

Fanning felt the sweat running down his back and sides. The feeling of lovelike urgency grew inside him. These people were of his generation: his audience. They would know him. It was almost as though, finding them here in the wilderness near the Arkansas state line, he had received a sign: a sign as clear as Thomson's home run ball, rising in flight.

He decided to test them right away.

"I see you folks are from New York." He put all the vibrancy he could muster into his famous voice. In the small room it seemed almost strident. People often recognized him just by his voice.

It seemed to be working. As one, the man and woman turned to him, smiling and nodding their heads.

Encouraged, Fanning extended his hand.

"Fanning's the name. L. C. Fanning."

He watched.

"Howdy *do*," said the man in a booming voice that made Fanning jump. "Hearty's the name. My real name's Donald R., but my friends call me Hale. Hale Hearty."

"Hale *Hearty*," the woman repeated pointedly, with a smile for Fanning.

Fanning turned to her. "And you must be Mrs. Hearty. My name's Fanning," he said. He paused. "L. C. Fanning."

"Oh yes," the woman cried. "Oh, yes. I'm the Little Missus. I'm Hale's Better Half. I'm *Mrs*. Hearty."

"Co'-Cola." The waitress pushed a plastic cup full of amber slush in front of him.

"Thank you," said Fanning. He cleared his throat. To the man, he said, "Well, now, how about those New York Nats anyway?"

The man said, "I'm sorry?"

The waitress said, "Fitty-fi' cen's."

Fanning reached into his pants pocket and slapped three quarters down on the counter. He glared at the waitress until she shuffled away.

He turned back to the silver-haired man with a smile on his face.

"The New York Nats," he repeated. There was no reaction in the man's face. Fanning was conscious of long shadows. How long had he been away? How much time had passed? His hand on the Coca-Cola glass was trembling.

"You mean the ball team." The man named Hearty grinned as though he had just solved a riddle, a brainteaser that Fanning had thrown at him. "We don't know about any of that," he said. "We're Angelenos, see. Why, we've just recently relocated to New York. But we put in most of our time in Los Angeles." He pronounced the *g* hard.

Fanning felt as though he had somehow been tricked. He was sweating hard now. "Well, you must have gone out to see the Nats when they come out to play the Dodgers."

"Of course *I* was born and raised in Kokomo, Indiana," put in Mrs. Hearty. "But Hale's an Angeleno all the way back."

"But I guess you must have heard a Nat game or two since you came to New York," said Fanning.

Mr. Hearty looked thoughtfully into his own Coke glass. "Well, I tell you, sir," he said after a moment. "The Missus and I are *doers*. That is, we don't believe in sitting around on our duffs. What we like to do is just pile in the car and go, see."

"It's a blessing to get away and see how people really live, without all the conveniences we're used to," said Mrs. Hearty. "Ours is such a vibrant country, and I wouldn't want to live anywhere else in the world." She turned to her husband with a radiant face.

"Myself, I'm a play-by-play man for the New York Nats." Fanning tried to make it sound like an afterthought. "I'm on the radio. Cover the baseball team, oh yes." He pulled a White Owl out of his shirt pocket. Mr. Hearty nodded and smiled.

"I don't know if you heard me," said Fanning. "I said that I am a major-league baseball announcer from New York City."

Hale Hearty winked and gave a sharp nod of his head.

"I like New York City," observed Mrs. Hearty, "but I miss the climate of Los Angeles. But I wouldn't live anywhere else in the world except the good old U.S.A., and we've been all over."

"Well, I'll tell you where all the top action is," said Hale Hearty. "Fiber optics. That's my game. Now you're a fellow in the communications trade. This is the stuff that's gonna transform the whole cable television setup. Boom! I've seen the stock triple in the last two years. Why, it is floating not one but two equity offerings." He reached over and put a hand on Fanning's shoulder; Fanning flinched. "Now you talk about an exciting bidniss to be in. Come on over to fiber optics." He winked.

Fanning clenched his fist on the counter and fought to keep himself from leaping at Hearty's throat.

"I don't suppose," he said through his teeth, "that either of you has ever heard the name Turtle Teweles."

Hearty sucked his teeth. "It doesn't ring a bell. Unless it's that new industrial supplies plant they're putting up over in Jersey."

It took a moment for Fanning to realize that he was on his feet; that the smiles on the faces of the two people were distorted with a kind of nervous fear.

He was looming over them, his breath coming in rasps.

He checked himself. Brought his wristwatch up to his face and made himself concentrate on the time.

In a few hours it would be twilight. In a few hours Robyn Quarrles would be taking the microphone by herself at Busch Memorial Stadium in St. Louis.

Fanning took the unlighted White Owl from his mouth and placed it on the counter, as gently as a man placing a bouquet on a fresh grave.

He looked at the two friendly faces, still dim above the pool of sunlight. He said, as distinctly as he could manage:

"I'm sorry. There has been some mistake. I don't know you people after all."

Mrs. Hearty grinned and nodded. "Of course on this trip we're just about living out of a can of beans," her dim mouth said. "We can't seem to get in with the young people and have them tell us where the good restaurants are."

Fanning crossed the Arkansas state line on a country road in the late afternoon.

The day had passed by quickly. He must have been in the diner for longer than he thought. It was late. Time had slipped away from him.

His only hope now was to reach Turtle Teweles. Without Turtle, nothing else hung together anymore. Nothing made sense. But Turtle would come back with him and be on hand for Fanning's Day. He was sure of that.

If he could only find Turtle. If only Turtle were at the place Fanning knew he must be—at the Bowl-A-Wile in the little town that Fanning had circled on the map.

If only Turtle were there.

This was the first time that Fanning had considered the possibility that Turtle might not be present at the end of his search. The thought made his hands go clammy on the wheel. In all his imaginings of what might go wrong on this journey—delays, wrong turns, car trouble, an accident, a stickup—Turtle had emerged at the end, inevitably, as visible and corporeal and eternal as a catcher squatting behind home plate when the pitcher turns to throw.

But now with the late-afternoon sunlight playing tricks on his eyes, he wasn't sure of anything. Black shadows laced the country road, cast by trees and barns. The alternating patches of light and shadow made the windshield, bug-stained now, seem to flicker, and he strained to concentrate on holding to the pavement. The blacktop road soared and dipped and curved. He wasn't used to this kind of driving. The woods and the pastureland that had seemed so open to him in the white afternoon, so emblematic of the lost America he craved, now glared at him in an angry luminous green under a red sky. White-frame churches, Baptist and Nazarene and Pentecostal, shone like burning sheet metal. He kept his eye on the speedometer; he was doing the limit. He passed boarded-up grocery stores and discount liquor stores and dust-caked ballfields and mobile homes. But he saw few people. The countryside had the empty sullenness of a vast stadium when the team was out of town. A black pickup truck shot up out of nowhere and hung on his bumper for a while, nosing across the center line and back again. Fanning scanned the rearview mirror. He expected for a wild moment to see Turtle's grinning face. But the face that looked back at him was the face of a cold-eyed girl. Fanning swerved to let her pass, his two right tires kicking up a funnel of dust as they dropped off the pavement. She was around him and gone in a flash, without looking back. Blond hair. He beat his fist on the wheel and screamed a curse, but no sound came from his throat. In an hour Robyn would be on the air.

*   *   *

She had known something was terribly out of kilter as soon as she arrived at the ballpark and discovered that Fanning was not there. That had been an hour and a half ago. Fanning was never less than two hours early for a game. She had delayed any action at first, praying that there was a reason for this exception; that he would somehow show.

When there was no sign of him forty-five minutes before game time, she alerted Danny Breen.

"No problem," said Breen. "You know the drill by now. I'll whip up some extra background material for you. Fasano pitched last night; Pachelbel won't be using him tonight. I'll see if Tommy'll send him up to the booth to do the color. You'll do fine. No problem."

"The problem," said Robyn, "is that L. C. Fanning is missing."

"Really?" said Danny Breen. "How can you tell?"

She steeled herself and walked into the pressbox area and asked each writer whether he had seen Fanning that day or heard whether he was ill. The writers grunted their noes without looking at her. Then she polled the press crowd still in the lounge. Then she called the hotel. And then she telephoned the police department to file the missing persons report.

She hurried down to the playing field to tape a pregame interview. She encountered Bogart Humphries in the dugout.

"Fanning didn't show up tonight. I'm worried about him. He may have had a heart attack or something in his room and nobody would know it."

Humphries, his arms folded, cap low over his eyes, made a hissing noise.

"That man didn't have no heart attack. I wouldn't be surprised if he didn't just go on and fly the coop, the way his buddy done."

"What makes you think that? That's crazy."

Humphries studied his highly polished baseball shoes. Then he turned his head to spit a line of tobacco juice—a trait that Robyn loathed—before he replied.

"Maybe Fanning can't take the competition."

"What competition?" Humphries had lapsed back into his country-boy cadences, to her further annoyance. She had come to him for advice, reassurance—not smirks and riddles.

Arms still folded, he rolled his eyes to her under the bill of his cap.

"Shee-it. Man loves your ass. Way I hear it, he can't handle the fact that Bogart Humphries been beatin' out his time."

"What?"

Two or three players at the far end of the dugout turned, grinned.

"Hey, keep your voice down." Humphries glanced about, frowning.

"I want to know what you mean about 'Bogart Humphries beating out his time'! That's a disgusting thing to say, and furthermore I'd like to know how Fanning is supposed to know about us!"

"Hey. You know. Word gets around. I gotta run my sprints." In a sudden motion Humphries adjusted his cap, clattered up the dugout steps, and trotted out toward right field, a rippling chorus of shouts following him along the box seats.

But he didn't run fast enough to escape Robyn Quarrles's shocked, piercing cry:

"You pompous phony puffed-up . . . *bastard*!"

Now, just minutes before game time, Robyn stood at a pay telephone on the causeway that led to the WERA broadcast booth. If she chose, she could see a slice of the green outfield bathed in the stadium light, and above the wall, fans moving in their ceaseless scurry. But her head was bowed and her face was toward the wall.

The public-address system boomed with the starting lineups, so she held a finger to her free ear. On the other end of the line, tracked down at last by a WERA operator, was Jeffrey Spector.

"Well, I mean I thought you'd want to *know*. Your number one announcer is *missing* and . . . sure, I can. Of course I can. That's not the point. The point is that L. C. Fanning has simply dropped out of . . . well, thanks, Mr. Spector. Thanks a lot for your concern."

By that time she was talking to a dead line. She turned away from the telephone and walked with short deliberate steps toward her broadcast booth, her head still lowered as if in thought.

When she saw the Nats pitcher, Fasano, seated in her old place at the second mike, she did not hesitate.

"Out."

"Huh? Hey, Danny Breen sent me up here to—"

"Get out. Get out of this booth right now."

She didn't want to deal with Fasano. She didn't want to think about L. C. Fanning, or Bogart Humphries, or Jeffrey Spector, or any other man. Their fears, their vanities, their idiocies repulsed her.

Only one thing mattered to Robyn Quarrles at this moment:

The game.

Darkness had come by the time Fanning approached the Arkansas town where Turtle lived. Only a narrow ribbon of orange hung on the horizon, receding under the rich cobalt of country night, like a memory.

Fanning's neck and shoulders ached. Cold sweat matted his shirt to his ribs. His throat was giving him trouble. It throbbed with a new kind of ache, dry and pulsing at intervals—a weakening radio signal, now, on these night airwaves.

He had the window down and his elbow thrust into the cooling dark air, and when he slowed to make the turn onto the "Business Route" that would take him into the town, he became aware of crickets in the sudden silence. He stared upward at the yellow blinking intersection light with fascination, as though looking at a legendary character in the flesh. Turtle had told him about this light, illuminating the pavement and the desolate sumac beyond, and now Fanning beheld it; it was real. Turning toward Turtle's town, he felt a shudder coming over him, at least partly delicious, and he passed his hand back over his damp hair, as if to set it in place.

What lay before him was a desultory collection of shapes in the darkness: small buildings, houses with the lights out, parked cars, a darkened grocery—the town had gone to bed. Something on three legs flashed in his headlights; a glimpse of illuminated eyes, and it vanished. The town seemed entirely to have festooned itself along the two sides of the narrow macadam road. There were two dull streetlights, one of them bringing up the colors in a Coca-Cola ad in the window of the grocery—an out-of-season Santa Claus, cheeks red and beard white, taking a swig.

Fanning slowed the car to a crawl and ducked his head, alert for clues to the whereabouts of the Bowl-A-Wile. Now the scent of the town came into his nostrils. It was a mixture of rust and gasoline and a sweet mulch, as of a creek backed up or old leaves rotting. The scent inexplicably brought tears to Fanning's eyes. Like the ribbon of orange at the bottom of the advancing night, it had the essence of memory.

He must have cruised the length of the town—about four blocks—a half-dozen times before he spotted the Bowl-A-Wile.

Actually, he heard the place before he saw it. He became aware of a muffled thud of music. At first, he thought it might be coming from somebody's radio. But then, wheeling the car around on the asphalt lot in front of the hulking grain elevator that dominated the town, he caught a flash of violet neon among trees, perhaps a hundred yards back off the road, on a rise of land littered with jagged shapes—rusting farm equipment.

Hitting the accelerator harder than he'd intended—the tires screeched on the asphalt—he swung the car about so that the headlights pointed toward the wisp of neon. The headlights were too far away to do any good, but peering through his bug-spattered windshield, Fanning was able to satisfy himself, after several minutes, that the swaying tree branches in front of the light concealed a half-extinguished script of neon tubing that had once spelled:

BOWL-A-WILE

He gunned the small car onto the macadam road, then slammed on the brakes, looking for the turnoff up the hill. Fortunately the road was otherwise deserted. It took him another fifteen minutes of retracing his route up and down the road, in ever lengthening laps, before he finally discovered the turnoff—fully a mile outside the town, and around the bend of the sloping hill on which the establishment lay.

He spotted several rows of cars and pickup trucks in a makeshift lot illuminated by what looked like strings of Christmas tree lights. He pulled off the macadam road and stopped the car at the foot of the dirt lane leading up to the lot. He reached a nervous hand inside his pocket for a White Owl, but he had smoked them all. The inside of the windshield was filmy with tobacco smoke.

Now he could see the shape of the Quonset hut, glowing in the night—the sky was filled with stars. Turtle Teweles was inside there. He knew it. He waited until the trembling in his sides was under control. He rehearsed the things that he wanted to say. Then he reached down for the ignition, switched it on and at once heard the angry *buuuuuuurrrrrrrp!* of an engine that was already running.

He eased the car up the dirt lane, his heart going as fast as it had on October 3, 1951.

The country music thudded out from a jukebox inside. The ear-splitting throb of the bass seemed to make the very building vibrate like a tuning fork. Fanning pushed his bulk slowly from the car, the Ambassador on his head. He stood for a moment in the loud night air. He glanced upward at the skyful of stars. He tried to remember the last time he had stood out in a country night. The sudden awareness of years shocked him.

He shuddered against the memory and looked upon Turtle Teweles's Bowl-A-Wile, a spectral entity now in its ineffable closeness. In the black night—given relief by a single window at the front, from which yellow light poured—Fanning could see that the roof of the hut was crescent-shaped, an elongated rind of aluminum not more than thirty yards deep and scarcely twice the height of a man. This must be the bowling-alley part. Lashed, welded, and hammered to the front of the crescent was a smaller cabana made of corrugated scrap metal. Several beer cans littered the loose gravel near the entrance, a screen door yawning open like the lower jaw of a drunk. Fanning paused a moment before plunging through this entrance. It appeared as though the town's entire male population were stuffed into the little sardine can of a tavern.

He opened the screen door and stepped through, to a raucous enclave thick with jukebox music, ripsaw laughter, cigarette smoke, and men with dangerous eyes. He smelled stale beer and sweat and something else he could not distinguish, an aroma both acrid and sweet.

He spotted Turtle at the pinball machine.

There he was—the familiar balding crown, the elongated chin, the hard intelligent eyes. Turtle's long arms, more sinous than Fanning remembered, gripped the sides of the machine as he shook it with a violence that made a mockery of "Tilt." The rattle of Turtle's pinball machine competed with the country-music din for primacy in the general uproar.

Fanning gave a yelp and squeezed his way between two tables, each occupied by a gaggle of beery men in cloth hats like baseball caps. He forced his way toward the throbbing pinball machine, his hands outstretched. It was only when he was within four feet of the figure, on the verge of calling out Turtle's name, that he realized the man was a stranger. He turned his head, by degrees, to survey the crowded tin can of a room—to determine whether anyone had noticed his near embarrassment. Now a fresh confusion: It seemed to him that every man in the tavern had Turtle Teweles's face. Could they all be his relatives? A sweet and acrid sickness took hold of his throat, then coursed into his belly, and the room seemed to break apart, then run like liquid into colors of orange and yellow, and he saw the silver face of Hale Hearty grinning at him, uncomprehending, unlistening, and he knew then that he had found his way inside a kind of giant radio, and that all these faces were the inhabitants, the voices that lived there as he had known they did in his boyhood . . . *Ladies and Gentlemen of the Radio Audience*! . . . but the volume was too low; you could barely hear the thing from down the road, and no wonder Hale Hearty couldn't hear him, his *tubes* were giving out. . . .

He had lurched and felt his way up to a small corner of the bar, and wedged himself upright between the wall and one of the four occupied stools, and had ordered himself a beer, before it hit him with the weight of desire itself that the bartender was Turtle Teweles.

They had locked eyes at least once before, when Fanning ordered his beer. But Turtle hadn't even recognized him. . . .

Now Fanning gaped at Turtle, ogled him, wooed him with his eyes.

He hadn't changed, and yet he had. Gone were the flashy clothes that Turtle had affected as an announcer. He had on a short-sleeved shirt of some faded plaid design and a pair of stained khakis, over which he had tied an apron. He was moving up and down the short bar with a rolling gait, setting out bottles of beer and raking in change in short, professional movements. He seemed neither aloof from his clientele (as a baseball celebrity might be expected to seem) nor particularly involved with them. His face had lost its seamed, anxious expression. He looked like a man at peace.

When Turtle drew near, absently chucking quarters in his palm,

L. C. Fanning, blissful between tears and laughter, reached a paw far over the bar top and grabbed Turtle by the elbow.

"Why, you old owlhoot!"

Turtle turned absently, a man distracted from private thoughts. He gave Fanning a cordial nod.

"Turtle! God dammit, it's me! It's L.C.!"

When Teweles looked back at him again, the eyes were penetrating but noncommital. Fanning waited for the flash of recognition, the sudden lunge, the old Turtle Teweles ribald grin, the uproarious cry.

What he got instead were three blinks. Turtle's eyes were as opaque as a reptile's.

The country song on the jukebox had a contemporary beat: *"Got*-cha, *got*-cha, *got*-cha, *got*-cha.*"*

Turtle said, "Well, hello, L.C."

With something like a sob, Fanning blurted: "Why I was just in the neighborhood, and I thought I'd come around and see how the other half lived."

Turtle lowered his eyes to the beer in front of Fanning's heaving chest. It happened to be a Heine Meine.

"You all taken care of, now, are you."

"Turtle, for God's sake, it's me! It's L.C.! Can you hear me, Turtle?" In the din of the place he could barely hear his own voice, and he wondered wildly whether anything was coming out. But the warm bulk he'd been leaning against suddenly shifted. The man on the stool next to him slid out of the way with a curse and muttered, "Don't go gittin' you balls in an uproar, Grand-daddy!"

Fanning crashed onto the vacant stool without being aware of the motion. Turtle was staring at him fixedly now, like a man coming out of hypnosis.

"Do you recognize me, Turtle? Turtle, god dammit, do you hear me?" He groped crazily in his mind for the speech he'd rehearsed— all about his plan to get rid of Robyn, ruin her name so she would no longer be around to torment them. About how essential it was for the two of them to be together in the booth again. About the rhythms, the undefined but nonetheless sacred rightness of things that must be restored, to make it all come out pure and redeemed on the last day of the season, on Fanning's Day.

But all he could think to say now in the uproar of the tin tavern, this garbled inside of the giant radio set on the side of the nighttime Arkansas hill, was: "Turtle, can you hear me? Do you understand me, Turtle? Turtle? Do you hear me?"

CHAPTER

21

BY THE TIME FANNING RE-
joined the team, in Houston,
it was as though the apparatus of the Nats baseball coverage—the ball
club's front office, its public relations staff, the statisticians, the
sportswriters, the radio and the television contingents—had adjusted
itself to compensate seamlessly for his departure. It was as though
L. C. Fanning had not been a part of this interlaced community for a
generation.

Only a little less than two weeks had passed since he had left the
entourage unannounced in St. Louis. (As Turtle Teweles had left it in
St. Louis in June.) But upon his return he immediately felt as though
vast gulfs of time now hung between him and his identity. He felt
like some dim abstract fading statistic, some numbed memory, some
familiar, half-noticed shape at the corners of the eyes of the hustling
preoccupied regular citizens of the pressbox. Time, in his absence,
had leapt ahead of him, as though gratefully released from his own
stubborn hold; and now these people, his former friends and his acquaintances still when he had left, seemed to be enveiled in more sig-

nificant duties, more telling missions, than would allow for their slightest acknowledgment of his reappearance.

No one rushed to greet him when he stepped off the Astrodome press elevator, punctual as usual to his own clock, a precise two hours before game time. No one asked about his health, his state of mind, the possibility of crisis in his personal life. (Danny Breen, passing him in the causeway, raised a quick quizzical eyebrow, looked ahead, and hurried on.)

No one remarked on his appearance—for L. C. Fanning was a shockingly different man from the dandy who had strutted the baseball world these forty-two years gone. In just twelve days he had lost weight. The newly loose skin hung in folds beneath his eyes. The crescent of jowl now looked like a deflated balloon. There were little hyphens of dried blood, razor nicks, on the crescent (where never before had the pomaded flesh betrayed the least hint of tonsorial error). On his cheeks and chin were small outcroppings of white whisker.

More unsettling than his physical condition—for anyone who, knowing the announcer, had bothered to study him closely in his reemergence—was Fanning's attire.

Put simply, Fanning's clothes were a disgrace. Shoes unshined, jacket creased with tributary wrinkles like the palm of a hand, unpressed trousers at odds with the jacket, the floral-patterned shirt festooned all down the buttons with chalky white accretions of food, or worse. He stank of sweat and old cigar smoke. His eyes, bereft of dark glasses now, had an unfocused, haunted look. Only the Ambassador, the antique of a broad-brim hat still mashed atop the back of his head, retained a measure of dignity, of decorum. Perversely, it seemed now to be the one anchoring facet of Fanning's appearance, the one surviving link with contemporary awareness.

To anyone, that is, who made it a point to notice. But no one noticed. Fanning was absorbed instantly, mutely, back into the fabric of pressbox society. The matter-of-factness was in its way more of a blow to him than outright resistance might have been. He felt like a man returning to his job after years in prison, or in a hospital, and finding that not a single colleague had noticed he was gone.

Robyn had noticed.

When he stepped into the Nats' broadcast booth, she jumped up and came to him, her hands outstretched. "We've missed you. My goodness—you're thin!"

He had several things to say, and they all came up at once, and he couldn't get any of them started, and so the two of them just stood there looking at one another, holding hands.

"Did you, ah—find him?"

Her perception jolted him. He opened his mouth to make up some kind of lie, some pretense of not understanding what she was getting at—and only nodded. Another moment passed.

"Well." She gave his hand a final squeeze. She gestured toward his microphone. "We've kept things the same for you. Welcome back."

But things were not the same.

She was as beautiful as ever, and as meticulously made up. Her cheekbones fairly glistened, her eyeshadow matched the shade of the festive scarf with which she had bound back her hair. But it seemed to him that the femininity had drained from her expression. Her eyes were quick and darting, the shapely mouth now set in a firm line. Fanning detected a hard resonance in her voice, a resonance that was confirmed as the game began and he listened to her announce the play-by-play with a new crispness, a detached efficiency that somehow turned his heart to lead.

A shift of primacy had occurred. Robyn owned the booth now. It was she, not Fanning, who was the Nats' number one announcer. He was number two—the backup, the middle-innings man, the color—and even this role, it was tacitly clear, he filled at her pleasure. There was nothing he could do about it.

Her new, officious manner was merely a ratification of the transfer. During the game Robyn alluded to Fanning's return with a professional obliqueness that muted the question of his absence—she even threw him several leading lines, which he fielded mechanically, working himself back into the tapestry of the broadcast.

But there was no question as to who controlled the rhythms—the rhythms!—and who responded, subserviently, a tolerated guest in the realm he had so long ruled.

The Astrodome! What a fitting spot he'd picked to come back to, Fanning thought. The place had always made him half dizzy with revulsion; unnatural metallic blister on the Texas skin. Like being trapped inside a pinball machine. No sky, no sun, no rain, no breeze, no grass, no place (it had always seemed to him) to put your feet, drop a butt, stretch out and enjoy a game the way baseball was meant to be enjoyed . . . ah, well. Nobody else ever mentioned it anymore. He was the only one left, he guessed, who still felt scaly when he saw those cantilevered walls like the insides of a peeled orange closing over him. Especially considering where he'd been over the past days, the Astrodome felt like a weird punishment, a final judgment of hard, cold, curving truth.

After the game he felt a powerful urge to talk. The loneliness welled up in him and he ached to invite Robyn over to the Astroworld for a drink—he wanted to tell her about his odyssey out of Arkansas, as though the telling might confer a kind of tangibility on his feverish recollections—transfer them out of mad imagining, into the manageable realm of accomplished human fact.

But Robyn was gone from the booth before he could collect his wits—with a businesslike nod to him she strode out into the departing maw, melded with them, became one *of* them, and Fanning was left alone to confront the giant orb of the Astrodome, which, its trickle of humanity bleeding into the crevices, hovered at the black edges of his mind in its sepulchral Astrosilence.

He left a minute after she did.

He had finally found the wherewithal to steady his manic bawling and say to Turtle, there in the mad sweaty orangelighted noise of the Bowl-A-Wile in the deep night of Arkansas:

"I've come to take you back with me. Come on now, you old peckerwood, come back where you belong! Come finish out the season with your good friend and runnin' mate L. C. Fanning, we'll ride the kilowatt range! Come home, Turtle!"

And Turtle had said (looking through him with bland reptilian eyes):

"This is where I belong. This here is my home."

And Fanning had wailed: "I'll take care of the girl. You just leave the girl to me."

And Turtle, wiping a glass with delicate fingertips, his voice sinking now into the country-music swamp of noise:

"It's finished, L.C. You got to know when it's finished."

And Fanning (the last card): "They're gonna have a Day for me, Turtle! Turtle, why don't you come on back and be up there alongside of me in the booth when they have my Day?"

But Turtle had turned to talk to one of the others at the bar, a slit-eyed man with gold teeth and black fingernails, the two of them leaning almost nose to nose across the bar, (like a single man looking close into a mirror) talking in rhythms that L.C. couldn't decipher through the *got*-cha country-music beat. And he thought of a swimmer who had fought his way through dark green waters to reach a drowning friend, only to see the friend slip below the surface and out of reach at the moment of rescue—but which was the swimmer and which was the drowning man?—and it seemed that too many other voices were talking; there was static in the air, thick as the cigarette smoke that now tortured his throat, and there wasn't much room for him at the bar, and after a while he placed a dollar bill under his bottle of Heine Meine beer, and didn't wait for his change, but made his way out of the Bowl-A-Wile and into the cool night air of Arkansas. He was a big tipper.

How he traveled then. Fatigued, groaning with dry bonesore torpor, he found the little rent-a-car in the dark lot under the Christmas-tree lights, and he eased it down the hillside dirt road onto the blacktop highway, and the turn he made was east.

He drove through the night, picking up a big all-night station out of Cincinnati, his body cold in the car with its bug-stained windshield, but warmed by the glow from the radio dial.

He drove on a northeast line toward Mississippi (but only because that was where the road happened to take him; Fanning had no plan), the wheels hitting tar ridges in the pavement with the regularity of hammer blows—*Got*-cha, *got*-cha, *got*-cha, *got*-cha. He passed darkened farmhouses and was aware of mysterious points of light, like lanternlight, that glowed out from secret specific places, and of the black arrested skeletons of machinery. Little enclaves of human energy that he'd never know anything about. He began to remember similar feelings he used to have years ago, traveling across the nation by railroad train, with a major-league ball club, him the Boy Announcer, unable to sleep in the majestic transcontinental night—how he'd peer out the window, cupping his eyes, watching the shape of a farmhouse ride by, wondering (with less vanity than with a kind of mirthful astonishment) whether his voice had been *there,* inside that house. . . .

On the radio the Cincinnati announcer (a voice Fanning thought he recognized; he just couldn't connect it with a name) said that to take them up to news time they'd hear a little bit of music designed to keep all the night owls there awake, and he put on Glenn Miller's "In the Mood."

The music drove some of the emptiness from Fanning's soul; he rolled down the window and let the chilly night air suck at his arm. Immediately he felt a great hunger for breakfast. It was as though a presence had entered the car, an old friend—those trombones—and in his half-dreamy consciousness, alone on the highway, Fanning came to the discovery that all the friends in his life had been like "presences"—disembodied values, notes on a scale. The sleeping ballplayers on the overnight trains. Eleanor. Turtle. Bobby Thomson. His waitress, Ceceline. His father. All of them—no more and no less real than a Glenn Miller recording, or a home run, or a fancy new sport coat. His loneliness tonight was different only in intensity from his loneliness of the days of the wealth of his fame. The orange glow.

If he needed Turtle for the last days of his career, the days leading up to the Day, he might, by God, be forced to reinvent him.

Fanning crossed the Mississippi border before dawn and drove through towns with names like Russellville and Mechanicsburg and Crupp and Yazoo City. When the sky before him turned slate-gray with morning, he felt the grayness seep into his muscles. Heavy with fatigue, he took a room in a fourteen-dollar-a-night hotel in a small town on a railroad line. The night clerk, a man with greased-back hair and horn-rimmed glasses, charged him a two-dollar deposit on the key, and Fanning shuffled to the room with a wild euphoria surging under his weariness. The small room, smelling of rust and Coleo soap, seemed familiar, welcoming. He was on a high adventure into his own past. There was a reckless beckoning in the transient slant of morning light through the closed draperies. He had not felt so *on the road* in years. The last thing he noticed before drifting to sleep on the chemical-redolent sheets was an oddly domestic framed needlepoint on the wall. The needlepoint spelled the legend:

> ON FRIENDSHIP'S TREE
> GROWS SWEETEST FRUIT

It reminded him, deliriously, of another sign he had seen on another wall somewhere in his past:

> REALITY IS ONLY WHAT
> YOU PERCEIVE IT TO BE

Fanning motored eastward through the South for days after that. He had no plan. He knew, in a vague way, that he would rejoin the team at some point—but for the time being it seemed important to him to languish and drift, gathering his strength, focusing his addled attention on the great vindicating challenge that lay ahead: His triumphant final broadcast on Fanning's Day.

But all of that (he now realized, perched menially at Robyn Quarrles's side through the last, desultory weeks of the Nats baseball campaign) had been a mistake. Whatever strength he might have gathered from those balmy days in southern hotels, with their venetian blinds and their verandas and their card tables at which old women sat working jigsaw puzzles—his future!—and their offerings of luxurious early evenings spent savoring key-lime pie at adjacent coffee shops, the glass doors propped open onto the pavement with a brick, offering a view to the Trailways bus terminal sign—his past!— whatever strength, in sum, he might have gathered from all of this was as nothing before Robyn's imperial command of the broadcast booth.

The only thing left to him—the only redemption that made this shattering humiliation worthwhile—was the promise of his Day. And whatever the plans may have been, the Nats were certainly keeping it all a tight secret. There had been no publicity. There doubtlessly would be none. The word would be passed out discreetly, to participating merchants, to the invited celebrities and other old-timers (perhaps Turtle had received his invitation after all, perhaps his stubbornness was feigned, part of a plan—he'd show up at the last minute, strutting out to home plate, the ultimate Mystery Guest), to the fans themselves. Probably the season-ticket holders knew about it. But no one, not a soul, not Danny Breen or anyone, was letting on. (Perhaps that was the reason behind the silent treatment.)

And so L. C. Fanning drifted, dreamlike, into his last September.

CHAPTER

P ARKING METERS WENT UP IN
Brooklyn that fall.

Jimmy Durante published Schnozzola.

"Some companies forbade the tuning in of the game broadcast, but most executives figured that little work would be done anyway. Besides, the boss was just as tense over the play-by-play progress as the office boy."

The newspapers ran photographs of soldiers being carried down from Heartbreak Ridge.

A Philco midget-size radio went for $42.70.

(Random memories. From the last pure season. Crackling now in his brain, old electrical charges. Clear visions—facts that seemed important then, fragments of data from that world, not related and yet inseparable, each fragment possessing an energy that linked it with all the rest, forming a unified field, like the airwaves, like what he had understood about love. Popping alive again in his mind, pleasurable illuminations. Now that it was all over. Now that the last illusion had been stripped away and he sat, a foolish silent old man

on a chair in a booth, watching the last baseball game bleed into insignificance on an artificial field.)

Radios in prison cellblocks. . . .

"The barbershop without a radio was also one without a customer."

From Here to Eternity *was in its seventeenth printing. Harper and Brothers published Hesketh Pearson's biography of Benjamin Disraeli,* Dizzy.

Overcast skies. The threat of rain.

The thing was (oh, the memory still made him shudder with delight), the Giants had come from thirteen and one-half games behind the Dodgers beginning on August 11. On that day they defeated the Philadelphia Phillies 4 to 0. They did not lose again for sixteen days, during which time they won fifteen games and narrowed Brooklyn's lead to six.

The Giants began September by trouncing the Dodgers twice, 8 to 1 on September 1 and 11 to 2 on September 2. Over the next ten days they played relatively modest baseball, winning six games and losing four, two of those losses being doubleheader splits—with the Phillies and Cards.

On September 13 the Giants stood exactly where they had on August 27—six games behind the league-leading Brooklyn Dodgers.

There were seventeen days to go in the season. Thirteen games.

The Giants were to lose exactly one: 3 to 1, to the Reds, on September 20.

Now, thirty years later, Fanning could recite those scores as unerringly as a Michigan child reciting a nighttime prayer. (Good evening, Ladies and Gentlemen of the Radio Audience! . . .)

A two-game sweep of the Cubs, 7–2 and 5–2. A doubleheader victory over Pittsburgh, 7–1 and 6–4. An open date. Giants 6, Reds 5. Another day off. The lone defeat to Cincinnati. Now: three straight conquests of the Boston Braves, 4–1, 4–1, 4–3. Giants 5, Phils 1. Giants 10, Phils 1. An off day (Brooklyn loses; Giants are a half game out). Another off day (Dodgers stumble again—the National League pennant race is tied with two dates remaining).

(A photograph of Eisenhower "scanning European skies.")

September 29—Giants 2, Braves 0. Dodgers also win. September 30—Giants 3, Braves 2, behind Larry Jansen hurling all the way.

Dodgers win, in the fourteenth, 9–8 over the Phils, on a Jackie Robinson home run. Dodgers had trailed Phils 6–1, then 8–5. Robinson saved it in the twelfth with an electrifying inning-ending catch of a low line drive by Eddie Waitkus with the bases full.

"Now the play-off comes. For the next week, just as in the past few days, even the grimmest of worldwide news will have an over-shadowing rival in the whirl and clash of the great American game . . ."

Acting Mayor Joseph T. Sharkey, pausing at Grand Central Station, into a microphone thrust forward by L. C. Fanning:

"I don't think there will be much work done in this town for the next ten days!"

And quoted in the next day's papers. (Oh, the accolades . . .)

"New York rocked yesterday with the great schism of 1951. As the weary Brooklyn Dodgers squeaked agonizingly into a tie with the New York Giants for first place in the National League, the metropolis went quietly mad trying to figure out which radio station to listen to and which team to root for."

The Day The Earth Stood Still *opened at the Mayfair.*

Temperature in the middle fifties. For New York City, considerable cloudiness and not so cool Monday with highs in the middle sixties, moderate to southwesterly winds. Low in the mid-fifties.

October 1:

GIANT HOMERS BEAT DODGERS
IN PLAYOFF OPENER 3 TO 1

"The Polo Grounds Express, which started carrying the Giants from nowhere six weeks ago, is still traveling at terrific speed. . . ."

Bobby Thomson and Monte Irvin hit home runs for the Giants, both off Brooklyn hurler Ralph Branca. Andy Pafko homered for the Dodgers in the second, giving Ebbets Field fans something to cheer about. . . .

(Was it possible that it was going to end this way? Him silent in this cold booth, Turtle gone, the girl, oceans away to his left, chattering on, giving no sign that she'd be needing even a word from him . . . and he fought to keep his mind on the moment, on the game

bleeding out below him, but the past compelled him, and he let the old electrical charges take hold again.)

Bobby Thomson, speaking into L. C. Fanning's microphone about Monday's homer:

"I hit a fast ball for that homer; caught it right, too. Makes you feel good to hit 'em that way. Particularly in a spot like that. It was a great feeling when I saw it traveling into the stands."

The Giants had now won their last eight, thirteen of their last fourteen, thirty-eight of their last forty-five.

WHEELS OF COMMERCE, INDUSTRY TURN IN LOW AS WORKERS LISTEN IN ON RADIOS

"Even the banter was held strictly to between-innings pauses, and the occasional joker who tried to crack wise while the play-by-play was crackling was brusquely silenced with, 'Shut up or beat it!' "

Channel 9 televised the first playoff game; Channel 11, the second and third . . .

"A woman, in a housedress, sat in the Automat on the Avenue of the Americas near 42nd St., a cup of coffee and a small radio on the table before her. The set was turned low, and there was a crowd about it."

October 2:

DODGERS WIN 10–0 BEHIND ROOKIE LABINE
Robinson 2-Run
Homer in First

Ralph Branca chortles, "The magic number is down to one."

(Labine, a blond kid with a crew haircut, sits on a trunk and asks for a cigarette. Clem served two and a half years with the paratroops in Europe. . . .)

The Dow Jones tickers reporting the play-by-play on Wall Street. . . .

A forty-one minute break caused by rain late in the game. . . .

"Times Square assumed a Sabbathlike calm, with little motor traffic and only a scattering of pedestrians on the streets. . . ."

*   *   *

And now, three decades later, this day.

The weather was the same—cloudy, temperature in the fifties. Sabbathlike calm—yes, that would accurately describe the present mood at Flushing Stadium on this rarest of schedulings, a Monday afternoon, where exactly nine hundred fourteen customers had paid their way inside to witness the final game of the Nats' dismal baseball season, against the San Diego Padres.

Nine hundred fourteen.

Who were they? What untold combinations of loneliness, despair, escape, macabre humor, forlorn devotion, curiosity, crazed delusion, had produced this precise number, this specific collection of refugees from metropolis's baleful rhythms? What transient hotels, public schools, machine shops, taverns, hospitals, park benches, taxicabs, bleak sitting rooms were deficient in population units that, in the aggregate, would comprise this silent, scattered audience?

Flushing Stadium looked like an empty claw. The broken circle that described its grandstand sweep—the tiers bitten off at the foul lines—where the awesome scoreboard presided—seemed, in its emptiness, to have unclenched, to have yielded at last a long-held pretense of might. Devoid of festive humanity, the endless seats exhibited their bands of identifying bright colors, unpurchased ribbons at an abandoned fair. Peeling paint was visible from the press rim, as were dark pockets of ripped-out seats like missing teeth. The dye on the artificial outfield grass had faded in patches to a sickly aquamarine. Even the scoreboard had surrendered to the torpor of a bad season badly ended: the stereo music system was not working and, on the Other Games section, someone had punched up the typographical error "Atalanta."

Not even Danny Breen could find the semantics to portray this day as anything but what it was—a mockery of major-league technology and know-how. Nobody (as it had been clear for weeks) really cared to come out and amuse themselves with scoreboard pyrotechnics, pregame entertainment, fancifully named junk food, music, mascots, and sexily dressed usherettes. Not when there was a team like the Nats on the field.

This day.

Fanning edged forward in his metal folding chair. It was not his day. Not Fanning's Day.

(Well, he thought, with a private smile, not exactly. Not in your textbook manner of speaking, it wasn't his Day. But what was it he always liked to say: The game is never over till the last man is out.)

It was, in fact, close to that eventuality: two out in the bottom of the ninth inning of a supremely flatulent baseball contest between two major-league teams that clearly wished to be elsewhere. The Nats, true to form, were on the short end of a 6 to 1 score. Both teams hung about their defensive positions like insolent street gangs—furtive, sullen, vaguely embarrassed. There had already been six errors. San Diego's leading hitter, a third baseman by trade, was at the moment pitching an inning—a publicity stunt. To Fanning's left Robyn Quarrles clattered out the play-by-play with the detached efficiency of a teletype machine.

He had willed himself to believe the Day was possible right up until the moment when reality flooded in like hard sunlight on a dreaming man, the moment far beyond any reasonable doubt, the moment when denial itself became undeniable.

He had awakened before dawn in the apartment that was like a hotel room, and spent an hour making final corrections on the speech he had worked up for the occasion. (It was a glowing speech, full of affectionate remembrances, affable jibes at himself for memorable on-air bloopers, his list of the Ten Greatest Players He'd Personally Seen, his thanks to a list of people who had made his career possible, some thoughts about Baseball and the American Scene. Heartfelt tributes to Mel Pelham, "the Old Sergeant" and his early mentor; to "all the fine folks" at MetroCom and Radio Station WERA; to his fellow broadcasters. A section written in two versions, one beginning, "And a special note of thanks to my longtime partner and running mate, Turtle Teweles, who unfortunately could not be with us today. . . ." and the other beginning, "And as for you, Turtle, you old horsethief—now folks, I ask you, what kind of a guy would drop in at the last minute and help himself to some of all this free publicity. . . ."

(He had sketched in something of his retirement plans. The deal with his friend the radio station owner in Florida looked as though it were going to come through—nothing had exactly been signed on the dotted line, but Fanning knew the man would jump at the chance to have his name—and so he planned to drop some hint on the order of,

"You folks planning a vacation in the St. Petersburg area, now, you better know you haven't quite got rid of old L.C. yet. . . ."

(There were no recriminations, no hard feelings. No allusions to the changes, the difficulties, the behind-the-scenes acrimony, in this final season of his great career. A Day, after all, was for tying it all together, for cementing bonds; a Day was for nobility.)

He had been dabbing at the speech all summer, in longhand, at odd moments—alone in the booth an hour before game time, on the airplane, in hotel rooms after midnight. Just a week before he had gathered all the jottings and typed them into a script, using triple spacing and all capitals, the classic radioman style. Now, in this spare yellow lamplight, he had bent to his final flourishes. His lower lip moved with the words and his breath came in small irregular wheezes. The radio beside his bed was on; a woman's voice kept saying "Thank you" to what Fanning gathered, with the minute fraction of his mind that was devoted to the sound, was a Chiquita banana. An "accu-weather" forecast came on, and then a news announcer's voice said that although a cease-fire was in effect, violence continued. He wasn't really listening.

When Fanning had satisfied himself that the remarks were the way he wanted them, he had gone into the bathroom and spent the next twenty-five minutes shaving. He applied steaming hot towels to his neck and cheeks—for some reason he bled easily of late—and eased his straight razor through the coils of lather with strokes as delicate as those of an artist's brush on onionskin. It all had to be just right. No blemishes. Nothing to mar this closing day.

Then, patting his skin dry with a fresh white towel, he had opened his closet door, switched on the overhead light bulb, and reached for the suit.

It lay on a wooden hanger, still enfolded by the plastic bag that the salesman had slipped around it for him to carry out of the store. It was unlike any suit Fanning had ever owned. He had ordered it tailor-made for himself when the Nats were in New York for a home stand back in June. Now he carefully pulled it free of its wrapping, switched on the room's overhead light, and smoothed the jacket and trousers down across the surface of his bed.

The silk shone even in the room's dull light. The suit was a royal gray—dignified, subdued, and yet not so dark a shade as to seem funereal. Conservatively cut, with a row of functional buttons adorning each cuff, it was a suit that called up all of the underlying grandeur, the magisterial tide, of Fanning's forty-two years as a distinguished radio play-by-play man. (It was not as though he was abandoning his popular penchant for colorful clothing; but on this closing day, a more meditative note was called for.) He would wear it with a starched white shirt and a necktie of orange and blue—orange for the old New York Giants, blue for today's New York Nats. Should the symbolism go unnoticed, he was prepared to point it out.

After putting it on (and noting to his dismay the excess material that already gathered at the waist and the shoulders), Fanning realized that he had nothing more to do until game time. Six hours.

He took the suit off and replaced it on the hanger and sat listening to the radio, until he dozed.

He had sensed doom as soon as he arrived at the stadium. He sported a red boutonniere in his lapel. The Ambassador was in place on his head, and—an impulsive, nostalgic touch for the fans—he carried his aluminum net.

But there were no cars in the lot. No people. His name was not on the stadium marquee.

Inside the press gate, no one from the Nats' front office or from Radio Station WERA waited to escort him off to a battery of interviews or to a hospitality suite.

Still, as he rode the press elevator to the stadium's rim, Fanning held out hope. The possibility remained that the Nats people planned to hit him with a last-minute surprise. That was the way they liked to handle such affairs, after all—spring it on a fellow totally out of the blue.

And then he took his first look down at the playing field. And shut his eyes.

It was the absence of bunting that told him there would be no Day. That was the moment when reality flooded in, the moment when denial itself became undeniable.

No bunting on the walls. On Days, there was always bunting. Red, white, and blue. And a microphone at home plate.

He was standing at the top of a flight of concrete stairs that led down into the newspaper press section, his left hand resting lightly on the protective rail, contemplating the playing field where the Padres were taking infield, when every particle of air seemed to leave his lungs and the blackness exploded between his temples. A dizzying throb filled his mind; it lasted only an instant and then things were clear again, but in that instant the aluminum net and the attaché case dropped from his right hand and Fanning started to swoon forward. He gripped the protective rail with his left hand in time to prevent himself from pitching down the concrete steps—and, God knows, over the edge—but his sudden lurching motion caught the attention of several people. A boy in horn-rimmed glasses, the Nat statistician, came running to him: "Are you all right, Mr. Fanning?" Several writers hurried to his side, assisted him into a sitting position on the concrete steps.

"Hold on there, L.C."

"Steady."

"What's the problem, L.C.?"

"Get him a cup of water."

Fanning blinked and peered up into the faces. It struck him that he recognized them, every one. Why shouldn't he? He saw them every day. These were his friends, the men in the pressbox. Men he had counted as bosom companions, until a time this summer that now seemed as far in the past as October 1951.

The expressions on the faces that looked back at him were of mingled concern and embarrassment. There was an urgency in the faces. Each looked as though it had a question to ask him.

Had he misread these men? Was it possible that he had mistaken their attitude when all the changes happened, when Robyn came into his life and Turtle departed? Had he just imagined their contempt, their hostility?

"No," he said aloud. He shook his head. Some of the black mists cleared. "No, I'm fine. Breakfast backed up on me, that's all. I'll be fine."

His voice, he realized, was gruff. But he meant it to be. He had not been mistaken. If nothing had changed, how the hell could they have ignored his Day?

They had humiliated him—worse, they had condemned him. He felt his entire career, all forty-two years, escaping like the heart's

blood through this terrible leak that was his pitiful, unstopped fi-
nale. All the passion, all the imagery, the sense of the palette, his
great, ongoing, half-articulated, half-mystical attempt to embrace the
quotidian rhythms of America in all his broadcasts . . . his private
vision of Thomson's homer, the comet bisecting the American century . . . gone, dissipating into the ether, infinitely dissolving. Mel
Pelham's face veered grotesquely into his mind's eye. (*Oh, the accolades* . . .)

Fanning sat on the concrete step until the men around him drifted
away. There had been an uncomfortable silence. So be it. The devil
with all of them.

After a few minutes he arose, dusted off the seat of his royal gray
silk suit, and walked, alone, toward the press lounge. His throat was
bothering him. He needed a beer.

Robyn was there. She caught his eye, hesitated, raised a hand in
greeting. He glimpsed the red fingernails. He did not acknowledge
her wave, but turned toward the bar. God, but he felt old.

She was standing in the center of a group of the press crowd. Some
of the men near her were the same ones who had tried to assist him a
few minutes ago. Fanning had noticed, since his return from the
quest for Turtle, that Robyn—incredibly—had been accepted into the
circle. The writers and broadcasters and front-office people were
treating her as one of them.

The poison spreads. Good thing he was getting out. On whatever
terms. He put his hand around a wax cup of beer, and saw that the
hand was trembling.

He could not shut out the conversation behind him. They were
ragging Robyn, but beneath the rough banter he could discern a con-
gratulatory mood.

"Just promise us one thing," a man's voice was saying. Dorton's.
"When you get there, you're not gonna do any of them goddamn
nauseating slow-motion *vignettes* on some fag quarterback, right,
with the goddamn theme music in the background, for chrissake, like
'I Did It My Way.' You hear what I'm saying?"

"That's right, Robyn. Tell those network stiffs to just cut all the
candy-ass and kick the ball off and play the freakin' football game."

"No, no. Robyn's gonna be down there on the field between

plays. Interviewin' the guys on their favorite way to make bouilla-baisse. Ain't it right, Robyn?''

"Hey, Robyn. Don't let these guys bullshit you. They're gonna be the first ones writin' to you for freebies. Fifty-yard line, Super Bowl. It don't matter if they have you doin' a striptease at halftime. You're gonna get great fan mail from all these mooches.''

"Never fear, gentlemen.'' Robyn's voice, tinged with the irritating new quality he had heard in it lately—a brittle pitch, hard and profes-sionally clipped, that had replaced her former humorous lilt. "Ms. Quarrles does not intend to further besmirch the hallowed traditions of sports announcing. Ms. Quarrles will be more macho than Pat Summerall, if not holier than the pope.''

"Drink to *that*.''

"Come on, Robyn. You can unbend this once. Chrissake. Red-let-ter day.''

And Robyn's laugh: "You talked me into it, guys. . . .'' The voices faded.

So she had landed a network assignment! Fanning pressed his fingertips to his temples, and the universe went red. The corners of his mouth jerked in spasmodic rhythms and finally settled into a hard grin. This was the final blasphemy.

This was the conquest of the airwaves themselves.

She had pulled it off. Consummated the cold-blooded design that he'd come to understand not long after she dropped into his life, liter-ally out of nowhere:

She had robbed him. Sucked the magic out of him; memorized it, enveloped it, *digested* it . . . she, who had no allegiance to the uni-verse of baseball, no communion with the people who followed it, no passion for unifying those two elements using the palette of the air-waves. She had marched into his broadcast booth like a marauding commando, snatched up the skills she needed, and now was moving on to rejoin that nefarious army that (Fanning could see now) had been advancing steadily on him, across all the years, while his own attention was turned inward, toward the unchanging imperatives, the guaranteed renewals, of the game itself.

And he had helped her. Pleaded with her to stay.

The nefarious army . . .

The Breens, the Spectors. All the technicians who were arranging a new universe . . . a universe of bogus grass under bogus skies and teams of strangers in stadiums like insulated cities.

Robyn's world.

Not at all like the world that existed on October 3, 1951, when Bobby Thomson hit the home run and life was green and grand.

This afternoon he would give them that world.

Afterward, he could never recall for sure the exact moment at which that astonishing notion crossed his mind. It could have blossomed at the moment when he learned of Robyn's ascension.

Or perhaps the seed had been gestating in him all summer, since the first night she addressed the microphone and the imperatives of his final season were irrevocably altered.

Or maybe the seed had been planted far back beyond this culminating season, back beyond Robyn's time, back in the last pure season, at the instant Thomson's comet bisected the century (it actually rose in flight!) . . . perhaps right then the logic of L. C. Fanning's valedictory moment on the airwaves had been ordained.

All he was sure of, as he drained the foam from the last free cup of Heine Meine beer he would ever take, and began his last stroll to the broadcast booth, was that he had hit upon his salvation.

And that his salvation depended (why had he not always known it? perhaps he had) upon a simple piece of radio equipment.

It was known as a ''Y connection'': a length of insulator cable that ran between the public-address announcer's booth, two doors away, to the Nats' home radio broadcast booth. One end was permanently attached to the stadium loudspeaker system. The cord extended through the intervening booth, bound innocuously to a trunk line of electrical wiring. Its other end lay on the floor beneath the WERA microphones. It needed only to be affixed—with a penknife and screw—to one of the Electro-Voice mikes, and the announcer had immediate access to the Flushing Stadium loudspeakers as well as to the airwaves.

Fanning had seen the cord connected by the stadium engineer countless times over the years. It was used whenever some ceremonial occasion called for the WERA play-by-play team to address the stadium crowd as well as the radio audience: Old-Timers days, Father and Son games, commemorations, Fourth of July observances.

It would have been connected for Fanning's Day.

Well, by God, he thought. Now it would be.

And thus L. C. Fanning sat silently beside Robyn Quarrles while the last ball game of his career bled on into oblivion. Silently while the woman on his left, glutted with her victory, chattered away like some Teletype machine, hopelessly efficient, heedless of him. . . .

Not for long.

Two out in the bottom of the ninth inning.

Do or die. Now or never. It was time.

He reached down and felt along the floor. He could tell without looking when the right cable came within his grasp. Pressing the end between his knees, Fanning opened his attaché case and rummaged until he found a small, folded pocket knife. He opened a flat-edged blade.

Unobserved by Robyn, Fanning set about connecting the wire end to his Electro-Voice microphone.

It couldn't have taken him more than fifteen seconds. He closed the case, cleared his throat. He released an involuntary chuckle that drew a quick scowl from Robyn. He placed both elbows firmly on the microphone shelf. As it happened, Bogart Humphries was just digging himself into position at home plate. Humphries held up one gloved hand for time as he studiously kicked and scuffed his spikes into their proper place. It could have been the god damned World Series the way Humphries twisted and twitched, shimmied and spat, arranging himself with all the self-important exactitude of a man hell-bent upon adding one last, precious negotiating point to his season's totals. . . .

Well, thought L. C. Fanning, *excuse the hell out of me, Mr. Humphries, but . . .*

"LIGHT UP A CHESTERFIELD!"

A clarion voice trumpeted across the empty claw of Flushing Stadium. The words flashed, almost visible in a blaze of energy like sunlight, through the sodden afternoon.

"LADIES AND GENTLEMEN! YOUR ATTENTION, PLEASE!

LIGHT UP A CHESTERFIELD AND RETURN WITH ME TO THE
THIRD OF OCTOBER, NINETEEN FIFTY-ONE!''

The voice shimmered, electric with an orange brilliance of its own.
It echoed off the seats, the scoreboard, the outfield wall. It undulated
with a thrilling urgency that caused scattered fans in the lonely stands
to turn their heads, searching. Bogart Humphries jerked, grabbed his
helmet, and slammed it on the ground. The Padres gaped. The plate
umpire swiveled. Held up his arms for time.

For time. Fanning slid his body forward on the chair until his chest
pressed against the microphone shelf. He swiped at the knot of his
necktie, yanked it low. His hand went to the crown of his Ambassador and he shoved the old hat to the side of his head. He was ready
for action.

"Ladies and Gentlemen! To set the scene for you! It is the *Polo
Grounds*! It is the bottom of the *ninth* inning of the third game in the
historic National League playoff series between the New York Giants
and the Brooklyn Dodgers! The *Giants* . . . coming from *thir*teen
and a half games out to tie the Dodgers on the *last day* of the season!
A demented Hollywood scriptwriter in the *last throes* of delirium
tremens would not have *dared* to pen anything so completely fantastic as the way this pennant race has come down to the finish!''

He was conscious of footsteps scuttling in the corridor. Then
Danny Breen's voice, pitched to a falsetto shriek:

"L.C., have you gone crazy? Robyn, what's he doing in there?''

He could see that Robyn was standing, staring down at him. There
was a lopsided grin on her face.

Robyn turned toward Breen. Others had gathered behind Breen to
stare; Fanning could hear them. Robyn's next words traveled along
Fanning's spine like an electric current:

"He's *announcing,* you stupid son of a bitch! What does it *sound*
like he's doing?''

He took a quick stock of the situation on the field. The game had
stopped—evaporated, as it were. Players, coaches, managers, and
umpires drifted trancelike away from their positions, out of the dugouts. They formed a cluster of disbelieving humanity in the center of
the infield.

And then the present dropped away, and Fanning beheld in a part of his mind's eye a Rheingold sign above center field, and a Longine's clock that showed the time of day. The Polo Grounds came up around him, and he had work to do:

"So it has come down to *this inning*! The two ball clubs *tied* at one game apiece . . . and the *Dodgers* behind Big Don Newcombe *holding* on to a four-to-one lead here in the last of the ninth inning! But *don't* go away, the Giants have something cooking! Alvin Dark *opened* the inning with a scratch single off the glove of Gil Hodges. Then Don Mueller singled to right with Dark racing to third. Monte Irvin popped to first base, so with one out the veteran Whitey Lockman is the batter! General Omar Bradley and General Matthew B. Ridgeway have landed in *Korea* to survey the *military situation*! In *Gatlinburg, Tennessee*, the GOP governors are thumping the tub for Dwight D. Eisenhower as the Republican Presidential nominee in 1952! The *pope* has warned of the possibility of a *Third World War*! The dollar of 1941 is now worth fifty-seven cents, Martin and *Lewis* are at the RKO, Turtle *Teweles* is a young catcher and my wife, Eleanor, God *bless* her, is at home with the *radio* on! So *listen*, god dammit, listen, Ladies and Gentlemen, because it'll *never again* be as good as it is now!''

He paused again and listened. The shock of his voice echoed off the Flushing Stadium girders. The Polo Grounds girders. A team in dusky blue-gray flannels had replaced the San Diego Padres. Billowing uniforms, the trouser legs pulled high on the knee. Blue uniform caps.

He held back for a beat, two beats, three beats. Timing was everything now. Transition.

Behind him, Breen muttered: "Well, for chrissake, somebody's got to disconnect him. This is insane.''

And Robyn, immediately: "Danny, this is the greatest public relations stunt you have ever pulled at this ball park. If you let it go on, you're famous. If you stop it, you're a joke in every newspaper in the country.''

Fanning turned and looked at her. She returned his gaze. She smiled. She raised a hand and made a circle with a thumb and finger. Somehow he was not bothered any longer, by the red fingernails.

He gave her a slight nod. What the hell. He gave her a grin.

And then L. C. Fanning went back to work.

He felt the authority grow in him; the old exhilaration flowed back into his veins, the sensation of *control*, as though the stadium itself were a mighty instrument and he was the artist, the soloist, and the microphone his reed.

A baseball inning thirty years dead had sprung before his eyes. The power of it rushed into his veins: a transfusion.

He didn't need a scorebook. Notes. Reminders. Promptings of any kind. It was all in him. The part of him that neither Robyn nor any of the rest of them could ever unlock. He was going to give it to them free.

Fanning, it seemed after all, was going to have his Day.

"So *light up a Chesterfield*! And we'll see what happens here! *Lock*man the batter! Whitey's had, uh—one hit today . . . and a sac-rifice. . . . *New*combe out talking to Reese, talking to Robinson . . . they're talking about the best way to *pitch* to Lockman. . . . *Bobby Thomson* is off to the right of home plate."

On the mound, Fanning saw the dark hulking form of a pitcher—a Negro—the sweat shining on his long face. At the plate, feet to-gether, a silver-blond man in a white uniform, orange trim on the dark lettering. The man, lean and lithe, young, waving his bat at Don Newcombe . . .

"First and third occupied, one down. . . . *Lock*man is the fellow who *has* to get on! He represents the *tying run!* Big Newk *stretches*! The *pitch* to Whitey . . . and he *swings* and fouls it back as he went for a high fast ball . . . *that's* the kind of ball that Whitey can hit for distance . . .

"It's four to one *Brook*lyn, this is the last of the ninth inning with *one* out . . . it's the last of the ninth inning in *more respects* than . . . you've ever seen! The last of the ninth inning of *nineteen fifty-one*! *Mueller* with his lead. Alvin Dark doing *like*wise down the third-base line. The *pitch* to Whitey . . ."

The lean young man uncoiled.

"A *LINE DRIVE BASE HIT* TO LEFT FIELD! *HERE* COMES ALVIN DARK SCORING! DON MUELLER TRIES FOR THIRD . . . *LOCK*MAN TRIES FOR SECOND . . . *LOCK*MAN IS IN THERE, HE REPRESENTS THE TYING RUN . . . AND THE DODGERS LEAD IS NOW FOUR TO TWO!"

Fanning paused, to allow a phantom crowd of thirty-four thousand, three hundred twenty to roar itself silly. Behind him, as over a great distance, he heard someone whisper, *"Damn. . . ."* Someone else coughed discreetly, covering it with a fist.

But now a flurry at third base, a man rushing onto the field with a black valise in his hand, caught Fanning's attention.

"And Don Mueller might have hurt himself sliding into third. Whitey *Lock*man! . . . doubled into the left-field corner. And *Bobby Thomson* will be the Giant batter . . . Don jammed his ankle . . . sliding into third, Doc Bowman is out there. . . .

"Whitey Lockman doubled over third base. Chuck Dressen walks off slowly! . . . Whitey *Lock*man who, with time out, goes over to look at Don Mueller . . . the boy that the Giants and Giant fans refer to as Mandrake. . . ."

And now a presence at home plate: a tall young athlete, lanky, almost frail beneath the shimmering billows of his white uniform (the shimmering tinged with an orange glow that seemed to Fanning so familiar, something bygone and yet eternal) stood working the spikes of his right shoe into the batter's box. He drummed his bat lightly on home plate, then raised it lightly above his head, where it shined in a brief arc.

The jersey bore the numerals "23."

The Scotsman. Edinburgh-born Bobby Thomson. A premonition seized Fanning: he suddenly sensed what was approaching. A desire, an ecstasy, washed through his blood, and his voice became a magnet, drawing all the fragments of the great splintered pallette of a country together, across the airwaves; one last time . . .

"So, *Bobby Thomson* . . . with the score four to two . . . will be batting with runners at second and third. And . . . Lockman at second, one of the fastest of the Giants . . . will represent the tying run. I've never seen anything like this one! . . . in a long, long time. In something like a hundred years . . . and I've only been around for ninety-nine." He allowed a chuckle into his voice. Break the tension.

At third base, men bearing wooden slats; a flash of yellow-white canvas. The men kneeling.

"Mueller seems to have hurt himself, and Doc Bowman's working on him . . . are they gonna bring the stretcher out, yes, they are. They're gonna have to take Mueller out of the game. . . .

"Don is gonna be removed from the field on a stretcher! We did *not* see him slide into third . . . I was watching *Pafko* as he tried to *back*hand the ball to throw to second base to get *Lock*man . . . and, uh, the Dodgers have *another* conference out there, and Chuck Dressen is . . . making up his mind whether to bring in powerhouse *Ralph Branca* . . . or Clem Labine. Don Mueller is being *carried off the field*, and he will get a tre*men*dous ovation. . . . from this *big crowd at the Polo Grounds*.

"So, don't go anywhere, willya not? Light up that Chesterfield, stay right with us . . . and we'll see how Ralph Branca will fare against Bobby Thomson and then Willie Mays to follow.

". . . Jim Hearn, warming up in the bullpen. He has not appeared in relief this year. . . . Clem Labine . . . throws in the bullpen, along with Carl Erskine. And Bobby Thomson is on the biggest spot of his entire baseball career. Bobby, who did not have much minor-league experience, has never been involved in a pennant race as yet. This is the biggest spot for him in his entire history! . . . and he'll be up there against Big Ralph Branca, swinging."

Now the moment neared. The sacred trajectory, the peak moment in American time . . . the comet . . . the ball would *take off* . . . would actually *rise in flight*. The young L. C. Fanning was seized with a feeling that had no plausible explanation in the brief span of his years: a feeling of redemption . . .

"A *home run* would win it for the Giants! And win the championship! A *single* to the outfield would more than likely *tie up* the ball game and keep the inning going! . . . So *Leo Durocher* . . . comes over and *talks* to Bobby . . . the *Dod*gers lead it four to two. And *Willie Mays* walks slowly out of the dugout; he'll be the *next* Giant hitter."

The bearlike Negro pitcher trudging off toward the dugout, head down. Another pitcher, the defiant numeral "13" on the back of his blue-gray jersey, making the long walk in from the visitors' bullpen.

"Branca, on the spot, he knows it . . . the big boy from Mt. Vernon, New York . . . with a slight cold . . . *wipes* off the perspiration from his brow . . . and the Dodgers play their infield deep. There's no double-play possibility on a ground ball.

". . . And Ralph Branca will come in. They're gonna put, uh— Clint Hartung in to run for Mueller. . . . Hank Schenz returns to the bench . . . and *Ralph Branca* . . . makes the long walk from the bullpen.''

Now an odd transmutation in the stands below: it seemed to Fanning as though the entire Polo Grounds crowd—all thirty-four thousand, three hundred twenty—had somehow coalesced behind home plate: had drifted from scattered lonely outposts about the stadium to huddle in a space where less than a thousand might normally stand. A sudden impulsive community; strangers unified. They were on their feet, looking—not at the field, but up, at him.

And the field itself . . . at the edge of Fanning's consciousness, glimmers of a wispy second image there: like ghosts, another collection of ballplayers had gathered. They wore strange uniforms, tight on their bodies, and their hair mushroomed beneath their caps. They milled on the baseline where Clint Hartung took his lead. Some of the ghosts flipped baseballs. Others balanced bats in the palms of their hands. Like the coalesced crowd, they were looking up at him.

He heard footsteps again outside the cubicle behind him; heard the knot of onlookers shift and give way; heard Danny Breen's half whisper:

''I just talked to Spector, Robyn. Kid knows what he's doing. He's got this on all the MetroCom stations and he's getting clearances every minute around the country.''

Around the country! A coast-to-coast hookup! Fanning's mind flashed to the Arkansas town. . . .

But low now. Low and steady. Build the moment:

''. . . Clint Hartung is at third base, Whitey Lockman is at second, the Dodgers lead four to two . . . and Ralph Branca, who has won thirteen ball games on the year . . . thirteen and eleven. He's given up eighteen home runs. Bobby Thomson against the, uh, Brooklyn club . . . has hit a lot of long ones this year; he's had seven homers.

''Billy Cox is deep! *Bobby Thomson!* . . . who has had, uh—two out of three! *Jim Hearn* in the Giant bullpen! Bobby *Thomson,* up there swingin' . . . he's had *two* out of three, a *single* and a double . . . and *Billy Cox* is playing him right on the *third base line!*''

America paused, waited. Held its breath. Fanning reached up to adjust his Ambassador. It was gone. Somebody behind him must have lifted it from his head; a souvenir. His hand came down on bare skull: his own skull. He was surprised at his skull's texture: so dry and brittle for a man so young.

He wheeled around to search the faces behind him for the culprit. What he saw was the same face, endlessly repeated: pale, featureless, like a mask.

He turned back to the action on the field.

Instantly he saw that a grotesque thing had happened to the Giants and the Dodgers: *they were no longer young.* Their bellies had suddenly bloated. Their arms and legs had withered. The lightning passage of time, which he had feared as a boy in his Michigan bed, had now transpired. There was darkness where a light had been.

He could see the details of their faces as clearly as though someone had pressed a mirror to his eye: could see the latticework of veins in the noses, the thinning hair beneath the caps, the half-moons of flesh at the jowls. Thomson himself—a preposterous man in middle age, clad in the uniform of a boy, attempting to act out a hopeless dream.

A dark sea seemed to break over Fanning. A force was trying to wash him loose from his moorings, drown the orange glow, send him swirling into oblivion. He would not let it happen. His voice would save him. Gripping the microphone shelf with his fingers against the swelling tide, he kept his voice even:

"One out . . . last of the ninth . . . Branca pitches, Bobby Thomson takes a *strike call* on the outside corner. Bobby hitting at two ninety-two . . . he's had a *single* and a *double* and he drove in the Giants' *first* run with a *long fly to center.*"

Now.

"*Brooklyn leads it* four to two . . . *Har*tung down the line at third, *not taking any chances*! . . . *Lock*man, with not *too big* of a lead at second, but he'll be *running like the wind* if Thomson hits one . . .

"Branca throws . . ."

The aging figure in the white flannels swung . . . *and the ball leapt off Thomson's bat and rocketed out to left field, a sinking line drive.*

"THERE'S A LONG DRIVE TO LEFT, AND I BELIEVE . . . I BELIEVE . . . I BELIEVE . . ."

No.

"PAFKO AT THE WALL . . ."

No! He had had his day! Thomson's comet belonged in its own time.

It was time now to let go.

Fanning said into the microphone: ". . . And *Pafko . . . makes the catch!*"

Time itself fell silent.

The Brooklyn Dodgers and the New York Giants faded into an orange glow. In the sudden clarity of Flushing Stadium no one moved. The San Diego Padres and the New York Nats stood on the field like frozen men. The little knot of fans behind home plate remained as though transfixed in the attitudes they had struck when Fanning started to call Bobby Thomson's drive: some with arms upraised, some embracing, some with mouths wide, exultant.

And then, slowly, like wax melting, the fans wilted back to life. Some shook their fists. Some cursed. Their voices didn't carry through the window glass. Some tore their scorecards to shreds and flung them helplessly toward the booth, but a faint breeze (moderate to southwesterly winds) caught the shreds and blew them like scraps of confetti against the sky, where they shimmered and were gone.

In the booth, Fanning felt the silence behind him like a frozen scream of rage. Breen was the first to speak, and his voice was thick with a wound.

"God dammit, Fanning . . . that's not the way it ended! What the hell are you trying to do to us? *That wasn't the way it was supposed to end!*"

A little of Breen's voice was feeding into the microphone and echoing like a tinny banshee shriek through the emptying stadium, so Fanning reached over and yanked the connecting cable free. He realized that his white shirt was soaked through with sweat, and he could feel the dampness on his new gray suit.

His throat was giving him hell.

He turned toward them. There was anger in their faces, but it was a dull, sullen anger.

He started to speak, but realized he had one thing left to do. The air mike was still live. He turned back to it and spoke into it for the last time.

"That about wraps it up from Flushing Stadium. For Robyn

Quarrles"—he paused—"Turtle Teweles and myself, this is L. C. Fanning saying . . . *so long!*"

He straightened, and once again turned to face the people who had crowded in the door.

Breen asked again, softly this time, "Why?"

Fanning studied them.

"Because, gentlemen, a thing like that . . . a moment like that . . . it happens only once. You can't bring it back. You can't keep living it. It would have been . . . *wrong* of me to . . . disturb it . . . try to bring it to life again. It belongs . . . in history."

He could tell that not one of them understood.

Danny Breen lifted a hand, let it drop. "Then why? . . . Why did you even bother to . . . ?"

Fanning smiled. He considered.

"Because I just wanted to test the equipment. Just one more time, gentlemen, I wanted to test the equipment." In his mind's eye he had a vision of an orange glow that flared for an instant, and began to fade.

"Well, you had your little fling, didn't you. I'm surprised at you, L.C. You'll be damned lucky to get out of this without a lawsuit."

He didn't answer, and after a minute the men before him went away.

He stood gazing at the doorway long after they had drifted off, the writers, the statisticians, Breen, the Nats front-office people. . . . He would miss them. He loved them. They did not know it, he thought, but he had done them a favor. As they had done him.

It was a while before he realized that Robyn Quarrles still stood beside him. When he turned to her, it struck him what a fine-looking young woman she actually was. She would go far in broadcasting.

"I owe you a great debt of thanks—" he began.

She placed a finger on his lips. "And I owe you. Just tell me one thing. I wasn't born then. How did it end, really?"

He leaned across and whispered the magic into her ear:

"Toot-toot-tootsie, *good-bye!*"